CH00689672

THE PHANTOM
AND
THE FRAUD

THE PHANTOM AND THE FRAUD

LINDA DORRINGTON

1795631 Ontario Inc.

This book is a work of fiction. Any references to historical events, real people, real places or institutions are used fictitiously. Other names, characters, places or events are the work of the author's imagination and any resemblance to actual events or places or persons living or dead, is entirely coincidental.

Copyright © 2020 by Linda Dorrington

All rights reserved, including the right to reproduce this book or portions thereof, in any form whatsoever.

ISBN 978-1-7770806-0-0 (Paperback edition)

For Andy and our girls;
Ashleigh, Bryony and Courteney

Chapter One

Mungo Joudry's impatience grew. He stared across the lake into the misty distance, seeing nothing. He was not a patient man. But then she didn't know that. He had been waiting almost twenty years, now these last minutes seemed interminable. And she was late.

He'd slept on the boat, or rather wished away anxious hours until morning, wondering if she would come. And hoping that the boat's owner wouldn't. Eventually he'd got up, groping for his glasses, and made his way up the narrow stairs, the cold stiffening his legs. He needed coffee, preferably intravenously.

Now he stood inside the bridge, trapped in anticipation, peering through the murk. He thought back to that unexpected glimpse of her three days previously and to what had driven him away from her years before. He thought about the choices made and decisions avoided which had brought him to this moment.

His ritual visit to the market was something he looked forward to each week. It was part of his routine which, although regular as clockwork, held for him the pleasure of opening an unexpected gift. The sights, sounds and smells, the ever-changing mosaic of people touching this, tasting that, and the overheard snippets of conversation allowed him to feel, for a few hours at least, that he too belonged.

After his meagre shopping he generally picked up a newspaper and coffee and sat down to sip, savor and people watch. He enjoyed the buskers, particularly the short Hungarian glockenspiel player. He always found some spare change for him.

The only person he really knew at the market was Frances. She was a struggling actress who made strange clothes when she was 'between jobs', which was most of the time. Her creations looked like they were intended for elves rather than people. Whilst she seemed to attract a lot of interest, she seldom sold anything. Part of him identified with her, he could tell that she was a peripheral too.

"Any luck today?" he asked, placing her coffee, black with one sugar, on the table.

"Nah, but one woman said she might come back for the green leggings," Frances replied. "How've you been doing? Written anything new?"

"Oh, you know, I'm always tinkering with a new piece. Don't know why. No one ever hears them." Just then his eye was arrested by the glint of something sparkly. Instinctively he turned to look, and at the base of a long slender neck was a beautiful emerald radiating in a beam of sunlight. His eyes travelled upward to the face of the wearer and he was shot through with a jolt of recognition.

"Why don't you find a string quartet or something...?" Frances was saying.

"I'm sorry Frances, I've got to go." Without volition, he followed her. He was sure it was her. That red hair was unmistakable, and she still had a faint dusting of freckles on her nose. What was she doing in Toronto? There was a young man with her. He didn't recognize him, though he struck a familiar chord.

He followed them through the crowds, keeping her in view but careful to stay out of sight. She still had that same proud cast to her brow, the pronounced cheekbones, the soft vulnerability of her mouth which belied a weakness otherwise hidden. Her piercing green eyes matched almost exactly the emerald at home just above the swell of her breasts. His breath quickened, a combination of some deep-seated sensual memory and his anxiety at the thought of being seen.

He spent most of his life as an invisible and silent observer, an unseen participant in other people's lives. He couldn't just walk up to her, here in this place, after all these years. What would he say? Would she even want to speak to him? He had acted purely on impulse. He had not expected to see anyone from his past again and certainly not here. A moment of panic overtook him. One wrong move now and everything could unravel. Yet he continued to follow her progress through the market.

The young man was just taller than her, with a head of thick curly brown hair. He had on a tan colored corduroy jacket, well worn. They had an easy familiarity about them which suggested years of togetherness. Mungo felt a twist of jealousy.

They made their way through the comfortable chaos of the market with the eyes of first-time visitors. They stopped and tasted, questioned and marveled over the fresh fish and meat with the wide-eyed wonder of children at a fun fair. He watched them buy bread and cheese, sample olives. At a flower stall the young man picked a carnation out of a bunch and stuck it behind her ear.

Eventually they sat at the same table he'd occupied not an hour earlier and sipped steaming cappuccinos. Now they people watched, remarking occasionally on the passersby. He'd have to be very careful. No longer absorbed by the shopping she could easily notice him. He had situated himself opposite a fish counter, partially hidden by a pillar covered with advertisements for hand-knitted baby booties, artisan cheeses, dog walking and window-cleaning, and a missing person poster.

From his vantage point he could surreptitiously study her. He saw the carriage of her head, the gloss of her hair and the feisty glint in her eyes. Yes, it was definitely Alexia. He could see the years on her face, but she still looked lean and strong. Even formidable. He wondered what had brought her here, to a place where he had thought he would be safe. What had she been doing all these years? Had she wondered about him as he had about her?

Standing shivering on the boat Mungo remembered how he had followed her from the market last Saturday to a small hotel and watched as she and the young man disappeared inside. Still uncertain of what to do, he had retreated to a coffee shop nearby. By the time he'd finished his coffee he had decided. He asked the barista if she had some paper and a pen. Borrowing from the words of Leonard Cohen he wrote:

"I saw you this morning.

You were moving so fast.
Can't seem to loosen my grip
On the past.
And I miss you so much.
And there's no one in sight.
And we're still making love
In my secret life."

He signed it simply, Mungo, and wrote down his cell phone number. He folded the page and wrote her name, Alexia Bantry.

The surge of adrenalin coursing through his veins as he left the coffee shop made him feel almost light-headed and he was barely conscious of the walk back to the hotel.

He asked the man behind the reception desk whether they had a guest registered under the name of Alexia Bantry. Mungo's anxiety mounted in the few seconds it took for the man to check the computer. It seemed that he'd found the record but then looked up placing a regretful smile on his pale face.

"I'm sorry sir."

"But is she staying here?"

"I'm sorry sir," the young man repeated, "It's against our policy to give out information about our guests."

"I'm not looking for information about her. I just need to know if she's registered here. I have a note for her." Mungo tried to keep the desperation from his voice. He felt sure that the man was assessing him based on the rising flush in his face and the pulse pumping in his neck. "Wait a minute…try Alexia Forsythe. I just need to know if she's here. Please."

After a pause the young man reached out his hand and said, "If you leave it with me, I'll see that she gets it." Mungo handed him the note and watched as the man picked up a pen in his delicate pale hands, crossed out Bantry and wrote Forsythe in its place.

Mungo's attention returned to the present as he saw lights draw closer through the early morning haze. He pushed his glasses further up his nose and squinted through the mist. Idiot, he thought. That can't be her; she'd approach from the land, if she came at all. He looked at his watch. He wiped his hands down his pants. Despite the chill he felt clammy all over. He rummaged through his bag and poured a mug of coffee from the thermos he'd filled earlier. He wished he'd thought to bring some whisky. He could do with a shot to steady his nerves, warm him up.

He wasn't sure if the shake in his hands was from the cold or fear. So much depended on how he handled this meeting. He'd given up, relinquished hope and eventually let go of the desire for vindication. Until he saw her last Saturday. Suddenly it was like he'd woken from a deep sleep, his heart started again, his eyes refocused on the world around him and he started to think. He allowed himself to dream about the possibility of recapturing something of what he had lost.

Chapter Two

He felt rather than heard Alexia's arrival on the boat as it moved slightly in the water when she stepped aboard. So, she had come after all. In a moment of panic he was tempted just to stay where he was, hiding, perhaps she would leave, and he could forget the whole thing. Instead, he turned and made his way quietly from the bridge to the deck below.

She was dressed in slim fitting jeans and a thick cream knitted sweater, her red hair tied up in a ponytail. She was looking back at the dock.

"Having second thoughts?" he asked.

She turned and looked at him, "Actually, yes...I almost didn't come. It was a shock getting your note. I thought you were dead...or something," her voice trailed off. She wrapped her arms tightly around herself and looked back at the dock, the wind flipping her ponytail into her face.

He had chosen the boat because he wanted a place they could be entirely alone. He knew it would be available. The Beringers never took it out during the week. Besides, Mungo thought Blake was in Munich and Nancy never used it when he was away. Now he found himself wishing that they were in a public place, surrounded by the distraction of other people having normal conversations, instead of here where neither of them could escape without causing embarrassment.

"I can't stay for long. I've got to go soon,"

"Alexia, you're more beautiful than I remembered. I mean, I'm sorry. What I meant to say is; its cold. Let's go in. I've got some coffee. We can talk." He rubbed his hands down his pants then quickly put them in his jacket pockets, as if hiding his hands would hide his nervousness. "Please."

After a moment she nodded, and he opened the sliding door from the deck.

"Please, have a seat. I'll be right back."

He went up to the bridge to fetch his thermos. He paused and looked out across the lake again. The visibility was improving as the weak wintry morning sun started to burn off the mist. He took a deep breath and headed back downstairs.

It was a large cabin cruiser with three private staterooms and a comfortable galley and living area. He'd often stayed on the boat, sometimes for a couple of weeks, when he was sure that Blake and Nancy were away, or the weather would prevent them from taking the boat out. The last time he'd spent a few days there he'd found a tube of lipstick between the cream leather cushions of the sofa and a floral headscarf on the bridge. He knew these weren't Nancy's, so he took them away. Blake is getting sloppy, he'd thought. Or perhaps he doesn't care anymore.

Alexia was on the sofa looking tense. "What do you want Mungo?" she asked. "Why now? What happened to you? You just disappeared and now you reappear just as suddenly. I was so angry. I *am* angry."

"I had to leave. There were reporters everywhere. I couldn't go home. I was so confused. Crazy. I'm sorry. It was all so long ago. Where is Oliver? Look, let me pour you some coffee and let's just take our time.

There's so much to talk about," he said, fetching mugs from a cupboard in the galley, but not wanting to take his eyes off her.

"I told you, I can't stay long. I don't even know why I agreed to meet you. I shouldn't have. So why did you do it?"

Mungo put the mugs on the coffee table and sat down heavily, the weight of all the years bearing down on him. She clearly still believed that he had done it. How could he make her understand?

He reached for the thermos and poured them each some coffee.

"I have sugar," he said.

"No this is fine," she took a sip.

"Still watching your weight," he said, regretting the words almost before he'd uttered them.

Her eyes narrowed into pinpoints. "So, what do you want to talk about?" she said. "You certainly owe me an explanation."

"Come away with me," he said, "just for a few days." He saw the reaction on her face and immediately realized his mistake. Get a grip, you idiot, he thought. Why couldn't he say the right thing?

She put her mug down and stood up. "This is all wrong. I've got to go. I thought you were crazy after what you did. Now I know you're crazy!"

He had to keep her on the boat. This would be his only chance to get through to her. He had to make her understand. He needed her to know what he had given up and, even more; he needed Oliver to pay for what he had done. She was moving towards the stairs and each step she took loosened his fragile grip on the future.

"Wait! Alexia please!" he called out. "You're right. Of course, you must go. But before you do, I want to tell you what really happened."

She turned, "I know what happened Mungo. You are a cheat and a fraud. And a coward who literally couldn't face the music and ran away."

"I am a coward. I have been running and hiding all these years. But I am not a cheat. There is something I want to show you and then you can go. Please just sit down and wait for a minute. That's all I ask, just a few more minutes."

She relented and sat down. He hurried up the stairs. "I'll be back in a moment." On the deck he went directly to the dock line and quickly untied it. Then he climbed the stairs to the bridge and took hold of the wheel. The key was already in the ignition. He turned it and felt the engine throb into life. It was risky, but he could move the boat rapidly away from the dock before she even made it out onto the deck. He pushed hard on the throttle and the boat surged forward.

Chapter Three

The taxi turned into the quiet tree-lined street and stopped outside a large grey stone-clad house. Elizabeth Carey was tired and felt stiff as she extracted her tall frame from the back seat. She paid the driver and tipped him generously. "No thank you, I can manage," she said, declining his offer to carry her overnight bag up to the house. It had been a long night. What was meant to be a brief trip to see a client had been delayed some eight hours by flight cancellations.

She was relieved to be home and decided that, as it was already almost noon, the office could do without her for the rest of the day. A few instructions to her paralegal by phone would be enough for him to proceed.

She opened the front door and stepped inside, experiencing the familiar sense that the house had not been alone. It felt fresh and welcoming. That was something she had grown to love about it. Even when she'd been away for a few days or at work all day, the house seldom got that empty neglected feel the way houses do when they are unoccupied for long periods. She put her bags down, kicked her shoes off and walked into the kitchen.

Her first thought was of Caprice, her cat. He had not been fed last night, or this morning, because of her delayed return. She expected to find him anxiously weaving around her legs in search of food and attention. Instead Caprice was lying in his usual spot on the wingback chair capturing the weak winter sunlight from the kitchen window. Elizabeth perched on the edge of the chair, stroking the cat.

"Hey mister, did you miss me?" He gave her a slightly baleful, speculative stare and stretched into her embrace. "Aren't you hungry then?"

She looked across to his bowls and litter box. That's odd, she thought, he still had food and water. "Haven't you been eating? Are you sick?" Instead of taking a break this afternoon she'd have to take Caprice to the vet. She saw her afternoon drain away in the vet's waiting room hoping for a gap in his schedule.

She picked Caprice up, her fingers imbedded in the soft fur, enjoying the feel of his lithe body under her hands. Caprice purred softly. She wished somebody would do this to her. She looked at the cat closely. "Do you know, I think you are just fine? There now, go and eat something," she said putting him down. The cat bounded away flicking its tail in the air and walked right past its bowls.

She switched on the kettle to make a cup of tea and then remembered that she'd probably have to go out for some fresh milk first. Checking the fridge, she was vaguely surprised, but pleasantly relieved, to find a carton of milk that felt almost full. She was always so preoccupied with work, she must have been mistaken. Or perhaps she was just getting old.

She sat down with her tea and wondered what to do with her afternoon. It had been so long since she'd been home on a mid-week afternoon. The house felt quiet and still, as the street had done when she'd arrived. The only other living creature around was Caprice. That's why she'd got the cat five years ago. And cats, they'd said, are easier to tend to than dogs, more independent. She didn't feel so bad about leaving him for long hours while she was at work or away on business.

Elizabeth finished her tea. She would call the office, she decided, have a shower and then spend the afternoon clearing out the storage room in the basement. It was a big project and one that she'd been putting off for a long time.

She stepped out of the shower feeling refreshed. Bending down she towel-dried her shoulder-length brown hair and flipped it back over as she stood up. She was tall and big-boned, with good proportions and, without much effort, had managed to maintain a good figure for a thirty-nine-year-old. She'd always thought that she had a plain but pleasant face and, when she took the trouble with some make-up, she even looked attractive. Most days she just brushed her hair off her face and quickly dabbed on some moisturizer. She was always in the office by seven-thirty and generally only got home at seven in the evening, sometimes later. Her sister, Rebecca, had always been considered the pretty one and she'd married quite young. Elizabeth's career had always come first but recently she had begun to wonder if she had made the right choice.

Pushing these vaguely uncomfortable thoughts aside, she dressed quickly and headed downstairs. The house was too big for her, but she loved the leafy neighborhood and had bought the property partly as an investment. Also, it was a solid manifestation of her hope that one day she might have a family to fill it. That had been nine years ago and still she lived here by herself with only Caprice for company.

Elizabeth didn't use the storage room much; there were plenty of other more accessible rooms in which to put unused items. She had been in the room a couple of months earlier while the furnace was being serviced and decided then that it could do with dusting and a clear out. Today was the day.

She was about an hour into the job when she came across the unfamiliar suitcase. Like everything else it was fairly dusty, and it had been shoved against the wall at the far end of the room between some large boxes. She was puzzled. She had never seen it before. She pulled it out and heaved it onto one of the boxes. She brushed some of the dust off it and stood with her arms folded looking at it for a moment. Strange. She didn't recognize it as one of hers. It was medium sized, dark brown with leather trim. It looked quite old with buckles on the faux leather straps.

Elizabeth struggled with the buckles; the straps were stiff and unyielding. "Come on, you," she muttered, "get out of there," she said between gritted teeth. Gradually she worked the straps free of the buckles, undid the brass clips and flipped open the lid. Clothing. Men's clothing. Elizabeth lifted out a creased navy-blue sweater. She held it up to the light, "What the hell?" It had obviously been folded up for a long time. Just then Caprice appeared and leapt onto the opened suitcase. The cat gave the slightly musty smelling contents a sniff and then jumped off, clearly disinterested.

Elizabeth unpacked a pair of trousers, a few long-sleeved shirts and a dark, olive-colored corduroy jacket. She shrugged and was about to put the contents back in and toss the suitcase on the throw out pile when she noticed a brown leather folder at the bottom.

She took it out and opened it. A hand-written musical score, pages and pages of it. Elizabeth flipped through the pages quickly. She could read music well and saw that it was a complex piece. It appeared to be original, with corrections and notations in the margin. She flipped the pages back and forth, scanning them. She hummed a few bars. Wow! This was different, beautiful. Elizabeth shoved the pages back into the leather portfolio quickly, dropping a few. Dammit. Picking them up with fumbling fingers she left the room and slowly made her way up the stairs, paging through the music.

Three years earlier when she had been made a partner at her law firm she had bought herself a baby-grand piano in solitary celebration of her achievement. She loved to play, and her ability had improved with the purchase of the piano. She set the music down on the keyboard and looked through the stack of pages. It appeared to be a sonata for a full orchestra. The music was not named and there was no indication of the composer. She put the manuscript on the stand and started to pick out the notes on the keyboard.

Chapter Four

Mungo heard her footsteps thundering up the stairs but he kept his focus on navigating the boat through the marina. Suddenly he felt her weight on his back and he fell forwards over the wheel as she flung herself into him. The boat veered to the left as the wheel turned under their weight. He tried to shake her off, but she clung to him like a limpet.

"What the hell do you think you are doing?" Stop the boat! Now! Turn back!"

He felt her nails digging into his neck, scratching. He'd forgotten how strong she was; a dancer's strength.

"Get off me! You'll make us crash!" He straightened the wheel correcting their course. He took a breath and pushed hard on the throttle, at the same time forcing his weight backwards. As the boat launched forwards she fell backwards onto the polished teak deck.

He looked over his shoulder. She sat, defeated, and breathing heavily, silent tears coursing down her cheeks.

"Don't do this Alexia. It doesn't have to be like this. All I want is to talk to you. After what happened you owe me that much."

"After what happened?" she screamed. "After what you did, I don't owe you anything!"

Mungo stared straight ahead, the boat was moving forward at speed. He grew quiet and still. They were almost out of the marina now and heading into the lake. His anger solidified his resolve.

He looked back at her again. He saw her register the hardness in his eyes.

"Let's get something straight right now and listen well," he instructed. "Eighteen years ago I lost everything I cared about, everything I had worked for, because of you. You owe me at least a hearing. When you have heard what I have to say, I will take you back."

Her eyes flashed around the bridge quickly. She folded her arms.

"And don't think you can jump off and swim away," he said. "The water is far too cold, you'd never make it."

"You've changed Mungo. I don't even like you anymore."

"People do what they have to do," he shrugged. "I didn't ask for any of this, didn't plan any of it. What about you? Did you get what you expected?"

She pulled her knees up toward her chest and wrapped her arms around them. She was so vulnerable suddenly. He wanted to sit down on the floor next to her, take her in his arms, stroke her hair and reassure her. He could still remember the feel of her lips, full and soft.

He remembered so well the five days they'd spent together all those years ago almost as if it had been yesterday. He'd examined those few days from every angle over the years, at times joyfully savoring every moment, at others filled with self-recrimination knowing that he'd brought his failure upon himself.

She had been intoxicating. From the moment Oliver had introduced them at Nick & Toni's Cafe he'd lost himself to her. He could see that Oliver was besotted too. Alexia was from England, a second-year student at Juilliard, studying dance. She was graceful, funny, clever and caring all at once. She radiated beauty and charm. When she walked into a room all heads turned to her, men and women. The fact that she was oblivious of her impact only added to her magnetism.

There was only one problem; she was Oliver's. Oliver had thrown himself into the relationship like he'd never done before. Mungo and Oliver had been best friends since they were eighteen. They'd met during their first year at Juilliard and since then Oliver had sampled and charmed his way through many young women in their circle, leaving countless broken hearts in his wake. Alexia was the first girl whom Oliver had allowed into his heart. As Oliver's love and happiness grew, so Mungo's pain and jealousy mounted.

He'd withdrawn and focused even more on his work. It became all-consuming and he rapidly progressed through his master's degree in music, using all his spare time to compose. He knew he was writing ground-breaking material, pushing the boundaries of modern classical music, but he was scared that it wouldn't be understood or accepted.

He had been determined to finish the sonata before showing it to anyone, before it would be played. He shared the smaller more conventional pieces with his supervisor and others, but not this, his major work.

Oliver too was studying for a master's degree in music, though his passion and ability were nowhere near that of Mungo's. Oliver's music was technically sound, but it lacked the powerful range of emotions which Mungo wove into his. Where Oliver's recitals were faultless but banal, Mungo's were unpredictable and emotional which lent them a captivating brilliance. Oliver's compositions were competent and correct; Mungo's transported each listener on his or her own journey.

Their brief affair had taken place two months before Alexia and Oliver's wedding. The wedding was set for just after graduation and the symphony performance at Carnegie Hall.

Once a year Juilliard put on a performance at Carnegie Hall of the works of a carefully selected handful of their most gifted students. That year Mungo was to conduct his sonata before and audience for the first time. It was also the first time that Juilliard had featured the work of just one of their students, the work being considered, by the panel of judges, so magnificent that anything else performed on the same stage on the same night would be diminished in comparison.

He remembered so well his one night of glory. How short it had been. The performance at Carnegie Hall had been everything he had hoped it would be, and more. The critical acclaim had been overwhelmingly positive. As he'd conducted the orchestra through his sonata he'd felt the unifying power of the music embrace him, the musicians and the audience and transport them all as one to a mystical place. As the last note died away a deafening silence fell upon the hall for what felt like minutes and then, suddenly, as if orchestrated, the audience erupted in applause as deafening as the silence had been.

He had been elated. He could still feel it now, after all these years; it was tangible, dizzying.

The after party had been attended by all the cultural, corporate and political elite of New York. He'd been surrounded by people wanting to shake his hand, congratulate him, hand him another glass of champagne. He'd had more women kiss him in one night than he'd had in his entire life. Reporters sought him out for comment and television cameras panned the room locking in on him as he moved through the crowd. A music producer pressed his card into his hand, imploring him to call so that they could discuss a recording contract.

He'd kept scanning the room for Alexia. She was stuck to Oliver's side, as if attached, smiling, talking and nodding. Finally, she looked across at him, their eyes met momentarily, then she looked away. He'd been hurt and puzzled. Neither she nor Oliver had acknowledged him that evening. He supposed that they were making space for those people not usually a part of his regular circle. He'd felt someone nudge his arm and turned to greet the music critic from the New York Times.

He turned, startled, his reminiscences interrupted when Alexia stood up, bumped his arm, brushed her jeans down and shivered. The boat made rapid progress through the dark grey water. He eased back on the throttle and slowed it down.

They had both calmed down and they stood side by side staring out into the distance, each absorbed in their own thoughts. Together they watched a flock of large birds drawing closer and then pass overhead, flying back to the north shore of Lake Ontario. The mist had thinned and the sun, now quite high in the sky, was penetrating the clouds.

"Where are we going?" she asked. "I didn't know you were interested in boats. I suppose there is a lot I don't know about you. When did you get it?"

He wasn't ready to tell her that it wasn't his boat. That would lead to too many other questions. And the truth was he didn't know where they were going. He hadn't planned this. He'd imagined them sitting together in quiet comfort talking, dissolving the years and distance between them. Subconsciously he'd even thought that things would be the same as they had been the last time they were alone together; that transcendent combination of passion and tenderness. He saw now how misguided he'd been. "Stupid. Stupid," he muttered under his breath, shaking his head.

"You're not listening. I think we should go back. Please."

"No. We'll drop the anchor in a while and then talk. After that, we'll see. Are you hungry? Go down to the galley and see if there's anything to eat."

He chose the nearest bay and dropped the anchor. He stood for a few moments, enjoying the stillness. But for the lapping of the water against the sides of the cabin cruiser, everything was silent. He felt the tiniest glimmer of warmth from the sun and watched its reflections play across the gently rippling surface of the water. The past had erupted into his present in the last week like a stone hurled into a still lake and the concentric ripples were expanding, out of reach and out of control.

He thought about Alexia downstairs and felt a sense of excitement surge through him and concentrate itself in his groin. Nobody knew where they were. He loved that. It had become his art form, moving in and out of peoples' lives without their knowledge. Now she was part of it too.

Chapter Five

They sat across from each other at the small table in the galley, the debris of an improvised meal between them. Alexia had found a tin of salmon, canned vegetable soup, a box of slightly stale crackers and they'd washed this down with black tea. They'd eaten in tense silence mostly, neither of them really knowing how to break the silence or bridge the gap.

Finally, pushing his plate away Mungo stood up and said, "Come." He could see the hesitation, fear even, in her eyes. She looked around, as if for an alternative, a way out. Eventually, with a shrug, feigning nonchalance Alexia stood up and followed him through to the sitting-room area and sat down on padded bench against the wall. He went to a cabinet behind the highly polished bar counter and pulled out a bottle of Macallan 18 single malt whisky. It was an 18th anniversary of sorts, he thought. He knew he was breaking one of his own cardinal rules. He always used his own supplies, but this was different, this was special. Grateful for Blake's refined tastes, he took out two crystal glasses and splashed the richly aromatic amber liquid into them. He dropped two cubes of ice into each glass and watched the whisky swirl around them. Mungo carried the clinking glasses over to the sofa and handed one to Alexia.

"Cheers," he said raising the glass "to us."

"There is no us, Mungo. But thanks for the drink."

Mungo sat down, sipped his whisky. "I had to do it, you do see that. You left me no choice."

He saw her face flush. He wondered if it was the whisky or her natural fairness that allowed the color of her anger to be so visible in her face.

"I had nothing to do with it. I was so disappointed in you Mungo. You had everything going for you."

"Yes, I did. Until Oliver stole it from me. God I was blind. I trusted him. He was my best friend. At first, I couldn't go back because of the reporters. They were everywhere, camped out outside my apartment building. And I just didn't understand what he was doing." His words came out in a rush, restless creatures finally released after eighteen years of confinement. "Then when I figured out how he'd got the manuscript; it could only have been through you, I knew I could never go back. Nobody had access to that music, not even my professor. It was my handwritten original. The only person who could have picked it up was you, when we were together. So, you see, I couldn't go back and plead innocence, not without Oliver and the whole world finding out about our affair. I was confused, devastated. Sometimes I even thought that you had given it to him deliberately. Most of the time I didn't know what to think. In the beginning I stayed away because I didn't know what to do. And then it just seemed the easiest option. Time passed. You and Oliver got married. I had to do it, to protect you. Eventually it was too late to return. Don't you see that?" He took a large mouthful of whisky, felt it burning all the way down the back of his throat.

She was shaking her head. "What? What are you talking about? It was his manuscript. You took Oliver's manuscript. Everybody knows that. You ruined yourself Mungo."

He dropped his head into his hands. He felt weakness flood through his muscles as the enormity of what she was saying hit him. If she didn't believe him, no one else ever would. God, what a mess. No wonder he had let it be for so many years.

Finally, he looked up at her. He had to make her understand, he had this one chance. He saw her hand shake as she sipped her drink. "Alexia, please, please listen to me. It was my work. Mine. I'd been working on it for two years. Only one other person knew about it, my supervisor. I showed it to him just before I submitted it to the judging panel for the Carnegie performance. My supervisor never defended me. I don't know why. I suppose he thought I was a fraud too. You still don't get it, do you?" He looked into her eyes, seeking for some sort of recognition. He saw only confusion, doubt. Well, doubt was better than certainty that she was right. He pressed on, "That long weekend, those five days we had together... They were the happiest of days of my life."

It was fall. Oliver had been called back home to Seattle; his mother was ill. Mungo and Alexia had naturally gravitated towards each other. The evening Oliver had left for Seattle they had a casual dinner together. Afterwards, without even discussing it, they'd walked to Mungo's apartment, he'd played the piano for her and when he'd finished he'd sat next to her on the sofa. Making love to her was as natural and seamless as breathing.

The next morning they'd woken and made love again. After breakfast they'd walked in Central Park. The color of her hair matched the color of the trees and since then he'd never been able to see the fall colors without thinking of her. He remembered the fresh, crisp chill in the air, saw her running towards him arms out stretched, her dress and her hair flying in the wind. He'd swept her up, twirled her round, kissed her long and deep. Those five days passed in a blur of sensual delight and happiness beyond anything he had ever experienced.

He brought his eyes back to her face, his voice urgent for understanding, "You had to leave so quickly? Remember the call from Oliver? He said he had been trying to get hold of you. He was worried. You weren't answering. He asked me if I'd seen you or heard from you. He said he was coming back early, that he was in the taxi on his way home from the airport."

She nodded. "I was so scared. I hated myself then. We both loved him. He trusted us. I just had to get out of your apartment. Pretend it hadn't happened."

"I've spent eighteen years pretending it didn't happen. But it did, and it changed everything." Mungo said, fighting to keep the bitterness out of his voice.

"We betrayed him." The unshed tears in her eyes sparkled.

"Yes, and he betrayed me. He destroyed me. At first, I couldn't figure it out. How had he got hold of my manuscript? I was always very careful with it. Not even my supervisor saw it right until the end."

"Are you saying that he stole your work, that he got it from me?" She shook her head; her face was starting to take on the same red tinge as her hair.

"That's exactly what I am saying. How else could he have got his hands on my original? They had a photo of it in the newspaper. It was on television too. It was my manuscript. But he was clever. He had added comments and notations in the margin in his handwriting."

"But why would he...I wouldn't have..." He could see the bewilderment on her face. She picked up her glass, held it in both hands to stop them shaking.

"Don't you see, somehow he found out about us. It was his way of getting even. And it worked. He discredited me professionally and drove us apart. I only worked it all out much later," said Mungo, "after the fog cleared and my hangover lifted." he added ruefully. "For the first few days after the concert I was in a daze. I didn't know what was going on or why. And I was pretty drunk much of the time, for months really."

"But I didn't take it. Why would I?" Realization dawned on her face. "Oh my God, did you think I slept with you so I could get my hands on your manuscript?" Her voice was shrill now.

"I wrestled and wrestled with it. I couldn't believe that you would have done it deliberately. I thought that maybe you took it by mistake when you grabbed your things from my apartment. Remember you'd been working on an assignment there. Your papers were all over the place you probably picked my papers up with all of yours. But by the time I'd worked that out it was too late. How would I explain it to Oliver, my professor, the music faculty, the media? And I knew that it would all come out. You were getting married in a few weeks. I couldn't do that to you. I didn't want to hurt you. I wanted you for myself, but not like that. I loved you Alexia."

She stared at him, silently. The red flush replaced by an almost transparent pallor in her face. He got up and refreshed their glasses.

"My God, Mungo... What, what did you do? Where did you go?" she asked, her voice quavering.

"The next morning, after the concert I had a huge hangover. I'd fallen asleep in my tux and woke up to find myself on the sofa. I felt ill. Too much champagne and then all the other drinks afterwards, I suppose. I switched on the TV. I wanted to hear the reviews. But there was Oliver on TV. Being interviewed. He was saying that I'd plagiarized his work. He was all indignant and enraged, waving my manuscript under the nose of the interviewer. I thought I was still asleep, having a nightmare. When I had to rush to the bathroom to be sick I knew it was for real." Mungo paused, swallowed a steadying gulp of whisky.

He went on, "The phone started ringing. Without thinking I picked it up. It was a reporter from the New York Times, their music critic. I'd spoken to him the night before at the party. He was mad, demanding why I'd made a fool of him. He'd published a fantastic review of the performance in the morning's edition, he said, and now this. I didn't know what to say, what was going on. My head was thumping. I put the phone down and it immediately started ringing again. I had to get away, to think. I left the apartment. I never went back."

Chapter Six

Nancy Beringer stood in front of them. They were a fairly new group; fidgeting, adjusting things, re-positioning their seats, exchanging a few nervous comments here and there, trying not to stare at her too closely, too obviously.

She dropped her robe to the floor, raised her left leg up onto the platform thrusting her hips forward at the same time. She put her shoulders back and rested her right hand on her hip. With her chin raised she looked directly at them.

She loved challenging them in this way. She was immobile, passive but always totally in control. Without saying a word she had them at her command. They had to capture her, represent her, reproduce her. And she knew that they would struggle.

Nancy didn't do this for the money. She did it for the sense of power it gave her and because she knew it would enrage Blake. And she liked the fact that this act of exposure was, at the same time, a secret. Occasionally she wondered what she would do if he ever saw her in a painting, but she knew this was unlikely. Blake didn't appreciate art; he just acquired it. He had an agent who represented him at auctions or brought him recommendations of what he should buy so he never browsed the galleries himself. For him art was an affectation. Sometimes she felt that she was one of his affectations too.

She'd stumbled upon this quite by chance. She often visited art galleries and enjoyed the variety of work on display at the university exhibitions. On one occasion a few years ago, she'd gone in search of the washrooms and strayed from the public area. At the landing at the end of a dusty wooden staircase she'd come across a student bulletin board and, pinned to the board amongst the advertisements and notices, had been a small flyer offering to pay students to pose for the life classes. On impulse she'd torn off the tab of paper with the contact number and called the next day. The art teacher was very happy to engage her. Mostly they had young models, he'd said, and he was delighted that his students would have an opportunity to study a more mature figure. Apparently, there were many firm young bodies willing to put themselves on display for money, but not many middle-aged women. And she'd kept herself in good shape. It was a requirement of the wife of a high-profile CEO, as Blake often reminded her. He had never balked at paying her spa bills as long as she looked good when he needed her on his arm.

It had grown from there. She now posed for a few art schools in and around the city. Blake was so busy and self-absorbed that he'd long since lost interest in how Nancy filled her days and his frequent business trips freed her up even more. Besides, she had her position on the Board of the Ontario Symphony Orchestra and she did enough committee work in between so that she always had something to say if he asked.

Her mind wandered as the art teacher walked between the students' easels, clarifying his instructions and demonstrating technique. This had become a form of meditation for her; the complete stillness of it, her slow deep rhythmical breathing, the sound of brushes scratching the canvas. She'd even grown to love the smell of the art studio, the paints and solvents.

Today though she was finding it difficult to relax, to settle into the pose and regulate her breathing. Sven had joined the class. He'd come in late and set up his easel at the back of the room. She was aware of his concentrated gaze on her each time he looked up. He appeared to be about fifteen years older than the other students and his maturity held a certain fascination for the younger students. While his age set him apart from the rest, his relaxed confidence and sense of humor broke down these barriers. But more than this, the whole class was in awe of his talent, especially the teacher. They didn't know much about him; only that he was from Sweden.

She thought about the unexpected encounter last week with Sven. The class was drawing to a close and she had just put her robe on and tied the belt. Covered once again, she had stretched out her neck and arms when he approached her.

"You must get stiff standing in the same position for so long."

"Oh, I'm used to it. Besides, it gives me time to catch up with my thoughts," she'd laughed.

"I've made good progress today. Thank you. I was wondering if you would mind sitting for me. Privately. I have some ideas for another painting. I think you'd be the perfect model."

Nancy had been surprised by his request, even a little flattered, but she wasn't about to make a decision so quickly. "Can you give me a few minutes to get dressed? We can talk afterwards."

"Of course, of course...I'm sorry, I should have thought..."

"I'll be right back." She'd gone into the adjoining room to change and when she came out he was waiting for her in the corridor outside.

"Would you like to get a coffee?" he'd asked.

They'd gone to a coffee shop across from the campus and sat sipping lattes, watching the students come and go through the steamed-up windows. It was a damp day in early spring with intermittent patches of wet snow. They'd watched pedestrians pick their way through the puddles and scurry to avoid the slush sprayed up by passing cars.

She had tried to study him unobtrusively over her coffee mug and felt a bit sheepish when he'd caught her eye. He was lean and fair with slightly scruffy sandy blonde hair and short stubble on his chin. What she really liked was the light tan and fine lines on his face. She could see from the crows' feet around his eyes that he'd done a lot of smiling and spent a lot of time in the sun. When he looked at her it was with unwavering eyes. The eyes of an artist, she'd thought.

"So, you want to paint me." Her tone had been somewhere between a challenge and an invitation.

"You are a good model. Patient and you seem to enjoy doing it. The bone structure in your face is good."

She squirmed inwardly as she remembered how he had studied her so closely that she'd felt as if he were touching her. Her uncertainty and curiosity about him were mixed in equal parts. She'd wavered, saying nothing.

"It's not so easy to get models." He'd filled the silence again. "You have a strong presence."

"Why did you leave Sweden?"

"I was in the tech industry in Stockholm, a successful start-up, made some money, got bored. Then I got into freelance writing and did some travelling for a while in Africa and South America. I met somebody from Toronto, thought it was as good a place as any for a man wanting a change. She didn't work out, but I liked the city, enrolled in an art course and here I am." He'd smiled. "So, will you pose for me?"

She'd turned from him and looked out of the window again. It was one thing to pose for him in a group setting, but she wasn't sure about a private sitting.

A woman had passed close by the glass on the other side, so close that Nancy could see the frown lines on her face and feel her anxious intent. She'd felt like an unintentional voyeur but kept looking anyway. The woman, completely unaware of Nancy's close observation, was pushing a baby in one of those large old-fashioned navy-blue prams that they made new to seem old for parents who were nostalgic for their own childhoods. Or perhaps for those preoccupied parents who felt that traditional baby paraphernalia would somehow anchor their distracted parenting in solid values. Still Nancy had hesitated, conscious of his gaze as focused on her as hers had been on the woman on the other side of the glass. He'd answered her question about Sweden, but something about it felt evasive.

Eventually she'd turned back to him. Although they were a table-width apart, she felt that he could see more of her than what he'd already seen beneath her clothing. She had been relieved when he'd sat back and scratched his chin, his fingers rasping his stubble.

She came to a decision. "I have a boat. It's here at the marina. We could go there."

They'd agreed to meet the following week after the class. They'd finished their coffees pulled on their coats and parted outside the shop each going in opposite directions.

Now here she was preparing to go to the boat with a man she hardly knew. No wonder she was feeling nervous. She had posed so often for groups and yet never felt inhibited or anxious, but Sven's gaze was getting under her skin, making her feel acutely aware of each exposed inch. Suddenly it didn't feel so impersonal any more, and she didn't feel quite so in control.

Nancy dressed quickly after the class and found Sven waiting for her outside the building, a new canvas and a portable easel leaning against the wall and the leather bag in which he carried his paints hanging from his shoulder. He was smoking a small cigar, staring up at the bare branches of a large beech tree, his eyes narrowed against the smoke and the whiteness in the sky. He smiled when he saw her and dropped the remains of the cigar, stamping it out. He picked up his things and they walked towards the car park.

"I'm glad you haven't changed your mind. I was worried," he said.

Am I that transparent, Nancy wondered?

"Also, we never discussed your fee. I will pay you, of course, for your time."

"Yes, I know. We can talk about it later," she said unlocking the trunk of her blue Volvo S60. She didn't know why she was doing this. It certainly wasn't for the money. They climbed in and made small talk about the art school as she drove through the midday downtown traffic to the harbor. He was curious to know how long she'd been modeling for the school and how many classes she sat for each week. She told him she'd been doing it off and on for about seven years and steered the conversation into more general observations about the art school.

At the marina Nancy strode purposefully along the dock, Sven following a few paces behind as he studied the range of boats on either side of him. The surface of the water had a slimy sheen and the air rising off it felt dank and heavy. Suddenly she stopped opposite an open space between two large yachts.

"That's odd. I'm sure this is where we moor it. Unless Blake has moved it? Or I suppose I could've got the wrong spot. I haven't been here since last summer." She looked around quizzically. Perhaps they'd been assigned a new berth. "Let's try across there," she said pointing to a dock opposite. It's called *The Ice Queen,* a cabin cruiser about fifty-feet long, I think." They retraced their steps along the dock, the wind whipping her thick wavy shoulder length fair hair around her face giving her a distracted demeanor. Sven paced the dock behind Nancy, fighting to keep the canvas from taking off in the wind.

They walked up and down for a few minutes. Eventually Nancy stopped. "Well that's it; it's definitely not here. I was sure Blake said he had had it put back in the water after the winter. He is always anxious to get it into the water at the first signs of spring." She rushed on, trying to hide her concern and embarrassment "I'm sorry. I just don't understand it. Blake is in Munich this week and we hardly ever take it out mid-week. I can't think what's happened to it, unless he has lent it to someone without telling me." She kept scanning the docks to see if she'd somehow missed sight of it.

Sven reached out his hand and moved a strand of hair from her face tucking it behind her ear. He turned her face toward him. "That's okay Nancy. We can do it another time. It's a bit cold today anyway. Come on, let me buy you lunch."

She hesitated just a moment and then nodded her head. "I need to speak to the harbor master first to see if he knows where the boat is."

They walked up to a cluster of buildings near the street entrance to the harbor. The yacht club was based there alongside a lawn bowling club that was deserted at this time of year. They found his office and stuck their heads in the door.

"Excuse me, Errol," said Nancy.

"Mrs. Beringer, come in, come in." Errol Joynt hastily stubbed out a cigarette. "Sorry, I know I'm not supposed to smoke in here, but I don't get many visitors this time of year, you know," he said standing up.

"That's okay Errol. Don't worry about it. I uh… We needed the boat today," gesturing toward Sven, "but I can't find it. It's not there. Do you know where it is?"

"Haven't noticed it gone particularly Mrs. Beringer. But can't say as I've looked today though," he said making as if to look through the window opposite his desk. "It's still fairly quiet this time of year. Mostly people putting their boats in and getting them ready for the season. Maybe Mr.

Beringer…?" he suggested. He stopped. Errol had seen Blake Beringer bring women to his boat often. And he'd seen the same woman with him a few times in the last couple of months. He didn't like to say anything to Mrs. Beringer. But it seemed now she had a bit on the side too. Young, attractive. *Money can get you anything.*

"No, I don't think so. He's in Munich. That's why I'm worried. Normally he'd tell me if he'd offered it to someone. I'll call him when I get home. He probably just forgot. But please call me if you find out where it is. You have my numbers?"

"Will do. Don't you worry Mrs. Beringer. I'm sure it's fine. I'll keep an eye out and call you if I see anything."

The scent of her perfume lingered and mingled with the cigarette smoke in Errol's office. He sat down and leaned back in his chair, put his feet on the desk and regarded their retreating backs speculatively.

Chapter Seven

Mungo put his glass down and looked across at Alexia for some sign that she believed him. She was still but for the steady rise and fall of her chest. She stared at him silently. He wished she would say something. There was so much more he wanted to tell her but suddenly he felt depleted. Even more than that, he felt mildly depressed.

This whole thing had been a waste of time, a mistake. In the few days since he'd seen her at the market he had recovered his sense of purpose. He'd had such high hopes for this meeting, hopes that he'd hardly allowed to crystallize into coherent thoughts. But he'd ruined it, taking her off in the boat like this, against her will.

But nothing had changed. Who can blame her, he thought wryly. He leaned forward and ran his fingers through his hair. She's believed for years that I am a fraud and now she thinks I'm an abductor. What is she expecting next?

Sitting up he looked past her through the sliding doors leading to the deck and saw clouds gathering in the sky and the wind whipping the surface of the water. It was getting late. He decided to give her some time to process what he had said.

He went out on the deck and felt the chill wind grab hold of his open jacket flapping it against his body. He had left the boat in neutral, anchored and drifting slightly in the wind. He pulled up the anchor and then, up on the fly bridge, he turned the boat and headed back home.

Odd, he thought, that he should think of going home when he didn't really have a home. He had a routine, certainly, and little rituals that gave him comfort and a semblance of normality. But he hadn't in fact had a home since that day he'd left his apartment in New York.

His life had been so well planned up until then. But then he'd lost his direction, and he had just allowed himself to drift into things as they came upon him, like Blake and Nancy.

He still composed in sporadic bursts, but these bursts were thrust upon him when the urge to write was greater than the pain induced by the loss of his musical career. At times he was able to find solace in the music and at others it was so unbearable that, for months, he actively avoided it. When he was in one of these states of avoidance he could not bear to hear a snatch of music on the television or even those tinny electronic tunes played on the phone.

He wondered about Alexia's home. They hadn't even spoken about the ordinary things. Where did she live? What was she doing now? Was she still dancing? What about Oliver? Who was the man she was with at the market? Did she have any children? Why was she in Toronto?

He watched the water breaking round the bow, frothy bubbles forming on each side of the boat as it pushed through. Water was so mesmerizing. Sometimes on the weekends when he had nowhere to spend the day he would go to Niagara Falls and stand for ages at his favorite spot, leaning against the railings just where the water flowed over the edge, and stare down into the clear rushing blue until he felt merged with it.

For the past three years he had been composing a concerto for piano and cello which he called *Water*, trying to capture its different qualities in the three movements. Lost in thought, he was replaying bars of the music in his head as he watched the boat cut through the water when he was roused by Alexia's arrival on the bridge next to him. She had loosened her ponytail and was rubbing the back of her head and massaging her temples as if to rub away a headache.

"Did you ever stop to think about the ramifications of running away like you did and the effect it had on me, on the rest of us?" she asked. Her arms crossed now, her gaze fixed upon some unseen spot in the distance.

"I spent the first few days in an alcoholic funk, hardly aware of where I was or what I was doing. When I came out of it I found myself on the outskirts of Toronto. I was numb. I didn't care about anything. It was like part of me had died. I just went through the motions." He turned to her, his eyes appealing for understanding. She said nothing.

"Thinking about it now, I can see that I was depressed. Much later, when I started to care enough to figure things out it was too late. So I just stayed here. It seemed easier than raking up all the pain again. Fighting with Oliver, trying to clear my name. All the publicity. And you would be dragged into anything I did to clear my name. By then you and Oliver would have been married. Think of what it would have done to you, Alexia, if I'd come back, if Oliver had found out about our affair?"

"We tried to find you Mungo. We filed a missing person report with the NYPD. But in view of the fact that your disappearance seemed voluntary they were not very motivated to search for you. Crime was pretty bad in New York back then. They had more critical issues to fill their time with."

A missing person report; this was news to Mungo but given the circumstances it was to be expected. He suppressed the urge to interject. He wanted her to keep talking.

"Juilliard paid for a private detective. They kept searching for about six months, I think. Oliver and I got so tired of answering their questions over and over again. The school was so embarrassed about the whole thing. Juilliard had never seen a scandal of that scale. There was intense speculation for months, in the music school and in the arts media, about why you had done it. A few people did speak out in your defense, but you were not there to back them up or to speak up for yourself. Eventually your absence underlined your guilt." She turned and focused her icy green eyes directly on him, accusing him.

Mungo said nothing; he just regarded her for a long moment and then gazed at the skyline of Toronto as it drew closer. Saying sorry now seemed so inadequate. His regret was too huge to be captured in that one word.

"About ten years after you disappeared, the New York Times Magazine did an investigative feature on the scandal. They tried to track you down but drew a blank. They rehashed the whole story, interviewed anyone who would speak to them about you. Everyone had a theory about why you had done it and where you were. I refused the interview. I thought you were dead. I thought you must have killed yourself. It was awful." She drew in a deep breath.

He felt that nothing he said now could wipe away their pain and undo the lost years. His desire to unburden himself had been so strong, yet now he discovered that there were no words which could do it justice. Despite his silence, or maybe because of it, she continued.

"Oliver spoke to *The New York Times*. We fought about it. We were fighting about a lot of things in those days." She laughed bitterly. "It's ironic, it was the last straw. We weren't happy. He was sour and frustrated. He'd not been able to compose another piece after *The Phantom and the Fraud* as the media had named the sonata. He was angry all the time. He started drinking heavily." She paused, a distant expression on her face. "Anyway, I told him to drop it, not to do the magazine interview. He wouldn't listen to me. Things escalated. Shortly after the article came out it was proposed that a sort of tenth anniversary concert be held at Carnegie Hall. I told Oliver not to allow it. But he got really excited about it and got involved, enjoying the publicity. It kind of rejuvenated him. And by then Juilliard had recovered from the scandal and saw the publicity as a good thing. But it made me unhappy. It's like that music had become a cancer in our lives and in our marriage. I couldn't listen to it without thinking about you and feeling angry and hurt. And Oliver could never live up to his one spectacular composition. He'd spent years feeling like a failure because he could not write another one as good. The drinking got worse. I left him just before that tenth anniversary concert."

They stood watching the lights of the Toronto skyline gradually approach, Alexia's arms folded tightly across her chest against the cold and her memories. As they drew closer to the harbor Mungo said, "Alexia, I'm sorry about taking off like that...I mean earlier today not then, when...well, of course I am sorry about that too. But what I mean is...God, I'm making a mess of this. Thank you for coming with me today, for talking to me..."

"You didn't give me much choice, Mungo."

"I know, I know. That's why I'm sorry. I know I handled things badly. Well, that's an understatement," he added ruefully. She kept quiet; her silence was as recriminating as anything she could have said.

She watched him as he navigated the boat back into the harbor and pulled it towards the berth they'd left that morning. Mungo asked her to go up on deck and throw the fenders overboard to protect the boat as he nudged it up against the dock. He switched off the engine and went on deck to fasten the mooring lines.

He stood up and turned to face her. He tried again. "Alexia, thank you for today. And I really am sorry it turned out like it did. I wish we could start again. I've been wishing that for years. I know it's not possible. Just tell me; do you still think it was Oliver's work? Do you still think I am a fraud?"

She raised and lowered her shoulders in a deep sigh. "Mungo, I don't know what to think. I need to think. It's been too much. I need to go now. People will be wondering where I've been." She turned and stepped onto the dock, gave him one quick glance over her shoulder and ran.

"Alexia wait!" he called. "How long will you be here? Call me. Please." He watched her until she disappeared from view then he turned and went inside to tidy up and remove all traces of their presence.

◆◆◆

From his reclining position with his feet on the desk and a cigarette clamped between his lips, Errol Joynt watched, though the dirty window of his small office, the silhouettes of the couple on *The Ice Queen*. He took the last few draws on his cigarette then leaned forward and stubbed it out adding another butt to the already overflowing ashtray. He flicked through a tatty Rolodex then picked up the phone and dialed Nancy Beringer's number.

Chapter Eight

Elizabeth became aware of a dull ache in her left shoulder. She looked at the clock on the mantelpiece. Two hours had passed since she'd sat down at the piano. The music had challenged and absorbed her. It was like nothing she'd ever heard before and she had struggled with it, but the more she struggled the more she wanted to hear it in all its fullness. She stretched out her shoulders and stood up. She went to the window and peered out into her garden. Most of the trees were bare but she thought she could see the promise of spring in the tiny buds which were starting to emerge. The bare branches cast long wiry shadows out across the still dormant grass.

Coming to a decision Elizabeth turned and went into the kitchen. She picked up the phone and dialed her sister's number.

"Rebecca, hi, it's me. Yes, yes, I'm fine thanks. No, same as usual but the flight was delayed which is why I am home this afternoon." Elizabeth hated inconsequential chat on the phone but felt obliged to ask after her sister's husband, Ian, and the two boys.

Rebecca and Ian lived an hour and a half out of Toronto in a small town where they ran a store which sold furniture made by the local Mennonite farming community. Elizabeth and Ian had never really warmed to each other, Ian having rather traditional views on the role of women. Elizabeth suspected that he found her independence threatening and worried about her influence on Rebecca. Their visits to Toronto were infrequent. When they did come to the city they stayed with Elizabeth and all three of them were silently relieved when the visit was over.

Rebecca had spent a weekend with her sister two months previously to celebrate Elizabeth's birthday and they had gone to the theatre to see a musical.

Elizabeth tried to concentrate while Rebecca talked about the boys' progress at school and sporting achievements and Ian's dissatisfaction with the fact that his business was not growing as he'd hoped. Eventually, impatience getting the better of her, Elizabeth cut in.

"Rebecca, remember when you were last here?" she asked. "Do you, did you…You didn't go into my basement storage room did you? I mean did you leave anything behind?"

"No, why would you ask?" said Rebecca, defensive and annoyed. "You always do that, you know. You are not really interested in anyone else but yourself. I don't know why you bother to call."

"I'm sorry Rebecca, it's just that… Well, it's rather peculiar. I don't know what to make of it. My flight got in late and I spent most of last night waiting at the airport, so I decided to stay home this afternoon. I've been clearing out the storage room in the basement and I found a suitcase which isn't mine. It's full of a man's clothing. And there's this leather folder with hand written sheet music. A sonata. Rebecca, I've been trying to play it on the piano. It's amazing."

"No. I don't know anything about it. Are you sure? Perhaps you've just forgotten. Perhaps someone asked you to keep it for them? You know how forgetful you are about anything other than your work. Why do you think it would be mine?"

"You and Ian are the only people who ever stay here. Mrs. Gibson next door feeds Caprice for me occasionally and waters the plants if I'm away. I'll ask her. It's just so strange. I haven't cleared out the basement for a few years. It could have been there for ages. I just can't think how it got there. It's kind of creepy."

"Aah, I bet you've had a man stay over that you're not telling us about. You probably have a stream of them in and out of your place which you're keeping secret," her sister teased.

"Oh, come on, Rebecca. Why would I call you up to ask you if I knew who had put it there? I'm serious. It's weird."

"I'm serious too Elizabeth. I wish you would find someone. You're what, thirty-nine already? You can't go on like this forever you know; working yourself into an early grave with no one to share your life with. There's still time to find someone. You could still have a baby. They've found ways to make it safe for older women. You just have to look up from your work for a while and observe the world around you. You are attractive, successful. Who wouldn't want you?"

"And what? End up like you stuck in domestic drudgery with a disgruntled husband and two grubby ungrateful little boys."

There was silence at the end of the line. Elizabeth realized she had gone too far; she'd hit on all Rebecca's soft spots. *Truth is*, she thought, *this is exactly why I can't maintain a long-term relationship.* The very things that made her an excellent lawyer made her a bad friend and partner. The only reason Rebecca was still around was because she was her sister.

"Rebecca, I'm sorry. I didn't mean that. I really didn't. You're right. It's just that we've been over all this so many times. I don't know what to do. I'm just not like you. I always mess things up by saying the wrong thing. Like I did just now." She bit her bottom lip and paused, hoping that Rebecca would accept her apology.

"That's okay," she heard the tired resignation in her sister's voice. "It's obviously not my suitcase. And I'm pretty sure it's not Ian's but I'll ask him if he knows anything about it and let you know. I've got to go. The boys need help with their homework." She hung up.

Elizabeth put the phone down slowly feeling a heaviness settle itself in her body with the knowledge that she'd widened the gulf between them by a few more inches. She had always been the more aggressive and ambitious of the two sisters with an inner drive that propelled her, while Rebecca was more content with the world around her, and her place in it. Elizabeth loved her sister and needed her and, particularly after their parents' death, they'd learned to accommodate each other's differences, until Rebecca met Ian.

Elizabeth was frustrated for Rebecca. She knew that her sister could accomplish so much more if she were not held back by Ian. Rebecca was good with people, she was creative and engaging and had some innovative ideas about marketing their business, but Ian was very dismissive of her suggestions. If he could only see that freeing Rebecca to contribute more would help them both; she would be more fulfilled, and they would both be more successful. But any attempt Elizabeth made to suggest this was met with hostility and defensiveness by Ian and forced Rebecca into her default placatory role.

Elizabeth went through to the hallway and pulled on her coat and a pair of shoes. As she stepped out the door she was met with a bracing blast of arctic air. She glanced up. There was a soft white haze gathering in the sky. An early spring snow fall was on its way.

Mrs. Gibson stood in her doorway shaking her head, her soft grey curls bobbing around her lined pink face. "No, dear. I haven't been around to feed Caprice. Sorry, I didn't know you were away." She pulled her long-knitted cardigan more closely around her. "Do you want to come in?"

"Just for a minute." It wasn't fair to keep the old lady freezing in the open doorway. She stepped in and felt the stale cloying air wrap itself around her as the smell of vegetable soup and damp penetrated her nostrils. "I wasn't planning to be away long, but my flight was cancelled. I got back this morning," she surveyed the hallway quickly. The place was dusty and the carpet beneath her feet was dirty. *The old lady really needs some help with this place*, she thought. *Or she should move into a retirement home. But it's not my concern. Her children should be seeing to it.* "Mrs. Gibson, I was wondering, do you still have the key I gave you a while ago?"

"Yes dear, I think so. I haven't used it for a long time. Let me see…" she shuffled through to a room leading off the hallway, the heels of her slippers dragging on the floor. Elizabeth heard her opening and closing drawers, rummaging. She came back with the key. "Here it is," she said, clearly pleased with herself. "As I said, I haven't used it for a long time, not since you went on that long holiday last year to, where was it?"

"Portugal," Elizabeth filled the old lady's memory lapse. "You wouldn't perhaps have left anything in my house, would you? In my basement? I know it seems odd, but I've found an old suitcase and I can't think how else it could have got there."

"No, no, dear. Why would I do that? I know people think I'm going dotty. My children tell me all the time that I should sell this house and move into one of those care homes. Samuel was here just yesterday trying to persuade me to move to a new place they're putting up for old people. But I said no. I'm not going to live on the twelfth floor of some modern apartment block overlooking an intersection. No trees, no space. It's too impersonal. No this is my home. I said to him I don't..." she stopped herself with an abashed smile. "Sorry I know I go on a bit. What is it dear, what did you say you'd found?" Her watery blue eyes stared at Elizabeth through her glasses.

"That's okay Mrs. Gibson. It's an old suitcase. It looks like it belongs to a man."

"No, no. It's not mine." She was thoughtful. "Where did you say you found it?"

"In my basement, in a storage room amongst some boxes." Elizabeth explained starting to feel that the conversation was getting her nowhere.

The woman shook her head sadly, "I've never been in your basement. I hardly ever go into mine. The stairs are too much for me. It's all I can manage to get up and down the stairs to my bedroom these days." Her face brightened a little. "Perhaps it belongs to your brother? Why don't you ask him?"

"I don't have a brother. I only have a sister. You've met her, remember?"

"But I saw him just the other day. I waved at him and he waved back. He does sometimes," Mrs. Gibson insisted.

"What do you mean? Who waved at you? I don't have a brother. Are you sure?" Elizabeth stared at her, alarmed, insistent.

"I, I don't know dear," said Mrs. Gibson, becoming flustered. "I just, I just thought he was your brother. I'm sorry." Her eyes were even more watery than they had been a few minutes previously.

Elizabeth took a deep breath. "No, I'm sorry Mrs. Gibson. It's not your fault at all. It's not you. I'm just a bit worried about this. Could we sit down for a minute?"

Mrs. Gibson nodded and turned toward a doorway leading off the entrance hall. She showed Elizabeth into a dark, over-furnished sitting room and sat down in a floral armchair, switching on the table lamp next to her. In the half-light from the lamp Elizabeth thought she appeared so small and vulnerable, engulfed as she was by the stuffed armchair. She was again struck by the thought that the big house was really too much for the old lady but brushed this aside bringing her mind back to more immediate matters.

"You say you've seen a man at my house. When was this exactly?" asked Elizabeth struggling to keep the urgency out of her voice, not wanting to upset the old lady further.

"Well from time to time really. I couldn't say exactly. A few days ago, I suppose. I see him sometimes."

"Okay, this is important," Elizabeth was all business now. "Can you tell me what he looks like? Where do you see him?"

"He seems nice." She said vaguely. "He waves at me sometimes."

"How old is he? How tall is he?" Elizabeth's impatience was growing.

"He's quite tall. Handsome. He reminds me of my father. He has lots of shiny grey hair, and glasses. When I was a little girl I used to love running my fingers through my father's hair. It was thick and wavy and very silver. I only knew him with silver hair. My mother said it went grey when he was still a young man. It suited him. I can still see it. Sometimes I remember…" Her eyes teared up. "I'm sorry dear. I'm not feeling very good."

Elizabeth realized that she was not going to make much progress with this conversation. All she was doing was upsetting the old lady. "Don't worry about it, Mrs. Gibson. I should get going. Are you going to be alright? Shall I call someone for you? Remember, if you ever need anything, I'm just next door."

"No, no dear. Don't do that. I'm fine. If you call them they will just try and make me move to one of those homes. They think I need help. They don't understand; this is my home."

Elizabeth thanked her and said good-bye. She made her way back up the path to her front door, more concerned about the old lady than before. *My brother? Her father? The old lady has been hallucinating, definitely losing it.*

Chapter Nine

It was dark and a light snow fell as Mungo left the boat. After the day spent with Alexia he felt his aloneness more acutely than usual. The sense of anti-climax drained his energy and he was unsettled. Where should he go now and what should he do?

He worked most nights as a janitor at the library but was not on duty this evening. He liked the job. It didn't pay much but then his living expenses were minimal. It was quiet, and he was left in peace to dust, vacuum, tidy shelves and read. He'd developed an efficient routine over the years and got through the work quickly. The job afforded him both privacy and time to recline undisturbed in comfort in his favorite seat at the end of the aisle between architecture and fishing. Once he'd finished the night's work he would pick a book from the shelves, sit down and enjoy the silence of the dimly lit library with a drink poured from his thermos and eat his sandwich. Usually he made it himself, but if circumstances prevented the use of a kitchen he'd buy a take-out on his way to work.

He decided to head for the gym near Union Station where he had a membership, mostly because it gave him access to their showers and locker facilities. He had a hot shower and retrieved a clean shirt and jacket from his locker. He walked back uptown, his hunger driving him toward Figaro's for dinner. He enjoyed walking in the city, largely unnoticed and unknown. He'd often walked the streets in New York when he lived there, taking in the energy and observing the focused purpose with which most New Yorkers went about their lives. New Yorkers pushed their way through the crowded streets aggressively; so intent upon their own goals that nobody else appeared to matter. Torontonians also moved through their city with a sense of purpose, but Mungo believed that their purposeful appearance was more a convenient veneer that allowed them to avoid contact with others. They were isolated, he thought, not so much by their own goals but more by their reserve, choosing to ignore rather than to risk this discomfort of saying the wrong thing.

Tonight, instead of enjoying the walk he was aware only of his deep sense of dissatisfaction with the day, and more disturbingly, with his life. He pushed his way through the double doors at Figaro's. If he was lucky they might even have their opera cabaret on. The thought of a meal and some music lifted his spirits a little.

He stepped into the softly lit colorful interior and paused a moment to take in the sense of having entered another world. He loved the flamboyant theatrical décor, the rich colors, the unexpected pools of light that spilled out from the lamps and wall sconces and reflected on the red, purple and green silk tablecloths. As he made his way through the restaurant towards his favorite table, he felt enveloped by the generous drapes of velvet that lined the walls between the gilt framed portraits and shrouded the private boxes above him. From his table he had a good view of the theatre style restaurant with its balcony seats and boxes and dress circle.

He sat down appreciating the strains of Puccini's *Nessun Dorma* emanating from secluded speakers. He sought the center of the restaurant where he saw a cello and an alto saxophone on stands next to the piano. He breathed a sigh of satisfaction. It looked like there would be a performance tonight. His eyes wandered up to the ceiling and he was studying the Michelangelo-styled murals when he was interrupted by a tuxedo-clad waiter on his right.

"Good evening, Mr. Mungo. Will you be joining the ensemble this evening or just dining?"

"No, no. Just dining thank you," he replied. "Is Patricia in?"

"She hasn't come down yet, sir. We expect her a little later." He handed Mungo a wine list and the menu. "It's our set opera menu tonight, sir. I hope that's in order?"

"That will be fine," said Mungo. He cast his eye over the menu selecting one of the four main courses available. "I'll have the shank of lamb for the main course and the Bordeaux cabernet sauvignon." He sat back to listen to the music while he waited for his meal. The background music moved on to The Anvil Chorus from Verdi's *Il Travatore*. He checked his watch, the opera cabaret would start soon.

Mungo was halfway through his meal and deeply absorbed in the music when Patricia sat down in front of him. She had a strong presence; her restaurant was an extension of her dramatic personality. She had short spiky ruby red hair, a deep suntan and striking eyes. She favored long bright dresses that flattered her full figure and large breasts. Her deep rich voice and throaty laugh carried across the restaurant and all eyes invariably turned toward her as she moved between the tables, stopping occasionally to greet guests.

She was the only friend Mungo had made in his years in Toronto and this was entirely a result of Patricia's persistence and generosity rather than anything he did. He had become something of a regular at Figaro's and she had spotted him at his favorite corner table four years previously. Mungo had squirmed under the attention of her determined hospitality when she had initially spoken to him. He had been so uncomfortable the first time she had fixed him with her smile and vectored in on his table, that he had not dined at Figaro's for three months after that. Reflecting on it, he was sure that the more he had tried to brush her off the more determined she had become to win him over with her charm.

Gradually over the months Patricia had thawed him out. He found that her knowledge and passion for music matched his and he began to look forward to their conversations. Arriving early one night for dinner Mungo heard that the string quartet was short a violinist and would have to cancel their performance. Having learned that he had a musical background, Patricia persuaded him to fill in for the missing violinist and he found he loved performing for an audience again. Since then, occasionally when one of the scheduled musicians was unexpectedly delayed or unable to be there, Mungo filled in for them.

After one such evening Patricia invited Mungo to go upstairs to her apartment above the restaurant for a nightcap. She was a large and sensual woman, a few years older than he, and in spite of himself he was drawn to her warmth, generosity, humor and her love of music.

Her apartment was decorated with the same dramatic opulence of the restaurant below. The living room was dominated by a beautiful Bechstein grand piano positioned beneath a single soft light. While she had poured them each a whisky he had sat down and played Rachmaninoff's Piano Concerto No. 3.

When he had finished Patricia had, without a word, firmly taken him by the hand and led him to her bedroom. Initially too surprised to object, he soon found himself unable to resist her. He soaked up her generous sensuality with a thirst so deep it frightened him.

Since that night, they had established a friendship but one in which he revealed very little besides his love of music. There were no demands made and no commitments. She spoke, and he listened, he played music and she listened. Sometimes the music underlined the loss of his own career, inducing more pain than pleasure and he stayed away for months. They made love and they satisfied each other. His visits to Figaro's; although unpredictable and erratic, always ended in her bed. She had no idea where to reach him and never questioned him about his absence when he suddenly re-appeared. He suspected but never asked about her other lovers.

"You look tired," she said from across the table. Patricia poured some wine from his bottle into one of the unused glasses on the table and took a sip allowing the dark red liquid to roll around on her tongue before swallowing. "Margot does such a good job of *Carmen*." Her eyes followed his to the singer in the middle of the room.

He put his knife and fork down. Her words brought him back from the reverie in which his thoughts of the day with Alexia merged uncomfortably with his memories of Patricia. His eyes rested on her, suddenly overcome with the uncomfortable urge to tell her about his day. His desire to talk did battle with his habit of reticence. Finally, he picked up his glass. "Cheers. It's good to see you."

"What is it, Mungo?" she asked.

"I can't talk here," he replied. They sat for a few minutes in silence, listening to excerpts from *Carmen*. She stood up, lifted her glass, took a final sip and, raising it in a salute to him, said "I'll see you upstairs later." He nodded and picked up his knife and fork.

When he'd finished his meal, he paid the bill and made his way to the back of the restaurant and up a flight of stairs behind the kitchen. At the top he passed by the 'Employees Only' door and entered a set of double doors marked 'Private'. He breathed in the comfortable abundance of the room. He relaxed in the refuge of its privacy and felt Patricia's presence everywhere even though she was still in the restaurant below.

He walked around for a few minutes, examining the eclectic collection of paintings, the books on the shelves, the mementos from her travels and the photographs of her with notable musicians who had performed in her restaurant or dined there. There were photographs of her son and her grandson. Patricia's only son, she'd told him once, had died in a motorcycle accident. He was young and had left behind a wife and a five-year-old son. The boy lived with his mother in North Carolina and Patricia visited them once or twice a year.

Mungo poured himself a whisky and walked to the window overlooking the street below. He was glad to be here in Patricia's home as he watched the falling snow diffuse the light from the street lamps and gather on the sidewalk. He thought back over the events of the day, how differently it had turned out from what he had imagined. Did Alexia believe his innocence? How could he convince her of the truth? After so many years of hiding he suddenly longed to have someone look him in the eyes and know him.

He wasn't sure how long he'd been standing there when Patricia entered and approached. She gently removed the glass from his hand, took a sip and put it down. "Something's bothering you," and without waiting for a response from him she said, "Come."

He wanted to tell her, even if Alexia didn't believe him, maybe Patricia would. Instead, wordlessly he followed her to her bedroom and watched as she went through her ritual of candle lighting. He wondered what music she would put on and waited in anticipation. Then he heard the first soft slow unmistakable strains of Ravel's *Bolero*.

One of the things he loved about her was her sense of drama and atmosphere. His life had been so devoid of normal relationships for so long that he'd stopped thinking about the possibility of love. But yes, he did love this about Patricia. She paid keen attention to all the details, like the candles she was busy lighting and the music she chose. That was partly what made her so successful as a restaurateur. The food, the décor, the ambience, the music and her guests were all given the focused attention of a lover.

When he entered her rooms, he entered a world in which the rhythms of music and their lovemaking were all that mattered. For Mungo it was an escape in every sense of the word and it was just what he needed tonight.

Tonight, as always, Patricia was as generous in her lovemaking as she was with everything else in her life. She gave richly of herself and took from others as hungrily as she gave. She was tender and voracious at the same time and making love to her was as exhausting as it was satisfying. She drew him into her deeply and repeatedly and he found himself totally lost in her sensuality until there was room for nothing but the experience of their bodies hot and merged, like liquid. When she came he knew that the pleasure she experienced did not just concentrate itself in her lower body but radiated outward until she shuddered from top to toe, letting out a loud cry of unrestrained ecstasy. This triggered Mungo's own orgasm and he released himself fully to it, carried away by wave after wave of pure pleasure.

After a while she got up, as he knew she would, and he watched her walk to the kitchen, oblivious of her own nakedness. Her footsteps were soft, and the curves of her body accentuated in the soft candlelight. He felt relaxed and content, as he hadn't done for weeks. He was comforted by the domestic sounds of her moving about in the kitchen, the fridge door opening and closing, glasses being placed on a tray. He knew what she would be preparing and looked forward to her strange post-coital delicacy.

She returned to the bedroom with a tray and handed him a bottle of champagne to open. Once he'd done this she filled their glasses and handed him one. Then she gave him half an avocado, liberally sprinkled with sugar, and a spoon. She took the other half and sat next to him on the bed as they spooned out the creamy greenish fruit.

That first time they'd made love he'd been surprised when immediately after their coupling she had served him the sugar encrusted fruit. He'd hesitated and watched intently as she'd scooped it out and slowly swallowed it down in the candlelight. "Go on, try it," she'd said. "There's nothing else quite like it."

"I'm sure there isn't," he'd replied wryly. He'd eaten avocado with salt and pepper, as a dip, chopped up with peppers and onions, covered with salad dressing, every which way but never covered in sugar scooped straight out of the skin. As he'd taken his first mouthful he was aware of the contrast of the creamy fruit and the sharp crunch of the sugar crystals. And yet, surprisingly, the flavors harmonized. It was as if, he thought, the avocado had been waiting for years for the strong crunchy sweetness of the sugar to fully bring out its subtle flavor.

After his emotional day on the boat with Alexia he was grateful for the quiet companionship of Patricia and they sat side-by-side eating the avocado, sipping the champagne and watching the candlelight flicker against the walls as the music played on in the background.

"What's on your mind?" Patricia asked as she swallowed the last scoop of her avocado and set the empty shell down on the tray.

His gaze was still on the window, watching the snowflakes drifting down in the streetlight outside, "I've been hiding. For years. Here in Toronto," he said, finally turning to her.

She nodded. He felt her uncomplicated acceptance of the world around her and, not for the first time, was envious of her generous acquiescence.

"Something terrible happened and I had to get away. I didn't plan it. I left New York and found myself in Toronto. I just never went back. I'm a fraud. I've been living a lie for almost twenty years."

"*The Phantom and the Fraud*," she said and nodded again. "I know about it Mungo. I read about it many years ago. Then you started coming to the restaurant and the first time you played for us, when you filled in for Carlos that night he was sick, I knew for sure who you were. I figured you'd tell me when you were ready."

"Well, no, that's not what I mean. I mean, I am that Mungo, but that's not why I'm a fraud." He couldn't go on. How to explain to her about his strange existence? After a long pause he said, "It didn't happen the way you read it. It's my music. I composed it."

He climbed out of the bed and crossed the room to the small table beneath the window. He lifted the lid of her humidor and selected a Bolivar. He clipped the end and lit the cigar. One of the many things he'd come to appreciate about Patricia was that she had very few rules and they did not include rules about not smoking in her bedroom.

He drew on the cigar and blew the smoke onto the window where it merged on the inside of the glass with the opacity of the snow-diffused light on the outside. There was quite an accumulation now on the sidewalk and the thin tracks in the middle of the road were deepening each time a car cautiously squelched past. He watched the Figaro's patrons as they stepped from the doorway. All instinctively cast their eyes skywards, as if seeking confirmation that what was happening on the ground was, in fact, coming from above.

His mind was drawn back to his first experience of Toronto, treading the streets and trying to figure out exactly where he was and how he'd got there. His recollections of that journey were still clear despite the passage of time.

Chapter Ten

With his back to Patricia, staring out of the cigar-fogged window onto the Toronto street, Mungo instead saw Manhattan and started to talk. He told her about Oliver's betrayal. It still burned him as if it had happened yesterday.

"I walked around the streets of Manhattan for hours. I was so shocked. I couldn't believe he would do something like that to me. I ended up in a bar, had something to eat and far too much to drink. A real cliché, I guess, the drunk trying to drown his sorrows," he looked over his shoulder at Patricia, as if for confirmation.

"What did you do?" was all she said.

"I sat there for a long time, mindlessly watching the TV above the counter. The local news came on. I was right up there, in the headlines. They showed scenes from the concert the night before and Oliver was interviewed. The bastard. All his false outrage about how he'd worked for so long on the sonata and then I'd taken credit for it. They had music critics, people who'd attended the concert, anyone they could find all giving their opinion. They showed my apartment building, there was this big group of reporters and photographers all clustered around waiting for me to show up. That's when I knew, I couldn't go back, at least not until the dust had settled."

"But if you were innocent, why didn't you speak up, why didn't you tell the truth?"

He paused, long enough to take a deep draw on the cigar. "The thing is, I wasn't innocent, not really. To begin with I was just so shocked. I didn't know what the hell Oliver was playing at. I mean, he was my friend. Why would he do this to me? It only came to me later that Alexia must have picked the manuscript up accidentally at my place when we had our brief affair. Oliver must have found it. To prove that it was mine, I would have had to explain how Alexia would have got hold of my original. I didn't want to expose her. So I had to shut up about it all."

"And move to Toronto?"

"Well, I didn't plan that either."

He explained how, when he had left the bar it was dark outside and he'd continued to walk. Near the Lincoln Tunnel he'd hitched a ride with a truck driver who seemed delighted to have some company. He introduced himself as Chaz and asked Mungo where he was going. Mungo had replied "Wherever you take me."

Chaz passed a quick glance at Mungo, sizing up the situation and nodded, "You got it," apparently satisfied with what he saw. They talked for a few hours; or rather Chaz had talked while Mungo feigned interest. They stopped somewhere along the way at a roadside diner for a late-night meal. When they climbed back into the truck Mungo had dozed off and Chaz nudged him and offered the relative comfort of his bunk in the back of the cab. Mungo had gratefully crawled in, too tired and too drunk to care about the dank sweaty smell of the bunk as he sank into a deep sleep.

He was unsure how long he had slept but when he woke up and emerged from the dark confines of the bunk the truck was still moving, but at a slower pace. He peered out of the window, smeared with the steam of hot breath and grease, onto an industrial wasteland patched alternately grey and white with snow and dirt.

"Where are we?" he asked Chaz. "How long have I been sleeping?"

"A long time mate. I was hoping for company. No such luck. You slept for about eight hours."

Mungo stretched. Despite the relative comfort of the bunk he was stiff. He rubbed his hand over his chin and felt the sharp stubble. He tried to remember when last he had shaved or showered. He studied his once elegant tuxedo. It would never be the same again. "Where are we?" he repeated. They appeared to be in the industrial outskirts of a big city, but not one he recognized.

"Toronto," came the reply. "This is where I let you off, mate." He saw the confusion on Mungo's face. "Unless you wanna do the return journey with me. Gotta off-load first and catch a few hours kip though. The truck rolled to a slow stop, the wheels crunching on the gravel ice mixture in the parking lot outside of what appeared to be a warehouse. "You can hang around here if you want. Or go for a walk or something. We passed a diner a few blocks back. Don't mind sharing my bunk with you but not while I'm in it." He laughed.

Mungo shook his head. They climbed out of the truck and he was jolted wide-awake by the icy blast of air that hit his face. He observed Chaz closely, seeing him clearly in the early morning light for the first time since they'd met. He too could do with a shower and shave.

"I don't understand," Mungo said. "I don't have my passport or anything. Didn't they stop you?"

"Nah," Chaz shrugged. He hitched his jeans up, they were fighting the battle with gravity, not finding adequate purchase around his hips hidden somewhere under his large belly. "I travel this route just about every week. The guys at the border know me. I just cruise through. Sometimes if I've got time to kill I stop near the border post overnight and we play poker when some of the guys get off shift. Say, you could join us," he added brightly.

"No, no thanks. I don't play poker. I'll just get on my way. I, uh…look thanks for the ride. And I'm sorry I wasn't much company. I've had a rough couple of days, probably needed the sleep."

"No problem, mate. You gonna be okay? Where you headed?" He looked at Mungo quizzically. "Like I said, you want a ride back I'll be leaving here in a few hours. Don't mind giving you a round trip. Two for the price of one." He chuckled at his own witticism.

At this Mungo reached into his pocket and pulled out his wallet, feeling uncomfortable and not quite sure whether he was expected to pay for the journey.

Chaz put up his hand, "Nah, I was joking man. No charge. No charge."

"Hey Chaz! You made good time." A man wearing blue coveralls approached them from across the parking lot. "The guys are ready to off load. You want a coffee inside?"

Mungo decided it was time to move on. He shook Chaz's hand, said thank you again and, with a brief nod to the man in the coveralls, he turned and left.

He moved off into the street, not knowing where he was or where he was headed. He just kept putting one foot in front of the other. Cars and trucks passed him on the road with a swish and a splash of slush, their headlights shining into his eyes through the early morning gloom. He found his way to a main road and walked in the same direction as most of the traffic, assuming this would take him towards, rather than out of the city. He was chilled to his skinny bones and hungry, aware that he must be a pathetic, curious sight to the commuters heading into the city, tramping along in his rumpled tuxedo on a freezing cold winter morning.

After some distance the industrial buildings gave way to a residential suburb and he walked on trying to decide what to do. He was off the main road now and trudging along a side street, shivering uncontrollably. The traffic had picked up as people were emerging from their homes and heading for work. He spotted a glass-enclosed bus stop and sheltered from the chill wind on the bench inside. While he was sitting there he noticed a couple emerge from the front door of a house diagonally opposite. They kissed good bye on the front doorstep and the man climbed into a BMW 733i and drove off. The woman walked a couple of blocks in the opposite direction and disappeared down some stairs leading to what he assumed must be a subway entrance.

As Mungo sat there it dawned on him that the house was probably currently unoccupied. His hunger and need for warmth propelled him and he found himself walking towards the house glancing up and down the street which appeared to be momentarily deserted. He walked purposefully up the drive and around to the back of the house. He tried the back-door handle. Locked. He shivered and scanned the garden, nervous. He lifted the doormat under his feet. Nothing. Felt around on the top of the wall lamp to the right of the door. Still nothing. He shifted a cracked flowerpot, its blooms long since withered in the chill air. Success. He picked up the key, brushed the dirt off it and inserted it into the lock. Yes. The lock gave way.

Mungo stepped into the warmth of a kitchen lined with wooden cabinetry and his salivary glands immediately responded to the smell of toast still lingering in the air. He was tempted to find something to eat but decided he'd best make sure there was no one else in the house.

He crossed the room and peered through a door to the right that gave way to a dining room. A highly polished cherry wood dining room suite stood in the middle of the room, adorned by a large bowl of dried hydrangeas. A doorway on the other side of the kitchen led into a hallway from which he could see the front door. He moved cautiously into the hallway. His footsteps seemed unnaturally loud as the hardwood floor creaked here and there under his feet. To the right, off the hallway, was a living room, comfortably furnished with a deep green and gold sofa, two armchairs and a television. Heavy drapes partially obscured the view from the window to the small front garden and the street.

Across the hallway was a pair of double doors, closed. Mungo was fairly certain the house was unoccupied but felt a nervous stir in his stomach nonetheless as he reached for the door handle. He turned the handle, the door opened inwards and he found himself staring into a pair of imperious dark eyes. He was breathing heavily and felt a cold damp sweat break out on his brow. He cursed himself silently for being so easily startled.

The portrait on the wall behind the desk was of a young man, but the unforgiving eyes and the severe set of the mouth beneath the dark moustache suggested a maturity at odds with the firm skin tone and lean young face. He took in the rest of the room. Two easy chairs were positioned in front of a window that matched the one in the living room. The wall to his right was lined with floor to ceiling shelves, filled with books but for a few photo frames. He stepped toward these and studied the pictures. The largest was a wedding photograph of a couple he gauged to be about his age, both smiling into the camera, the woman round-faced, with long fair hair and the man sporting a noticeable moustache. He returned his scrutiny to the portrait. Definitely the same man. He turned and left the room, conscious of the portrait's unwavering stare at his retreating back.

At the top of the stairs Mungo found three bedrooms, one was clearly the main bedroom and bore evidence of habitation. A robe hung over the back of an armchair in the corner of the room and the dressing table was home to some perfume bottles and jars of cream. A pair of men's slippers was neatly placed on the floor at the foot of the bed. He walked across to the bedside table nearest him and picked up the book lying there; Iacocca, Lee Iacocca's autobiography written with William Novak.

The other rooms appeared to be guest bedrooms without any signs of recent occupation. The bedrooms were separated by a small bathroom, in which the air was damp with a soapy scent. A few water droplets trailed down the glass shower door. Mungo reached out and touched one of the towels on the rail behind the door. This too was damp. As he turned to leave the room he caught sight of himself in the mirror above the basin.

His eyes were sunken in dark hollows and under the black stubble on his chin, his face was sallow. His mouth tasted sour and he was suddenly aware of the rumpled pants clinging abrasively to the hair on his legs. Impulsively he stripped off, dropping the clothes in a heap at his feet. He climbed into the shower and stood for a few moments enjoying the sensation of the warm water beating down on his head and shoulders and coursing down his body. He scrubbed himself vigorously working the soap into a creamy lather. When he stepped out of the shower he hesitated a moment before reaching out for one of the towels on the rail and dried himself quickly. Examining his face again in the mirror, he decided that a shave could wait until he could purchase his own razor. He dressed, combed his hair, hung up the towel and did a quick inspection to make sure that everything in the bathroom was as he had found it.

Downstairs in the kitchen he found the bread and put a couple of slices into the toaster. He had his head half buried in the fridge where he found butter and cheese and was just contemplating whether he could make a fresh pot of coffee without leaving any trace, when he was startled by the loud jangle of a telephone. He jerked his head out of the fridge and stared, transfixed, at the instrument on the shelf near the hallway door. He held his breath; willing his heartbeat to slow and the noise to stop. He was afraid that the ringing would bring someone running to answer it and expose his trespass. Then he heard the answering machine click on and a woman's voice, "You've reached Blake and Nancy. We can't come to the phone right now. Leave a message and we'll get back to you." He drew in a deep breath.

Another voice followed. "Hi Nance. It's me, Janine. I know you're not there right now, but I just wanted to confirm things for the weekend. Jacob and I are so glad you and Blake will be joining us. We have a big crowd coming up and it will be fab. We're all meeting at the club for dinner on Friday at seven. No need to bring anything, we have everything sorted. Just don't forget your skis. The snow's going to be great this weekend." The machine clicked off.

Mungo decided to forgo the coffee and ate his toast pacing round the kitchen, anxious now to get out of the house but still uncertain of where to go. He tried to figure out what day it was. Thursday, he concluded. He wandered back into the hallway, toast in hand, and saw a closed door under the staircase. He opened it and descended a darkened staircase arriving in a recreation room of sorts. There were a few old leather sofas, a small television, a coffee table and some boxes against the wall. Through a doorway on the far side of the room he entered a storage room. It housed some old armchairs, a dust covered desk and a narrow bed pushed up against the wall. There was also a filing cabinet, a floor lamp and more boxes. Through yet another doorway he found the furnace room.

As he made his way back up the stairs a nascent thought nudged itself into his consciousness. He switched off the light and closed the door. Back in the kitchen he wiped the breadcrumbs from the counter and replaced the butter and cheese in the fridge. With a last scan of the room he left the house, locked the door and put the key in his pocket.

Chapter Eleven

In the week following her discovery of the manuscript Elizabeth worked on the sonata each evening after work. In fact, as each day drew to a close she became restless in her office and eager to get home to her piano and the mysterious music. Her paralegal and her personal assistant, who shared an office just outside hers, speculated out of her earshot, that she finally had a man in her life.

The music had a capacity to raise her emotions in a way that she had not experienced for years, so dulled had she become by her sterile routine. Elizabeth knew she could not do the sonata justice on her own but was driven to perfect it and longed to hear it played with the backup of a full orchestra.

At her desk in the office, she finished scribbling a note on a file, scanned her email inbox one last time and decided that what remained could be left for the following day. She switched her computer off, removed and replaced her shoes with the more comfortable ones she used for commuting. Picking up her briefcase and purse she left the office.

"Sam, I've emailed my comments on the draft Jameson agreement to Clive, with a copy to you. If he calls after I've left, tell him I'll be in first thing tomorrow morning and will answer any questions he has then," Elizabeth said to her paralegal as she passed his desk. "I have to leave now, I have a dinner this evening. See you tomorrow." Sam and the P.A. exchanged meaningful glances as they said their goodbyes to their boss.

At home Elizabeth fed Caprice, had a shower and got ready for the dinner. It was a fundraiser she'd agreed to attend in support of a charity that was working to build a hospital in a remote part of Brazil. One of the partners at her law firm, Brian Palmer, was married to a Brazilian woman who was on the advisory council of the charity and he had sold a number of tickets on her behalf. Elizabeth was not particularly in the mood but, having made the commitment and bought the ticket, she felt obliged to go.

♦♦♦

Nancy was upstairs in the bedroom moving her things from the purse she'd used that day to a black and gold satin evening purse when she heard the front door close and the heels of Blake's shoes strike the hallway floor. She came out on to the landing and looked down over the banister.

"You're cutting it fine," she said. "We're due at the dinner in thirty minutes."

"What dinner?" said Blake, the lines of irritation on his face matching his tone of voice. She saw realization dawn on him. "Oh, for God's sake Nancy! You can't seriously expect me to go to a black-tie dinner now." He dragged his suitcase toward the stairs and started heaving it up.

"You've known about this for weeks Blake. It's not like I'm springing it on you at the last minute. And besides, you decided to extend your trip by two days." She stepped aside to let him pass as he reached the top of the stairs. In the bedroom he hefted the suitcase onto the bed and turned to face her.

Nancy said, "It's up to you Blake, but don't expect me to make your excuses. All the big pharmaceutical companies will be represented; they've all put money into this hospital, and I've made sure we will be at the same table as Jeremy Wilkes and his wife. I thought you were after that position as the Head of the Ethics Committee. He's a key decision maker, as I understand it."

"Christ," he said running his hand through his hair. He flung his jacket onto the bed and headed for the bathroom tugging at his tie. Nancy smiled smugly at his back and continued transferring things to her evening purse.

Half an hour later they were weaving through the traffic headed downtown in Blake's Porsche. Nancy watched the wipers slashing rhythmically across the windscreen in front of them.

"Did you lend the boat to anyone last week?" she asked Blake.

"No, why? Who'd want to take it out in this weather?" he said peering through the rain relentlessly hitting the windscreen. It had been cold and grey, alternately snowing or raining for weeks. It would be so good to get some sun, he thought. He was wondering if he and Jessica could coordinate their schedules for a week away in the Caribbean without raising suspicions when Nancy's voice cut through his thoughts.

"Blake are you listening to me? I told you. Errol, the guy from the harbor, called last week to ask me if we were using the boat. Someone took it out, he said, but he was puzzled because he knows we don't usually go out this time of the year. He called later to say it had been returned. I do wish you'd tell me these things. How can I see to things when you don't keep me informed?"

"I didn't lend it to anyone. Who would want to go out...?" he stopped. *Oh shit!* Christine, he thought. She loved the boat. He knew he should never have got involved with her. She was too needy. But so bloody sexy. *I really must get her transferred. As far away as possible. God, what I don't need now is for her to find out about Jessica. She could ruin everything, everything. And I am so close to the Ethics Committee appointment. Shit, if Christine gets out of control I'll lose my job and the Ethics Committee appointment. If Nancy finds out all hell will break loose.*

"Blake, are you okay? What's going on?" Nancy was staring at him intently. He could feel her gaze as he kept his eyes fixed on the road and the raindrops. He tried to take a few unobtrusive deep breaths. He felt as if she could see right through him, right into his soul.

"Nothing. Nothing. I'm fine, just tired. I told you I don't feel like going to this dinner tonight. And I, ah, I think one of the guys from the office could have taken the boat out. I offered it, but I didn't really think he would take me up on it." He hoped this would allay any suspicions.

"Well, you should have told me. And as for this evening, this is for you Blake, not for me. You've always wanted an appointment to the International Pharmaceutical Federation. And the Head of the Ethics Committee would put you right in the hot seat, in the center of things. It's all about ethics and social responsibility these days. If you hit it off with Jeremy Wilkes, who knows?"

♦♦♦

The evening had been a long one and while the meal had been excellent, the speeches and acknowledgements of the donors had seemed interminable. Elizabeth had enjoyed the entertainment though; a jazz pianist and a soprano eased the tedium with individual performances between the courses.

Elizabeth was making her way across the banquet hall occasionally stopping to say good-bye when Brian came up and took her arm.

"Elizabeth, thank you so much for coming, but before you leave there is someone I want you to meet. You play the piano, don't you? You must meet Nancy Beringer. She's on the Board of the Ontario Symphony Orchestra. She arranged the musicians for tonight."

They walked across to a small group who were talking and laughing. Elizabeth recognized Blake Beringer, he was the CEO of Founder Pharmaceuticals and was often quoted in the business media. He seemed to elicit a mixed response from people being both lauded and criticized for his aggressive approach. Brian introduced them, and Elizabeth shook hands with them both and was immediately drawn to Nancy who was poised, almost regal, and yet a warmth emanated from her.

"Brian tells me that you were responsible for this evening's musical entertainment. It was superb. Such a nice idea to alternate the jazz piano with the soprano," said Elizabeth.

"Thank you. I do a lot of work in the arts community and I always like to find opportunities for new artists to perform. The soprano is just twenty-three, but such a talent. We will hear a lot more from her in the coming years I think. You play the piano, Brian tells me."

"Yes, but purely for my own pleasure," Elizabeth felt abashed and wished that Brian had not mentioned her to Nancy. "I'm nowhere near performance standard. But I do love it."

Blake cut in, "Excuse me." He looked from Elizabeth to Nancy, "we really do need to get going darling. It's been a long day and I have an early meeting tomorrow morning."

"Oh yes, of course," replied Nancy. "Blake has just got in from Munich and barely touched down before I dragged him out to dinner," she said, flashing an insincere smile in Blake's direction. They headed to the exit together and said good-bye.

Chapter Twelve

Mungo left Patricia's apartment while she was still sleeping. He was anxious to leave before she woke and worried that he had told her too much the night before. She had listened to his recounting of the past in silence and when he'd finished all she'd said was, "You have even more secrets than I thought. I've suspected for a long time who you really are. If you're innocent, then you owe it to yourself to come forward and clear your name."

"Patricia, it's not that simple. Don't you think I would have done that at the time if it had been possible?" He looked at her, appealing for understanding but saw just frustration in Patricia's face. "There was a woman, I couldn't speak out, it would have damaged her..."

"Aah, of course, a woman. Well the way I see it, the only thing that is stopping you now is what you're currently guilty of, trespassing.

She was right, of course, he thought as he walked quickly toward the subway station. The early morning air was cold but clear, it promised to be a bright day once the sun rose fully. He got on a train and headed north. It was filled with early morning commuters, some reading the paper, others trying to eke out a few more minutes sleep, their heads lolled back, mouths gaping uncontrollably. Still others were lost in the electronic devices plugged into their ears or the images on the tiny screens that apparently kept them connected with the world yet actually seemed to isolate people more than ever from the person right next to them. Those who were not otherwise occupied, simply stared straight ahead looking through or past each other, effectively rendering one another invisible, which is how Mungo felt much of the time anyway.

He arrived at Elizabeth's house shortly before eight having interrupted his walk from the subway station near her home to buy some bread and cheese. He walked quickly up the drive hoping to evade the inquisitive eyes of Mrs. Gibson next door. She was a sweet old thing but was becoming too interested in his comings and goings. They were now on 'waving terms', which was not something Mungo wished to encourage, but it was difficult to avoid acknowledging her without raising her suspicions, and so, when she saw him he waved and smiled confidently.

As he approached the garage he peeked through the small window in the sidewall. It was empty. *Good.* Using his key, he unlocked the back door. Caprice immediately sprang off his favorite chair and wove himself between Mungo's legs purring loudly.

"Hello mister," he said and bent down to stroke his silky fur. "Haven't seen you for a few days? How've you been? All quiet here, is it?" he said, glancing around.

He put his bag of shopping down on the counter and walked through to the study at the front of the house. Elizabeth's briefcase was not on the desk, which meant that she was probably at work.

Back in the kitchen he switched on the radio and got the coffee maker going. Soon the room filled with its delicious aroma. He unpacked his shopping and set about making himself an omelet and toast.

Once he had finished his breakfast he washed the dishes and repacked everything as he had found them. He replaced the remaining groceries in the shopping bag and headed down to the basement. In Elizabeth's guest bedroom he dropped his backpack on the bed and stripped off. He had a long hot shower in the adjoining bathroom and washed some of his clothes by hand in the basin and put them in the dryer.

He went upstairs, poured himself another coffee and sat down at Elizabeth's desk. He shifted the wooden in-tray on the desk and found the small notebook she used to record her passwords. Quickly flipping though it he confirmed that she had not changed computer password. While he waited for her computer to boot up he picked up the phone for the landline and dialed into her voicemail. There were no new messages and one saved one. He wasn't sure if this was one he'd already heard but pressed one to hear the recording. It was a message from her sister.

"Elizabeth, its Rebecca." She sounded terse. "I'm calling because I said I would. I've spoken to Ian. He knows nothing about the suitcase. He doesn't know what you are talking about. Well…" she hesitated. "I guess that's all. Let me know if you find out anything more about the music." *What was Rebecca talking about, music, a suitcase?*

He listened to it a second time then shrugged and resaved the message. He started perusing Elizabeth's emails. Nothing much of interest. Her life was really becoming very narrow, he thought, somewhat guiltily. A few years previously she had dated occasionally, but not since the last jerk. He was relieved. He didn't think any of the men she had dated were good enough for her; that often happened with professional women, the older they got the fewer eligible men were available. And those that were available were losers or too young.

He thought back to her last relationship. He was sorry she had been hurt, but really it was for the best. If she'd known he'd saved her from a fraudster she would be grateful. The jerk, Trevor, was a real loser. Mungo could see that. Why couldn't Elizabeth? Mungo had done some checking up and had caught him out in some lies. He said he was in real estate, but when Mungo enquired he wasn't even registered with the real estate board. No, the guy was a real passenger, trying to get a free ride on her back. He was glad he'd overheard their last argument. And the next day when Trevor had sent two-dozen red roses and an apologetic note Mungo had destroyed them before Elizabeth got home. She never knew, and she never saw Trevor again.

He was paging through the program on Elizabeth's desk, from the Brazilian hospital fundraising dinner she had attended the night before, when he was startled by the doorbell. *Damn, who could that be?* He approached the study window to see who was on the front porch. The doorbell rang again. After a few moments he saw Mrs. Gibson navigate the stairs down from the porch and make her way round to the side of the house. *Oh hell.* She wasn't giving up. He crossed the hallway and stood just out of sight of the kitchen windows. He heard her knocking on the back door.

"Hello, hello. I know you're there. I saw you arrive. Elizabeth was asking about you. Hello," the old lady shouted.

Mungo stood absolutely still. He found that he was holding his breath. *What? What was she saying?* Elizabeth was asking about him! For a moment he was tempted to open the door and confront her, but he thought better of it. She knocked a few more times and finally left.

He suddenly felt exposed and fought the urge to leave immediately. She'd seen him arrive; she would no doubt be watching to see if he left. He felt trapped. This house, which had been a sanctuary for so long, now felt like a threat. *The bloody woman!* He would have to stay away from the windows. He had planned to work on his composition at the piano today, but it was too close to the living room window. She might come back again.

He went down to the basement. At least there was no way she could see him down there. He loved Elizabeth's house and the Beringer's place was only available to him erratically since Nancy no longer worked full time. This new wrinkle was really upsetting his routine. Everything had worked out so well for so long. *If it weren't for the old busybody next door.* If only he could shut her up somehow. Perhaps he should go and talk to her, allay any suspicions. He could try and find out what she meant about Elizabeth asking about him.

He removed his clothes from the dryer and packed up his few belongings in the small backpack which he took everywhere with him. He needed to sleep. He was working that night and he'd hardly slept the previous night. He'd spend ages spilling his guts to Patricia and then lain awake worrying about having said too much.

He stretched out on the guest bed in the basement. He would just lie here for long enough until he thought Mrs. Gibson would no longer be watching out for him and then he'd leave. Eventually he drifted off to sleep, his thoughts of Alexia merging into a confused jumble with Patricia, Elizabeth and Mrs. Gibson.

He was not sure if it was the music or his dream that had woken him. He'd had a vivid disturbing dream in which he was playing the piano before a large audience and then he was both playing and watching himself playing the piano. As he watched himself play, the person he observed became

Oliver. He tried to rush across to the piano to yank Oliver from his seat but felt that he was being held back. He turned to see what was restraining him and stared straight into the green eyes of Alexia. Her gaze had immobilized him, trance-like. Then she kissed him, and he kissed her back strongly, holding her tight in his arms. While he held her, she transformed into Patricia. Patricia was whispering something urgently into his ear, though he couldn't make out what she was saying. He broke free of her hold and rushed toward Oliver, remonstrating with him. As he approached the piano, Oliver dissolved before his eyes. Mungo looked around, the concert hall was empty, the lights dim, and he was totally alone.

He was fully awake now, yet the music from his dream played on. His music. Someone was playing one of his early sonatas, one he'd composed in the early years following his flee from New York. He hadn't played it for more than ten years and he'd certainly never heard anyone else play it. He'd forgotten about the piece. He'd hidden it with some of his old things in Elizabeth's basement years ago. *Of course, that was the suitcase Rebecca mentioned in her voicemail. She must have found it!* He sat up with a jerk, alert now. He wondered what else he had left lying around to be found. He was getting too complacent. He would need to scout around and make sure he hadn't forgotten anything else. But not tonight.

The music nudged its way back into his consciousness. It was beautiful. It really needed the back-up of a full orchestra though. It must be Elizabeth at the piano. She was doing a fine job of the sonata too and it was a particularly difficult piece. The timing was awkward in places but that was what made it so unexpected, so exciting. He wanted to rush upstairs and give her some direction, to fine-tune things.

He checked his watch. Five-twenty-five. What was she doing home so early? He hadn't intended to sleep and certainly not for so long. He was tired; it was because of the anxiety and sleepless nights leading up to his confrontation with Alexia on the boat and the wakeful night at Patricia's.

Mungo had to get out of the house. He was due at the library at seven pm. This hadn't happened before. If he was in the house while she was there it was always because he had planned it, and he was very careful. He was losing control. She was upstairs. And he was trapped. He went into the bathroom leaving the light off because it activated an extractor fan and the noise could be heard upstairs if the house was quiet.

After relieving himself he realized too late that he could not flush the toilet without risking her hearing the sudden rush of water. He should have waited until he got outside. *Idiot.* He really needed to think. He quietly lowered the seat and added some toilet paper. Hopefully if she found the unflushed toilet Elizabeth might think she'd forgotten to flush.

Back in the room he sat down on the edge of the bed with his head in his hands. The music continued to drift downstairs. He thought back through the day. He was sure he hadn't been back in the study after Mrs. Gibson rang the doorbell. He pictured the scene. He'd been at the desk. With a coffee cup, the computer switched on. Reading the program for the fundraiser. The doorbell rang. *Dammit.* He hadn't removed the coffee cup and he'd left the computer on. It would have gone to sleep now, but that was not how Elizabeth had left the room. He was really losing it. It was all because of Alexia. He had to get her out of his mind. And he had to get out of the house.

If he was really careful he could do it. But he needed to do it soon, while she was still playing the piano. She'd be concentrating on the music and would be less likely to hear him. If he could get across the hallway from the basement stairs and into the kitchen without her turning around he might be able to do it.

He got up and carefully smoothed the bed covers. Hooking his backpack onto his shoulders, he cast a quick look back at the room and made his way to the stairs. He knew which ones creaked and avoided those. At the top of the stairs he stopped and peered across the hallway. Elizabeth was still playing; he could see part of her back through the opening into the living room. His pulse quickened. I can do this, he thought. As he stepped into the hallway Caprice appeared and rubbed herself against his legs, mewing. *Shit. Bloody cat!* He stepped back onto the staircase and flattened himself against the wall, the cat still with him.

"I know, I know, you're hungry Caprice," he heard Elizabeth say. He bent down to stroke it. The mewing changed to purring. "I'll feed you in a few minutes," she said, the piano keys still sounding out his notes. He had to get out of there before Elizabeth stood up. He stuck his head forward; she was still focused on the piano. *Now.* Mungo forced himself to slow his movements and his breathing as he crept through the hallway as stealthily as Caprice herself. When he got into the kitchen he stood still, waiting, listening. Had she heard him?

The cat walked into the kitchen, mewing again, back at his legs. He heard the piano stool scrape against the floorboards as Elizabeth pushed it back. *Here she comes.* He hoped that the back door was still unlocked, as he had left it when he entered that morning. He darted across the room. The door opened easily and he pushed through, closing it quickly and more noisily than he would have liked. The light from the kitchen window spilled into the garden. He moved to the side and tucked himself alongside a large globe cedar. His breathing was rapid and loud in his ears. He waited.

As he expected, a moment later the door opened. Elizabeth was silhouetted against the light, peering into the garden. "What is it Caprice? Did you hear something too?" She paused a moment, shook her head and stepped back into the kitchen. He heard the lock fasten.

Chapter Thirteen

As a director of the Ontario Symphony Orchestra, Nancy spent at least one day a week at their offices. She had been busy for a couple of hours with the Admin Manager, reviewing expenses, signing cheques and discussing some human resource issues. She was not responsible for the orchestral staff but the board members were often invited to auditions of new musicians and approved the performance repertoire put forward by the musical directors for each season.

The phone rang on her desk. She saw the call was from reception. "Yes, Jennifer?"

"There's a Mrs....a Ms. Carey here to see you. She says she doesn't have an appointment but would very much like a few minutes with you if you are free? She says you met at a dinner last night."

Nancy glanced at her watch. It wasn't ideal. She was having lunch with Sven in forty minutes, but she supposed she could fit it in if it was quick.

"That's fine. Tell her I only have twenty minutes, so I can see her briefly. Do you know what she wants? No. Okay then. Just show her in." She put the phone down. *Carey, Carey?* It rang a bell, but she just couldn't place the name.

As soon as Elizabeth walked into the office Nancy recognized her. Of course, Brian Palmer's law partner. Oh well, couldn't do any harm to spend a few minutes with her, Brian was always a very generous contributor to her fundraising efforts.

"Well, this is a surprise," she said, softening her words with a smile. "Please sit down," she gestured to a small cream leather suite in front of the desk.

"Thank you," said Elizabeth, "and I must apologize for appearing like this without an appointment or anything. This is a rather spur of the moment thing."

"No problem," said Nancy graciously. "I'm just sorry I don't have much time right now. It's nice to meet you again. It was a wonderful function last night. Brian Palmer is such a strong supporter of the arts. Have you worked with him long?"

"I've been with the firm for about ten years and a partner for three." Elizabeth stopped, appearing uncertain how to carry on.

Nancy, sensing her ambivalence said, "Is there anything I can do for you?" She smiled. "I'm sure there must be a reason for your visit."

"Well, actually, yes of course there is," said Elizabeth extracting from her bag the thick pile of manuscript pages she had photocopied at her office that morning. She held the manuscript on her lap, reluctant now that she had brought it here, to release it. She suddenly felt possessive, afraid of it falling into the wrong hands and of losing control of it. Her lawyer's brain kicked into gear and she started thinking of copyright and non-disclosure agreements. What if someone else took credit for the work? There was no name on the piece, no indication of the composer. Or what if she and the OSO contravened the composer's copyright? She realized now that she really couldn't hand the manuscript over to the OSO just like that, with no formal understanding or agreement between them. On the other hand, her desire to find out who the composer was equally matched her desire to hear the sonata played in the grand setting it deserved with the backing of a full orchestra.

Finally, she said, "I know this is going to seem strange, but a few weeks ago, when I was clearing out my basement, I found this manuscript. Well not this one, this is a copy. I have no idea how it came to be in my basement, where it came from, who it belongs to or who composed it. But I've been playing it and it's magnificent. It should be heard. It should be played professionally, in an auditorium in front of thousands of people. It is one of the most beautiful pieces of music. I don't think it's been performed before.

But then, you'd be a better judge of that." Elizabeth stopped; she realized she had been speaking more and more rapidly, fueled by her desire to get this music heard. She paused, took a breath. "I've been working through it on my piano at home. It is lovely, complex and the timing is very tricky, but well, I was wondering…when I met you last night, it occurred to me that perhaps this is something the OSO would be interested in?"

Nancy smiled again. "That is unusual," she said. "Are you quite sure there is no indication of the composer?" She held out her hand for the manuscript. "Perhaps it is a known piece. I'd have to look through it and hear it played to be sure if it is new. Of course, if it is new, and is as good as you say it is, that would be quite something." Her eyes shone, unwavering, on Elizabeth.

Elizabeth was becoming embarrassed by Nancy's outstretched hand and annoyed with herself at only thinking of the copyright implications once she'd sat down in front of her. She fanned through the pages and handed Nancy the top third. That would be pretty much the first movement, she estimated. She said, "I know you don't have much time right now, and I have to go too. I'll leave you with those pages, and my card. If you are interested in the piece, please give me a call and we can discuss it further. Also, if you have any ideas as to who the composer might be, I'd be very interested. As you can imagine, I am very keen to discover how this music came to be in my basement. I know it was not there when I moved into the house and it was certainly not there the last time I did a clear out."

"I will review the music and pass it on to the right person here. I will be in touch as soon as I have some news."

They both stood and said their good-byes. Nancy watched as Elizabeth left her office, her intrigue rather more piqued when she realized that Elizabeth was, in fact, reluctant to part with the photocopied manuscript.

Nancy left the office building tugging her brown coat around her against the wind, her head full of the brief conversation she had just had with Elizabeth Carey. She doubted that the music would be any good. The real problem would be how to let Elizabeth know without offending her while preserving her good relationship with Brian Palmer. As Nancy approached the restaurant where she and Sven had agreed to meet she became aware of a light bubble of excitement in her stomach, a feeling that had become less and less common in recent years. She pictured Sven waiting for her, his blue eyes gleaming out from the lines around his weathered face. She was just two blocks away when suddenly a car pulled up and stopped alongside her. The driver rolled down the window and called her name. It was Sven.

"Get in," he said.

Nancy looked ahead toward the restaurant then back at him. "Well, okay, but we're almost there. I can walk."

"Get in." He leaned over and opened the passenger door. Nancy climbed into the car.

"This is a surprise," she said. I thought we'd agreed to meet at Phillipe's."

"We did. I changed my mind," Sven replied as they drove past the restaurant.

"Where are we going? I have to get back to the office right after lunch. That's why I picked Phillipe's. It's close by." Nancy was feeling just a little unnerved. She was used to being in control, and when it came down to it, she really didn't know much about Sven.

He reached out and patted her leg reassuringly and then left it there. "You will see. It is a surprise." Nancy watched his tanned hand on her leg. She was surprised by the unexpected intimacy of this, he was a relative stranger after all, but she found she was enjoying the sensation of his long fingers drawing imaginary circles on her thigh and pushed aside the thought of Blake and her twinge of misgiving at this sudden change in direction.

◆◆◆

Blake Beringer slammed his way out of the Founder Pharmaceuticals boardroom, stomped past his assistant and into his office throwing the folder he'd been carrying onto his expansive desk. In the privacy of his office he allowed himself a deep relieving sigh as he stood at the window and studied the familiar Toronto skyline. Two sides of his office were windowed, and he had impressive views north and east of the city. Taking in the panoramic view used to give him a sense of pleasure and a sense of power but now he barely noticed the office buildings, large condo towers and slow snake-like crawl of the traffic heading out toward the snow-covered countryside beyond.

That bloody Simon Parnell is becoming a real nuisance, thought Blake. No, more than a nuisance, he is becoming a threat. I should never have agreed to his transfer to Canada.

The thought of Simon's transfer reminded him of the problem with Christine. He had to get her moved. Quickly. Before she could do damage. She was so clingy, the kind of woman who was bound to snoop and gossip. All hell would break loose if she found out about Jessica. Maybe he should finish things with Jessica too. Really, he was being bloody stupid. And God knew he was not a stupid man. Why couldn't he keep away from the women he worked with?

Most of the time, he allowed himself to believe that it was the women who couldn't keep away from him. They were drawn to his powerful sexuality, his authority, his strength, his wise leadership of the organization. What was a man in his position to do? They needed him, they wanted him. They proved that he was indeed invincible, that he was entitled. In taking them sexually he was only taking his due. He could, in fact, have any woman he wanted. Which woman had yet denied him or brushed him off? These women were indeed his right. This too was a form of leadership, of guidance, of generosity even. He was fulfilling their needs, providing emotional support and sexual release. And he was always attentive, caring, interested in them and their careers. He bestowed professional advice as generously as he did expensive gifts. This was his reward for the determined and arduous job he did.

It was, however, in the unguarded moments just after waking, early in the morning or in the middle of the night, when the mind is at its most exposed, soft and permeable, that the piercing clarity of what he was doing and who he was shot through his thoughts like a sword. These moments of brutal honesty jolted him into wakefulness more effectively than a bucket of ice-cold water in his face. It was then, before he fortified, reassured and re-built his walls of self, that he knew he was deluding himself. It was not so much these women who needed him, as he who needed them.

They were the proof that he was indeed a man, not just any man but a powerful man, one to be admired and obeyed. He was a man to whom men deferred and women succumbed. Indeed, his many mistresses in the workplace had not passed the notice of his male colleagues. They knew. And their awe and deference were communicated through the silence of their tacit complicity. In those early morning moments of unadorned self-knowledge Blake Beringer knew his weakness was such that while he needed these women they were using him as he used them.

He also knew that an affair with the head of Founder's legal department, while he was running for the Ethics Committee appointment, was just about as stupid as one could get.

His heart pounding rapidly now, he stepped across to his desk and hit the button on his phone that connected him with his assistant.

"Yes Blake?" He heard Diane's voice.

"Can you get Christine Hayes up here? I need to see her as soon as possible."

"It's lunch time Blake." Diane patiently reminded him. The condescending way she drawled out his name grated on his nerves. "I'm sure she'll be out of the office now. I'll try her after lunch." *Why was it that whenever he needed something urgently his people were always on lunch? Why couldn't they take a sandwich at their desk as he did most days?*

His thoughts returned to Simon Parnell and the four-hour long executive committee meeting they'd just finished. *What a frustrating fucking waste of time that was!* Blake felt ready to explode. Blake thought the guy derived tremendous satisfaction from thwarting his efforts to initiate anything, make changes, drive productivity and improve performance. Before Simon arrived, Blake was able to forge ahead with the support of the executive committee on most things. But over the past year or so Simon had managed to change the dynamic on the committee to the point that previously loyal supporters of his were now questioning his decisions and, this morning, had actually voted against his proposal to expand the east Toronto manufacturing laboratory.

It was clear now that Simon wanted his job and he was running his mission like a military campaign. During the coffee break, after it became apparent that things were not going Blake's way, he had taken Chris Redford aside for a quiet word. His long-time friend and confidant had sheepishly acknowledged that Simon had been to see him last week, while Blake was in Munich, and had presented an alternative set of figures and a new proposal which, Chris agreed, was much more solid than what Blake was suggesting.

Every time he turned his back Simon had the knives out. How the hell was he supposed to do the job of a CEO if he could never leave the office or the country on business? Truth was, Blake conceded, that for too long now he had been more preoccupied with his dalliances than his job. His eye was no longer on the ball. He had become complacent and there was no room for complacency in the corner office. A few years ago his vigilance would never have allowed him to put forward a proposal that ran the risk of being outvoted. No, Simon had definitely undermined his position and he had to be neutralized. But first he had to get Christine Hayes transferred. Fortunately, the head of HR had helped find a spot for her in Calgary. Now he just had to persuade her to take it. And to stay off his bloody boat and out of his life.

Chapter Fourteen

Nancy sat pensively next to Sven. A quick lunch with Sven would be harmless enough, justified even, considering what Blake got up to, but she hadn't bargained on driving out of town to some unknown destination with him. And let's face it, she thought, I hardly know him.

He turned the radio on to a jazz station and continued to excite the nerve endings on her leg, almost absent-mindedly. While she was uncomfortable with the growing silence between them, Sven appeared quite content, peacefully distant. After a while she spoke up. "Where are we going? I'm expected back at the office this afternoon. You might be a free agent, but I have responsibilities."

He shot her a look and, as if he had been reading her mind, he said "I just thought we should get to know each other a bit. Don't worry we're almost there. We're going to have a picnic." He squeezed her leg.

"You're crazy, it feels like mid-winter. Nobody picnics in mid-winter and I'm not dressed for the outdoors. I think we should go back." She was the crazy one for getting into the car with him. Her eyes were on the stark landscape surrounding them. They were about thirty or forty kilometers north of the city, the snow-covered farmland yielding periodically to the trees that, although they had prior claim to the land, were losing an economic battle, for which they were ill-equipped, with the developers. Restless, she removed her cell phone from her purse, more out of habit than anything else, and checked the time on the screen. "How much longer are we going to be? I've got to make some calls." She was striving now to keep the unease from her voice.

The effort of keeping her voice level had forced the tension into her body and she thought he must have felt it in her leg because he started massaging her thigh all the while keeping his eyes on the road. "Relax Nancy, you don't always have to be in control. You might find you enjoy it. It is all about trust isn't it? Who do you trust, Nancy Beringer?" Briefly taking his eyes from the road, he turned to her, the weight of his question heavy between them but softened by the curve of a self-deprecating smile.

My God, who did he think he was, this... this sun-tanned foreigner talking to her of control and trust! He didn't even know her. She brushed his hand off her leg. "I need to get back to the office," her voice was shaking now as much as the hand that brushed his from her leg.

"We're here," he said as he turned the car into a long-graveled tree-lined drive.

Sven pulled the car up in front of a shabby but well-proportioned old Tudor- style farmhouse, the snow crunching under the wheels as they drew to a stop.

"Where are we?" said Nancy, making no move to open the car door.

"This is my place. I'm renting it for a while. I come here to get away from things. Sometimes to paint and to write. It is beautiful, and peaceful, but I must warn you; it is very basic. That is why it will be a picnic. Come, let's go in."

"Look Sven, I don't have that much time and I don't appreciate you changing our plans without consulting me."

"I'm sorry. I just wanted to surprise you, do something fun, a nice change..."

Now she felt like a silly school girl out of her depth. Perhaps she was over-reacting? "Okay," she said uncertainly, looking at her watch. "I can only stay for an hour and then I have to get back."

He got out of the car and came around to open Nancy's door. "Come. I will show you around. We will have our picnic and then we will return. I promise."

She gathered up her purse and pulling her coat around her, reluctantly took his hand as he helped her from the car. Too late they both realized that her city shoes were no match for the deep snow between the car and the front door of the house. As her ankles sank into the snow, he apologized and reaching down, put his hands behind her knees and under her arms, and lifted her up. She gasped and grasped him around his neck, feeling certain that they would both fall. No one had lifted her like this since her early twenties.

"No, Sven. Put me down. I can walk."

"Aah but those beautiful shoes and those delicate feet...no I can manage."

Once inside the house she saw what he meant by basic. It was a large house in need of repair. Someone had started work in the kitchen and living room where the wooden floors had been sanded and the rooms repainted. The kitchen was furnished with old farm style loose cabinets rather than fitted cupboards. Sven returned to the car and fetched a basket and a brown paper bag containing their lunch. He put them down on the large oak table in the kitchen.

"Take a look in there," he said gesturing to the shopping bag. "I'm going to turn on the water mains."

She unpacked the fresh bread, cheese, pate, red wine and a tub of seafood chowder he had bought in Toronto.

"We will have to heat that," he said walking back into the kitchen. He wore khaki chinos, a blue denim shirt and a thick cream sweater. The blue shirt collar mirrored the blue in his eyes. In spite of herself she felt her mood lighten.

She wandered around the house while he lit the fire. "You can explore upstairs if you like," he called to her, "my paintings are up there." The living room, dining room and study were downstairs and upstairs there were four bedrooms and a bathroom. Not much work had been done upstairs and only one of the rooms was furnished with a double bed, chest of drawers and desk. There was a worn red and blue patterned rug on the floor. The light which came into the room was soft and filtered through the cream drapes drawn across the window.

Across the hallway Nancy pushed open a heavy wooden door into a room that was awash with color. Canvases in various stages of completion lined the walls and were propped up against every available space. She wondered why he had chosen this room as his studio, the window was small, south-facing and the light was poor. She walked across to the window and gazed out at the view of a small frozen pond surrounded by snow-covered trees. Beyond that she could see an elevated tree-covered ridge. The room smelled strongly of oil paint and thinners and the floorboards creaked as she walked across them.

She turned to study the paintings. His work was prolific, and she immediately responded to the energy in his canvases. The paintings were flamboyant and unexpected, fluid and bold. There was nothing constrained about the choice of color, subject or treatment. The brushstrokes were big and broad, even ill defined; yet the paintings had such visual depth, some of them even creating the illusion that she had entered the picture. She was drawn immediately to a huge painting; the petals of a crimson flower, a Rose of Sharon, occupying at least a third of the canvas in the foreground, beyond it the purplish-blue peaks of a mountain range rising in the distance. The immediacy of the flower juxtaposed with the moody, misty distance of the mountains was remarkable. Nancy was not sure how long she had been studying this painting when she became aware of hot breath on the back of her neck and turned to look straight into the eyes which had seen and painted this incredible picture.

"They're beautiful, really good, but why haven't you signed them? Do you exhibit them?"

"No. I don't. My work is writing. I paint as a hobby, because I love it."

"But you must. These are fantastic. They must be seen Sven." She was insistent. She walked across to another ceiling high painting of a woman and a dog walking along a beach, the wind whipping her red coat around her legs. Nancy could almost hear the waves and feel the wind in her face. "You must exhibit these."

Sven walked to the window, his back to her, apparently giving what lay beyond his full attention. His arms folded, mute and resolute.

"I know a lot of the galleries in Toronto. Let me talk to them for you. I know they will want to show this work. And there are many people who would buy them…"

"It is cold up here, let us go and sit by the fire and have our lunch." He turned and left the room. She followed him downstairs, silently resolving to continue the conversation later.

Downstairs she could smell the comforting wood smoke and hear the crackling of the fire. Already the lower part of the house felt warmer. They went into the kitchen. He had laid a tray with their meal and she helped him carry the plates and glasses into the living room. The furniture in the room was rudimentary and mismatched, but comfortable, however in the spirit of a picnic, they sat on a rug by the fire.

He poured the wine and handed her a glass. "Skål," he said, smiling at her. "You were angry with me earlier. I hope you have forgiven me now? Are you glad you came?"

"Yes, I was. I resented your suggestion that I am a control freak. I have things to do, responsibilities. You can't just expect me to drop things and let people down on a whim."

"Aah, think about it. What is the worst thing that can happen? You miss a meeting or two? So what? Be honest, what really annoyed you was not that other people might need you but rather the fact that we are not doing this on your terms."

She felt her face flush with anger but before she could say anything he reached out and patted her hand. She was not to be so easily mollified and looked away. He may be right, but she was not going to give him the satisfaction of agreeing. She posed for artists on her terms, at her convenience. If he thought she was going to pose for him today, he would be disappointed.

As if reading her mind, he said, "If I were to paint you today, I would want grey stormy seas around you, wind and waves. Other times I see tranquil turquoise as the right backdrop, sometimes I see you walking in the rain. Always water. Always changing. But we are not here to paint today. Today we eat and talk, and I take you back to Toronto."

She was not to have the pleasure of refusing to pose for him. He was really quite infuriating. What exactly did he want from her? What, for that matter, did she want from him?

"Tell me," he said, "How long have you lived in Toronto?"

"All my life. But that's more a question for you, a newcomer to the city. How long have you been here?"

"About six months," he replied. "How long have you been married?"

"Too long, probably."

"Have you always lived in the same house?" He tore a piece of bread from the baguette and handed it to her. "Here, have some cheese," He pushed the plate toward her.

"Well, yes, the same house since we were married. We've renovated it," she caught herself, "What's this, twenty questions?"

"I am just interested. I have travelled around a lot. I wonder what it is like to live in the same house for such a long time."

Nancy felt defensive. "We have a cottage near Haliburton and a boat. We spend a lot of time there. We have both had busy careers and travel a lot too." She decided to change the subject. "You said that you are a writer, what kind of writing?"

"Oh, I do a bit of freelance work to keep the money coming in. Mostly feature length investigative pieces."

"A man of mysterious talents," she said. She was curious about him, now even more so than before.

"What are you writing at the moment?"

"It is a story that dates back almost twenty years. I am not sure that anything will come of it. I am still in the research stage. If I finish it, I will see if I can sell it." He topped up their wine. "Tell me about your work at the OSO."

"I had an interesting meeting this morning with a woman I met at a fundraising dinner last night. She claims to have found an unnamed musical score in her basement and says that she has no idea how it had got there."

Sven propped himself higher on his elbow, his interest clearly piqued. "Is it any good?"

"She seems to think it's brilliant. She plays the piano and has been working through it. The reason she brought it to me is because she believes it should be performed by an orchestra and heard by multitudes."

"She really has no idea who composed it?"

Nancy shook her head. "She says she found it a few weeks ago during a clear out of her basement. It may not be anything of note. But I'll give it to our musical director and see what he thinks. Perhaps he can identify the composer. But what really struck me," she added, "was Elizabeth's insistence that the music be performed so that others can hear it too. That's true of your paintings upstairs. They should be on display so that others can enjoy them. Why don't you exhibit them?"

"Elizabeth who?" queried Sven.

"Elizabeth Carey."

"Elizabeth Carey," Sven repeated her name as if committing it to memory. "What do you know about her?"

"Not much. Just that she's a law partner at a firm in Toronto. I was introduced to her by a friend of mine."

By the time they had finished their lunch, Nancy felt the comfortable deep heavy lethargy in her limbs that follows a satisfying meal and a good bottle of wine enhanced by the warmth of the fire.

Sven's conversation was interesting and varied. They spoke about books, music, politics and art. She tried to draw him out about his life in Sweden and about the woman who had attracted him to Toronto, but he so skillfully side-stepped the questions that she only realized long after the conversation had moved on that he had failed to answer her.

Mostly what Nancy had enjoyed about the afternoon was the laughter. Sven made her laugh out loud, like a school girl, his eyes dancing with merriment like the flames in the fire. She felt bathed in a tonic of reckless abandon, a lightness of spirit and joy that liberated her from the seriousness of her daily life. It was sad, she thought, that she and Blake no longer made each other laugh. It was one of the things that had attracted her to him. She suddenly remembered the time and stood up. "Thank you for the lunch Sven, but I really should be getting back now," she said, and they started clearing up the dishes.

When he dropped her back at her office she thanked him for the extended lunch and looked ruefully at her watch realizing that it was probably not worth going back up to the office. He leaned across and gave her a quick kiss on the cheek.

"Let me know what happens with that music," he said as she climbed out of the car. By the time she had gathered her things, stepped onto the sidewalk and turned to wave, his car had pulled away into the stream of traffic.

Chapter Fifteen

Mungo passed a distracted night at the library failing to derive the usual peace he enjoyed amongst the book-lined shelves. The work itself was easy enough, mindless in fact. But this night he found himself wishing for something more challenging and absorbing, something to transport him away from the thoughts bouncing off the walls of his brain. Every time he latched on to one and tried to wrestle it into something manageable so that he could examine it for a solution, it reflected onto another thought and then he was chasing that one round and round.

His most immediate problem was where to go when he left the library at seven in the morning. He didn't feel like returning to Elizabeth's house and risking a repeat of yesterday's close shave. He knew Blake must be back from Munich and would be at the office, but he wasn't certain of Nancy's movements. Although today was her OSO day she sometimes varied this routine.

He left the library through the rear door ignoring the three or four vagrants who sheltered independently in the building's recesses. Nobody ever bothered them, and he knew that as the day matured they generally shuffled off in search of food and the avoidance of accountability elsewhere. Even though he did not have a home of his own, he never categorized himself with the growing number of street people in Toronto. Today, however, he felt displaced.

He could go to a hotel; he wasn't destitute like these people. Yes, that's what he would do. He would check into the hotel Alexia was staying in. That would solve two problems at once. He hadn't heard from her since their episode on the boat and was anxiously hoping for a call; some sign that she believed him.

What she represented now was a connection with his past, and perhaps if he could grasp that, it would provide a means to a future in which he could reclaim his legitimacy. He had never intended this parasitic way of life to become permanent, but once he had stumbled into it, entropy had settled in and it became easier to carry on as he was rather than conceive of a new life. Also, he had a half-formed notion that in consciously constructing a new life he would, by default, have to let go of his past life and his brief brush with international acclaim. He had never reconciled himself to that. In the first few years after the incident he had not been able to face what he had lost, and in the subsequent years, after the pain had subsided, he was in the grip of apathy.

If he was honest with himself, he never expected to go undiscovered for so long. It had become a kind of game with him, a challenge to see just how long he could live as an uninvited, unseen guest in other people's lives without getting caught.

When Mungo arrived at the hotel he learned that Alexia had checked out a few days previously and his desire to check in there evaporated instantly.

"You couldn't perhaps give me a forwarding address for her, could you? It's just that we're old university friends and I would very much like to stay in touch with her," Mungo asked the same skinny-faced young man who had been at the reception desk the last time he was there.

"I'm very sorry sir; we absolutely cannot give out information about our guests."

Mungo's disappointment was such that he felt suddenly quite weightless, the purpose of the last few weeks disappearing as quickly as the news that she had left with no further word. He thanked the man, turned and left the hotel. In need of comfort and familiarity he decided he would take his chances at the Beringers.

Mungo had breakfast at a greasy spoon restaurant that served all day bacon and eggs. He wanted to be sure that Nancy would be out of the house, socializing, shopping, fundraising, posing or whatever else she did these days, before he got there.

In the early years he had had more time at their house and had learned much about them. He read their mail, sifted through papers on their desk, medical reports, bank statements, investments and vacation bookings. He monitored their interests and acquisitions. He even felt he could discern their moods and energy levels by the care they took of their home. It was remarkable how much you could learn about people just by going through their things. This was how detectives worked, he imagined, when they had to figure out the motives and means of a crime. He had regretted Nancy's decision to stop working full time. Not only because it made his life more uncomfortable since her routine had become erratic, but also because he believed she should maintain a degree of independence from Blake, both emotionally and financially.

It was clear to Mungo right from the beginning that Blake was more interested in himself and his own success than he ever was in his wife. During those years when they had struggled, and eventually given up trying to conceive a baby it had become increasingly apparent to Mungo just how unsupportive and unconcerned Blake was of Nancy's need for a child. Yes, Blake went to the clinic, submitted to the often embarrassing examinations, the awkward conversations about sperm counts and ovulation, performed on demand when the time was right and paid hefty amounts for two rounds of in-vitro fertilization. But his heart wasn't in it and when Nancy would have tried one more time, Blake put his foot down. No more.

In the years that followed, they had both focused on their careers and more recently, as Blake had progressed further up the corporate ladder, he had started to cheat on Nancy. When Mungo had first discovered this he was hurt, angry and even jealous on Nancy's behalf. He thought of ways to expose Blake's infidelity. It was when he realized that in so doing he would be the deliverer of her pain and not her protector that he changed his tactics and instead covered up Blake's little slip-ups. In shielding them both he felt that he was part of their marriage and that he had earned a vested interest in the relationship.

When he'd finished his meal and a second cup of coffee he caught the subway to the Beringer's house. They had done a lot to improve it since he'd first arrived there, and he felt an almost proprietorial pride as he surveyed it from the bus stop across the road, checking for any signs that might indicate one of them was home.

The postman had already been, and some mail was protruding from the box. This meant Nancy was probably not home. Using his key, he entered the house through the back door and did his usual quick, quiet scout around to make sure he was alone. Upstairs he had a shower in Blake and Nancy's bathroom. Even though they had added a guest suite he preferred to use theirs. He felt more at home that way.

While brushing his teeth he wandered into Nancy's closet. She'd done some more shopping he gauged from a few new dresses hanging there. He saw her gold and satin evening purse hanging from the inside door handle. Toothpaste was dribbling from his mouth down his hand. He rushed to the bathroom to rinse and returned to the closet. Opening the purse, he found lipstick, tissues and a folded program. Interesting…she'd been to the same Brazilian hospital fundraiser that Elizabeth had attended. Well, Toronto society wasn't that big, he supposed. They were bound to cross paths at some stage.

Across at the bed he sat down on Blake's side and perused his current reading matter. *Ethics and the Business of Biomedicine* by Denis G. Arnold. So, Blake must have made it to the short-list for the Ethics Committee position. Mungo had often read Blake's bedside books, curious to get inside his head and see what was occupying his thoughts. In this way he had learned a lot about the man's priorities, political views, intellectual aptitude and preference for bio-tech thrillers when in need of escapism. He put the book down; this was a tome which Mungo did not presently have an appetite for.

He went down to what he considered to be his bedroom in the basement but was really a spare room in which the Beringer's stored odd furniture, Christmas decorations and boxes of old tax receipts. He set the alarm on his watch for three in the afternoon. He would normally sleep longer but with the scare at Elizabeth's yesterday he felt caution was in order. He stretched out on the springy narrow bed and quickly fell asleep.

♦♦♦

Things had gone from bad to worse for Blake at the office and the discussion with Christine had gone seriously awry. When he'd finally got her out of his office he did something he very rarely resorted to. He told Diane to cancel his remaining meetings for the day and headed for home.

He kicked off his shoes just inside the front door. In the study he slung his jacket over the chair and put the day's mail and his briefcase on the desk. Instead of feeling relieved, he found that he was agitated, and the afternoon's vacancy heightened his unease. All he had wanted while he was at the office was the refuge of his home. But now that he was here, in the silence of the house, he felt trapped with his problems. He found himself wishing that Nancy was home.

He paced around the room for a few moments, repeatedly running his fingers through his hair before flopping himself angrily into one of the armchairs by the window. He stared up into his own severe hostile eyes. It was as if his other self in the portrait was accusing him, reminding him of his mistakes and where his selfish pursuit of success at all costs had gotten him. They should get rid of that bloody portrait. He didn't like it and it didn't even resemble him any longer. When he was a young man it seemed like such a fitting, mature and noble thing to have, but now, from its lofty self-important position on the wall, it only served to remind him of his hubris.

He stood up and headed for the drinks cabinet in the formal living room. His hand poised over the gin bottle, the voice of self-preservation reached his consciousness and instead he turned and went into the kitchen where he downed a glass of filtered water.

He was upstairs changing when he heard the insistent repeated chiming of the doorbell. *Who the...?* He finished dressing quickly and thundered down the stairs coming to a stop in the hallway. He didn't really feel like talking to anyone, and it couldn't be for him as he was not usually home this time of the day. *Damn.* He remembered he'd left his Porsche in the driveway. He approached the door softly and as he put his eye to the peephole he heard Christine's voice: "Open up Blake. I know you're there."

In an involuntary jerk he thumped his forehead painfully on the door. *Hell, what is she doing here?* He had to get rid of her. He opened the door, rubbing his forehead, ready to go on the offensive.

"Look Christine, I don't know what you think you are doing here…"

"You had better speak to me Blake. If you don't I can make things very messy for you." Her handbag was slung over her shoulder and her arms crossed implacably.

She was right of course, and what he didn't need was a scene on his front doorstep. He opened the door wider and she pushed past him.

"Mmm, very nice," she said surveying the hallway and peering past him into the living room. She walked in, and dropping her bag onto the sofa, said, "Pour me a drink."

"You can't stay Christine. This is not the time or the place." Then trying to sound more reasonable he added "Look, I understand that you are feeling aggrieved and you are quite right, we do need to sort this out but let's do it tomorrow? What about lunch? We'll have a nice meal at Giuseppe's and talk things through. You'll see; it will all work out for the best."

"You are not in a position to determine the time or place Blake. And you don't understand. I can't be bought off with a lunch at Giuseppe's." She sat down. "Now pour me that drink. I'll have a gin and tonic."

There was nothing for it; he would have to go along with her in order to get rid of her. He fixed them each a drink using the time to try and figure out what to do with the woman.

◆◆◆

The distant chiming of the doorbell penetrated the recesses of Mungo's sleep. He lay still, listening for confirmation. Yes, it was definitely the front doorbell. Well, he would just ignore it. Whoever it was would go away soon enough. He tried to reach back for the relaxed vestiges of sleep when he heard the unmistakable sound of footsteps thundering down the stairs above. He sat up, totally alert now. *What, two days in a row!* He heard the muffled tones of Blake's voice, and a woman's. He couldn't hear what they were saying but they sounded adversarial.

Judging by the footfalls on the wooden floor above they'd moved into the living room. Mungo knew that if he positioned himself beneath a certain return air vent in the basement ceiling he would be able to hear the conversation in the room above.

"You think you can just toss me out like so much used goods?" the woman was saying.

"Of course not, Christine. It's not like that. We're neither of us adolescents. You knew the situation going into this. I'm a married man. I have responsibilities. I have my position to think about, my job, and it's not as though I have not looked after you…"

"Oh yes Blake, I know the situation and I also know about Jessica. A man in your position with your responsibilities should think a little more carefully before diving in and out of bed with every passing fancy."

"Who the hell are you to judge? You didn't hesitate to sleep with the boss!" Mungo could hear the exasperation in Blake's voice. Uh oh, thought Mungo, wrong question Blake. Blake went on, "That job in Calgary is an excellent step up for you. You will be heading up the western sales division. You would not have been due that promotion for at least three years. And we'll pay the relocation expenses, set you up in a furnished apartment for three months until you find your own place. It's a chance for a new beginning Christine." Blake was almost pleading now.

"The thing is Blake, if you are going to buy me off you are going to find that I am a lot more expensive than that. You want to sweet talk me at lunch and then sweep me under the carpet in Calgary. I don't think so. I've got other ideas."

"Don't be ridiculous Christine. I'm not buying you off, I'm offering you a promotion for God's sake," Blake's voice was rising.

Mungo knew now who the woman was. Blake had been having an affair with Christine Hayes, an assistant regional sales manager, for about eighteen months. At just about the time Blake was finding her too cloying and demanding, Jessica was appointed as head of the legal department and Blake quickly lost interest in Christine. During their affair, Blake had often taken Christine to the boat, which was a nuisance for Mungo.

"And I'm offering you a reasonable solution to this little problem." Mungo could hear that the balance of power was in Christine's hands. She sounded like a woman in control. She had come prepared. Mungo was worried for Blake. But more importantly, he was worried for Nancy. Watching out for her had become second nature to him. If Blake was threatened, then so was Nancy. He heard footsteps crossing the floor, bottles clinking against glass. *No Blake don't, you need a clear head for this*, Mungo implored silently.

There was a pause. Mungo could picture the scene above, Christine waiting for Blake's response, offering him nothing more until he asked what she wanted to make her go away. Mungo figured that she wanted him desperate to make a deal. He knew from going through the documents that Blake brought home from the office that Founder had sent Christine on many sales and negotiation skills training courses and she knew how to seal a deal. She was putting their training dollars to good use, Mungo thought wryly.

◆◆◆

Upstairs, Blake glowered at Christine, her long golden legs attractively crossed as she sat complacently on his sofa. The sofa Nancy had chosen, their sofa. He was suddenly filled with rage. He wanted the bitch off their sofa and out of his house. He fought off the urge to physically haul her out of the front door. He felt the pulse jerking in his neck as if his anger was trapped there and trying to break free. He took a gulp of the gin and tonic. He had to get a grip.

He walked across the room, affecting nonchalance but fooling neither of them. He would not sit down. He would not pour her another drink. He would set the terms.

"Okay Christine, I get it that you are hurt and that you feel I have treated you badly. I am sorry. I didn't plan for anyone to get hurt. But you knew right from the outset what the situation was. I have never misled you or made promises I couldn't keep…"

She cut in sharply, "This is not about me being hurt Blake, this is about you being stupid. Everything has a price, including your stupidity. I know you are in the running for the Ethics Committee appointment. I also know that the Founder Board would not tolerate a sexual harassment case against their Canadian CEO. Imagine how Founder Pharmaceuticals would look in the same headline with #MeToo?" Blake felt a chill go down his spine. She continued "I have spoken to Caroline Sharpe. Oh, I know she has left Founder and that you had a thing with her too, but she is more than willing to join me in pressing charges against you if that's what it comes to. And who knows, perhaps Jessica will come around to our way of thinking too? Then there is Nancy, of course, how do you think she will react to all the terrible publicity, the humiliation? I also know the, shall we say, the lengths you went to last year to get the permits from the Indian Government." She let that sink in for a moment.

"You can't prove any of this." Blake's voice was hoarse.

"Maybe, maybe not, but the scandal itself would be enough to ruin you. You see, I have nothing to lose and you Blake, you have everything to lose."

"What do you want from me Christine?"

Chapter Sixteen

Mungo lay for a while on the narrow bed in the dark recesses of the Beringer's basement trying to control the anxiety gnawing at his stomach. He needed to be quiet and calm and to think. The house above him had become silent and Christine had left. Christine's demands of Blake were outrageous; not only did she expect the promotion and transfer, but she demanded eight hundred thousand dollars in cash from Blake as well.

Mungo's instinct was to go upstairs and counsel Blake, to offer comfort and advice but, of course, that was out of the question. What he should do was leave the house quietly while Blake was distracted and before Nancy returned.

He got off the bed and put his few things into his backpack. He then moved back to the return air vent under the main part of the house and listened carefully for a while. He could make out Blake's footsteps above and the periodic clinking of bottles and glasses. Blake was drinking, heavily it seemed, judging by his repeated trips from the study to the drinks cabinet in the living room. Mungo checked his watch. Five o'clock. It would be another hour or two before Nancy got home. If Blake was losing himself in liquor it would be easier to get out of the house unnoticed. He would give it another hour or so before attempting his exit. He remained where he was listening to the pattern of movement on the floor above.

While he stood there his mind played out the various scenarios and their possible outcomes for Blake. Part of him felt that Blake was only getting what he deserved but the other part of him hated the thought of Blake trapped by the fear of scandal and falling victim to the unscrupulous avarice of

Christine Hayes. And of course, once she really got her claws into him, it would never stop.

What options did Blake have? Either pay up and keep paying up. Or call her bluff and allow her to do her worst, confess and lose everything he'd worked for. Maybe he could find some other way to silence her? The more Mungo thought about it, the more certain he became that she had to be silenced. But how?

After some time, Mungo became aware that Blake was no longer moving around upstairs. Perhaps he had slumped into an alcohol-induced sleep? Mungo quietly climbed the plush carpeted stairs that led from the basement to the main floor. He opened the door at the top of the stairs slowly and listened. Although it was growing dark outside Blake had not switched on any lights. Good sign, thought Mungo. He was inclined to peek into the study to see how Blake was doing, but that would really be tempting fate. He'd had too many close shaves in the last few days. He'd never come so close to discovery before. Perhaps this was a sign that it was time for him to make a change. Quit while he was ahead.

He moved easily from the basement entrance into the darkened kitchen and, from there, to the back door. He slipped out quickly, closing the door with a soft click behind him. Outside in the early night air he breathed in deeply and then let out a sigh of relief. He was getting too old for all this stealth and he was making serious errors in judgement, but only since he'd become so preoccupied with Alexia and reliving the past, he thought.

Relieved at having exited the house unnoticed, he strode confidently towards the driveway. As he rounded the corner of the house he was blinded by a pair of headlights as a car turned into the drive. He jumped back into the shadows of the house. Nancy! Had she seen him? Very likely, he would have been lit up like a statue in the headlights in front of her. He needed to hide before she came investigating. He heard her car door slam and footsteps crunching up the driveway. He swiveled around, panicking. He was on the back deck with only a few potted plants and garden furniture for cover. He made a dash for the stairs into the garden but turned back realizing he would come face to face with Nancy. The only option was to jump over the wrought iron railing that surrounded the deck and duck down on the ground. He leapt quickly over the railing on the far side, feeling the pull of a muscle on his inner thigh as he jumped. He landed on the snow below with a soft crunch and lay still, waiting, breathing. He heard the rhythm of her footsteps crunching across the snow on the deck. *Please God let her not venture into the garden or peer over the railing.* His heart was racing. He tried to still his breathing. He could feel the adrenalin coursing through his body. This was really getting too much for him.

"Blake," she called. "Blake is that you? What are you doing out here?" Of course, she must have seen Blake's car in the driveway. After a moment, he heard her walk across the deck away from him; he raised his head and saw her leaning over the railing and squinting into the garden opposite the back door. Then she turned and headed back to the driveway. He heard a car door slam again and the beep as she locked the car.

Mungo lay very still in the crisp snow for a few long minutes, the cold penetrating his jeans and stiffening his legs. Eventually he decided it was safe to leave the garden, but this time he would be very cautious. As he stood up he felt the pain of the pulled muscle sear through his inner thigh and up into his groin. He immediately went slack and tried to rub it away, but only for a moment; there was no time to indulge his pain.

◆◆◆

Nancy pushed her way through the front door. "Blake. Blake!" she called with growing insistence. She dumped her briefcase on the floor and pushed open the double doors leading to the study on her right. The room was in darkness but for the dim streetlight penetrating the windows, curtains un-drawn. The first thing she saw was the blank space on the wall opposite, where, for so many years, Blake's portrait of youthful severity had hung.

She looked sharply across the room. He was stretched out in one of the armchairs by the window, the streetlight casting a grey gleam across his face heightening his angular nose and sunken eye sockets. His mouth hung open and his head flopped slightly sideways in a position that would surely have been too uncomfortable to allow sleep in any state other than inebriation.

Her eyes travelled down his arm slung down the side of the chair toward the floor and she saw the portrait at his feet. The face that stared up from the floor now transformed into something grotesque by two sharp slashes through the canvas. A paper knife lay on the floor, slightly underneath the chair as if trying to hide from sight.

Nancy launched herself onto the floor at Blake's feet. She picked up the portrait. In the slashed face she saw their slashed hopes and dreams, their irretrievable youth, the children they had never had, the anger, arrogance and hurt which now lay between them. "Oh no, Blake, why?"

◆◆◆

Mungo worked steadily and silently but for the noise of the vacuum cleaner. An observer would have admired his absorption, but all the while he was eradicating the day's dirt and dust from the library his mind gnawed away at Blake's predicament.

If this were a movie, he thought, Blake would conspire to have her killed, or even do it himself. He wondered if Blake was capable of doing it or if he would pay someone else to do it. And how would he do it? With a gun, his bare hands, drowning, drugs or an intentional accident? There were so many options. Mungo suddenly straightened, rubbed the stressed muscle on his inner thigh and switched off the vacuum cleaner. This was ridiculous. He must stop this thinking. Blake was not going to kill anyone. And neither was he.

He retrieved his backpack from the janitor's office and settled down in his favorite chair. He unwrapped the sandwich he'd bought from the all-night deli. Asparagus, brie and bacon on an olive bun. He poured some wine from his thermos and bit into the bun. He munched for a few minutes, occasionally sipping the chardonnay, appreciating the combination of flavors. He remembered the first time he had eaten this combination together.

He'd come across Nancy's party planning notes on her desk one day about a year after he had taken up residence with them. She'd written out a guest list – seventy-five people - sent out invitations, hired a caterer, Classy Cuisine, and had been considering their proposed menu options. It was when he was perusing these that he got the idea. One of the appetizers was described as bite sized rice crackers topped with a wedge of brie, crispy bacon and an asparagus tip. Mungo had paused to think; he might be able taste them for himself and, more importantly, get a closer glimpse into the Beringer's life.

He had picked up the phone and called Classy Cuisine to find out if they needed part time serving staff. He impressed the manager with his clear quick answers to the basic questions and secured an interview for the next afternoon. The rest was easy. He was hired on a part time basis and ensured that he was allocated to the Beringer's function three weeks hence. It had turned out to be an excellent means of supplementing his income, allowing him to work mostly in the evenings when the Beringers, and then later, Elizabeth were home and he needed to be out of the house.

As the day of the party drew nearer his excitement mounted. He had been observing the Beringer's life from behind the scenes for almost a year. Now he would get to participate. He longed to face them and to be seen by them, to look into their eyes and speak to them. Could he get away with it? The thought thrilled him. He knew so much about them already and they did not even know he existed.

He knew that two months previously Nancy had stopped taking her contraceptive pills – he found her completed package along with four unopened ones in the bathroom garbage bin. He knew that Blake's father, Jackson, was seventy-two and suffering from Alzheimer's in a nursing home. He knew that Blake had an older brother and sister and that he was close to his sister but rarely spoke to his brother. He knew the names of some of their friends and acquaintances, but now he would get to see them for himself.

He had pulled out his shabby, travel-weary tux from his backpack and shook it out. Deciding it was beyond restoration he had purchased one from a charity shop and felt quite the part when he arrived with the other staff at the Beringer's.

Nancy opened the door and stood before them like a goddess in a stunning deep cut long plum-colored dress with a gold buckle gathering the fabric between her full breasts. The porch lights radiated off her golden hair and Mungo had the sense that her spicy perfume carried her charisma, which held the catering team mesmerized as they stood like peasants on her porch. It was a moment before the catering manager was able to close his mouth, swallow and then introduce himself and his three staff members.

Nancy showed them through the house and led them to the kitchen. The house was beautiful with flowers, candles and Herb Alpert's *Rise* carrying on the air. As they prepared the appetizers Mungo was careful to approach the kitchen as if for the first time, occasionally asking Nancy where she kept this or that and opening cupboards unnecessarily before finding a particular dish or utensil.

Mungo was in the dining room setting up the serving area, repositioning a vase of flowers and shifting candles when he caught sight of Blake through the doorway to the living room. He still had his moustache in those days. Mungo felt mildly resentful of his height and purposeful stride that lent him an air of authority that was hard to ignore.

"Come here gorgeous," he had heard Blake say. Nancy, who had been just out of sight, crossed the room to him and he put his arms around her. "Don't ever forget, you are the most beautiful woman in the world. And you are mine." Mungo watched as Blake lowered his mouth to Nancy's and his hands moved down her back coming to rest on the curve of her buttocks. Blake raised his eyes and looked straight at Mungo, challenging and triumphant. Mungo had the impression that Blake had been aware of his presence in the neighboring room and was consciously parading his sexual authority. Mungo returned his stare for a moment before turning away to his tasks.

Before long the house was filled with greetings, chatter, laughter and music, creating that cacophony which signals a successful party. Mungo moved through the crowd unobtrusively offering trays of canapés while a colleague served champagne and filled wine glasses. He was infected with the excited buzz of the gathering but feigned disinterest while paying keen attention to the snatches of conversation he caught during his rounds with the appetizers.

"…well, yes. The divorce was finalized two months ago. Two years and two months it took to get out of it. I didn't want to at first, thought we could work things out. Isabella was determined but by the end I think she was changing her mind," said a well-dressed paunchy man, pausing to pop a tasty morsel from Mungo's tray into his mouth.

"So, you weren't tempted at that stage to reconsider, to get back together again?" asked his companion, a long-limbed man who seemed to be dodging the swathe of floppy red hair which kept falling across his freckled forehead.

"God, no. By that stage she'd shown herself to be far too fickle. Some other poor sod can deal with the vagaries of her moods." He greedily swallowed from his glass of whisky as if to underline his good fortune.

Mungo turned away from the pair, lingering on the edge of a group next to them.

"I quite like being on my own. Have the house to myself now to do as I please. It's much too big for me but I like the neighborhood and I'm not inclined for a big move just yet." Mungo offered his tray around to the neighboring group.

He returned to the kitchen to replenish the tray and found a frenzy of activity. His colleagues were in the final stages of preparing the main course. From one serving station in the dining room they would be doing a Thai stir-fry and from another they would be cooking various sauces for Italian pasta. He picked up the asparagus, bacon and brie platter and headed for the door. As he opened it with one hand, the other balancing the tray, he was surprised to find Nancy about to enter the kitchen. They both did a side-step to allow the other to pass and in a gawky comedy of mutual incoordination Mungo almost tipped the platter down the front of Nancy's dress. Righting it quickly he inspected her dress to make sure he hadn't messed on it and found himself staring straight down her cleavage. Embarrassed, he looked up, directly into her eyes. His embarrassment grew, and he tried to move past her, stuttering out an apology. She put a hand on his arm and he returned his gaze to her face. Instead of hostility, her eyes were sparkling with amusement.

"Don't worry about it." she said. "Everything is going really well. Thank you."

He nodded and thanked her. As he stepped into the dining room he was conscious of a certain satisfaction bordering on smugness. He had somehow landed in the right home and felt indebted to Nancy. He was even more determined now to make sure that the evening was a success.

Mungo approached a group of people in the hallway who were intent on listening to a humorous story. The storyteller, a glamorous older woman, bore a striking resemblance to Nancy. This must be her mother. He offered his tray around the group. "… and just as the lights went on and the curtain rose a bat flew from the rafters above, blindly flapping and flailing, finally coming to rest in Andrea's big wig. Of course, she was as terrified as we were amused. She screamed and pulled at the wig, dislodging it to show her untidy mousy crop underneath. The audience thought it was the best thing they'd ever seen. There we were, all set for a dramatic opening but instead, absolute hilarity." She paused to enjoy the group's laughter. "Andrea stormed off the stage. Clearly, we couldn't go on with the show without the lead, so the curtain came down and the lights went off. It was about ten minutes before Jack O'Donaghue, the director, could persuade Andrea to return to the stage."

When the laughter died down, a person in the group asked her what her next show would be.

"Julian and I are taking the winter off," she said, raising a delicate hand to move an imaginary strand of hair from her face. "We've rented a house in Tuscany. He has some writing to do and I need a break. When we return in May we start rehearsals for *A Big Deal*, which opens in October."

Mungo moved on. Nancy's parents would be away for the winter and presumably their house would be unoccupied. The evening was proving very fruitful indeed.

Reminiscing in the darkened library, Mungo stretched his legs out and topped up his wine recalling another conversation he had overheard the night of the Beringer's party. He had been clearing plates and glasses from the hallway when he saw a man step into Blake's study. He was so grey and gaunt that he appeared illusory. Mungo hesitated near the doorway wondering whether he should ask him what his business was in there when he heard Blake himself say, "Rupert, I'm so glad you could make it. I know you love jazz; we have a jazz quartet arriving later so stick around for a while."

A jazz quartet would round off the evening perfectly, Mungo thought. Nancy had such good taste. He carried a stack of dishes to the kitchen and returned to the hallway for some more. He heard Rupert say to Blake, "Well, we are very discreet. We mostly work undercover within organizations rather than as observers from the outside. I have two veteran investigators who work with me. Our projects tend to be long-term, although occasionally we take on a short-term contract." He coughed, then cleared his throat. "Now is not the right time to discuss this, but I'll give you my card and we can talk next week."

Mungo returned to the kitchen before Blake and his guest emerged from the study. It sounded like he was a private investigator. What did Blake need to discuss with an investigator, Mungo wondered, feeling a twinge of disquiet. He later returned to the study on the pretext of clearing glasses and found the business card identifying the man as Rupert Benson, Director of Strategic Solutions.

Mungo had never discovered the reason for which Blake had needed an investigator and concluded that it must have been work related. Now, however, sitting in the quiet library mulling over Blake's latest problem he wondered whether the time wasn't right to contact Strategic Solutions. And if not them, then someone equally discreet who could dig up some background on Christine Hayes. If she was the kind of woman who would resort to blackmail, then the chances were she had engaged in other unethical, even illegal activities. Yes, that would be a good first step. He would do it. Once he had some dirt on Christine Hayes, he would find a way to get it into Blake's hands and he would be able to neutralize her.

Restless with excitement now that he had found a solution, he wanted to act immediately but this would have to wait until the morning. Unable to sit still, he packed away what remained of his meal and finished the cleaning. This time, he worked with a lightness of step and spirit which made the remaining tasks a pleasant backdrop to the tune that was forming in his head.

A strong trumpet, but smooth and soft, soaring to a top C. He heard it gently, but ever so clearly, carry the orchestra further and further as other instruments joined. Now there was a strong subtle base coming in from the deep background, thrumming the rhythm. Gradually the first violins came in supporting the trumpet, then the second violins picking up the harmony, now some cellos, percussion now adding to the soft vibration of the base, the pace picking up, the trumpet leading the way into the higher notes, then suddenly dropping off. He could hear this rhythm starting to repeat itself building up each time, adding more instrumentation and increasing the pace until finally the trumpet leads them all into powerful resolution, its last enduring slow note lingering in the air. Mungo realized he was standing motionless, mop in hand, listening to the music in his head. He needed to get this down before he lost it and rushed to the librarian's desk in search of pencil and paper. He pulled up a chair, sat down and started scribbling notes on the page.

Chapter Seventeen

Nancy was not looking forward to the meeting and, following Blake's breakdown the night before, a stressful confrontation was the last thing she needed. But having taken the plunge and sent the partial manuscript to Alfonso Ghiradelli, the OSO's musical director, she had no choice but to see it through. Nancy had reviewed the manuscript and was intrigued not only by the promise of the music, but by the glimmer of a story behind it.

Financial support for the OSO had been dwindling in recent years and with it their capacity to market the performances and attract top-notch musicians. This might help stop the downward spiral. Nancy had a flair for attracting publicity and felt instinctively that, if what Elizabeth Carey had told her about finding the anonymous manuscript in her basement was true, this was bound to pique the interest of the media and put the OSO firmly back in the musical spotlight.

She could see the headlines now: *OSO Performs Magnificent New Mystery Symphony*. She pictured herself giving interviews about how the music came to light and speculating about who the composer might be. The potential for publicity was exciting. She must set aside her antagonism towards Alfonso and persuade him that this was just what was needed to turn things around for the organization.

Right from the beginning Nancy and Alfonso had rubbed sparks off each other and things had become steadily worse finally erupting in a nasty confrontation at a post-performance party a couple of years ago. Nancy considered him an opinionated, self-absorbed musical purist who did not understand the mood or needs of the audience and he had written her off as an interfering board member who did not know enough about music to justify her position on the board. Since their embarrassing public spat, for which they had both been chastised, they gave each other a wide berth.

Now, for the good of the OSO, she told herself, she would have to overcome her prejudice and distaste. She felt a renewed surge of anger, remembering the summons from his assistant that morning. He would be willing to see her for a few minutes in the auditorium at 3 pm, after the rehearsal. Any other reasonable individual would call to schedule an appointment at a mutually convenient time, but not Alfonso. Everything was always on his terms and on his turf. She swallowed the bitter taste of her pride, picked up her folder and set off.

As she stepped into the darkened auditorium, her eyes were immediately drawn to the only pool of light in the vast room. Alfonso's head of thick curly black hair shone in the spotlight like so many curling, writhing snakes as he shook it wildly, tapping out the rhythm of the music on the stand in front of him while issuing instructions to a young cellist who sat before him, her bow quivering on the instrument between her shaking knees as she tried over and over again to get the music right.

What a beast, Nancy thought. Before she could stop herself, she strode up the aisle shouting, "My God, Alfonso, can't you see she can't give her best like that? No one can function properly when they're being bullied!"

He turned and glowered at her from his lofty height on the stage. By the time she reached him she was breathless with effort and rage. Still he stood, staring down at her, not even bothering to respond. The young cellist sat transfixed, eyes wide, bowing arm poised above the bridge, apparently uncertain whether to continue playing or take the opportunity to scramble out of the auditorium. Nancy stood below him her chest rising and falling. Finally, her breath caught in her throat and she coughed, breaking the spell that held the three of them frozen in the pool of light from above.

Alfonso spun around, a thick strand of hair falling across his pale face. He raised his baton and pointed it directly at the young woman.

"*You* may leave," he said.

She scraped her chair back, picked up her cello and rushed out, her footsteps erratic as she disappeared into the backstage shadows.

"How dare you come in here and tell me how to handle my musicians?" His voice was low and menacing.

Nancy could see the small droplets of sweat highlighting his face. With the suddenness of a slap, she realized that despite her resolve to treat Alfonso with tact, she had already antagonized him. If she handled this any worse, he would refuse to even consider the new composition and blow their chances. She took a deep breath. "You are quite right, Alfonso, I'm sorry. I shouldn't have stormed in like that. Would you like me to come back another time?"

He stood above her for a moment, clearly unsure how to respond. Nancy was aware that he was set for a shouting match and she had just changed the moves in the game, putting him momentarily on the back foot. She watched carefully as the indecision wrestled itself across his face. Should he pursue the argument or allow her to take their meeting in a different direction? To argue in the face of her apology would appear churlish, at best, but to give in and accept would be to put her in control of the discussion. She had long experience in dealing with artists and understood something of what drove their creative genius, what held them there and what they perceived as threats.

In Alfonso was the unstable mix of real raw talent, a deep sense that he was never quite reaching his potential, and a fear that others might well be better than him. Were this confined to his music he would be far easier to manage, but like many artists, the fight between talent and self-doubt ploughed its way into every area of his life producing an arrogant but insecure man. Nancy knew it would not be so easy to bring him down from the tower of his indignation and she also knew that he was too smart to be easily manipulated.

He turned away from her and shuffled the score on his podium. "I was just getting somewhere with that girl when you burst in. You, you're not a musician, you wouldn't understand." He waved his arm in the air theatrically underlining his exasperation, his back still to her.

She thought it prudent not to point out to him that she played the piano passably, and waited in what felt like subservience, while he continued to sigh and shuffle his papers.

Eventually he turned around, looked down at her and said, "Now what is it you want from me?"

"I thought you wanted to discuss the anonymous composition, the one that I sent you…"

"Aah, yes," he interrupted, "your *mystery* music," his unnecessary emphasis on the word mystery giving it a sarcastic tone. "You want *my* orchestra, the finest orchestra in Canada and certainly one of the best in North America to perform a new piece, of dubious origins, by an unknown composer when there are other far more worthy compositions which we have yet to perform here? What do you think we are doing here, Nancy? While you sit in your ivory tower dreaming up new ideas, do you think we are the guinea pigs?" His Italian accent grew thicker as he worked himself up into a lather of self-righteousness. "The classics have been good enough for the world for centuries, but now, now they are not good enough for you and your board." Both his hands now were in full use, appearing as spectators on the sidelines, waving and bobbing in support of his argument.

Nancy could feel the control slipping from her grasp. She had to stop him. She had seen him rant like this before and the longer he went on the more convinced he became of his rightness until he had so fortified his position that there would be no getting him down from it.

"Alfonso," she said, grasping onto the first idea that occurred to her. "Why don't we go to the coffee shop to discuss this? Let me buy you a cappuccino. Please." This was humiliating. Now she was pleading with him. She held her breath. She watched his eyes dart to the doors at the back of the auditorium and then to the music he held in his hands. He gave his watch a significant look and then finally shrugged his shoulders, his black curls quivering around his face.

"I only have twenty minutes," he said.

Nancy imagined that it was petulance rather than perspiration oozing out of his pores. "That's fine. That's great," she said, feeling the stiffness of the forced smile on her face.

They were seated in soft armchairs, their cappuccinos on the low table between them. This was better, she thought. She stood a reasonable chance of winning him over here and at least she was no longer at the disadvantage of having him tower above her from the stage. The silence hung between them for a few moments. Clearly, he was not about to put her at ease with small talk. She sipped her coffee and, using both hands, set the large bowl-shaped cup down carefully in the saucer.

"I know you're very busy, Alfonso, but have you had some time to consider the music?" she asked, hoping she'd struck the right deferential tone.

"Do you think I would waste my time in a meeting with you if I hadn't gone through it?" Without waiting for her answer, he continued. "Of course, I have gone through it. I have played the part for piano and, in fact, what you interrupted in there," he jerked his thumb over his shoulder toward the coffee shop door, "was the cello solo which comes in at the end of the first movement."

Now it was Nancy's turn to be surprised. She was thankful for the large coffee cup that partially shielded her face from Alfonso's dark eyes. Momentarily lost for words, she took another sip and then looked at him. "I said I was sorry. I'm sure you know…No, I know you know what you are doing, but I just thought…"

"It's magnificent." He cut her short. "Where is the rest of it?" He demanded.

Nancy was too shocked to question his sudden change in opinion about the music. She knew he was temperamental, but this was something else. "I don't have it. Didn't you read my note? The manuscript doesn't belong to me, to the OSO, I mean. A woman I met recently brought it to my office. She found it in her basement. She has no idea how it got there or who composed it. We'd have to talk to her. She only gave me the first movement."

"What? What do you mean you don't have it?" he exploded. "What am I supposed to do with only part of the composition? You want me to reorganize my repertoire for the season around a partial score?"

"Alfonso, please. Keep your voice down. People are staring."

"People are staring! People are staring? And so, I must keep my voice down? I am Alfonso Ghiradelli and you are telling me to keep my voice down?"

"I'll speak to her and tell her we're interested." Nancy rushed to calm him. "We will have to come to some sort of agreement. I'll have to get legal advice. I've never dealt with anything like this before. We don't know who it belongs to or who wrote it. But we'll get the manuscript if you are willing to perform it?"

"Yes, yes get it. As soon as possible." He was looking past her now, his eyes distant. "This, this could make my career."

Nancy dismissed the soft jangle of the warning bell growing in her mind. He'd agreed. That was the main thing. She would have to manage the rest.

"Well, I was thinking that it's such an intriguing story, and if the music is as good as you say it is, then it would be a great opportunity to infuse new life and public interest in the OSO. Just think, Alfonso, of the fundraising opportunities…"

"Yes, yes. I can see all the opportunities," he said, his eyes still focused elsewhere. "Just get the music."

Chapter Eighteen

Alexia stretched her neck out left then right, as far as it would extend, enjoying the relief that it brought to her aching muscles. She walked across to the barre, lifted the towel from the rail and wiped first her face and then her neck. Then she bent to the floor, picked her phone up and switched off the music playing through the wireless speakers in the studio. With the sudden silence in the room she realized just how tired she had become of hearing the same piece of music over and over again.

She had been working on her routine for two hours without interruption and wondered if she would ever be ready for the performance which was now only weeks away. Her body knew that the pace she had set herself was unsustainable, but her mind was still refusing to acknowledge this. Her warm-ups were taking longer and her injuries more frequent. What was worse was that she knew she had not had her mind on the dancing this morning.

In fact, ever since the encounter with Mungo on the boat in Toronto she had been unable to focus properly on her work, and it was showing up in the rehearsals. The artistic director had taken her aside after yesterday's rehearsal to ask her what was wrong. Her timing and precision were off, she was clearly distracted, he said. That was why she had booked studio time this morning to go over it again. Now, all she felt was drained and disheartened, and no less distracted.

She went down to the changing room, stripped off and stepped into the shower. After a quick rinse she wrapped a towel around herself and entered the sauna. She ladled some water over the hot coals and the air became clouded with steam. She sat down. The heat from the wooden bench penetrated the tight muscles in her buttocks and her back, the steamy air warmed her from within and she sank back allowing herself to relax for the first time in days.

This was the place where she did her best thinking. If she timed it right she could have the sauna to herself. She felt safe here. The moist cedar scented air enveloped her, and she closed her eyes.

By the time she stepped out of the sauna Alexia had made up her mind. She had another quick shower, partially dried her hair, dressed and left the studio with a new resolve. As soon as she was in the car and had eased into the traffic, she hit speed dial on her phone. He picked up after two and a half rings.

"Mum, I'm in class," his voice was a low whisper, "I told you I can't talk in the middle of class."

"I know Sebastian, but this is important."

"Everything's always important with you. I can't talk now. I'll call you when my class is over."

"Wait. Can we meet for lunch? Today?"

"I've got classes all day," he said, his voice heavy with resignation.

"Surely you get a break for lunch?"

"I can see you between two and three."

"Okay, a late lunch then. I'll reserve a table at Nick and Toni's. See you there." Alexia ended the call and noticed for the first time the slow-moving traffic along the Henry Hudson Parkway. Once she passed the George Washington Bridge things picked up. She checked the time on the dashboard clock. Good, at this speed they should get to Riverdale in time for her to change, book the restaurant and pick up her own car for the drive back into the city.

◆◆◆

Mungo stood and stared up at the building, his eyes squinting against the sunlight reflecting off the wall of windows rising high above him. He wondered if he was even visible to someone looking down from the top.

Before leaving the library the night before he'd searched the internet for private investigators and come up with a handful of choices. The Strategic Solutions website was indeed discreet to the point of being extremely vague about the services offered. In the end he had chosen a company called Van Buuren and Co. He was concerned that, while investigating Christine Hayes, Rupert Benson would be sure to unearth damaging information about Blake, his own client and the person Mungo was trying to protect. Van Buuren and Co's website advertised a full spectrum of corporate and private surveillance and security services with a special focus on legal and accounting clients.

Now that he was here, he was stalled by doubts. Perhaps it would be safest for him to stay out of the mess Blake had created for himself. However, even though they did not know him, the Beringers and Elizabeth had become his surrogate family and you help family, right? Plus, he hated the thought of Nancy being hurt because of Blake's poor judgement.

His reverie was broken when two people who were trying to flag down the same taxi jostled him from behind. Stumbling forward he took the plunge and pushed his way through the revolving glass doors. He stood inside the gleaming marble and chrome lobby, dwarfed by its inhuman scale, the echo of disembodied voices and footsteps surrounding him.

Conscious now of his casual attire among the business suited crowd crisscrossing the lobby, he quickly dug into the pocket of his anorak and pulled out the folded paper on which he'd written the details. Van Buuren and Co., twenty-third floor, Meredith Salinger at eleven thirty. He found the bank of elevators marked floors twenty-one to thirty and pushed the up button. Mungo seldom had reason to go into Toronto's towering office blocks, but this was certainly not the setting he'd expected for the office of a PI. Instead of the imagined seedy neighborhood, down at heel buildings, creaky floorboards and dusty staircases, he was being effortlessly transported to the upper heights of this monument to capitalism.

A discreet brass plate identified Van Buuren & Co. He tried the door. It was locked. This was his last chance to change his mind. But before he could do that a buzzer sounded and the door clicked open. He stepped into a spacious room, its walls lined with modern art and leather sofas that looked as though they were never occupied.

To his right was a sleek reception counter and he approached the young woman who was busy there. "You must be Mr. Jameson to see Meredith Salinger," she said, with a humorless professional smile.

"That's right."

"Please take a seat, she'll be out in a moment."

He moved to the middle of the room, too unsettled to sit, an unhealthy mixture of impatience and anxiety creeping up in him like mercury in a thermometer. He ran his hand through his hair, feeling the coarse wavy strands between his fingers and smoothed it down. He walked towards the bank of windows opposite and looked through the vertical blinds seeing only the corresponding windows of another office block. What was the point of an address like this if you didn't even have a view, he thought irritably? He'd give it another minute then he was out of here. It was a bad idea, he thought, he was opening a can of worms.

Just then a door to his left opened and a woman entered. "Good morning Mr. Jameson, Meredith Salinger. Pleased to meet you." She extended her hand and gave him a tight smile.

He was faced with a sudden urge to back out of the room and cancel the whole thing, but politeness forced him to raise his hand and shake hers.

"Come this way please," she said.

She turned and led the way through the door. Hanging all the way down her back almost to her waist was a single thick braid of chestnut hair. Mungo found the disproportionate swaying braid disconcerting against her petite but muscular form as he followed her down the long hallway.

She opened a door to her right and showed him into an office bathed in bright light from the large window behind the desk. She sat, offering him the guest chair opposite. He was momentarily disoriented by the sunlight streaming into the room and looked away from her and the window while his eyes adjusted. The room had the impersonal feel that often characterizes contemporary decor.

She reached for the blind pull behind her and angled the blinds so that the sun was no longer in his eyes. "Is that better?"

He nodded, "Yes, thank you."

"Perhaps I should start by telling you a bit about myself and our agency and then you can tell me what brings you here."

Mungo noticed again the insincere smile which briefly occupied her face. He felt a trickle of sweat run down his side from his armpit.

She stood suddenly and held out her hand. Confused he didn't know whether to shake her hand again. Perhaps she was terminating the meeting and he could get out of here.

"Let me hang up your jacket," she said.

Was it that obvious that he was sweating, he wondered as he removed it and she hung it on the back of the door.

"Would you like a coffee, Mr. Jameson, before we start?" she said, returning to her seat.

"Sure, that would be great." He was relieved to have the momentary diversion.

She pressed the intercom button on her phone, "Jared, could you bring in a tray of coffee for two please?" Then, to Mungo, she said, "We have six investigators at Van Buuren and Co, supported by a number of researchers. My background is military intelligence. Most of our staff members have come from the security or IT fields. In our business, discretion is a top priority..."

She was interrupted by a soft chime and responded by pushing a button. The door clicked open and a lean bespectacled young man walked in with the coffee.

"Thank you, Jared," said Meredith. "Jared this is Mr. Mungo Jameson, a new client."

Mungo stood, and they shook hands, "Pleased to meet you," he said.

"Jared is my researcher. We've worked together since before he completed his master's in computer science."

"Let me know if you need anything else, Meredith," Jared said and left the office.

Mungo sat down as she handed him a cup of coffee and pushed the cream and sugar across the desk toward him.

"How long have you been doing this?" Mungo asked.

"Van Buuren and Co. was started some twenty years ago by Dieter Van Buuren. I have been with the company eight years. We don't advertise widely, so most people who seek us out usually know what they are looking for. Most of our clients are law or insurance firms and we have a large forensic accounting function. We have a small private client practice which I head up." She leaned back in her chair and took a sip of her coffee, "So Mr. Jameson, how can we help you?"

"I have a friend who is being blackmailed," began Mungo, realizing the moment he uttered the words how disingenuous he sounded. How many clients must come to such an agency claiming to be representing a friend? "He really is a friend," Mungo went on, the hollowness of his words reverberating around the room. She looked at him, offering nothing. "What I mean is, he is not me. And he's not a friend exactly. But he is someone I know well, very well and I know he is being blackmailed."

Still she looked at him.

"I would like to help him, but he doesn't know I am here. I hoped that you could get some information on the blackmailer which could be used to keep her quiet."

"Don't you think it would be a better idea for him to request our services?" she finally said.

"It's complicated. He doesn't know that I know he is being blackmailed." Mungo picked up his coffee, his hand shook slightly.

"You do realize," she said, "that we charge by the hour. The less information you give me, the more I will have to find out for myself and the longer it will take to solve your problem. And the more it will cost you in the end." She sat back in her chair. "Now why don't you tell me as much as you know? From the beginning."

Chapter Nineteen

As he surfaced from the muggy depths of sleep the first thing Blake became conscious of was the thumping in his head. He lay very still in his bed, squinting against the light. He surveyed the room, the curtains were still drawn, and the house was silent. Nancy must have left already. *Shit! What is the time?* He sat up straight and instantly regretted the move. He grabbed the clock off his bedside table as he sank back down on the pillows, one hand rubbing his forehead.

It was eleven thirty in the morning. He had little recollection of the night before and no recollection of how or when he had got to bed. Nancy must have brought him upstairs. *Oh hell*. That was the last thing he needed. Now Nancy had something else to chalk up against him. He realized he was naked under the sheets. She must have undressed him. His clothes were nowhere in sight. The warmth he felt towards her surprised him. She always took care of the details, always had things so well under control.

Suddenly he remembered Christine Hayes' visit and the blackmail threat. A wave of nausea rose from within his gut and he pushed his way off the bed in one swift movement and dashed for the bathroom. When he'd finished spilling his guts into the toilet he lurched over to the basin and rinsed his mouth. He looked up into the mirror and was overcome with a self-loathing so strong that he felt he would be sick again. He remembered now; it was the same disgust that had driven him to destroy his own portrait.

What else had he done last night? What had he said? How much did Nancy know? He opened a drawer under the granite vanity and scrabbled around until he found a bottle of ibuprofen tablets and swallowed two.

Blake returned to the bedroom and sat down on the edge of the bed waiting for the tablets to take effect. It was then that he saw the envelope propped up on Nancy's dressing table. He went across and picked it up, looking for a long moment at his name in Nancy's distinctive script across the front. He was not sure he wanted to read what was inside. Eventually he opened it and read:

I've had enough Blake. It's time we called it quits. We will talk about it this evening when I get home, and once you have sobered up. I called your office and told Diane that you are ill and will not be in today. She will cancel your appointments.

He dropped the letter onto the dressing table, conscious now of being cold. He crossed the room to his closet and dressed quickly. He would shower later; first he needed coffee.

He stood and studied the garden from the kitchen window while the coffee brewed. It was a beautiful garden even now at the end of winter it retained a certain charm. Again, he thought of Nancy. She had designed it and overseen the work of the landscapers. She kept it in good order. The blooms in spring and summer were perfectly sequenced for continuous color. His eyes settled on the corner she had earmarked for a play gym, the corner where eventually they had planted a maple instead. It had grown into a magnificent tree. He turned away and watched the coffee drip through the filter into the pot.

◆◆◆

As Alexia navigated her way through the Manhattan traffic to West 67th Street, she played out different scenarios in her mind and tried to work out the best approach. There was no telling for sure how he would react, he could be temperamental and volatile, even impulsive, but he also had his father's sensitivity for other people and often surprised her with his perceptiveness. She couldn't control his reaction, but she could control herself and she would just have to make sure that no matter how he responded, she would stay calm and reasonable.

Sebastian was already at the table when she arrived, his violin case propped against the chair next to him. He stood to kiss her. She couldn't resist the urge to ruffle his disheveled thick wavy hair. He was tall and lean, and his cream linen shirt hung untucked over his jeans, a dark green sweater hung open over this and he had a thin brown plaid scarf around his neck.

They sat down, and he picked up his beer and swallowed. He looked across at her sheepishly, wiping his mouth with the back of his hand. "Sorry. I've ordered you a chardonnay."

She smiled at him and the waiter appeared with the glass.

"So, what's so important that you had to see me today?" he asked.

Alexia sipped her wine, rolled it around in her mouth for a moment feeling the refreshing prickle as it awakened her taste buds, and then held up her glass and said "Cheers. To us."

He raised a quizzical eyebrow but clinked her glass anyway. She glanced around the restaurant and felt comforted by the coziness and familiarity of the place. It had changed very little since she used to frequent it with Oliver and Mungo and the others. This was where she had first met Mungo. It felt right somehow that she and Sebastian talk here.

She remembered how torn and confused she had been in those days. So much is expected of young people, before they are ready for it. She looked back at her son and wondered what conflicts and confusions he might be dealing with in his life. In some ways he appeared so grown up and self-composed, so equipped for the life he had chosen, and yet she knew that much of this was pretense, a part of the process of maturing. You wore the mantle of maturity, hoping to carry if off and convince those around you until slowly, imperceptibly, it became a reality. If she had it over again, she would do things differently. She knew now about misplaced commitment, but it was too late.

"Mom," Sebastian's voice broke through her thoughts, "what is it you need to talk about? I have to get back to class soon."

"I have some news. Well, it's not really news I suppose, but it's news to you."

"What, have you met someone new? Are you getting married?"

"No, I've met someone old. Someone from my past." She cast her eyes down at the table and ran her fingers slowly across the grainy wood, feeling the ridges and patterns under her finger tips.

"So, are you seeing him?" Sebastian looked around, trying to catch the eye of the waiter.

"No, it's nothing like that." She picked up her glass, prevaricating. "He was... a friend of your father's. They were as thick as thieves until..."

"Not that guy who stole Dad's music? The one who disappeared, Mungo Joudry?"

"Well, yes, but he claims he didn't steal the music. He says it was his composition. That Oliver was the one who lied about it."

"Oh, come on Mum! That's neat, after all these years! I thought he'd vanished anyway, ran away guilty! We still study Dad's piece and the story behind it. Everyone knows it's Dad's composition. But no-one knows what happened to the guy? Where'd you see him?"

Just then the waiter appeared, and they quickly glanced over the menu and gave their orders, he for a pizza and she for the roast chicken salad.

"So, he showed up at last. Where?" Sebastian leaned back in his chair and settled his gaze upon his mother, arms folded.

"Toronto." She fiddled with her wine glass, then smoothed out an imagined fold in the table cloth.

"And?"

"Well, it was all a bit strange really. He spotted me, at the market that day you and I were there together."

"What, I don't remember this."

"No, we didn't actually see him. I didn't know he was in Toronto, or where he was, for that matter. Anyway, apparently, he saw me and followed us to the hotel. He left a note for me at reception."

"Seems odd," said Sebastian unfolding his arms and reaching for his glass. "Why'd he follow you, why didn't he just talk to you at the market?" He swallowed what remained in the glass and beckoned the waiter for a re-fill. "Why didn't you tell me before?"

"I don't know exactly, Sebastian. I didn't meet with him until after you'd gone back to New York. He is a bit of an odd guy, always was. You know he ran away after your father accused him of stealing his work. He just completely vanished. Juilliard even hired a private detective to search for him, but nothing, not a word, and then suddenly a few weeks ago he pops up in Toronto. After nearly twenty years." She shook her head, her eyes focused somewhere on the past, beyond her son's shoulders.

"What did he want with you?"

"At first I was unsure. I didn't call him back to begin with, but I suppose, eventually, curiosity got the better of me and I called. The truth is, I was in love with him. I loved Oliver too, I was engaged to Oliver, but I was totally in love with Mungo. He was incredibly talented, deeply artistic. He could make music like nobody I knew. Everybody recognized his talent. It never made any sense to me that he would plagiarize."

"Hah! You picked the wrong guy to fall in love with."

She nodded, "Yes, well, I certainly married the wrong one."

The waiter brought their meal and they spent a few minutes savoring the food.

"The thing is," Alexia looked at him steadily until he raised his eyes from his plate and met hers, "I think he might be telling the truth. I think maybe he *did* compose *The Phantom and the Fraud*."

"Seriously!" Sebastian flung the piece of pizza he was holding down on his plate. "What is this? This guy, this Mungo, steals Dad's work, gets caught out and then goes into hiding. Then he pops up one day, twenty years later, claiming innocence." He wiped his hands down on his jeans then ran them through his thick hair. "This is crazy! Look I don't have a lot of time; I've got to get back to class." He reached down to pick up his violin case.

"Sebastian, wait. Please. There's more." Her eyes appealed to him across the table.

He sighed and sat back in his seat, picked an olive off his pizza and put it in his mouth.

"He told me a lot of things when I met him a few weeks ago. I didn't want to believe them either, but the more I've thought about them, the more sense they make. I think he's telling the truth and if that is the case then he has been done a terrible injustice. And he did it for me. That's the worst part of it all. We owe him."

117

"I don't owe him anything! What are you talking about?"

"You owe him your talent. He is your father. Not Oliver but Mungo. Mungo Joudry is your real father."

Sebastian was very still, his face pale and intense. He stared at his mother, studying her as if confirmation of her words could be found in her light freckles and the lines on her face. Someone opened and closed the door to the restaurant creating a quick draft which blew a strand of Sebastian's hair into his face. He brushed it aside and Alexia drew in a long breath.

Finally, he pushed his chair back roughly and stood up. He grabbed his violin. "I'm leaving. I'm going to be late." He strode to the door.

Alexia sat for a moment, watched him leave. Then she grabbed her purse, pulled out some money and left it on the table. She was still struggling into her coat when she caught up with him on the corner of West 67th and Colombus Avenue. She grabbed his arm, "Sebastian please, let's talk. We can't leave it like this. Running away isn't going to help. He ran away, and he lost everything; his career, me, his friend and most importantly, you." He looked down at her and allowed her to pull on his arm and turn them towards Central Park.

♦♦♦

The crisp clear air invigorated Elizabeth's steps as she walked through the downtown area towards the market, taking in the Saturday morning activity. This morning the traffic had not deterred her, she'd not minded when a man had zipped into the parking space she had been staking out and she'd generously doled out about five dollars in change to the homeless man who had accosted her as she left the parking lot. The city seemed to share her optimism and the aroma of coffee beckoned her.

She stepped into Starbucks and was immediately enveloped by the cozy neighborhood charm, which seemed to be the stock in trade of the international coffee chain. People were lounging in shabby chic armchairs reading the Saturday papers, propped up at tall tables sipping lattes and standing in the queue, which extended all the way to the door.

The night before, she had received a call from Nancy Beringer who said the first movement had been favorably received by Alfonso Ghiradelli and that the OSO would like to review the remaining manuscript in order to make a final decision.

"But just between you and me," Nancy had breathed into the phone, "he loves it! He could hardly contain himself. And what Alfonso wants, Alfonso gets. So, if the rest of the music is as good, we will be changing our repertoire for the spring season."

"Well, that's just wonderful," Elizabeth said, "I knew the OSO would want to perform it."

"If we are going to include it we will have to get on to it right away. They are already well into rehearsals for the spring season. What are the next steps? How quickly can we move on this?"

Elizabeth told Nancy that she had already consulted with an intellectual property lawyer at her firm and that she would have a draft agreement for Nancy within a few days. She said that, in view of the fact that the originator of the work was unknown they would need to apply for an orphan works license and that special clauses would have to be included in the agreement to protect both Elizabeth and the OSO. She said that her colleague was researching this.

Elizabeth left the Starbucks, a steaming latte in her hand and a spring in her step, sub-consciously humming a few bars from the sonata. She'd taken the unusual step of inviting some colleagues around for dinner and anticipated a few hours of culinary inspiration as she wandered around the market.

Chapter Twenty

Mungo arrived at the back entrance to Figaro's and pushed his way in through the door stamping the snow off his boots on the rubber mat in the small vestibule before entering the kitchen. He paused for a moment, observing the organized chaos. He often thought that the work of a chef was much like the job of a conductor. Timing is critical, the best ingredients essential if the goal is more than mediocrity, but it is in knowing what to introduce when, and how much is enough, that really distinguishes the good from the sublime. Mungo stood in quiet admiration as he watched Patricia's head chef, Paulo, orchestrating the activities in his kitchen. Paulo greeted Mungo in his typically gruff manner and said that Patricia was out, but that Mungo could wait in the restaurant. He promised to have someone bring Mungo a drink while he waited.

Mungo loved having Figaro's to himself before it opened, to sit in the dim interior and think or read or make music.

Today he sat down at the piano and removed a folded wad of pages and a pencil from his pocket. He laid them on the piano smoothing out the creases. Head bowed over the keyboard he started to play, slowly at first, stopping every now and then to make some notes on the page, and then with increasing speed and intensity. Often, he played the same refrain repeatedly, with minor variations until he was satisfied. Then he would stand suddenly and pace around the room seeing nothing, running his fingers through the waves in his hair and then lean over the piano on his left arm as his right hand picked out another riff. If he liked what he heard, he would sit down and his left hand would find the chords to support the right hand's melody.

He worked like this for two hours, intermittently playing, scribbling and pacing, the coffee which had been placed on the table to his left long since cold and forgotten, oblivious to the mounting panic in the kitchen next door and the repeated trips in and out of the room as the waiters readied the tables for dinner.

Eventually, he straightened, placed his hands on his lower back and stretched backwards, feeling the release of tension from his neck and shoulders.

He heard Patricia's voice from behind: "When are you going to stop hiding?"

He turned. It was hard to see her in the darkened restaurant, but he knew she was sitting at her favorite table tucked slightly out of sight yet offering a full view of most of the restaurant.

"I think you are more afraid of success than failure. You have embraced failure, Mungo, and wrapped yourself in it like a comfortable blanket."

He moved toward her table and sat down opposite her, elbows on his knees he dropped his head down into his hands.

She did not release him from his distress by offering further comment to alleviate the impact of her words; she simply sat, watching him.

Finally, he looked up. "It's too late now. I had my chance and I blew it. I should have spoken up years ago."

Patricia slowly poured a glass of champagne from a bottle on the table and pushed it towards him. He watched the bubbles rise to the top, burst at the surface and become nothing. Just like me, he thought. She topped up her own glass and then lifted it in a toast, "To the greatest musician the world has never known." She took a sip. "I don't want you to come here again Mungo. Until you are ready to take up your life and reclaim your place in the world, I don't want to see you. I can't stand to see you waste your life any longer. I know how talented you are and it's painful to see you squander it like this. As a friend, I'm asking you to step out and claim your rightful place in the world. You may have buried your pain, but I can't." She stood up and walked away. Mungo watched her retreating back, the only sound the soft swish of her long skirt as it brushed against her legs.

He sat in the empty restaurant for a long time. When he finally left it was dark outside and the first patrons were being shown to their tables.

Mungo stepped onto the boat, his backpack over one shoulder and a bag of groceries in his hand. It was cold and he was desperate for the familiar comfort of the boat after Patricia's painful words. He crossed the deck to the sliding door, unlocked it and slid it open just wide enough to step in. He switched on the light and crossed the seating area to the galley beyond. He stopped short as he approached. Blake's bottle of Macallan 18 stood on the counter, almost empty.

Alarm rippled through his body. He'd not been to the boat since the day with Alexia. Could it be that he'd left it out? We only had two glasses each. I'm sure I cleaned up. Yes, yes, I did. We had lunch. I cleared everything away. Someone has been here.

He scanned the room. Nothing else was disturbed. He quietly set his bags on the counter and moved to the stairs. He peered down. It was dark and quiet. Muscle by muscle he descended the stairs. It was probably nothing, but his near escapes in the past few weeks had reminded him that he couldn't afford to get too cavalier.

The door to the main sleeping cabin was closed. He reached out and turned the handle slowly then pushed the door open. Blake was sprawled across the bed on his stomach, his face twisted toward the door. Mungo backed quickly into the narrow hallway his heart thumping against his ribcage. There was no reaction from within. He leaned into the doorway again, this time taking in all of the small room. Blake hadn't moved. Next to him on the bedside table was a half empty bottle of Johnnie Walker. So, you started on the good stuff upstairs and then moved onto Johnnie Walker, Mungo thought. Then his eye fell on the pill bottle next to it. *My God Blake!* He launched himself across the small space and snatched up the bottle. Lorazepam. Mungo didn't recognize it, but clearly printed on a sticker across the label were the words 'Warning. Not to be taken with alcohol.' The bottle was not quite empty, but Mungo had no idea how many Blake may have consumed.

"Blake! Blake!" he said, all anxiety about his own discovery vaporized. No reaction from Blake. Mungo leaned over him. His breathing was shallow and irregular, but he was breathing.

Mungo was uncertain what to do or if it was even serious. Should he just leave Blake to sleep it off? Would he sleep it off or would he just drift off into eternity? How many pills had he taken? Mungo studied the bottle in his hand again and gave it a shake. Blake stirred and groaned.

"Blake, Blake, wake up,"

He groaned again but seemed unable to open his eyes or raise his head.

"Wait, I'll get you some water," said Mungo. He dashed into the bathroom. Confused images from movie scenes played themselves unbidden across his mental screen showing people trying to resuscitate those who'd overdosed, pouring coffee down their throats and walking them around to keep them awake. He returned with a glass of water. He rolled Blake over and tried to raise his head sufficiently to get some water into his mouth but all he succeeded in doing was splashing cold water down Blake's chin and onto his shirt.

He put the glass down. Water seemed innocuous in the face of what Blake had consumed. He needed coffee. And he needed help. Mungo clambered up the stairs. Should he call 911 or should he just make coffee. *Godammit.* He felt so ill equipped. Perhaps he should just take his things and leave. No-one would know.

He was suddenly jolted from his state of immobilized indecision by the insistent chirrup of a cell phone. It was coming from downstairs, it must be Blake's. Without thinking he took the stairs down two at a time following the sound.

The phone was in the pocket of Blake's leather jacket, which was hanging behind the bedroom door. He yanked it out fumbling for the answer button as he made his way back upstairs. Mungo hoped that the caller would come to Blake's rescue but instead he heard Christine's voice.

"Blake, where are you? Why haven't you been answering my calls? Don't mess with me." Mungo said nothing, trying to figure out what to do. "I mean business and I mean to get my money. Don't play games with me, I know you are there… Speak to me!"

Mungo finally found his voice, "Blake is ill. He can't come to the phone."

"Who is this? Where is Blake? Put him on I need to speak to him."

"He can't come to the phone right now. What do you want from him? Maybe I can help," He said.

"Yah right. He's just avoiding me. You tell him that I meant everything I said. If I don't hear from him by midnight on Tuesday, he should watch the morning news on Wednesday. I'm going public. I have nothing to lose and he has everything to lose." The call disconnected.

He stood staring at the now silent phone. Tuesday night, that didn't give them much time. Mungo heard a crash from down below. He ran down stairs. Blake lay across the small floor space between the bed and the doorway. He'd fallen and it seemed to Mungo that he'd hit his head against the door frame. *Could things get any worse?* He dropped to his knees beside Blake and tried to roll him over. He saw a red gash on his forehead. It didn't look too bad, based on Mungo's rudimentary knowledge of first aid, but it may need a stitch or two. Now he would have to call 911.

As he turned to go upstairs again for the phone he heard Blake murmur. He turned back. Blake was trying to sit up. Mungo grabbed him under his armpits and dragged him up into a sitting position, propping him against the wall. He clambered over Blake's outstretched legs and took the water from the bedside table.

"Here, drink this," he said holding the glass up to Blake's mouth and tilting it so that some of the liquid poured into his mouth. Blake swallowed, then swallowed some more. He drank until the glass was empty. "That's good, that's good. You'll feel better,"

"My head hurts. I need some pills."

"No! No more pills. How many did you take earlier?"

For the first time Blake looked at Mungo, his bleary vision clearing a little.

"Who are you?" he said.

"It doesn't matter. A friend," said Mungo, "You have had too much to drink, and taken pills. Then you fell and hit your head. Here let me help you back to the bed."

Blake allowed Mungo to pull him up and together they shuffled him back to the bed where he lay down. Mungo went into the bathroom and re-filled the water glass and pulled a hand towel off the rail. He handed it to Blake. "Drink some more." He gently blotted the gash on Blake's forehead with the towel, not removing much of the now congealing blood. "You might need a couple of stitches here," Mungo said.

"Who are you?"' Blake repeated, this time more insistently. "I don't know you."

"No, you don't, but I know you," said Mungo. "Wait here, I'm going to put some coffee on. It will help you."

Mungo went up to the galley and mechanically set about making coffee, trying to think of what he should do next. So much of his life had been a series of accidental events which he had simply responded to. Now he really needed to think and plan and take some proactive steps. He could just walk out and leave Blake to find his way to the coffee and his own way out of the mess, or he could expose himself and help Blake fix his problem, deal with this scandal. It was this last thought which decided him. He had allowed his own life to be ruined by running away from a scandal. This was his chance to put things right, at least for Blake.

He poured two mugs of coffee, sugared the one for Blake liberally and carried them downstairs.

◆◆◆

The smell of oil paint and thinners filled Nancy's living room. Sven would have liked to open the window to let some air in, but it was cold outside. He was pleased Nancy had agreed to this painting session at short notice. He stepped back and studied the scene with a critical eye. He knew he was on thin ice here. At some point she was going to want to see the portrait and truth was he was an amateur and certainly no portrait artist. But having used the art school to get close to her, he was now committed. At least until he had the information he needed from her.

The conversation with Nancy the other day, when she mentioned the music Elizabeth Carey had brought to her attention, was the first bit of hard evidence that Sven had found to support his theory that Mungo Joudry was hiding in Toronto. And it was his first real breakthrough in this story which he had been pursuing for months, at considerable personal cost. He hoped like hell that he could sell it to the *New York Times*, or one of the Toronto dailies. Better still, he'd like to find a documentary film maker and see if they could collaborate on the story. He could almost taste the success. But he was getting ahead of himself. He needed to confirm his theory, locate the elusive bugger, line up interviews...

"How much longer? Do you think we could stop for a while?" Nancy's voice broke into his thoughts.

"Of course, I'm sorry. I get so absorbed," he lied. "We can take a break, but you can't see it yet. It's a long way from finished."

"I'm going to the washroom. I'll be right back and then I'll make us something to eat."

"That would be great," he replied, pleased that he may have another few hours to draw her out. He smiled at his own pun and studied the rudimentary oil sketch he had started of her. At least he was trying, he thought. He'd got a pretty good rendition of the outline, captured some nice negative spaces and shadowed areas.

He was excited to think he had tracked Mungo Joudry to the right city. Though why nobody else had tumbled on this, he didn't know. Perhaps they had just lost interest. Since he and Nancy had last met he had found out quite a bit about Elizabeth Carey. He wondered if Nancy realized that she lived just a few streets over from her and Blake.

Sven had been watching the Beringers' home off and on for a few months and was almost certain that it was Mungo Joudry who had been coming and going from the place from time to time. He was pretty sure though that Nancy had no idea. Unless she and Joudry knew each other, moving in musical circles, as it were. Maybe she had been protecting him all this time? He really had to get to the bottom of this, and soon. If she had discovered a piece of his music and it was about to be performed, others might scoop him. If he could sell it just as the OSO did the inaugural performance, it could really make his name.

"So, are you pleased with your handiwork?" Nancy appeared in the doorway.

"Well, like I said, it's a long way from finished."

"Come through, you can keep me company in the kitchen. I'll pour us some wine."

"I'd like that, but what about your husband? Will he join us for dinner?"

"Don't worry about him. He's not here. I'm not expecting him back. At least not tonight," she said.

"If you are sure, Nancy. I don't want to put you in a difficult position."

"Yes, I'm sure. I could do with the company."

He sat down at the kitchen table and she poured them each a glass of wine.

"I have steak and salad and could bake a couple of potatoes," she suggested.

"Perfect, thank you. Just let me know what I can do to help."

"Nothing really. It's such a simple meal. Besides I have been reclining and you have been working for the past hour and a half. Just sit and relax."

"You have a beautiful home Nancy. It seems quite big for just the two of you. Have you ever considered downsizing or renting out a room?"

"No not really. We have got used to rattling around in here and quite honestly, I need my space from Blake. Though, now, things might change..." She stopped herself.

"Oh?" Sven raised his eyebrows.

"Oh, you know, things change, people change, we will have to see what happens," she said vaguely.

"So, you've never had a boarder or long-term guest to, ah, use up some of the extra space?"

"Goodness, no," she said. She looked across at him from the counter where she was chopping vegetables for a salad. "You're not wanting a room to rent, are you?"

"No, no. Sorry to seem so curious. I guess it's just that we are not used to such big homes in Sweden. A place like this in the city would often accommodate a few residents. Like London, you know, where they turn bigger old homes into flats."

"Fortunately, we still have space to spare in Toronto."

"What happened with that anonymous music you told me about last week?"

"I gave it to our musical director and he loves it. We're going to include it in the spring repertoire. The woman who gave it to me is sorting out an agreement. She's worried about intellectual property rights, particularly since we don't know who composed it and have to follow certain legal protocols."

"So, you really don't have any idea who composed it?" Sven asked.

"No, nothing concrete. But that's what makes it so appealing. The mystery of it. There is huge potential for publicity, to get people interested in classical music and maybe draw them back to the OSO. I'm working on a campaign. This may draw the composer out or identify him." She said, her back to him as she placed the steak on the gas grill, "The steak will be done in a couple of minutes and I hope you don't mind microwaved-baked potatoes, they're much quicker to cook."

Sven felt the pulse pumping in his throat. Too damn right, he thought. People are going to love the intrigue. His sense of urgency increased. He needed to break the story before the OSO campaign stole his thunder. He wished now that he could excuse himself and get back to work.

A few minutes later, Nancy brought the food to the table and sat down opposite him.

"Bon appétit," she said, raising her glass.

"Skål," he replied, and they clinked glasses. "Thank you, this looks delicious," he said, cutting into the juicy steak. "When do you plan to launch your campaign?"

"It will probably coincide with our usual run up publicity to the start of the season. But there will be a lot more work involved than usual. Of course, it all still needs to be approved by the board. We will have to fit in additional rehearsals. It's a piece which none of the orchestra members have played before and it is quite tricky by all accounts. Also, we will have to find a few soloists and all the good ones are booked up far in advance. So, I'm thinking we should open up the solo spots to the music schools and try and flush out some new talent. It will be another angle for positive publicity, you know, highlighting how much the OSO is doing to provide opportunities for young musicians, that sort of thing. But that is enough about me. Tell me about you."

Sven managed to steer the conversation onto generalities until the meal was over. When they had finished eating he helped her clear up.

"Thank you, again, Nancy. Your home has such a sense of history, yet it's not dated," he said as they walked through the formal living room. "I will just pack up my things."

Across the hallway was a pair of double doors, one slightly ajar. "That looks like a lovely room too," he said.

"Oh, it's Blake's study," Nancy said. "Go in, if you want." She opened the doors and they stepped into the room. Nancy switched on the light and the room was bathed in the warm glow of lamplight reflecting off the red walls.

surveyed the room and the portrait immediately arrested his gaze, sharp gashes distorting what would otherwise be an asymmetrical but balanced face. He felt instinctive regret for the destruction and stepped closer to the painting propped up against a wingback chair. He dropped to his haunches to study it more closely. It was beautifully painted. He shook his head.

"I didn't do it, if that's what you're thinking."

He heard Nancy's voice from behind. He turned and looked up at her, his face a question.

"It was him. Blake. He did it himself," she said.

Sven turned back to the painting. He wondered what could have driven Blake to slash his own portrait?

As if in answer to his silent question Nancy said "He was drunk. I got home on Thursday night, after we had been to your farmhouse, and found him slumped in that chair, a whisky bottle next to him and his portrait slashed at his feet."

"But why?" He stood suddenly and turned to her. "Thursday. You don't think he was angry because we went to my place?"

"No, no. Sven, he doesn't know. He doesn't even know you. He doesn't know what I do," she sighed. "Look, you don't know him, what he's like." She turned away and headed for the door. "Come on, this is not why you are here."

"Stop. Nancy, wait. This is important. He must be very unhappy, to do this."

"Yes, he is. We are."

Sven stared at her for a long moment until she turned and left the room. He picked up the painting and carried it across to the lamp to study it more closely. He recognized the artist. He was renowned for his portraiture and his worked fetched a great deal of money these days, as is always the case once the artist stops working. He turned it over and studied the back. It could be repaired, but it would be difficult, and it would never be the same again. The slashes were too long. He put the painting down and followed Nancy out of the room to say his good-byes.

Chapter Twenty-one

They spoke very little for the first hour or so. Mungo concentrated on getting coffee and water down Blake's throat. He was initially horrified when Blake started retching and dragged him into the small bathroom to try and contain the mess. On reflection he realized this was probably a good thing, he was getting rid of some of the toxins in his system.

He helped Blake clean up and supported him back to the bed. Blake propped himself up against the polished wood headboard and focused his bloodshot eyes on Mungo.

"Who the hell are you?" His belligerence was as strong and sour as his breath.

"I'm a friend," said Mungo. "I'm here to help you."

"What do you mean a friend? I don't even know you."

"But I know you Blake. I know more about you than you can imagine. I know more about you than Nancy does, and I probably even know you better than you know yourself. Because I see it all, and, unlike you, I am not blinded by the self-delusion which blinds you."

"What the fuck! Get out of here..." Blake interrupted, the red in his bloodshot eyes now spreading to his cheeks as he tried to raise himself more upright.

"And," continued Mungo undeterred "importantly, despite what I know about you I am still willing to help you. I am probably the only true friend you have Blake."

"I don't need your help. I don't know you. Get the fuck off my boat."

"Oh, but you do, Blake. What are you planning to do? Pay Christine off and then pay her again, and again? Do you think she will keep quiet if you don't keep paying up? She means business and she knows who the other women are. Against them, you haven't a chance." Mungo saw the shock register in Blake's face as it drained of color just as quickly as it had reddened. "And what about Nancy?" he went on, "have you ever stopped to consider her, the effort she has put into your marriage and your career? You would be nowhere without her Blake."

"Did she send you? Did Nancy send you? How does she know about this?" Blake voice was hoarse.

"Nancy knows nothing. That's partly why I am here. I've been protecting you two from each other for years."

Blake tried to clamber off the bed, galvanized by rage, his fists swinging wildly. His legs became entangled in the sheets, now partially lying on the floor. He stumbled and fell back on the bed.

"Fuck!"

"What about the Ethics Committee position with the IPF?" Mungo's voice was quieter now. "Are you really ready to throw that away? And in the wake of the #MeToo revelations, you will surely be ruined. Everything you have worked for over the past twenty years is about to go down the toilet Blake, and then what will you do? Have you even thought about it?"

Blake was sitting on the edge of the bed now, his head in his hands, between his knees. "God, my head hurts."

"You haven't thought about it, have you? You have just lost yourself in an alcoholic haze and you are hoping that when you come out of it all this will have been a horrible nightmare and you can pick up where you left off. You didn't used to be this pathetic Blake." He reached out and gave Blake's shoulder a shake. "You have to deal with this. You can't hide from it forever. Believe me; I know. At some point you will have to face it. You might as well do it now. The sooner you do it, the sooner you can get your life back on track." He paused and then suddenly, drained of energy, he sank to the edge of the bed next to Blake, his head in his hands too.

"What do you want from me? How do you know all this?" Blake's voice was hoarse.

Mungo ran his fingers through his hair, his eyes staring unseeing at the carpet beneath his feet. "I just want to help you Blake. It doesn't matter how I know you or who I am. Just accept that I am probably the only person who can help you get out of this mess right now."

There was a long silence. Mungo heard the water lapping softly against the outside of the boat. After a few minutes he stood up. "Are you up to a shower? You smell bad. You need one."

Blake nodded.

"Fine, you take a shower. I'm going upstairs. I have some calls to make. When I'm done we'll eat something and then we'll talk about how to fix this."

Mungo walked up the narrow staircase, went through the glass sliding doors and stepped out onto the deck. He drew deep lungs full of cool fresh air through his mouth and rested his eyes on the lights of the harbor front buildings reflecting in the inky water. He knew that in helping Blake deal with his secrets he would be exposing his own. Last chance, he thought. Then he took his cell phone from his pocket and dialed Meredith Salinger's mobile number. He was completely unaware of the man lurking in the shadows between two large boats opposite, watching and listening.

◆◆◆

Sven left Nancy's house in a restless state alternating between excitement and anxiety. He was conscious of the story gathering momentum, almost to the point that it was now out of his control. He had to get to Mungo Joudry before the other media did. He had exhausted all avenues online and now it required some good old-fashioned foot slogging. *But where to look?*

By a slow process of logic and elimination his research had brought him to Toronto. He had spent months attending classical music concerts, chamber concerts, identifying members of string quartets and nosing about in the lives of the OSO Board and orchestra. Finally, one night he had spotted a man resembling Joudry dining at Figaro's. He couldn't be sure because the lighting was low but there was something about the man that had struck him as familiar.

It was not the first time this had happened to Sven and sometimes he chastised himself for becoming obsessed and seeing the ghost of Mungo Joudry around every corner.

Years earlier in Sweden, Sven had succeeded in locating a missing ship's captain as part of an investigative piece for a local newspaper and this had given him a taste for how people manage to hide and why. It turned out that the ship's captain had been part of a human trafficking operation from Russia and the previous Soviet bloc countries into Europe. When things got a bit hot and he'd made enough money, the captain changed his identity and took up residence in Estonia. Sven had helped the Swedish police track him down.

Sven started reading up about other missing people and came across the search for Mungo Joudry. At the time he was still based in Stockholm, but when his job there came to an end, he started the search for Joudry in earnest.

As the cabaret performance drew to an end and diners got up to leave, he had planned to follow the man he thought was Joudry out of the restaurant. However, instead of making for the exit, Joudry had headed further into the restaurant. He assumed that Joudry had made a detour for the washroom, however, when forty-five minutes later he had still not appeared he had given up and headed home.

Since then Sven had regularly enjoyed a meal at Figaro's hoping to see him again. Apart from a good meal and some decent music, none of these visits had borne fruit.

It was still early in the evening and he knew that if he went back to his apartment he would crawl the walls with frustration; so instead, he had caught the subway downtown and walked to Figaro's. Once there he stood around outside for a while watching the door smoking one too many cigarettes. Just as he was becoming concerned that he would draw the wrong sort of attention as a loiterer and was about to head home he saw the man leave the restaurant. Now he was on full alert; he wasn't absolutely sure, but it looked like him.

Instinctively he straightened from his leaning position against the wall, dropped his cigarette and, crushing it underfoot quickly, set off after him. He followed Joudry at a casual distance, not wanting to draw attention. He watched him enter a local grocery store and leave shortly with a bag of groceries. He had continued his walk for some time with Sven following at a safe distance and sticking to the shadows wherever possible. After some time, it became clear that Joudry was headed to the marina. The closer they got the more convinced Sven was that this was his destination.

He recalled the day Nancy had taken them there only to find the boat missing. It was starting to make sense. Now that he was sure where Joudry was headed, he hung back increasing his following distance. He gave Joudry some time to enter the marina and when he thought the coast was clear he walked in. He walked past the harbor master's office, his head tucked into his collar and hands in his pockets as if hiding them would make him less visible as a trespasser. He caught the strong unmistakable whiff of fish and chips as he passed by and ventured a glance at the office. He saw, through the window, the man Nancy had called Errol reading a newspaper while he absently stuffed some chips in his mouth. Relieved that Errol's preoccupations kept him from his watch, Sven hurried past and quickly found *The Ice Queen.*

As he approached he saw the lights glowing from within. Convinced now that this was where Joudry had been hiding out, he decided to watch and wait for a while. While he watched he played out different scenarios in his mind. Should he confront and question Joudry? That might scare him off and drive him further into hiding. It probably made more sense to track his movements and get more answers that way. But realistically how long could he keep that up without getting noticed? Also, he needed to be sure he had the right guy. He would need to get some good photos to compare with those he had on file of Joudry as a younger man. He absently reached into his coat pocket for his pack of cigarettes when he heard the sliding door of the deck open and a man stepped out. Now was not the time to light up. He quickly shoved the cigarette packet back into his pocket and retreated further into the shadows. He saw Joudry pull out a cell phone and watched as he punched in some numbers.

♦♦♦

Meredith was dressed in what she thought of as her comfortable cottage clothes; fleecy checked pants and a soft cream argyle sweater she'd knitted for herself many years ago. She was using her own time to research her new client, Mungo Jameson. One of the things which distinguished Meredith as an exceptional investigator was her unerring instinct about people. And right from the first moment when she observed him waiting in the Van Buuren and Co. reception area she knew he was going to be an interesting client.

This was indeed proving correct. Besides an early morning run along one of her favorite forest trails and a quick trip to the local store for some grocery basics, she had spent much of the day researching him. It didn't take her too long to discover that, of the few Mungo Jameson's on record, her new client was certainly not one of them. Mungo was not a common name and soon she stumbled across news reports in the online archives of various newspapers, dating back almost twenty years, regarding the missing Mungo Joudry.

She came to the conclusion that her Mungo Jameson was the missing composer. But that is where her research started to draw blanks. She could find absolutely no trace of him in the intervening years from the time that he had performed the famous *Phantom and the Fraud* and then disappeared.

In addition to Meredith's instincts she was also a very gifted computer hacker. This was something she did not make known to her colleagues, but which had certainly propelled her to the upper ranks of Van Buuren and Co. Using her computer, she had spent hours that day figuratively prowling around the backrooms of many government departments both in Canada and the US, but there were no records of Mungo Joudry since his disappearance.

Her research revealed that a New York based investigation firm she knew well, Jaffer and McConvey, had been hired by Juilliard to find him and, after over a year, had produced no results, not even any strong leads. People had stopped searching for him. Interestingly his friend, Oliver Bantry, who claimed to have been wronged by Mungo, had never written another piece as great as *The Phantom and the Fraud*. Meredith learned that after some years of struggling to make a name for himself as a composer, Bantry had taken up a career in the advertising industry writing jingles.

Eventually the prevailing opinion was that Mungo must have committed suicide, possibly by drowning, and the body had never turned up. He dropped off the radar screen and people forgot about him. And then a few days ago he had walked into her office.

She straightened up and stared through the window into the darkness of the forest surrounding her cottage. She observed that the dark outside was about as impenetrable as the dark which surrounded the mysterious Mungo Joudry when her reverie was interrupted by the shrill sound of her cell phone.

Meredith cursed. She always switched it off when she was at the cottage. She must have forgotten when she got in late the night before. She had an unlisted landline at the cottage and only three people had the number. They hardly ever used it. She had made it very clear; it was for emergencies only. The ringing continued. She strode across the wooden floor to the table by the door where she had placed the keys with her phone and purse. She picked up the phone and saw it was from an unidentified caller. She was about to cancel the call, when on impulse she clicked the connect button.

"Yes?" she said irritably.

"It's Mungo Jameson here. I'm sorry to bother you on the weekend. It's just that, well…that matter I spoke to you about this week. It's become rather more urgent." He paused. She was silent.

Her irritability at being disturbed was fighting with her curiosity.

"Hello, Ms. Salinger, are you there?" Mungo tried to keep the urgency from his voice.

"Yes, yes. I'm here. What can I do for you Mr. Jameson? I'm not in Toronto this weekend but I'll see what I can do."

"We got a call from the woman. She has set a deadline of midnight on Tuesday. If he doesn't pay up by then she's going to the media."

"Look, we've seen this kind of thing before," said Meredith. "It's in her interests to keep the story quiet, that way she can extract more money out of him over a longer period. She's just keeping the pressure on. You will probably be able to negotiate an extension. She could sell the story to a newspaper but then she'll only get one payment, and there is no way they would pay what she is asking of your friend. You must be cool but give her the impression that he is panicked and is doing everything he can to get the money together. If she doesn't call again this weekend, then call her on

Monday, let her know that he is working on her request and is taking the matter seriously."

"Yes, that makes sense. I'll do that. But do you have any information on her yet? We need something, anything, to shut her up."

"We have assigned two of our best investigators to your case. I should have an initial report on my desk on Monday morning. If it's any reassurance, in my experience, people who are sufficiently unprincipled to blackmail, usually have a few skeletons of their own hidden away. If there is anything, trust me, we will find it. If not, we can work out a strategy for dealing with this. I suggest we meet on Monday afternoon. Come to my office at two o'clock."

"I'll be there."

◆◆◆

While Blake showered Mungo fixed them a simple spaghetti Bolognese using the groceries he had brought with him. Blake clambered up the stairs and flopped onto the sofa. Mungo was aware of Blake studying him with hooded speculative eyes as he deftly finished preparing the meal in the confined galley.

Mungo placed the plates on the small table and sat down gesturing to Blake to join him. Blake sat and reached automatically for the wine bottle. Mungo stuck out his hand and grabbed the neck of the bottle, shaking his head vigorously, and waving his fork negatively with his other hand.

"Oh no, it's orange juice for you tonight." He splashed some juice from a carton into a glass and pushed it across to Blake who slurped down half the glass before picking up his fork and spoon and tackling the Bolognese.

They ate in silence for a few minutes, Mungo warily watching Blake and wondering when he would have to answer the inevitable questions.

Blake rapidly consumed half the food on his plate before he raised his bloodshot eyes and demanded, "Who the hell are you anyway? And what are you doing on my boat? Did Christine send you?"

"When last did you eat?" said Mungo.

Blake slammed his utensils onto his plate splattering sauce, "Look, either I get some answers, or you get off my boat now!"

"Aah, that's the spirit. The old Blake is back."

Blake sat back and gave him a long, almost appreciative look, "Okay, so how about we start over and you tell me everything, from the beginning? Clearly, I don't need to introduce myself, since you seem to know so much about me, but it would be nice to know who you are and what you are doing here."

"Think of me as your guardian angel," said Mungo. "Someone who has been watching out for you for a long time."

"I don't need a bloody guardian angel! Stop talking in riddles and spit it out."

"Oh, but you do. A few weeks ago, Christine Hayes left a rather incriminating voice mail on your home number. I deleted it before Nancy got home."

"Bullshit."

"Three years ago, you forgot Nancy's birthday. When you got home that evening she met you at the door all dressed up for dinner and delighted with the lovely bouquet which the florist had delivered from you that day, along with the card telling her that you'd reserved a table at "Le Canard" for the two of you. You knew nothing about it, but you're a quick learner, Blake, and Nancy had no idea that you were on the back foot. You thought it was your assistant who'd made the arrangements, didn't you? Well, it was your guardian angel."

Blake just stared at him, speechless now. Mungo went on, "In February last year you and Nancy were supposed to go skiing with Janine and Jacob and other mutual friends. You told Nancy that you couldn't go because you had a business trip to Tokyo. In the end Nancy went without you. You took Christine to Mexico. When you got back, you left your boarding pass for the Mexico flight in your desk drawer in amongst some other papers. Nancy would have found it eventually, except I found it first and destroyed it."

"Christine has put you up to this, hasn't she?" Blake exploded. "You're part of it; you're in cahoots with her. Get off my fucking boat!"

Mungo stood up, picked up his backpack and started stuffing his things into it. "Have it your way Blake. In some ways that has been your greatest strength, but also your greatest weakness. You always get your own way, which is fine, until your own way is not the best way." He shrugged on his jacket, slung his backpack over his shoulder and went to the door. "I've engaged the services of a private investigator to look into Christine Hayes, but well, I guess you can handle this on your own."

"Wait. You haven't told me who you are. What do you want from me?"

Mungo turned slowly to face him. "Like you, I am a person with secrets. All I want is to help you. And if you think about it, you are not in a position to turn down help right now or lay down any conditions. Now you decide, either you can trust me, or you can't, but make up your mind because I'm not hanging around here indefinitely."

"Please...sit down," said Blake.

◆◆◆

On Monday, Elizabeth met with Nancy and one of the OSO's lawyers, Nigel Hawthorne, to discuss the mystery composition. Nancy was anxious to sort out the legalities as quickly as possible and get her hands on the music, but the lawyer was predictably cautious and asked Elizabeth to go over again and again how she had come by the music. He and Elizabeth agreed that any contract between her and the OSO would have to clearly set out the intellectual property rights and he said that he had applied for an orphan works license since they did not know who originator of the music was. He promised to review the draft agreement she gave him and get it back to her before the end of the week.

Once he left, Nancy set out her plans for deriving maximum publicity for the OSO through the inaugural performance of the mystery music. She asked Elizabeth whether she would be willing to participate in the media campaign that she and the OSO's Public Relations department were developing. She explained to Elizabeth that it would involve a search for the composer of the music and, she hoped, would attract the attention of the international classical music community and the public at large. She saw this resulting in a huge increase in ticket sales for the OSO and for invitations for the OSO to perform at other world-class venues. "It would mean," she said, her clear gaze fixed intently on Elizabeth's face, "that you too would be in the media spotlight." She paused to let her words sink in. Not getting an obvious adverse response, she pressed on, "You would be sought out for interviews; they may like to see exactly where you found the music. There would be speculation about you and how the music came to be in your home. It would even make an excellent subject for a documentary. The possibilities are limitless." She caught herself, realizing she may have said too much. She might have put Elizabeth off.

Elizabeth turned away and looked out of the window across the other side of the room. Finally, she turned back becoming aware that Nancy was watching her silently.

"Let's not get ahead of ourselves," she said. "I need to think this through carefully. I want the music to be heard, but I need to think about the consequences both for myself and the composer, whoever he or she may be."

"Of course, of course," agreed Nancy. "Everything must be carefully considered and covered by the agreement. I tell you what, why don't I draft a proposal setting out our ideas for promoting the performance and send it to you for consideration? We can work from that and when you are happy we can have it included in our agreement?"

Elizabeth eventually left Nancy's office and stepped into the frigid February air with her head spinning. What had she got herself into, she wondered, and was she ready for the changes this music was bringing into her well-structured, if somewhat boring, life? She had a strong sense that she was facing a turning point.

Instead of returning to her office, she called her assistant and told her to cancel her meetings for the rest of the day. Pulling her coat tighter around herself, she shoved her phone into her pocket and walked briskly in search of a coffee shop.

Chapter Twenty-Two

Mungo and Blake arrived at Van Buuren and Co. a few minutes before two o'clock. Mungo gave Blake a quick appraising look and thought that, considering what he'd been through in the past forty-eight hours, he seemed remarkably good. The only tell-tale signs being the gash on his forehead, which was healing nicely without any stitches, and slightly bloodshot eyes. Many men Blake's age looked like that on a normal day, thought Mungo, wondering how he himself looked.

All things considered, Mungo thought that Blake had accepted his sudden intervention in his life remarkably well, in large part probably because he was still suffering the combined ill effects of excessive alcohol and pills, but also because he really didn't have anyone else he could turn to.

As they stepped into the reception of Van Buuren and Co. Mungo said, "Now remember, let me do the talking. This woman is very good at what she does and will easily get you to say more than you want to."

"I hope you know what you're doing."

"So do I, believe me, so do I," was all Mungo said before the door opened and Meredith appeared.

Mungo made the introductions and they seated themselves in Meredith's office, a tray of coffee and a single folder, about an inch thick, on her desk.

"So," said Meredith, "your blackmailer is turning up the heat, I gather." She focused sharply on Blake. Before he could formulate a response, she went on. "That's a typical pattern in these situations." She shifted her eyes to Mungo. "Well, I've got good news and bad news."

"You've found something then?" asked Mungo, looking hopefully at the file.

"I always find it better to get the bad news out of the way first," said Meredith, again fixing her eyes on Blake who shifted in his seat and scanned around the room, as if for escape. Finally he crossed his arms. Meredith continued, "The bad news is that this woman, Christine Hayes, has accumulated much irrefutable evidence of your affairs, Mr. Beringer, not only with herself, but it seems with a number of other women too."

Blake was about to speak, and she raised a hand to stop him. "Don't ask me how I know. We can't reveal our methods or our sources. Just take it from me she has a strong position, which in normal circumstances would put you in a very weak position, but, this is where the good news comes in." She paused and looked at them both before continuing.

"Christine Hayes has an interesting history. She started out life as Christine Meyford, born in Vancouver, where she dropped out of high school and lived on her wits for several years. Her school records show good performance and a high IQ, but she fell in with the wrong crowd, started doing drugs and spent far too long in the rebellious teenager phase. Eventually she teamed up with a guy who, although criminal and unprincipled, stayed clear of drugs and he pulled her out of it. She started temping in and around the Vancouver area, doing office admin and clerical work. One thing led to another and she landed a full-time position with a pharmaceutical company, gradually working her way up. However, greed and impatience got the better of her and..."

"That sounds like Christine," said Blake bitterly.

Meredith raised a hand, "Please Mr. Beringer, let me finish. It appears, that she started to embezzle funds, small amounts at first and then, as her confidence grew, so did her greed. At a point she involved a colleague, as a bit of an insurance policy against discovery. She covered her own tracks so carefully that it would take a lot of determination to pin anything on her and would necessarily involve the colleague exposing himself."

She looked from Mungo to Blake, satisfying herself that she still had their full attention. "Things started to unravel when she was transferred to another division; she was no longer on the spot to effect the on-going cover-ups.

When things got hot she resigned, moved away and then set about changing her name. Meanwhile the colleague was blamed for the scam and, while he managed to raise suspicion about Christine Meyford, he could not provide unequivocal proof. The company failed to locate her. They fired the colleague, pressed charges and recovered a small part of the funds that they had lost over the previous five years."

"My God! What a witch," Blake exploded. He burst from his chair, paced up and down, the air in the office suddenly thick with his anger.

"Blake, come and sit down," said Mungo. "Have some coffee."

"Don't you tell me when to sit down," Blake said.

Mungo and Meredith's eyes met across the desk in silent agreement.

Ignoring Blake's pacing Meredith went on, "While her ex-colleague has been brooding for the past three years, hungry for revenge, and has yet to find full time employment, Christine Meyford has reinvented herself as Christine Hayes, embezzler turned blackmailer." She picked up her coffee cup and sat back, observing the two men. Blake returned to his seat.

"I'm amazed that you managed to find all that out so quickly," Mungo said.

"We are very good at what we do, Mungo. May I call you that? It's an unusual name. Not too many Mungo's around." She gave him a penetrating look. "And please call me Meredith. As I was saying, we are very capable. When we take on a project, and a client, we research *everything*." She let the emphasis hang between them for a moment. "Sometimes we find out rather more than the client bargained for."

"Well, this is rather more than I expected, I must admit." Mungo's eyes shifted from her to Blake and back to her again. He felt the pulse pumping in his neck. What was she insinuating, he wondered, or perhaps he was reading more into her comment than she intended? Seeking some tangible diversion, he reached for his coffee cup and took a loud sip. He swallowed then cleared his throat. "So how do you suggest we take this forward?" he asked, keeping the conversation focused on Blake's problem.

◆◆◆

Sven hung back a little and watched the man he assumed was Nancy's husband enter the office building with the man he was sure was Joudry.

He had returned to the marina off and on throughout the weekend to observe the activities on *The Ice Queen* and concluded that it remained occupied. Without somewhere to situate himself unseen, he had been unable to linger there so had walked past quickly from time to time.

From late morning on Monday he had hung about outside the marina hoping to catch sight of Joudry as he headed for his two o'clock appointment. Shortly after one o'clock an Uber had pulled in and stopped outside of the harbor master's office. Thinking quickly, Sven had flagged down a passing taxi and climbed in, telling the driver to wait. As he had anticipated, a few minutes later the Uber drove out with two men seated in the back.

"Follow that car," he had said to the driver, suppressing a smile as he uttered the clichéd line he'd heard in so many movies. They pulled into the traffic and made their way uptown, arriving at a tall office block near the intersection of University Avenue and Dundas Street.

He paid the driver and got out of the car. After a few moments he followed Joudry and Beringer into the lobby and watched them approach the elevators which served floors twenty to thirty-two. A woman and a bike courier entered an elevator with them when the doors opened. He studied the lights above the closed doors as the elevator passed through the floors. He noted the elevator stopped on floors twenty-three, twenty-nine and thirty-one. He returned to the main lobby area to check the directory of businesses occupying the building.

The twenty-third floor was home to a company called Van Buuren & Co and a well-known law firm, Crofts and Nighey. The twenty-ninth floor appeared to be a selection of medical suites with cardiologists, oncologists, psychiatrists and a few other ists. Floor thirty-one housed a firm of architects.

They are unlikely to have business with architects, he thought, and he couldn't imagine a scenario in which the two of them would be attending a doctor's appointment together, so they were either seeing the lawyers or the Van Buuren crowd.

He left the building and looked up and down the street, quickly spotting a diner serving all day breakfasts a few doors up on the opposite side of the road. He took a window seat which allowed him to keep an eye on the entrance to the office tower and ordered a coffee.

"Are you sure I can't bring you anything else?" the waitress asked as she poured the coffee. "Free refills," she added hopefully as she left the table.

"No thanks, I'm good," said Sven. He had his phone out and was entering 'Van Buuren and Co' into his search engine. He added cream to his coffee and absently stirred the cup as he read. "Private investigators, forensic accounting, internet security, remote surveillance..." This was getting more intriguing by the minute. He checked his watch; two twenty. He supposed he could safely assume they would be in there for at least an hour. He blew on his coffee and squinted across the building he had just left. His eyes travelled up the building and he mentally counted twenty-three floors. Were they seeing the law firm or the investigators? And why?

◆◆◆

Elizabeth sat at her kitchen table, a mug of tea in front of her, staring out of the window into the garden beyond. The house was quiet but for the sound of her fingernails absently drumming a rhythm on the wood. After a few minutes she got up and fetched her phone from her purse on the counter. Sitting down again, she dialed her sister.

"Hello, Rebecca, it's me, Elizabeth."

She heard her sister sigh, "Yes. I know it's you. We do have call display in the country, you know."

"How are you? How have you been?"

"Oh, you know, much the same. What did you call it last time? Domestic drudgery, I think."

"Look, I'm sorry about that. I really am. I don't know what came over me."

"Nothing came over you, you just said what you thought, same as you always do, without considering the impact you have."

"I've been worrying about you. I feel bad. I really am sorry. That's partly why I called." There was a long pause. "Rebecca, hello, are you there?"

"I'm still here." Rebecca's voice was heavy with resignation. "That's the problem; I'm still here. What was the other reason you called?"

"Do you remember the last time we spoke I told you about that music I found?"

"Yeah, in the suitcase. What about it?"

"I still haven't found out who it belongs to. But, the thing is, it turns out the music is really very good. It's amazing. I showed it to someone at the OSO and they want to perform it. They want to include it in their spring repertoire."

"What, but how can they do that? You don't know whose it is or who wrote it?"

"Well, that's just it. I need some advice. I need to talk it over with someone. I thought maybe you'd..." Elizabeth trailed off.

There was another long pause. Eventually Rebecca said, "You're asking me for advice? That's got to be a first. What advice could I give you, I'm just Ian's wife, remember."

"Oh, come on!" said Elizabeth. "Give it a break. Of course, I want your advice; you're my sister. You are the only person I have."

"Aah that's why. You have no choice. I'm the only person you can turn to."

"Rebecca, stop it! I respect your opinions. Your problem is that you don't respect yourself. You keep putting yourself down. You are worth so much more than you give yourself credit for. And you have let Ian undermine you for too long. When does he ever say or do anything which makes you feel valued or appreciated? When does he ever show respect for your views?" She stopped suddenly, realizing that she had said too much, again.

"Oh, God! I am so sorry. I don't know why I say these things. I really didn't want to do this again. I wanted to say sorry. I shouldn't have called. I'll talk to you another time."

She was about to disconnect the call when she heard Rebecca's voice, "Elizabeth, wait! Elizabeth. You're right." Elizabeth heard Rebecca's voice dissolve and become thin and small.

Now I've made her cry. "Are you alright? Can I do anything? I'm sorry…"

"Stop saying you're sorry. You're right. Things are not good here. It's Ian and the store and being stuck out here. This is not what I wanted. But he won't even discuss things or consider other options. I'm just so tired."

Elizabeth heard her sister sob. "Rebecca, why don't you come to me for a few days? You need a break. We can talk things through. I'll take a few days leave. I need a break too. And I really do need your advice about this OSO thing. I'm scared. I need to find out whose music this is, but I don't know how to do it and I'm not sure if handing the music over to the OSO is the right thing… Please come, we could have some fun, see a show, go to dinner, maybe some shopping?" Elizabeth held her breath, suddenly filled with excitement at the prospect of a few days with her sister. Rebecca's sniffing was the only response.

"Becky, come on, what do you say? Ian will be fine for a few days on his own. In fact, it would probably do him good to see how much you do for the family."

"But, the boys…," said Rebecca.

"The boys will be fine. They'll be at school most of the time anyway and Ian will just have to give the staff a few more shifts at the store while you're away. It won't kill him."

She heard Rebecca draw a deep breath, "Okay, okay, I'll come. I'll have to sort out a few things tomorrow first and then leave after that. I should be there by dinner time. I'll let you know which train I am on."

Chapter Twenty-Three

"So, what do you think?" Blake was hunched into his charcoal overcoat, his hands deep in his pockets. He and Mungo walked quickly along the street. An arctic wind funneled between the glass and granite skyscrapers encouraged them toward the stairs in the sidewalk which would take them down into the subterranean network below the city.

Before Mungo could respond, three youths pushed their way up the stairs between him and Blake, almost knocking his backpack from his shoulder as they laughed and jostled, spattering muddy water from the puddles.

"Infernal kids!" said Mungo, throwing a glance over his shoulder in the wake of the youths. "Sorry, I didn't mean you," said Mungo as he almost collided with a tanned blonde man hunched into his collar who was coming down the stairs close behind him.

"I know," said the man, "Thankfully, I'm no longer a youth." He side-stepped Mungo and continued down the stairs, head down.

"We need to talk about this." said Blake. "Let's find somewhere quiet while we decide what to do." They headed away from the subway and into the underground maze of marble and glass until they found a coffee shop.

Mungo watched Blake make his way toward the small table, a cup of coffee in each hand. "I'll do it," he said as Blake set the cups down and pulled out a chair.

"I've already paid for them."

"No, I mean I'll meet with Christine. I'll tell her to back off."

Blake tore a strip off the brown sugar sachet and shook it into his cup. Stirring it slowly, he said, "She doesn't know you. Why do you want to do it? It's my issue."

"That's the whole point. She doesn't know me. It will throw her off balance a bit, maybe even intimidate her. I'll tell her I'm your alter-ego." He gave Blake a wry smile.

Blake scanned the coffee shop. It was populated with business people either engrossed in conversation or communing with their mobile devices. "Isn't that the guy who bumped into you on the stairs?" he asked nodding toward a tanned blonde guy who was seated not far from them, his jacket slung over the chair next to him.

"I don't know; I didn't really see his face. My eyes were more at crotch height." They shared a laugh.

"Oh man," said Blake sighing and running his fingers through his hair. "I've got to get back to work. I haven't been there for days. They'll be wondering what's going on."

"Well, you can't just walk in now, without an explanation," Mungo said, "and what if Christine accosts you? What will you say?"

"What will you say if you meet with her? How do you know she'll back off?"

"I'll follow Meredith's advice. I'll tell her that I've hired a private investigator who has found out enough about her to put her in jail for fraud. I'll tell her that if she tries to contact you, or if any information about your relationships leaks out, she will have the police knocking on her door."

"You think she'll go for it?" asked Blake.

"We can only try. What's the alternative? Do you want to pay her off? You certainly can't bump her off."

"That's crazy."

"Exactly, so we have to try this."

♦♦♦

Sven checked his watch and was aghast at the time. Almost midnight. He suppressed a yawn. He found to his surprise that he was enjoying painting

Nancy. Even though he wasn't sure that he was getting an accurate likeness, he felt that he was capturing something of her attitude and aura. Oh well, he smiled to himself, if he couldn't sell the story of Mungo Joudry, he could try and sell his paintings; it would be about as lucrative a career. He had called Nancy earlier in the evening on the pretext of wanting to work on the painting, but really hoping to glean more from her about what was going on with Blake and if she knew he was with Joudry. He had found her quiet and preoccupied and eventually he stopped trying to get her to talk and just became more absorbed in the painting.

Nancy stretched. "You've stopped. Can I see it?"

"No, no. It's not finished yet." He tried to quiet the panic in his voice, along with the twinge of conscience about how he was misleading her. To augment his authenticity, he picked up a paintbrush and touched up her jaw line with a mixture of yellow ochre, raw sienna and the tiniest dab of Payne's gray. He loved Payne's gray, he was discovering that, unlike black, it could darken a color without overwhelming it.

He looked across at Nancy reclining on the sofa, her eyes closed now. She really was beautiful. He felt a mixture of gratitude and guilt that she was prepared to share her body with him in this way. This close observation of every line and curve, every beauty spot and blemish, every wrinkle and furrow. This was real intimacy and he knew that it took huge courage for models to expose themselves to such close scrutiny for hours. Not many people were up to it. She was special.

"I can feel your eyes," she said, her eyes still closed.

"I can feel your body," he said from the other side of the room.

She sat up and picked up her robe, stood and slipped into it. Tying it around her waist, she said to him "Stay with me tonight."

She walked past him out of the room. He paused a moment, undecided. Then he wiped off the brushes and placed them in a jar of thinners, switched off the lamps which he had carefully positioned to light her and his canvas, and followed her upstairs.

Sven stood on the threshold of the bedroom. A single light was on at the far side of the bed, casting a soft glow across the covers that she had already turned down. He heard her moving around in the adjoining bathroom, jars clinking, water running, an electric toothbrush humming. He felt like an intruder, a voyeur, and was about to turn and leave when she emerged from the bathroom.

"I thought perhaps you wouldn't stay. I'm glad you're here. I don't want to be alone. I've put a new toothbrush out for you," she said, gesturing towards the bathroom. "There are clean towels in there too. Take your time."

He watched her remove her robe and pull a silky nightdress over her head before climbing into the bed. The light clicked off.

Sven went into the bathroom and quietly closed the door behind him. There was a soft soapy smell lingering in the moist air. It was immediately clear which side of the granite vanity was hers and which was his. He picked up a bottle of Armani aftershave lotion, felt the weight of the clouded glass bottle in his hand. He opened it and sniffed the distinctive fragrance, a masculine scent, yet sweet enough to appeal to women. He had never met Blake, only recently observed him from a distance, but he could imagine that he was the sort of man who would wear Armani.

There were two electric toothbrushes on the vanity, next to each of the side-by-side basins. Blake must have left in a hurry, but it appeared he planned to return; he'd left many of his personal grooming things behind.

Sven looked up and caught his image in the mirror. Dark rings under his blue eyes, the creases on the outer corners carved deeply into his skin. He knew he was prevaricating. He was tired though, it would be so much easier just to sleep here and if he stayed, perhaps he could get Nancy to talk. He pulled off his clothes, roughly, before he could change his mind, and stepped into the shower.

Sven was momentarily disoriented when he woke up. It was only when he propped himself up on his elbow and surveyed the darkened room that he remembered where he was. By the time he had finished his shower Nancy was already asleep, so he had quietly crept into the bed next to her. He'd moved closer to her, curving his body against hers and enjoying her warmth and softness. He lay for a while listening to the soft rhythm of her breathing and the occasional creaks and groans of the house until he fell asleep. He must have slept very deeply because he had not been disturbed by Nancy while she slept or when she got up.

He straightened up and stretched before swinging his legs onto the floor. He was reaching for his jeans when he heard Nancy coming up the stairs. She was carrying a tray of coffee which he smelled even before she entered the room.

"No need to get up yet," she said. "Enjoy some coffee first. I hope you slept well."

"So well that I did not even hear you when you got up. Have you been up long? I hope my snoring didn't disturb you." He was suddenly conscious of his sleep rumpled face and the inclination of his hair to stick up at odd angles before he tamed it in the morning. He rubbed his face feeling the stubble on his chin and tried to smooth his hair.

Nancy placed the tray on the bedside table and sat down next to him. "You didn't snore and leave your hair, I like it." She reached out and ruffled it affectionately.

Sven caught her hand in his and kissed it. "You are a lovely woman Nancy. I don't know what's happened between you and your husband or why he's not here, but all I can say is that he is the world's biggest fool."

She withdrew her hand and poured their coffee. She had also made some buttered toast and handed him a plate. She opened the curtains and sat next to him on the bed where they ate and drank in silence for a few minutes. Sven watched the wintry sunbeams catch and highlight the dust particles in the air.

"I was thinking," said Sven, his eyes still following the dust dance, "that I could take the portrait of Blake and try and fix it, or if I can't do it I can find someone who can restore it. It won't be perfect, of course, but it would be good enough for you to hang it again."

"That's good of you Sven, thank you. I'm not sure if I want to hang it again, or if I even want Blake himself again. He may regret damaging it. I don't know. If it is repairable, I suppose you could try."

"What happened? Why did he do it? Did you have a fight?"

"No, nothing that would have precipitated that kind of act of, of... self-mutilation. It was awful to find it; to find him like that. He was drunk when I got home on Thursday night. Slumped in the study with the torn painting on the floor at his feet. I really don't know why he did it." She paused to think for a moment, "He has been acting a bit strangely recently. But then, to be honest, we don't see that much of each other. He travels a lot and works a lot. He does his thing, I do mine. That's not how things started out of course. When we were young we had a lot of fun together. We enjoyed just being together. Like all young couples, I suppose. We had shared dreams, we wanted the same things, children..." she trailed off.

"What changed? Where did things go wrong?" Sven prompted. He wondered if Nancy was watching the same dust particles trapped in their cylindrical streams of light. Streaks of light and shadow from the blinds slashed diagonally across the dressing table. He saw jars of cream, bottles of perfume and Nancy's hairbrush all painted in a series of disjoined shapes and blocks of color rendered uneven by the broken light, horizontal fragments in sharp focus, overexposed almost, in the light, and then suddenly receding ill-defined into darkness. He could offset the dark from the light portions creating a multi-dimensional, almost cubist effect. He would suspend the dust particles in layers of linseed oil applied to the bands of light, giving the painting depth and the perception of the dust being closer to the viewer...

"... felt wrong for so long that it is hard to pin point an exact moment, but if I'm honest I suppose...are you listening to me?"

"Yes, yes, of course." He turned to face her. *What was happening to him? Now he was starting to think like a painter!* "I was just watching the dust patterns. I am listening. I'm sorry, I was distracted."

"I never feel that Blake really listens to me. His mind is always miles away. Eventually I stopped talking to him, about things, the things that really mattered."

"You were telling me what happened, what went wrong."

"I haven't discussed this with anyone for years; I don't know why I'm raking it all up again now. We moved on, Blake and I. We just get on with our lives."

"It's on your mind now because you have reached a crisis point in your relationship. Or at least Blake has. Think about the portrait. Only a really unhappy person would slash a painting of themselves. It seems almost... suicidal." As soon as he uttered the words he regretted them. He knew that Blake was alive and well, but he couldn't reveal that to Nancy without revealing the fact that he had been following Blake and that he was in her bed under false pretenses. He was getting himself inextricably embroiled and, even worse, was the fact that he was becoming more and more attracted to her.

"Oh my God, Sven! I never thought of it like that. You're right. I haven't heard from him. I was so angry." She leaped from the bed and started pacing. "I left him a note telling him our relationship was over. When I got home he was gone. And quite honestly, I was relieved. I needed some time to think."

"Come and sit down." He reached his hand out toward her. "I'm sorry I said that. I don't know what I'm talking about. He was drunk, wasn't he? You said he was drunk. People do crazy things when they are drunk. He hasn't ever done anything like this before has he? I mean, shown suicidal tendencies?"

"No, no never. He's always been so driven and focused, and successful. He's at the top of his game. Why would he throw it all away? He's in the running for a senior position with the International Pharmaceutical Federation. You're right. He's probably just trying to teach me a lesson. He's trying to make me relent and call him, to beg him to come back. I'm sure he's on the boat. He likes the boat. It's his escape."

She sat down on the edge of the bed next to Sven. He put his arms around her and held her for a few moments. Her body sagged into his and he felt some of her tension release. After a while she pulled away and sat up. He moved some strands of hair from her face and tucked them behind her ear.

He poured them some more coffee and handed her a cup. "I've got some more work to do on your picture. Are you up to it today, or shall I come back another time?"

"I've got some work to do, so maybe another day?"

"Of course," he nodded, taking a sip of coffee, "What are you working on?"

"I'm meeting with the OSO's marketing consultants to discuss the publicity campaign for the music."

"Any further information on who might be behind it?" Sven asked, trying to keep his voice light.

"We've given a copy of it to the University of Toronto music department and they have their musicologists studying it at the moment. We'll get their report before the concert, but we'll keep it under wraps until the inaugural performance.

He saw her eyes light up with excitement and felt her energy. He wanted her. Now, more than anything. He suddenly understood what motivated those artists who painted the same subject repeatedly and he knew that painting her wasn't going to be enough. He needed to consume her, to absorb her, to be part of her. And after that he would be heading downtown to find out who it was that Blake and Joudry had been to see in the office tower or perhaps he would nose around the U of T music department.

"It's all part of trying to garner maximum publicity. I really hope that through this we can attract new patrons and membership. This could be a big turnaround for us," she continued.

A stream of light broke through the slatted blinds, landed on her hair and highlighted her cheek bone. He leaned forward and kissed the golden spot on her cheek. She turned her face slightly and his lips found hers. Slowly and softly his tongue outlined the shape of her perfect mouth. Her breath was soft on his face. He pulled back gently and looked deeply at her.

"Do you want me Nancy?" He leaned forward, put his hand behind her neck, gripped the soft hair in the nape of her neck. He whispered in her ear, his breath hot against her cheek "Do you want me? Do you want me more than anything you've ever wanted in your life? Tell me you want me. Tell me you feel it too." His tongue touched the soft skin behind her ear.

She brought her hands up to his chest, felt his warm hard flesh. She grabbed his head in both hands and her tongue found his. The weight of his body pushed her back onto the bed.

Chapter Twenty-Four

Mungo was accustomed to making his way around the city at night, long after most people were safely in their homes. He headed toward the docks on foot, giving himself plenty of time to find the warehouse Christine had specified when she called Blake earlier that day. She had accused Blake of deliberately avoiding her, since he had not been at work over the past few days. She wanted to meet at the office that afternoon, but Blake had refused saying that he did not want to see her there ever again. As he and Mungo had agreed, Blake told her that once they had concluded their transaction, she was to resign immediately from Founder Pharmaceuticals and that he would see to it that she was not required to serve out her notice. He did not tell her that he would not be the person meeting her late that night.

As Mungo approached the warehouse, he checked his watch. He was about twenty minutes early, just as he'd planned. Christine was probably expecting Blake to arrive in a car and so Mungo felt unobtrusive on foot. It took him a few minutes to walk past the large building and its parking lot to the south. It was his plan to give it a quick once over before going to the meeting spot on the east side of the building.

He noticed a cube van parked near the entrance of the warehouse and two other cars some distance from each other in the parking lot. Having scouted the area, and walked two blocks beyond the building, he turned, crossed the street and walked back up on the opposite side heading north. The wind was coming right off the lake and he was pleased to turn his back on it, his face shielded by the hood of his coat. When he reached the warehouse, he walked quickly along the perimeter of the parking lot and then made his way across it on the eastern side heading towards the building. He had only seen one car drive past about ten minutes earlier and it had been travelling north toward downtown, away from the docks.

He could see his breath forming little plumes of vapor in the air and the crunch of his shoes on the icy asphalt sounded uncommonly loud in his ears. He came to a stop alongside the building and looked around. Nothing. He checked his watch again. Exactly on time. He hoped punctuality was one of her virtues as it was far too cold to stand around the draughty docklands for long. He paced along the building trying to keep warm. There was a doorway further up and he walked toward it hoping it might harbor an alcove in which he could stand out of the wind. He was struck by the incongruity of its size, tiny in comparison with the walls stretching before, after and above it. However, it was flush with the wall and offered no shelter. He turned and walked back toward the corner from which he had just come. He would take another look at the parking lot in the hope of seeing Christine's car pull up.

Blake would be back at the boat, waiting anxiously for his call to confirm that Christine had been dealt with. He wished he were there too, in the warmth and comfort of the boat, with this bizarre situation behind him.

He hadn't really considered the possibility that Christine may not be deterred by the information Meredith had unearthed. But now that he stood there alone in the cold and dark, this thought seemed unavoidable. They didn't really have a plan B. Neither he nor Blake had wanted to broach the subject of what to do if this failed.

He was growing impatient now. And he was bitterly cold. He hadn't taken a taxi as it would have seemed odd getting dropped off in this part of town at this hour. He regretted it now. He stomped his feet, trying to keep the blood circulating in his toes, and blew into his gloved hands enjoying the momentary warmth on his face. He checked his watch again. He'd been waiting fifteen minutes. Something felt wrong.

He decided to turn and walk the length of the building and back down again. If she had not shown up by then he would call Blake and tell him it was a waste of time. He walked fast, trying to stay warm, feet crunching on the icy gravel, feeding his anxiety. It seemed so odd though, that she hadn't arrived. She had been so persistent, threatening Blake, and insisting on her payment. It didn't add up. Maybe she was here somewhere. Watching him. Maybe she saw that he wasn't Blake and had left. It dawned on him then that the whole plan had backfired. She had left without her money and was probably busy spilling the beans to some tacky reporter even now, as he stood in this darkened parking lot waiting for her.

He turned and started across the parking lot toward the road, no longer worried about staying out of sight. He was almost running, anxious to get out of the cold as quickly as possible, planning to flag down the first taxi he saw. As he neared one of the two parked cars he saw what appeared to be the silhouette of a person in the front seat. He slowed his pace. Perhaps this was Christine. Perhaps she had been here all along.

He walked slowly toward the car trying to see if it was her. He was breathing hard, his throat burning as he drew the cold air in. He couldn't tell from this distance, but it looked like a woman. She was wearing a hat, her head was bowed forward, her forehead almost touching the steering wheel. She must have fallen asleep waiting for him. He walked cautiously around the front of the car, staring into the windscreen. It was too dark to see properly. He came alongside the driver's door hoping he had been seen and wouldn't startle her. Still no reaction. He knocked on the window. He called out her name trying to rouse her. He was certain now that it was Christine. After a moment he opened the door and the interior light lit her up.

"Christine. I've come for Blake. I've been waiting round the side, like you said." Getting no response, he leaned down towards her. "Christine, wake up." It was then that he saw a single stream of thick dark liquid form a path from the side of her head down into her neck.

Mungo recoiled, stumbling over his own feet in his scramble to back away. He couldn't take his eyes off the scene in front of him, all the while instinctively backing away from the vehicle, its lifeless occupant lit up now by the car's interior light like a beacon in the parking lot.

Suddenly aware of his own vulnerability, he looked around. He was completely alone. Just then the mobile phone in his pocket shrieked into life and he groped for it, his gloved hands clumsy with cold and fear. He stabbed at the buttons awkwardly with thick fingers until the call connected. He raised the phone to his face, his eyes fixed on the figure in the car. "Yes," he said.

"What's going on? You said you'd call. Did she buy it?"

Thoughts whirled around his head. He was at the scene of a crime. The only person on the spot; a derelict warehouse late at night. This was not good. He could hear himself trying to explain to police that he had come to settle a score with a blackmailer on behalf of a man who had only met him a couple of days earlier. And the only other person who knew where he was, where Christine was, was on the other end of the phone. Slowly the familiar feeling of betrayal settled on him.

He walked up to the car and, with his boot, kicked the door shut.

"Everything is fine," he said. He switched off the phone, shoved it into his pocket and started to run.

◆◆◆

Blake lay back on the sofa feeling the soft comforting sway of the boat as it gently rocked with the motion of the water in the harbor. He stretched out and pushed his phone back into the pocket of his jeans. *Good. Things seemed to be going according to plan.* He started to feel some of the old Blake coming back. He was back in control. He wouldn't fall into that trap again. *Bloody bitch. She needed a lesson. Nobody screws with Blake Beringer.* His eye fell on the drinks cabinet in the corner of the cabin. There wasn't much left in there, but he might be able to rummage up a bottle of something. He straightened up to get off the sofa and then he stopped. No, he wasn't going back there. He was just getting things back on track. He would go into the office tomorrow and, now that Christine was taken care of, he'd get Simon Parnell under control. No more Mr. Nice Guy, the gloves were off. He felt a surge of power and optimism. He was still in the running for the IPF position and nothing was going to stand in his way.

His thoughts were interrupted by the sudden trill of his phone. He shoved his hand into his pocket and wrestled it out, hoping he hadn't cancelled the call in the effort. Thinking it was Mungo, he quickly hit the answer button.

"Yes."

"Blake thank God," he heard Nancy's voice. "Are you okay? I've been trying to reach you."

"I'm fine. Why wouldn't I be?" belligerent as ever.

"Well, it's just, the last time I saw you, you weren't so good. Remember? Mind you, I don't suppose you do, given the condition you were in."

"What the hell Nancy? Did you just call me to bleat at me? At this time of night? Because, if so, I can do without it."

"I've been worried about you. You haven't been home, you haven't been at work, and you haven't been answering your phone. You slashed your portrait."

"So, you leave me a note telling me it's all over between us, then you phone me to tell me you're worried about me. What gives? Make up your mind."

"Oh Blake, why do you always have to be such a shithead? You didn't used to be like this. What's happened to you?"

"Look, it's late and I'm not in the mood for psychoanalysis-by-phone. Can we do this some other time?"

"Fine. Just let me know when you are ready to talk. We've got things to sort out."

The phone went dead in his hand. He stood up and made his way to the bedroom. Tomorrow would be a long day and he'd need all his resources to square with Simon Parnell.

◆◆◆

Mungo's throat was burning, his thighs were burning, and he couldn't feel his face anymore. He was sure it was frozen into its grimace of horror, mouth wide, sucking the frigid air into his over-worked lungs. His feet were pounding the pavement, obeying some impulse of their own. He lost his traction on a patch of ice and his feet slipped out from underneath him. His arms and legs flailed about like some wild windmill, trying to regain his balance and grab onto something to break his fall. His right foot found some gravel and he steadied himself, sucking in vast lungs full of air. Suddenly he felt his stomach rise to meet his throat and he lunged forward, stuck his right hand out, leaned on the red brick wall next to him and vomited onto the sidewalk. As he watched the yellowish lumpy liquid pool itself in a hollow on the snow he had a sense of complete disconnect from the convulsions in his stomach, the numbness of his face and the bitter bile in his mouth. He was no more able to stop what was happening to him than an onlooker would be able to. Eventually the convulsions stopped, and his breathing slowed. He stood up and wiped his mouth on the back of his sleeve. He coughed and spat and stepped back. He glanced around; apart from a few parked cars, the street looked deserted. He kicked some snow over the vomit and started to walk on, his legs feeling stiff and awkward, like those of a tin soldier. A few paces on, a pair of wary eyes peered at him from beneath a mound of smelly blankets huddled in the entrance of a building.

"Bad night huh? Can you spare us some change?"

"Fuck off," said Mungo, quickening his pace.

It took him about forty-five minutes to reach the rear entrance to the library. By the time he got there his hands were so cold he could barely manipulate the key in the lock. Finally, he pushed the door open and stumbled inside. He made his way through the darkened passageways to the little kitchen used by the staff and slumped into one of the plastic chairs. He sat for a while in the darkness, allowing his body to thaw out and a measure of calm to return. Then he got up, switched on a light and made some coffee. When this was done, he poured himself a mug, found a half-eaten package of cookies in one of the cupboards and carried them to his favorite chair amidst the shelves of books.

Placing the coffee carefully on the floor next to his chair, he sat down and removed his boots. He massaged his cold feet back to life for a few minutes before sitting back with the coffee and cookies to restore his equilibrium and think.

Only Blake knew about the meeting with Christine. Had he somehow got there before Mungo and dealt with her in his own way? But why? They had a plan, they had enough leverage to get Christine off Blake's back. Unless Blake didn't think it would work. But he hadn't said he didn't trust the plan. He rubbed his hand across his forehead and gave his head an unconscious shake. He leaned forward and picked up his coffee, taking a deep slurp, feeling the warm liquid make its way down his throat. He stared straight ahead of him between the long aisles of books in the semi-dark of the library.

Fucking Blake had set him up. Had him on the spot. If anyone came looking he, Mungo, would be the guy. Once again, he would take the blame for a crime he didn't commit. Either that or be forced further into hiding. The bitterness of betrayal rose like bile in his throat. *Well, not this time Blake, not this time. This time the world would know who the real culprit was.*

He finished his coffee in one long draw, put his shoes back on and headed back to the staff kitchen where he carefully washed the mug and cleaned up behind him. Then he left the library, locking the rear door behind him. Once he was a few blocks away he removed his cell phone from his pocket, opened the back cover and levered the sim card out of the phone before dropping the card on the pavement and crushing it with his foot.

◆◆◆

Blake thrust his chin forward, rubbing his jaw line feeling for any stubble he may have missed first time round. Finding a rough patch, he ran the electric razor over the offending area one more time, all the while humming softly. He stood back and gave himself an appraising look in the mirror. He leaned forward again and gently touched the scar on his forehead. Not too bad, all things considered. He switched off the shaver and the female voice of the news reader carried through from the bedroom where he had the television on.

"... she was found early this morning in a vehicle parked outside the old Delmott and Wilson warehouse near the Toronto docks. Anyone with any information or who thinks they may have seen anything unusual in the area last night is asked to contact the Toronto police. The name of the deceased will be released once the next of kin have been informed."

Blake hurried into the bedroom, tightening the towel around his waist. He got into the room just in time to see an image of the Delmott and Wilson warehouse, with a cluster of cars and a group of police officers standing nearby, disappear off the screen. The image switched to the studio where the news anchor was saying "This is Toronto's fifteenth murder this year..."

163

"What the hell!" he said out loud. He grabbed his cell phone off the table beside the bed and dialed Mungo's number. He paced up and down the tiny room running his fingers through his hair waiting for the call to connect; receiving instead a recorded message saying, "The number you have dialed is not in service." *Shit! Now what?*

Meredith. He checked the time. Ten to eight. He could get up town and be at her office by eight-thirty. He hoped they would be open by then.

He dressed quickly in a suit and pulled on his coat as he stepped off the boat and hurried along the jetty.

"Everything okay sir?" Blake looked up and saw Errol Joynt leaning in the doorway of his office with a steaming mug of coffee in one hand and a lit cigarette in the other, the steam and smoke intermingling in front of his unshaven face.

"Yes, yes. Fine, thanks, Errol."

"You in a hurry? If not, I've got a fresh pot of coffee inside."

"Ah, no thanks. I'm on my way to a meeting. You really should give those up you know," he said, gesturing towards the cigarette and turning to walk on.

"That's what your missus says every time I see her too."

Blake paused, hesitated a moment and then continued. Something niggled. As far as he knew, Nancy hadn't been to the boat for eighteen months, even two years maybe.

"She okay then?" he heard Errol say behind him. Now he turned around to face the man.

"Ah yeah. Yeah, she's fine. What makes you ask?"

"It's just that she was worried when she came by here with that artist bloke looking for the boat." Errol slurped his coffee, eyeing Blake from over the mug.

"When was that?" said Blake trying to appear unconcerned but wondering what Errol was talking about. He made it sound like Nancy was at the boat regularly. *Artist bloke?* He'd have to remember to ask her about that. It would be good to get her on her back foot for a change.

"Don't worry, I didn't tell her nothing." He winked at Blake.

"Ah...Good. Okay. Look I've really got to get going." Blake started to move off.

"You see the news this morning?" Errol called after Blake. "There's been another murder. Not too far from here. You can't be too careful these days..."

Blake waved his arm dismissively, not wanting to get into a discussion about the murder with Errol, as he hurried out to the road his eyes scanning for a taxi. Despite the morning chill he felt the perspiration gather under his shirt.

He arrived at the offices of Van Buuren and Co. and headed straight up in the elevator alongside a cluster of smartly clad people who looked like they took themselves far too seriously. When he got there, he tried the office door. Locked. He pressed the buzzer and stood for a moment wondering if anyone was even inside given that he wasn't expected. He waited a moment and pressed it again. Should he try and call Meredith? As he pulled his cell phone out of his pocket he heard another buzz and the door clicked and swung open a few inches.

He stepped into the now familiar reception area which was devoid of occupants. He paused for a moment wondering whether he should head toward the door at the far side when it opened suddenly, and Meredith appeared.

"Can I get you some coffee, Mr. Beringer?" she said by way of greeting.

"I, ah... yes sure. Thank you."

"Wait here. I'll be right back," she said.

Blake walked across to the window and stared down on the rush hour taking place silently in the streets beneath him. Taxis vying for space between skinny bicycle couriers, more of the serious office workers walking rapidly with unseeing purpose, coats clutched close against the cold. He watched as, in her hurry on the crowded sidewalk, a woman was forced to step right over a ragged bunch of blankets underneath which a homeless person was trying to have a lie-in on top of a heating vent. From this distance, looking down on the self-important bustle of the city below him, Blake was struck with a sudden, melancholic sense of the pointlessness of it all. How tiny and anonymous they all were from his vantage point. Standing up there, looking down on the scene below him he felt for a moment as if his consciousness embraced them all, as if he was the only truly sentient one, as if he were the only one who could see the big picture. And he didn't like what he saw.

His reverie was interrupted by Meredith who stepped into the room with a tray of coffee and invited him to follow her down the hall to her office.

They sat down. She poured the coffee and handed him a cup, looking him directly in the eye, her question unspoken.

"Have you seen the news?" he said.

"Of course."

"I think it's her," he said.

"It is. We've checked."

"Shit! He didn't come back last night. I called him. He said everything was fine then he cut off. I can't reach him. What the hell do you think happened? What does he think he's doing?" Blake's voice rose and he slammed the coffee mug down on the table with a shaking hand, slopping some of it on the polished surface.

"Calm down, Mr. Beringer. I'm on top of the situation. Everything will be fine."

"Fine! What do you mean fine? This was not what we planned. What the hell happened? Who is he? I don't even know who he is."

"I'm investigating that too. There is nothing you can do now. I suggest you go back to work and resume your normal routine..."

"Normal, I don't even know what normal is anymore!"

"Please, Mr. Beringer. We are monitoring the situation closely and I'll be in touch with any new developments. For now, you just carry on as usual, that's the important thing." She stood up and smoothed down her skirt.

Blake was forced to stand too, not wanting to sit looking up to her. "You people are all the same, aren't you? You've got all the cards and you keep them close to your chest. Well, I'm the client here and I want to know what you know."

"Actually, Mr. Beringer, Mr. Jameson is the client, he engaged us, and he settled the bill this morning. The funds were deposited electronically into our account." She strode to the door and held it open for him. Blake stalked past her throwing her a black look.

Chapter Twenty-Five

S ven stood at the kitchen counter in his small apartment slurping from a mug of coffee and idly paging through the morning paper. Not much had grabbed his attention and his mind was half on how he was going to fill his day. He hadn't had much success the day before in trying to track down the right person to speak to at the University of Toronto music department. Part of the problem was that he was being necessarily vague in his enquiries, not wanting to give too much away about his theory on the whereabouts of Mungo Joudry. He was beginning to think that he should discuss it directly with Nancy, but if he did, she would probably become suspicious of his motives for befriending her. This was further complicated by the fact that he had slept with her. He shook his head, silently admonishing himself for once again confusing work and pleasure. It never ended well, and he never seemed to learn.

He turned the page, and then, with a sudden jerk almost spilling his coffee he flipped it back over. Something caught his eye and he quickly scanned the article. The police were looking for a tall slim man with thick wavy silver hair, wanted for questioning with regard to the murder of a woman, identified as Christine Hayes, found near the Toronto docks overnight. It was the description which struck him, and he walked across the open concept living room to his desk, opened a manila folder, flipped through a few photographs and picked one up. It was one he had taken a few days ago of the man he was now sure was Mungo Joudry. The image captured him from the side and slightly behind, walking away from the marina, tall, slim with unmistakably thick, silver wavy hair and a backpack slung over one shoulder.

Coincidence...or not? he wondered. His instinct as an investigative reporter taught him never to ignore a coincidence. He pulled out the desk chair and sat down, pondering and flipping through the other photos and papers in the folder. Snatches of the conversation he had eavesdropped between Blake Beringer and Joudry in the coffee shop came back to him. He was sure they had been talking about someone called Christine ...and Meredith.

He cleared some papers from his laptop and hit enter. The screen lit up. He opened the browser and typed in Van Buuren and Co. while the search engine found the entries, he sipped the dregs of his coffee and pulled a face. It was cold. He put the mug down and found the entry he wanted. From the home page he clicked on 'Our Team' and quickly scanned the list of about fifteen names. There was no Christine, but there was a Meredith, Meredith Salinger, VP Private Clients. He read the one paragraph biography. Impressive.

He picked up his phone and dialed.

"Van Buuren and Co. Good morning," he heard.

"Yes, morning. I'd like to speak to Meredith Salinger please," he said.

"I'm afraid that won't be possible. She is in a meeting right now."

He thought for a moment then said, "Does she have some time today for me to come in and see her? I just need twenty minutes or so."

"Well, she is quite busy, sir. Are you an existing client of hers or new?"

"I'm not exactly a client," he realized this might not be in his favor, "But I might become one."

"We generally need an hour for a first meeting, sir."

"Look, I might have some information which is useful to her. I only need twenty minutes."

"I see. If you come in just before noon she might be able to squeeze you in. What is your name please?"

He gave the woman his details and disconnected the call. He checked his watch. Good, he had a few hours. He needed to think about how to play this meeting.

◆◆◆

Elizabeth sat in the car with the motor running to keep the heating on. She had the car radio on but was only vaguely aware of the monotonous voice of the news reader. She was mulling over the pros and cons of handing over the music to the OSO, wondering if she was up to the publicity Nancy was hoping to gain. She was also staring at the station exit, watching for the familiar form of her sister to appear.

"...and now to local news. There has been a development in Toronto's latest murder case, the fifteenth murder this city has seen so far this year. The body of a young woman, identified as Christine Hayes, was found in her car early this morning. The car was parked at the Delmott and Wilson warehouse near the Toronto docks. A witness has reported seeing a man with thick wavy grey hair wearing a dark coat running from the area shortly after midnight and police are asking anyone with further information to come forward."

She saw Rebecca emerge from the station exit and climbed out of the car to wave to her. As her sister approached, dragging her wheeled suitcase behind her, she saw the defeated droop to her shoulders and was pleased that she'd persuaded her to visit. A few days of pampering in the city, away from the demands of her family were just what she needed. Elizabeth resolved to make sure that Rebecca had a good rest, some good food, good company and a trip to the spa while she was here.

They gave each other a quick hug and then Elizabeth opened the trunk and helped Rebecca stow her suitcase. They climbed into the car and Elizabeth switched off the radio.

"I'm so glad you've come..."

"Thank you for inviting me..." they both said at once.

"There's so much to tell you," Elizabeth said. "Would you like to eat out this evening, or should we stay in and I will cook us something?" Elizabeth asked as she put the car in gear and pulled out of the parking lot.

"Let's stay in," said Rebecca. "It will be a treat to be in your quiet, ordered home for a change. My place was chaos when I left, unfinished laundry in the machine, breakfast dishes, Samuel had left his homework on the dining room table, so I had to rush it to the school before I caught the train. Wow, the traffic in Toronto is getting worse and worse," she said looking around. "And Ian wasn't very happy about my sudden decision to come. I hope you don't mind, but I told him you were having some sort of crisis and that's why I had to come now."

"Oh well, it will only reinforce his opinion of me as a selfish woman who always gets what she wants," said Elizabeth, as she nosed the car into the stream of cars.

"Please, don't start. Things are strained enough as it is."

"I'm sorry, you're right." She reached out and squeezed her sister's knee in a conciliatory gesture. "I was hoping you'd want to stay in. I'll give you a little recital after dinner and you can tell me what you think of the music."

"You really are excited about this, aren't you?" Rebecca said taking the opportunity to scrutinize Elizabeth while she was focused on the traffic. "I've never known you to get so caught up in anything quite so much, apart from your work. It's all you seem to talk about these days. Watch out, there's a cyclist. Why do they always think they own the road, just because they're on a bike? They get so sanctimonious. Some people need cars. We couldn't manage without one where we are."

"Rebecca," Elizabeth took her eyes from the road and turned to face her sister, "wait till you hear it. It's a magnificent piece. And completely new. The OSO have been researching their archives, consulting with academics and everything, trying to track down who the composer might be. Apparently, it's creating quite a stir amongst the musical cognoscenti, and to think that it was lurking in my basement in a dusty old suitcase." A hoot from an impatient driver behind her brought her attention back to the road.

"Have you still got it, the suitcase?"

"Oh yes. It's got some clothes in it. A man's clothes. It's quite creepy really, when you think of it. I mean, how did it get there? I've asked everyone I know, anyone who has spent time in my house, that is, if they know anything about it, but nothing. No one knows a thing."

"Ooh, a real mystery," said Rebecca, "maybe I can help you solve it?" She paused, then said, "Speaking of mysteries, did you see the news this morning, about the woman who was murdered last night? I read about it on the train. Well, they haven't actually come out and said murdered, but that's the way it seems."

"Yes, I just heard it on the car radio. They're looking for a man with thick, wavy silver hair." She paused. "That's funny..."

"What is?" said Rebecca, turning to her sister.

"Oh, nothing, I'm sure it's nothing," she replied with a quick shake of her head.

◆◆◆

Alexia stood at the window of her living room observing the rain drenching everything on the street. She had a spacious apartment in Riverdale, a leafy part of the Bronx. After she and Oliver had split she had decided to make a fresh start and move out of Manhattan. She liked Riverdale, it was a good compromise between urban and suburban living. She went into the city most days but enjoyed being able to retreat from it at night. She was only one floor above ground level and liked the feeling of connection it gave her with what was going on outside. In Manhattan they had lived very high up and it had always made her feel isolated.

She was still worried about Sebastian. Even though they had spoken on the phone a few times since their lunch at Nick and Toni's, and he'd assured her he was fine, she knew she had turned things upside down for him. She knew he needed time to sort it all out and she wanted to help him. But right now, he didn't want to see her.

He was mostly angry with her for having waited so long to tell him the truth. The fact was he and Oliver had never really got on well. As far as she knew Oliver believed that Sebastian was his son, but sometimes she wondered if he suspected the truth. Perhaps that was what lay at the bottom of his strained relationship with Sebastian. She'd never told either of them the truth, until now. There'd been no point. Mungo had disappeared, some thought he'd died. There was no point in raking up the past and making things more complicated than they already were. She'd tried to explain this to Sebastian but that afternoon in the café he wasn't taking it all in. It was too much to absorb too quickly. She could see that.

As Sebastian had grown and his musical talent had flourished, so had Oliver's jealousy of his son increased. He was as jealous of Sebastian's talent as he had been of Mungo's. As Sebastian matured he resembled Mungo more and more. After the scandal, she'd removed all the photographs of Mungo so there was no visible reminder of him in their lives. Except for Sebastian, of course. But then, she was sure she was the only one who saw Mungo every time she looked at her son. If Oliver had wondered about Sebastian's paternity, he had never admitted it, even in their worst rows, and she was grateful to Oliver for this small act of mercy.

Since her meeting with Mungo in Toronto, she had been consumed with guilt about the unwitting role she'd played in the destruction of his career and in keeping his son from him. She'd known she was pregnant before she and Oliver married, and she knew it was Mungo's child. But she'd said nothing. She was in love with Mungo, but she had married Oliver. She had built her life on a lie and in so doing she had destroyed Mungo's.

She didn't realize the full enormity of this deception until her meeting with Mungo on the boat. At first, she had not wanted to believe him, she had fought the truth all the way back to New York and in the weeks since. But the more she examined it, the clearer it became to her that he was telling the truth. And now her need for the truth was insatiable. It was like she had finally come up for air after being submerged for a very long time. She'd told Sebastian the truth and now she owed it to Oliver and Mungo too.

She picked up the phone and dialed Mungo's cell phone number. There was a pause, then a click on the line, then a voice said: "The number you have dialed is not in service. Please try again later." She had tried his number repeatedly over the past day, but every time she got the same message.

Apart from this number, she had no idea how to reach him. She watched the raindrops hit the window and then slide down the glass, quickly replaced by new ones. The branches of the tree outside with its tender new green shoots swooped and swayed in the wind. She saw a woman walking on the sidewalk below her, fighting the wind for possession of her umbrella.

Then she picked up the phone again and dialed. She waited for the call to connect and said, "Yes please, I hope you can. I'd like to book a flight to Toronto."

◆◆◆

Elizabeth placed the last dish on the draining rack and dried her hands on a dishcloth. Rebecca was seated in the wingback chair near the window, Caprice on her lap, the soft glow from the light above catching the highlights in her hair. Smooth strains from Chris Botti's trumpet swirled around them from the sound system in the living room.

Rebecca looked up. "It's so lovely here Elizabeth. I can't tell you how much I need this little break."

"Yes, it is peaceful. But I do get lonely in this big house by myself. It's good to have your company. I need it too. Come, it's time for your private recital."

In the living room Elizabeth switched the stereo off and seated herself on the piano stool, shuffling the score while Rebecca stretched out on the sofa, placing her wine glass on the coffee table.

"Now, this is a bit different, I have to tell you. It is what I think they call neo-classical, so some of it might sound a bit discordant, but if you stay with it you will find that it pushes your boundaries in the most exciting way. It seems to fragment in places, but then it all comes together magnificently, in a new way to create something completely different out of the same components in the music. You have to trust the music, well, trust the composer I suppose, that he will get you there, you have to... you just have to listen. I can't wait to hear it played by a full orchestra..."

"Elizabeth, just play the damn thing."

Elizabeth breathed in deeply, closed her eyes for a second, opened them and began. The piece started suddenly, jarringly and very loudly. It was like a call to action which could not be ignored, sudden panic, adrenalin pumping and frenetic activity. Rebecca watched her sister's face as she beat the notes out, fingers flying across the keyboard. She could feel Elizabeth's energy pulsing through the music right into her own blood stream, the music connecting them physically, she felt her pulse quicken and her breathing speed up. She straightened up on the sofa, her foot tapping the rhythm, her eyes fixed on Elizabeth, she watched her chest rising and falling with the music and a small bead of perspiration form itself on the side of her forehead.

Just as suddenly as it had started, the pace slowed, and the tone of the music changed, becoming fluid, sounds merging into one another seamlessly.

The vivid energy drained itself slowly from her; she sank back and was filled with languor, a pleasant weakness seeping into her muscles.

The music continued its varied pace, never becoming cyclical, never failing to surprise, delight and at times terrify in its intensity.

Eventually Elizabeth was still, her hands resting on the keyboard. She breathed rhythmically for a few beats and then looked up. Her face was flushed, her eyes bright.

"That was more than music, Elizabeth. That was the closest I have come to having an orgasm without being touched."

"I'm so glad you understand."

"We must find him."

◆◆◆

"I'm sorry about the dust down here," Elizabeth said, waving her hand. "You wouldn't think I'd cleaned it recently." They were in the basement, each with a cup of coffee which they'd brought from the breakfast table. "This is exactly where I found it. Here just behind these boxes."

Rebecca scanned the small storage room, one hand on her chin the other holding the coffee mug. "You know, I don't think I've ever been in here. I mean it's not all that accessible is it?"

"You can get in to the basement from the stairs which go up to the garage. But I don't use that entrance. It's dark and dusty and full of cobwebs."

Rebecca leaned forward and lifted the flap on a cardboard box. "Oh my God, Elizabeth. I don't believe it. You've still got this thing?" She pulled out a tan colored threadbare teddy bear, holding it between a thumb and forefinger, an arm's length from her body. Its musty smell adding another dimension to the dank odor in the small room. "I threw mine away when I left for university."

"Stop poking in my things! Let me show you the suitcase, it's upstairs."

The suitcase lay on Elizabeth's desk. "It is quite old and battered. Could have been there a long time. Can I open it?"

Elizabeth nodded and watched as Rebecca unfastened the clasps. "I put everything, except the score, back in the suitcase just as it was when I found it." She watched her sister's face closely to see if there were any signs of recognition as she unfolded the navy-blue sweater, the pants, shirts and finally the corduroy jacket, laying them down on the desk.

Rebecca's hand thoughtfully stroked the ridged corduroy of the jacket. Then she picked it up and started going through the pockets.

"I've done it. There's nothing." Elizabeth said.

Rebecca looked at her and then down at the jacket again, examining the inside for the label. Harry Rosen.

"It doesn't tell us much, except that he bought it in Canada," Elizabeth said.

"They might be able to tell us when this jacket was made, when it was sold, that sort of thing." Rebecca said.

"Yes, but how can they connect the jacket to a specific customer?"

"You're absolutely sure no-one knows anything about this suitcase? Who have you actually spoken to about it?"

"Only you, Ian and my neighbor, Mrs. Gibson have ever had access to the house while I'm not here. I mean, I've spoken to the OSO people, of course, and one of my partners at the law firm about this, but they've never been here."

"What did Mrs. Gibson say?"

"She doesn't know anything about it either. But, she did say something a bit strange, which I dismissed because she is so old, and she gets confused. She really shouldn't be living on her own in that house."

"What did she say?"

"It's funny, but the way she described him was rather similar to that description I heard on the radio yesterday about the man they arc looking for in connection with that murder near the docks."

"Elizabeth what are you talking about?"

"She said something about a man with thick wavy silver hair, but she was confused, she thought she was seeing her father."

"Okay, wait a minute. Just tell me again exactly what Mrs. Gibson said."

"Honestly Rebecca, when you meet her you will see what I mean. She doesn't know what she is talking about half the time."

"But what did she say?"

"She said something about having seen my brother here. Mrs. Gibson does know I only have you, so you see, she is getting very fuzzy in the head. Then when I questioned her further she said he had thick wavy silver hair like her father and went on about how she liked to run her hands through her father's hair when she was a child. I think she was just having a flashback or something. She's probably getting Alzheimer's. Like I said, she's too old to be living alone."

"And what were you saying about the man and the murder?"

"Honestly, it's nothing. It was just that the way they described his hair on the news and the way Mrs. Gibson described her father's hair was so similar."

"I'm going around to talk to her. I might be able to get some more sense out of her," said Rebecca.

Chapter Twenty-Six

Alexia handed her suitcase to the taxi driver and climbed into the car. "The Pantages Hotel, Victoria Street," she said as they climbed in. Considering the short flying time from New York to Toronto, it seemed to take ages to travel between the two cities. She had to allow time to and from each airport, and endless hours to get through immigration and security. Now that she had finally arrived, she hoped that it would not be a waste of time and that she would be able to track Mungo down. Many people, including private detectives, had tried to find him years ago and he had eluded them, so she was not especially confident. She suspected that if he wished to remain hidden, he knew just how to do it.

She watched the passing traffic and industrial buildings near the airport pass in a blur as the taxi navigated its way through the Toronto highways. Parts of it were quite ugly she thought. The Canadian city planners did nothing to disguise the urban landscape bordering their highways. She watched the taxi driver fiddle with the knob on the radio and he said over his shoulder, "Do you mind if I put on the radio? What would you like?"

"Yes, go ahead," she said. "You choose, I really don't mind."

Static filled the air until he settled on a radio station playing some music. The traffic was stalled now on the highway. She looked at the car next to them and saw the driver was a young woman talking on a cell phone. In the back seat was a toddler happily chomping on a pacifier and wiping her sticky fingers on the car window. Alexia waved to the child who waved back and smiled broadly, allowing the pacifier to fall from her mouth. Alexia pulled a funny face and saw the child laugh; now waving both hands.

The taxi pulled forward and left the car with the laughing child some meters behind. Alexia became aware of a news broadcast on the radio.

"...the body of thirty-six-year-old Christine Hayes, of Toronto, formerly from Vancouver and an employee of Founder Pharmaceuticals. Police confirm that she died of a bullet wound to the head and are asking for assistance in identifying a man who was seen in the vicinity at approximately one AM. He is described as approximately six foot one, and lean, with very thick wavy silver-grey hair. In other local news, the Premier of Ontario announced today..."

"This is a shame, a terrible shame," the taxi driver said. "I have come to Toronto from Islamabad to get away from terrible things, but I find they take place here also. Who would do this, to this woman? No place is safe anymore." He said shaking his head.

"You're right," Alexia said, "murders take place everywhere, some places more than others. But to my knowledge, Toronto has never been the victim of a suicide bombing, so you are probably still better off here."

"Yes, but I have to drive a taxi! Do you know that in Pakistan I was a mathematics teacher? But they won't employ me here. They say my qualifications are not good enough to teach their children mathematics!"

Alexia made a mental note to give him an extra tip and picked up her cell phone. She didn't want to get drawn into a conversation about Canada's immigration policies. She dialed Mungo's number again but got the same recorded message. He'd given her this number and now he couldn't be reached? First, he followed her and left her a note, then he all but abducted her on his boat, and he'd been so insistent that she listen to him, and now he'd disconnected his phone.

◆◆◆

Nancy put down the phone and breathed a sigh of relief which quickly transformed into a feeling of triumph. She had done it, she had persuaded Elizabeth Carey to sign the agreement and hand the music over.

She had sensed that Elizabeth was wavering but had managed to reassure her that the publicity would die down within a few weeks. But not before

Nancy had achieved her objectives for the OSO. This, of course, she did not say to Elizabeth. She told Elizabeth that the OSO would arrange for her to have some media training and that everything would be well scripted before they put her in front of a TV camera or microphone.

She picked up her phone again, "Brendan, can you see if Jason Matthews of Quantum Public Relations is available for a call. I have a big project for him."

Just then Alfonso strode into her office. He walked across the office to the window, looked down at the street and then, as if seeing nothing worthy of his interest, crossed the room again and sat down on the sofa, uninvited.

Nancy felt the anger rise in a red flush on her neck. *How dare he?*

Before she could speak Brendan stuck his neck around the door and said, "I see you are...uh...busy. So, I'll just hold on that call to Jason Matthews?"

"Why don't you call him and see if he is available for a meeting this week," said Nancy.

"And you can bring us some coffee," said Alfonso to Brendan's retreating back.

Nancy felt that she should regain some control in her office.

"Actually, Alfonso. I don't really have time for coffee now; I was in the middle of something."

"I know what you were in the middle of," he said. "So, she has agreed. Good. When do I get the score?"

What, how could he know so soon? She had only just put the phone down from her call with Elizabeth.

"I assume that's why you are in such a hurry to speak to Quantum? To plan out the media strategy? I want *Entertainment Tonight, Arts and Minds, The Concert Hall*, CBC, all the national papers. I will handle the interviews myself. I am the one who is going to bring this music to life. You might have been the one who found it, but without me, it will be nothing." He stood up and paced the room again.

A sweet musky scent reached her nose, it radiated off him as pungently as his energy. He looked at her sharply, she saw the determination concentrated in his dark eyes. Nancy felt a liquid warmth spread through her, from her lower abdomen to her limbs, leaving her feeling pliable, open to opportunity.

Not unlike the way Sven had made her feel the other night. Get a grip, she thought, this is Alfonso, public enemy number one, not Sven!

He ran his fingers through his black curls, unconsciously preparing for the cameras. My God, the arrogance of the man, but she had to admit, he certainly had presence. The media would love him.

Brendan came into the office with the coffee which he placed on the table in front of the sofa. She got up from her desk and approached the table.

"Well, as the spring season starts in a couple of weeks, I suppose the sooner we start preparing the better. Thank you, Brendan, that will be all for now," she said as she sat. Since he was here now she might as well use the time to get him on side.

She poured the coffee from the French press and the aroma mingled very well, she thought, with Alfonso's own scent.

"If we get this right we will have the public salivating for the OSO, we will sell out all the tickets for the season as soon as they go on sale and I want to launch a campaign to attract new patrons. Also, have you thought about the soloists? It will be difficult to get the big names at such short notice, so I was thinking we should open up the spots to the music schools. We can promote this too. Another opportunity to showcase how much the OSO is doing to nurture talent…"

Alfonso studied her silently, appraisingly, sipping his coffee.

"There is so much sex appeal in this music, Alfonso, and the mystery surrounding the composer... it has all the perfect ingredients. The public will love it. And they will love you; you are exactly the right man to conduct this piece. This is the breakthrough we have been waiting for."

"Yes, this is just the breakthrough I have been waiting for." He reached forward and put his cup down, his face only inches from hers. "And I think, after all, you and I will make a very good team Nancy."

She picked up her notepad and they started to plan.

♦♦♦

Mungo bought a copy of *The Toronto Star* on his way into the subway station. He was headed for Elizabeth's house. He couldn't go back to the boat because Blake was staying there. Also, he couldn't stomach the risk of running into him at his house. He had allowed things to get way too close with Blake. Even though Blake didn't know how he had become involved, he had too many reasons to question everything now.

He found a seat between the morning commuters and felt the train lurch into motion as he opened the newspaper. Quickly scanning the first few pages, he found the crime report about Christine on page four along with an old headshot of her and a photo of the Delmott and Wilson building. As he expected, there wasn't much in the report, most of it covering the usual police reassurance that the investigation was on-going and that several initiatives were underway to address the increase in violent crime in the city. The newspaper trembled in his hands as he read the description of himself: tall, lean, early to mid-forties, with thick wavy silver-grey hair, vomiting on the sidewalk.

Mungo was about to snap the newspaper shut when he was interrupted by a finger pointing at the article. "This one seems different from the usual drug-related violence."

He looked at the man sitting next to him who had evidently been reading over his shoulder. He took Mungo's glance as encouragement to continue. "It seems more deliberate somehow. I mean, what young woman hangs around a desolated warehouse at the docks late at night? Most of these drug crimes happen outside night clubs, in crowds, or round the Jane and Finch area..." he tapered off. Mungo suppressed the urge to brush his hair back from his face, to try and tuck it out of sight. As if reading his mind, the man's glance travelled upward and settled on his hair.

The train jolted to a stop. Mungo clumsily folded the newspaper and got to his feet. "This is my stop." He made his way off the train as fast as he could, not hazarding a backward glance, and hurried along the platform, breathing hard. *Calm down, this is crazy. No one has reason to suspect me other than my suspicious behavior. I have to act normal, just like any other person on the street. And get my hair cut. Short.*

Up on the street he found a convenience store selling cheap tourist knickknacks alongside soft drinks and chocolate bars. He bought an over-priced Maple Leafs baseball cap and chewed off the plastic tie which attached the price tag. He shoved the cap on his head, cramming in as much hair as he could and pulled the brim low on his forehead. All he needed to do now was pull his pants down below his crotch and he could join the ranks of the disaffected youth, he thought.

As he approached Elizabeth's house he saw her car in the driveway and quickly stepped into the shadow of a hedge at the edge of the driveway. Damn! What was she doing at home this time on a week day? Her routine normally ran like clockwork. He was just wondering what his next move should be when he saw her front door open and her sister Rebecca appeared.

He watched Rebecca cross Elizabeth's garden and then walk up the flagstone pathway towards Mrs. Gibson's front door. She stooped down to pull a weed, an aggressive dandelion which was getting a head start on spring. He heard her curse under her breath as the tough plant snapped off in her hand, the root trapped somewhere beneath the flagstones. She straightened and threw the plant aside.

Mungo retreated further into the hedge. After a moment he peered around and caught a movement in the window of Mrs. Gibson's front room. Mrs. Gibson, no doubt, was still keeping an eye out. What a damn nuisance she had become.

The door opened.

"Hello, Mrs. Gibson, you probably don't remember me, but I'm Elizabeth's sister. Elizabeth Carey from next door? I'm Rebecca." Mungo heard her say.

"Yes, yes, my dear, I do. I saw you arrive yesterday, with Elizabeth."

"I wonder if I could talk to you for a few minutes. It's rather important. It's about the man you say you have seen at Elizabeth's house. Are you busy?" Mungo felt the blood pulsing behind his ears and strained to hear what they were saying.

"Me? No. What would an old woman like me be busy with? Please come in, I'll put the kettle on for some tea." She turned and shuffled into the house. Why was Rebecca asking about him? How did Elizabeth find out? His desire to know fought with his urge to get out of there before he was discovered. Making a quick decision, he turned and walked away as fast as he could.

◆◆◆

Rebecca noticed the dirty carpet beneath her feet and decided to keep her shoes on. It had been a few years since she had spoken to Mrs. Gibson and she was struck by how much the woman had aged. Elizabeth was right; she was too old for this place. The air was stale and there was an accumulation of things on every surface, all covered in dust.

"Sit down please," Mrs. Gibson gestured to one of the chairs around the kitchen table. "I'll just put the water on to boil. Please excuse the mess. I don't get visitors anymore. Just my children occasionally, but they don't like coming around. And it's not nice having them here anymore, all they do is try and persuade me to move."

"I'm sure they just want what's best for you."

"Yes, that's what they say, but how do they know what's best for me?" Her hands rattled around with the tea pot and cups. "Is Earl Grey alright?"

"That's just fine." Rebecca stood up, "Here let me help you..."

"Just you sit down," the old woman said, "I can do it. If I can't make a cup of tea, then what am I good for?"

"I'm sorry, I didn't mean to imply..."

"That's okay dear. Now tell me, what did you want to speak to me about?"

"Do you remember when Elizabeth came around to see you the other day; it was a few weeks ago, I think?"

"Yes, yes, I do. She wanted her key."

"Do you remember she asked you about a suitcase she found in her basement?"

"Yes, I told her I didn't put it there. I hardly ever go down to my basement; I might never get up again. Why would I go in hers?" She put the teapot, now heavy with hot tea, down on the table in front of Rebecca, slopping some of it onto the stained tablecloth.

Rebecca reached for a dishcloth and soaked up some of the liquid. "I know. She doesn't think it was you, but the thing is, we don't know who it belongs to and we need to find out. She said that you had seen a man around her property. Is that right? Can you tell me about him?"

Mrs. Gibson's hands shook as she poured the tea. She sat down heavily in one of the chairs, her face flushed from the effort. She looked across at Rebecca, her eyes watery behind the thick glasses.

"I know she thinks I'm crazy and that I am making it up. And well, I know I'm getting forgetful and I get confused sometimes. Just the other day I left my bathtub running and... oh..." She took a tissue from her sleeve and dabbed at her nose. "I only realized when I came out of my bedroom and nearly slipped in a puddle of water on the floor. It was already trickling down the stairs."

"You must be careful. You do need some help here, you know. This is a big house to take care of. Perhaps you can get someone to come in...?"

"I managed to get into the bathroom and switched the taps off. I mopped it all up. It's fine. I didn't slip." She looked pleadingly at Rebecca. "Really, it was all fine in the end. Here, drink your tea." She pushed a cup towards Rebecca.

"What were you saying about the man at Elizabeth's house?" Rebecca prompted.

"Oh, yes. I have seen him there off and on, for a long time. He comes and goes, during the day mostly. I don't have a lot to occupy me you know, my dear. And my favorite chair is the big soft one in the front room, by the window. The light is good there and if I'm not too tired I like to read there. I see people coming and going in the street. There's a nice lady from up the road who pushes her baby in the stroller most days, if it's not too cold. I wave to her through the window..."

"And this man, the one who goes to Elizabeth's house, what does he look like?"

"He reminds me of my father. He's tall and slim, but it's the hair. Not many men have hair like that. He has a young face, but his hair is silvery and very thick. It has a nice wave to it. I used to run my hands through my father's hair when I was a little girl, I loved it. It was strong, but silky. I think that's what appeals to me, the combination of strength and softness. Elizabeth is lucky to have him."

"But wait a minute, Mrs. Gibson. Elizabeth doesn't have a man. She is single." A mild feeling of panic emerged in Rebecca. "That's why I'm here. Do you know who he is? When last did you see him?"

"You don't believe me either. You also think I'm too old and confused," her eyes teared up.

"No, no, that's not what I meant to say. If you say you have seen someone there, then I believe you. It's just that this person is not Elizabeth's. She doesn't know anyone like that. She lives by herself. We really need you to help us find out who he is."

"He's a nice man, I'm sure he is. But I'll help you however I can."

Chapter Twenty-Seven

Sven shook Meredith's hand and sat down opposite her. "Sven Svenson," he introduced himself. "Thank you for fitting me in at short notice today."

"I just have a few minutes before I leave for a lunch appointment," she gave him a tight smile. "I understand that you have some information for me."

"I am looking for somebody and I have reason to believe that you may have met with him recently."

"And how does this constitute information which may be helpful to me?" Meredith asked.

"If he is who I think he is, he has been missing for many years and has been the subject of a scandal, possibly even a crime."

"How would you know who I have been meeting with? I'm sure you understand that the nature of our business is necessarily highly confidential."

"You are a private investigator and I am an investigative reporter. My methods and sources are just as confidential as yours are. I'm sure you don't expect me to disclose how I know what I know."

"Well, in that case, I don't expect we have much to discuss," Meredith stood up.

"Wait, just hear me out. I really think we can help each other," Sven held his hands out, palms facing her.

"That's assuming I need your help."

"How can you tell until you've heard what I have to say?"

She glanced at her watch and sat down. "You've got five minutes."

"I'm a freelancer. I try to go after the stories which other people forget about. There's less competition that way. A few years ago, I read a piece in a back issue of *The New York Times Magazine* about a composer who disappeared following an accusation of plagiarism," Sven said. He noticed the flicker of interest spark in her eyes. "He'd been a star student at Juilliard. There had been a big search for him, but no-one ever tracked him down. I didn't have much else on the go at the time, so I decided to do some digging myself." He paused, wanting to see if she was properly hooked.

She took the bait. "What did you discover?"

The fact that she didn't ask for his name confirmed for Sven that Meredith Salinger knew exactly who he was talking about.

"He had disappeared without a trace, so some people postulated that he had died. Possibly suicide, jumped off the George Washington Bridge into the Hudson River or something. He wasn't showing up on any of the US Government databases, no fingerprints, no criminal record, no banking, no UI, no tax, no driver's license, no medical claims, no death certificate, no marriage certificate, his dental records didn't match any John Doe's, no contact with relatives or friends. Nothing. Either he was dead, or he had left. I didn't buy into the suicide theory. I decided he had left but there was no record of him having left the US, so I figured he must have slipped out of the country illegally. It was a matter of figuring out where he could have gone without his passport."

She nodded.

"Canada was the obvious place to look as it shares an international border with New York State. I started in Montreal. I spent about a year there, but I didn't turn up a thing. About eight months ago I came to Toronto." He stopped suddenly. It was time to see what she could offer.

"And now you want me to find him?" she asked.

"I found him. I know he is here. I've seen him. I just don't know where he is right now, and I think he is involved in some serious shit."

"How did you find him?"

Despite his claim that he wouldn't disclose his methods, he found himself wanting to impress her. "Well, this guy was a musical genius right. Someone with that talent wouldn't be able to stay away from music. So, I followed the music. I went to symphony concerts, string quartets, jazz clubs, nosed around university music faculties, live music venues all over the city. Eventually I spotted him. I've been following him around, but he is as slippery as an eel."

"What exactly do you want from me then?"

"I followed him to your office, so I know he has been here. I want you to help me pin him down."

"Why would I do that, Mr. Svenson?"

"I don't know what his business is with you, but like I said, I think he has been involved in some serious shit and he is one strange guy. He may even be implicated in a murder. I could go to the police with what I know. In fact, I probably should, but I have spent years and a few thousand dollars on this story. I've almost got it nailed but before I can sell it, I need some proof. I need to locate this guy and I'd like to do it before the police do. I am prepared to trade information with you. It could save you time and money and if he is indeed involved in murder, it won't look good for your company when my story comes out." He sat back, crossing his right ankle over his left knee.

Meredith leaned forward and pressed the intercom button on her phone. "Jared, could you cancel my lunch appointment please. I'm going to be busy here for a while."

◆◆◆

It was getting dark by the time Alexia got to the harbor. She hoped she would remember which boat it was and that it was still moored in the same place. She hurried down the access road, past the little office with its dim light shining through the dirty window. She stepped onto the main boardwalk and started to make her way along it, the wind whipped around her, the sides of her trench coat flapping against her body. She grabbed hold of them and wrapped them around her, tying the belt to secure it. In her haste to get here she hadn't unpacked to find something warmer, but just dumped her suitcase in the hotel room and headed straight downstairs for a taxi. She walked up and down the jetties, the wind wrestling her hair free of its barrette and streaking strands of it across her face.

A few people were on their boats, packing up things for the day. Here and there she caught the aroma of food being prepared, but for the most part it was still too early in the season. If she could just remember the name of the boat? *The Ice Maiden? No, it was The Ice Queen.* It was starting to get dark and the air was noticeably colder. She couldn't walk up and down here all night. She turned to retrace her steps and was startled to find a man standing close behind her. She hadn't heard him approach.

"Oh, excuse me," she backed up a few steps. She tried to move past him but there wasn't enough room on the narrow jetty.

"Can I help you, mam?" the man said. "You look lost."

"No, I...uh. Excuse me please," she said, trying again to get past him. Realizing he wasn't going to move, she said, "I'm looking for a boat." She saw him raise a sarcastic eyebrow at her statement of the obvious and hastily added, "It's called *The Ice Queen*, I think."

"I know where it is, this way." He turned, and she followed. He lit a cigarette as they walked, her a pace or two behind him. "You can't be too careful around here after dark these days. Young woman was murdered a couple of nights ago, not far from here," he said. He turned his head, releasing the smoke to the side as he walked, and she caught sight of his craggy profile and unshaven chin. Not sure if his comment was intended to threaten or caution, Alexia said nothing, anxious to get away from him but with no way off the jetty other than to follow.

"So, you know the Beringers then?" he asked, apparently undeterred by her silence.

"What? No, I uh..." she tried to hide her confusion.

He stopped suddenly and turned to look at her. She couldn't read his face, silhouetted as he was in the light from a harbor lamppost behind him. "There she is," he said pointing at a boat diagonally across from them on a parallel jetty, *"The Ice Queen."*

Alexia watched the man walk away, reach the main access boardwalk, and enter the small office she'd passed on her way in.

She approached the boat and saw there was a light on inside the cabin. She paused on the edge of the dock and tried to tidy her hair. She smoothed her hands down her coat. She couldn't knock on the door from here. She wasn't expected so should she just step on board or call out or what? She could see the sliding door to the cabin was closed and the blinds were drawn. Seeing no other way to get his attention, she stepped on board and went across to the doors. She knocked on the thick glass, her knuckles making a dull thudding sound. She waited a few moments and then knocked again. No response.

After a few moments she pulled the door and it slid heavily, a few inches, on its tracks. She opened it just wide enough to slip inside. The cabin was empty, but she heard Corinne Bailey Rae's "Just like a star ..." coming from the sound system in the corner. He must be downstairs.

She went to the top of the stairs and peered down. She thought she heard the shower running. Halfway down the stairs she called out: "Mungo, is that you? It's Alexia. I need to talk to you, can I come in?"

The door to the bedroom cabin was ajar. She pushed it open. She heard the shower switch off. "Mungo, it's me, Alexia. I tried to call. We need to talk. I can wait upstairs if you like."

Just then a man emerged, completely naked, from the small bathroom, toweling his hair with one hand.

"What the...!" the man said, pausing only for a moment before continuing to dry his hair.

"Oh my gosh, I'm so sorry!" She backed away. "I thought you were someone else."

"Well, this is a surprise, but rather a pleasant one." He smiled. "Please, don't leave on my account." He wrapped the towel around his waist and tucked it in. "Who were you expecting?"

"I'm looking for Mungo, Mungo Joudry."

She saw his eyes light up, like a flash of electricity had shot through them before they became guarded.

"Joudry, you say, Mungo Joudry. As it happens, I'm looking for him too. After you, my dear," he said as he gently propelled her along the narrow passage to the stairs.

"I, uh, I don't mind waiting upstairs while you dress."

"I pride myself on never keeping a lady waiting. Wouldn't dream of it. Up you go," he said, giving her behind a nudge.

When they got upstairs he went to the small galley, gesturing her to the sofa. "Please have a seat." She watched while he deftly opened a bottle of white wine and poured two glasses. He came across and held a glass out to her. She could see small water droplets from the shower nestling in the hair on his legs. His skin smelled freshly of soap. She looked up. "Go on," he said, "I'm not going to jump you, I promise. You are the one who walked in on me remember."

She took the glass and he sat down opposite her.

"How do you know Mungo?" he asked.

"We go back a long way. I hadn't actually seen him for almost twenty years, until a few weeks ago when I met him, here, on the boat."

"Is that so," said Blake. He sipped the wine and studied her, offering nothing in return.

"How do you know him?"

"I don't, as it happens, but apparently he knows me. When was it, exactly, that you met him here?"

"It was about six weeks ago. I was in town for a show. He left a note at my hotel and, well, we met here and he, he took me out for the day...Do you know where I can find him?"

"Now that is very interesting," said Blake, anger lighting his eyes, "since this is my boat and he has no business being here, let alone entertaining his women friends here! I will have to have a little chat with Errol, he's the harbormaster, to find out what else has been going on in my absence."

"Look, I'm sorry," Alexia said, standing up. She removed a card from her bag and placed it next to the wine glass on the coffee table. "This has obviously been a mistake, but if you see him, I'd be very glad if you would get him to call me. It's really important that I speak to him." She opened the sliding door and stepped onto the deck.

"Well, get in line," Blake shouted behind her "I'd like to speak to Joudry too and so would the police. Apparently, he is wanted for questioning about a murder."

◆◆◆

Errol sat with his feet on his desk and a cigarette between his fingers watching the smoke idle its way to the ceiling of his little office. He saw the woman he had directed to *The Ice Queen* walking at a fast pace past his office and up toward the road. A few moments later a slim blonde man walked past too. There was something in his demeanor which piqued Errol's interest. He got up and moved to the doorway watching them. He could have sworn that the blonde guy was following the woman. I'd pay money to know what the hell is going on with the Beringers, he thought.

Chapter Twenty-Eight

ungo waited for about fifteen minutes after he saw Nancy leave the house and when he was sure the coast was clear, he went around the back, took his key out of his pocket and let himself in. Clearly his situation was becoming untenable and he was suddenly desperately tired of his itinerant lifestyle. As he let himself in, he knew these would probably be his last hours in the Beringer home. It was time to move on.

Everything was as he expected to find it. It was her OSO day, and all being well, she should be out the whole day. The only risk was that Blake would come back to the house for something, given that his schedule was unpredictable at the moment.

Mungo made himself some coffee and removed a wrapped sandwich from his back pack. Feeling as edgy as he was these days, he wasn't planning to stay in the house long. He would just have something to eat, take a shower, say his silent good-byes and figure out his next move. He considered his options as he had his breakfast.

He could go to the police and reveal what he knew about Christine and her blackmailing of Blake. But that would mean that he would expose himself and the plagiarism issue might come to the fore again. Blake would become their main suspect, and this would probably destroy his career and marriage. Nancy would have to deal with the fallout. But what if they didn't believe him and charged him with the murder of Christine instead. No, it was just too risky.

The other option was to ask Meredith Salinger to act as an intermediary and get her to tip off the police about Christine's blackmail plot, embezzlement history and change of name. If they hadn't already figured that out. Hopefully, he could stay in the background and she wouldn't reveal his involvement. He wasn't sure that he could trust her. He felt sure that, given her thoroughness, she had looked into his background too. He was comforted by the fact that, even if she had figured out who he was, she didn't know where to find him. No one did. However, the big issue was, did she think he had killed Christine? If she suspected him, then she wouldn't protect his identity.

The way he figured it, the only other option he had was to leave Toronto and start again somewhere else. Maybe somewhere warmer? He had saved most of his wages from working in the library and the odd catering job over the years and could afford to start a legitimate life somewhere inexpensive. Perhaps Mexico? He could rent a place; finally have a home of his own. He could buy a piano and compose. He could take his violin and maybe work as a musician in a restaurant serving tourists. The idea grew in appeal. Why hadn't he thought of this sooner? There was the passport problem. Living below the radar had its downside. He may have to stay in Canada.

Pushing the thought aside for the moment, he poured himself another cup of coffee and reached for Nancy's *Globe and Mail*. He paged though it, not finding anything new about the murder of Christine Hayes. He turned to the entertainment section and saw an article headlined '*OSO to Perform Anonymous Composition*'. Intrigued, he read on; 'A full-length sonata recently discovered in the basement of a Toronto home is capturing the attention of musicologists and classical music fans all over. The composer of the music is unknown, but those in the classical music fraternity who have heard it say it could be one of the best neo-classical compositions to emerge in the past twenty years.

According to research done by the OSO and the University of Toronto Department of Music, the piece has never been heard by an audience before. The composition, being dubbed *The Anonymous Sonata* will be debuted by the OSO this spring.

Followers of classical music are intrigued by the unknown origin of the music. It was found by Toronto lawyer, Elizabeth Carey, this past winter during a clear-out of her basement. She has no idea how it came to be there or who the composer is. "I have asked friends and family, anyone who has been in my home, but no-one knows anything about it".

Ms. Carey, herself a pianist, started to play the sonata and soon realized that she had something special on her hands. "I just felt that people needed to hear music as beautiful as this and so I approached the OSO."

"We quickly recognized the professional quality of the work and acquired the rights to perform the sonata," said OSO Board member, Nancy Beringer.

It will be conducted by Alfonso Ghiradelli, musical director of the OSO. Ghiradelli has worked with both the Vienna and Philadelphia Philharmonic orchestras. "This piece will attract musical talent and music fans from all over the world," he said. "We hope to find out who the great composer is."

According to Professor Joshua Naumetz, head of the Department of Music at U of T, "Our study of the music indicates that it was composed within the last twenty years or so. It is in the style of Glass or Bantry."

The discovery of *The Anonymous Sonata* has reawakened interest in the mystery surrounding *The Phantom and the Fraud*. This was conducted to great acclaim, and presented as his own work, by a young music student, Mungo Joudry, in an inaugural performance at the Carnegie Hall in 1996. Immediately after the performance, Oliver Bantry, best friend of Joudry, claimed that the work was in fact his. Joudry disappeared and has not been seen or heard of since.

"Who was the actual composer of the piece and what happened to Mungo Joudry? This remains one of the greatest mysteries in the modern world of classical music," said Prof Naumetz. "What has added to the intrigue is the fact that Bantry, who claimed to have composed the sonata, has never produced another piece of classical music. Some say that this serves as proof that Joudry was indeed the composer. But as Joudry never came forward to confirm the work as his own, the question remains open."

Mungo put the newspaper down and instinctively reached for his coffee mug with shaking hands. Finding he could not face another mouthful, he pushed his chair back and stood up. What the hell...he was getting so sloppy.

He had hidden that manuscript in Elizabeth's basement so many years ago; he'd even forgotten it was there. He paced up and down the kitchen. Things were closing in around him so fast and once again his instinct was to run. He forced himself to calm down. *Think Mungo, think.* He'd stick to his plan. First take a shower. Make sure he left no tracks. Make sure he didn't leave anything else from way back when in their basement, get his few things together and leave town.

He made his way up the stairs to Nancy's bathroom with a sense of sadness. This would be his last time here. It was his first place of refuge after he'd arrived so unexpectedly in Toronto. He supposed it was fitting that it would be his last. He'd really love to hear his music performed again. Perhaps he could lay low, go to the OSO performance and leave after that?

Mungo was relieved to be having his first hot shower in a few days, humming a few bars from his latest violin concerto, when he heard a sound. He went still, listening.

"Hey, Nancy, it's me, Sven."

What the hell? His heart pounded. Just when he'd decided to leave for good, now he gets caught out. Frozen in his state of panic, Mungo left the shower running and stood still. Perhaps the guy would realize he'd intruded and leave.

"I've come to pick up the painting for repair. Shall I wait for you, or I could join you in there..." the voice trailed off.

Through the steam and water streaked glass Mungo saw what looked like a fair-haired man standing in the doorway.

"Oh my God! You must be Blake. I'm so sorry, I am so sorry."

"Who the hell are you?" said Mungo, quickly realizing that he had been mistaken for Blake and there was a chance he could maintain his cover. "What are you doing here?"

"I'm so sorry. I'm leaving. I'm a friend of Nancy's. She asked me to repair your portrait. I'm an artist. I might be able to fix the canvas."

"I don't want it bloody fixed," shouted Mungo, mustering up some rage on Blake's behalf. "Get out! In fact, how did you get in?"

"Nancy gave me a key."

"Well, leave it on the hallway table when you go and don't come back!"

"I'm really sorry. I wouldn't have come if Nancy hadn't asked me to pick up the painting. I'm a friend of hers."

"The kind of friend that offers to share her shower! I get it. Now get out of my house," shouted Mungo.

Mungo stood in the shower and drip dried. He waited until the house was completely quiet and then left the bathroom and peered out of the bedroom window into the front garden. There were no cars in the driveway. He cleaned and dried the shower, dressed and packed up his few belongings. He glanced into the study. The damaged portrait of Blake was still there. The guy calling himself Sven had left the key on the hallway table, as instructed. Hopefully he had scared the guy off for good.

In the kitchen he removed his sandwich wrapper and cleaned the coffee pot and mug. He refolded the newspaper fighting his temptation to take the entertainment section with him.

All the while he thought about his predicament. Another possible course of action occurred to him. He could try and find Alexia. She was the one person who knew his story. She just might vouch for him. Perhaps in the weeks since they had met on the boat she had thought about what he'd said and recognized the truth. He was tired of this lonely existence and needed an ally.

He thought of calling Patricia, but the last time they'd spoken she'd made it clear that, unless he was prepared to come clean, she didn't want to see him. He'd never fully confided in her anyway, though he'd often been tempted. She knew about the music, but not about how he had been living.

He arrived at the library at about midday and went in the main entrance, through the adult's section and straight to the bank of computers available for use by the public.

He opened an internet browser and typed in 'Alexia Bantry.' Several results showed up, most of them mentioning her marriage and subsequent divorce from Oliver Bantry along with articles and posts about *The Phantom and the Fraud*.

He tried again, this time using her maiden name, Forsythe. Aah, this was more like it. Now the results dealt with her career as a dancer. He scanned a few sites, eventually landing on one for The New SoHo Dance Company which had her listed as both a lead dancer and choreographer. He went to the contact page and scribbled down their number.

The next stop was a wireless telephone company booth in the station where he bought a new pay-as-you-go sim card and had his phone reactivated. He sat down on a bench nearby and dialed.

"New SoHo Dance, can I help you?"

"Can I speak to Alexia please."

"She's not in today."

"Do you know how I can reach her?"

"Sir, we don't give out personal contact information for our dancers."

"When will she be back? Can I leave a message for her?" Mungo asked, trying not to sound too insistent.

"I'm happy to take down a message but it will be a couple of weeks before she returns. She's out of town."

"I understand," he said, his tone conveying the exact opposite. "I'm an old friend and I really need to get hold of her urgently."

The young woman on the other end sighed, "I am not allowed to give out personal information. We get lots of creeps trying to contact our dancers. I'm sorry, I can't help you. Good day, Sir."

"Wait, please!" Mungo held his breath for a second. He didn't hear a click cutting off the call. "It's really important that I speak to her. Perhaps you could call her and ask her to call me, Mungo Joudry. She knows me, she can decide if she wants to return my call. What's the harm in that?" It felt strange to him stating his real name for the first time in years. He'd been going by the name of Jameson and it had almost become his own.

"We-ell okay, I suppose," he heard the woman concede.

He quickly gave her his new number and spelled out his name. "Please tell her to call me as soon as she can."

◆◆◆

Back in her hotel room Alexia wracked her brains trying to remember as much as she could from the day on the boat with Mungo. Was there anything he had said which would give her a clue as to his whereabouts? And what was that guy on the boat talking about, Mungo wanted in connection with a murder? Ridiculous. He was odd, but she couldn't imagine he would murder anyone. It just didn't fit.

She switched on her laptop and waited for it to boot up. She really hadn't planned any further than finding Mungo at the boat. Then she remembered that he'd said that he'd seen her at the market when she was last in Toronto. She could wait until Saturday and she might just find him there, if it was part of his routine.

She logged onto her computer, opened a browser and searched 'Toronto murder'. She needed to find out more about this recent murder. It certainly seemed uppermost on the minds of the few Torontonians she'd spoken to since she'd arrived; the taxi driver and the man at the harbor, as well as the owner of the boat.

She scanned a few news articles quickly and saw why the boat owner would think Mungo may be involved. Most of the articles stated that the police were looking for a man who appeared to fit Mungo's description. She'd only seen him once in the past twenty years and that was six weeks ago. He certainly had the hair. So similar to Sebastian's, she thought, but his was still dark. Also, he was tall and still very lean, but surely that was not enough to make him a suspect?

She heard her phone ringing and quickly dug it out of her purse, rushing to answer the call before it stopped.

"Sebastian, hi." She was thrilled to see his name appear on the screen of her phone. He hadn't contacted her or taken her calls since their last meeting when she told him about Mungo. She had left him a voicemail telling him she would be in Toronto.

"Mom, I've got good news! I've been accepted to audition for the OSO's new spring performance."

"That's fantastic. What's the piece?"

"You know, *The Anonymous Sonata*. It's a new work. The OSO is squeezing it into their spring repertoire. It's a last minute thing so they have opened the solo spots to music students. I've got an audition!"

"I haven't heard of it. But that's great."

"Seriously! Where have you been? It's all over the arts and entertainment pages. It's by an unknown composer. It's never been performed before. Everyone's trying to figure who wrote it."

"That's so exciting. You've worked so hard. This is a real breakthrough for you. Next stop: the New York Philharmonic."

"Google it. You'll find all sorts of stories about it from the last few days. Everyone's trying to get an audition."

"When do you arrive? Do you want me to book you a room at my hotel? I'm at the Pantages."

"No thanks. I'll stay with Elliot. One of his friends has an apartment there. Besides if I get the part I'll need to stay for a few weeks. I'll give him some money toward rent. But I was wondering... Do you think you could help me out with some money? I hadn't exactly budgeted for this trip."

"All right, I'll put some money in your account. Let me know your flight details once you've booked."

"What are you doing in Toronto? I got your message. Have you got another show there?"

"No, it's not a show. I'll tell you about it when you get here."

They said their good-byes and hung up. Alexia switched her internet search from 'Toronto murder' to 'Anonymous Sonata.'

Chapter Twenty-Nine

Nancy had been fielding calls all day from the media, music students hoping to audition, and other orchestras curious about what the OSO had discovered. This is what comes from publicity, she thought. She had told Jennifer, the receptionist, to hold all calls for a while and was irritated when her phone rang again.

"Jennifer, I asked you to hold my calls..."

"It's someone called Sven. He says it's urgent. And *personal*..." Jennifer said.

"Oh, I suppose I had better speak to him then," she said, annoyed that he was phoning her at the office. "Put him through."

"Sven, did you have to tell the receptionist that your call was personal."

"Well, it is personal, and it was the only way I could get her to put me through. She was quite obstinate. Plus, you haven't answered my texts."

"I'm sorry. The phone hasn't stopped ringing all morning. Have you seen the news coverage about the new performance? It is creating quite a storm."

"That's what you wanted, isn't it? You should be happy."

"I am, I am. I just need to catch up with things. So, what's on your mind?"

"I think I may have caused a problem for you. I went around to your house this morning to pick up the painting. The thing is; Blake was there. He was in the shower. I thought it was you."

"Oh God, Sven! You went up to the shower! Why? This is not what I need right now."

"I'm sorry, Nancy. I just went up to speak to you. I thought I'd surprise you. Well, I surprised him instead."

"What happened?"

"He was quite angry. Told me to get out and leave my key on the table. He said he didn't want his portrait repaired."

"Oh God. I'd better call him. Things are not good, and this will only make matters worse."

"I'm really sorry, Nancy."

"I know. I'll deal with it."

Nancy arrived at the restaurant near Blake's office a few minutes early and was immediately shown to a table. She knew he was more likely to agree to meet if he didn't have to drive too far from his office. She had impressed upon Diane, his assistant, that it was urgent, and she had to see him today.

She looked up and saw him making his way toward her, weaving between the tables. He was already removing his jacket and looking harassed. He slung it on the seat back and sat down.

"What is it, Nancy? You know I'm really busy."

"I'm fine thank you, Blake, and how are you?" She studied him, assessing his sobriety.

"Okay, okay. I'm sorry. I've got a lot on my plate right now. Parnell's after my job. I have to watch my back twenty-four seven."

Just then the waiter appeared. They placed their order, Blake for his usual of flank steak and fries and Nancy for a salmon salad. He filled their glasses with sparking water and disappeared to the kitchen.

"Thank you for coming," Nancy began. "We have a lot to discuss..."

"I really don't have time for this now," Blake broke in. "Can't this wait..." He reached for some bread, carefully spreading butter onto it.

"You've never had much time for me, for us. That's the problem." She lowered her voice. "I asked to meet as a courtesy to *you* Blake. I wanted to explain, about this morning." She instinctively scanned the restaurant, checking to make sure there was no one she knew in the restaurant.

"What about this morning?" He looked at her blankly.

"You know, when you were in the shower? The guy who came in?" She stared at him.

202

"What guy? When? What are you talking about?"

Now it was Nancy's turn to look blank. "Were you, did you go home this morning? Did you take a shower?"

"I haven't been home since last week. Tuesday, Wednesday, was it? Remember you left me a note. Told me you wanted to end our marriage. So, I packed a bag and have been staying at the boat ever since."

"Wait a minute. So, you weren't in the shower this morning when Sven arrived?" Nancy's head was spinning. What was going on? Why would Sven tell her he'd walked in on Blake in the shower?

"Sven? Who's Sven? I've been at the office since early this morning." he paused, enlightenment crossing his face.

"What is it? Did you see him?"

"No-oo, but there's been a guy hanging around the boat. And I *was* almost caught in the shower the other day, but by a woman who was looking for him."

"What?" Nancy could see that he was hiding something. His eyes were darting from side to side as he spoke, something he did when he was dodging the truth.

The waiter appeared with their food and she waited until he had left the table. Blake immediately cut into his steak and forked some into his mouth.

"So, what's all this about? Why do you think I was home this morning? And who is Sven?" he said.

"Sven's a friend of mine. He's an artist. He offered to repair your portrait and I gave him a key so he could go and pick it up."

"What kind of friend would assume he could go upstairs while you were in the shower?"

"For God's sake, Blake, that's not important right now. He's just a friend and you're hardly one to start throwing stones."

"It is important. It's important to me."

"It's only important if our marriage is important," she said, her eyes challenging him.

He looked down at his plate and then back up at her. "I know I'm a selfish bastard and I haven't always done the right thing. But the fact is Nance, I do love you. I've always loved you. Sometimes it's like you're just too good for me and I'll never be whole in your eyes. And then I stop caring and just please myself."

Nancy was really surprised. This is not how she expected their lunch to go. She couldn't even remember when last Blake had told her he loved her. Something must be going on with him. Clearly her note telling him that their marriage was over had really shaken him up.

"Say something," he said.

"Well, this isn't what I expected. You've been so difficult and distant. I've put up with it for so many years, but I've finally run out of patience. And, besides, I've met Sven..."

"What are you saying, Nancy? Are you leaving me for another man?" His face was red with anger. "You sure pick your moments! I have so much shit going on right now." He grabbed the glass of water and took a few deep swallows. "God, I could do with some wine."

"Not now, you need a clear head for this discussion. About Sven, I've only just met him. And, face it Blake, you haven't been faithful to me for years. Do you think I don't know what's going on?"

"Oh, you don't know the bloody half of it!"

"Please, keep your voice down," Nancy glanced furtively around. She was relieved to see that most people were absorbed in their own conversations. She took a deep breath and a reluctant mouthful of salad.

Blake looked at her, "Let's try again. Let's try and make it work. I'll try harder. If I get the IPF position I could give up my job. I wasn't planning to, but maybe it's time. I could semi-retire. The IPF position is very prestigious but it won't be as demanding as my job at Founder. Then Simon-bloody-Parnell could get his way and we could spend more time together. We could do some travelling; go out on the boat in the summer..."

Nancy could hardly believe what she was hearing. Something had come over Blake. He'd never shown the least interest in cutting back on his career. This was so out of character.

"What did you say just now about a man at the boat and a woman who was looking for him?"

He was quiet. She could see his mind working, calculating how much to tell her. "Blake, what is going on? This is not like you."

Eventually he said, "The other night after you threw me out..."

"I didn't throw you out!"

"Okay, okay. After I found your note. I went to the boat and I got drunk..."

"You were already drunk Blake!"

"I know, I know. Do you want me to tell you or not?"

"I'm sorry, carry on."

"I was really out of it. I think I passed out on the bed. So, I wake up and there's this guy standing over me. Saying my name and trying to, you know, get me to wake up. I think I'd taken some pills. He seemed panicked."

"Oh my God, Blake! I had a bad feeling about you."

"It's okay. I'm fine. Look, I haven't even had any wine with lunch. I haven't had anything to drink since then."

"Who was he?"

"He said he was my friend and he was there to help me, but the thing is, I had never seen him before. But he knew all about me. All about us. And about..." he stopped. "It was really creepy. He knew everything."

"What are you talking about? What else does he know? You were probably hallucinating. Pills and alcohol will do that to you. You of all people should know that, heading up a pharmaceutical company!"

"Nancy. I wasn't hallucinating, I promise. Look, if we are going to start again; then I have to tell you everything. If I lose you, then I have nothing left to lose."

Nancy felt her stomach lurch. She put her knife and fork down. She couldn't swallow another mouthful. She noticed that Blake's food had gone cold as well, the gravy congealing on the plate. She prepared herself for the worst.

She looked at him. "Well?"

"I think he might have killed somebody. And made it look like it was me," he blurted out.

"What are you talking about? Don't be ridiculous!"

"I'm not Nancy. Just listen."

She heard the seriousness in his voice and scanned the restaurant again, checking. "Quiet. People can hear you."

He hunched over the table towards her. "Have you seen the news, about the woman who was killed at the docks the other night?"

Nancy had been so busy with her own media campaign that she had only paid the barest attention to anything else. She nodded, "I've just seen the headlines. What's it got to do with you?"

"She, that is Christine Hayes, the woman who was killed, she used to work for me. We had a bit of a thing. It was over." He paused. Nancy knew he was waiting for her response. She said nothing.

"I told her it was over." She still said nothing, her eyes cold. "It wasn't serious, Nancy, I promise. Anyway, that's when she decided to blackmail me. She knew I was applying for the ethics position with the IPF and saw her opportunity. She's jumping on the #MeToo bandwagon. She is a nasty piece of work," he grimaced "Or was."

"So, who is this guy? Why do you think he killed her? Have you gone to the police?"

"No! I don't want to get caught up in the middle of it. They will think it was me."

"But what has he got to do with it? Who is he?" she persisted.

"I don't know exactly. He was on the boat when I came around. He was trying to revive me. That's the first time I saw him."

"This is weird, Blake. Are you absolutely sure you didn't imagine this?"

"No. I don't know how, but he knows all about us, everything. Somehow he found out that Christine was trying to blackmail me. He offered to help. I was desperate. He seemed decent. I agreed. He took me to a private investigator, here in the city. A big outfit. They do forensic accounting, cyber-security, everything. They found out that Christine had embezzled money from her previous company in Vancouver, managed to lay the blame on someone else and then changed her name. She moved to Toronto and started working for us." He paused, checking her reaction.

"Go on," was all she said.

"The plan was that he would meet with her and, instead of giving her the money, he would tell her that we knew about her past and if she didn't get off my back then we would put the police onto her."

"How much money did she want?"

"Eight hundred thousand."

Nancy rolled her eyes, "Oh my God! That would be just the beginning."

"I know, right. So, we had this plan all worked out. He went to the meeting spot and he was supposed to call me once he had spoken to her. I didn't hear from him, so I called him. He said it was all sorted out. I thought he'd told her what we knew and that she would shut up. He didn't come back to the boat and then next morning I saw on the news that she had been killed."

Nancy felt like she was in the middle of a crime drama on TV. She used her napkin to wipe her mouth and then her forehead. She leaned forward and lowered her voice, "What does he want from you? He's probably going to blackmail you himself now. And eventually the police will come looking for you. They will find out about your affair with this woman and they will come after you. You must find this guy. What is his name?" She felt her panic rising, took a deep breath and sat back making a conscious effort to calm herself.

"He called himself Mungo Jameson. Bloody funny name, if you ask me. But then the other night this woman shows up on the boat, just as I was getting out of the shower and she says she is looking for Mungo Joudry. She says that he took her out on *our* boat a couple of months ago or something."

"What? What did you say she called him?"

"Mungo Joudry."

"Blake, do you know who that is?"

"No idea."

"He is that famous composer who disappeared about twenty years ago after being accused of plagiarism. With a name like that, there can only be one," she was almost breathless. "You must have seen in the news, we are, the OSO is about to perform a newly discovered composition and the pundits think it could have been composed by him. He has been missing for all this time and now he turns up on our boat!"

Chapter Thirty

"Are you expecting anyone?" asked Rebecca. She and Elizabeth, both still in their pajamas, were sitting in the kitchen having a second cup of coffee after breakfast, when the doorbell rang. They looked at each other across the table both hoping the other would volunteer to get the door.

"Nope. Not at this time of the morning." The doorbell rang again. "I suppose I'd better see who it is." Elizabeth got up.

She squinted through the peephole and was relieved to see that it was just Mrs. Gibson. Opening the door, she said, "Hello Mrs. Gibson. How are you? Please excuse my pajamas, we were just finishing breakfast."

"Yes, hello dear. I know it's early, I'm sorry, but there is something I thought you'd want to see." She held up the morning newspaper.

"Please come in. Would you like some coffee, or some tea maybe?" Mrs. Gibson followed Elizabeth into the kitchen.

"Oh, this is nice," she said. "What a nice sunny spot. Tea would be lovely" She sat down. "Nice to see you again, dear," she said to Rebecca. "Are you enjoying your visit with your sister?"

Elizabeth put a cup of tea down in front of her and offered the sugar and milk.

"I'm having a good break for a few days. It's like when we were young," said Rebecca. "And we have a little mystery to solve. I'm calling it 'The Secret of the Suitcase.' I feel like Nancy Drew." Rebecca laughed.

"Well, that's why I'm here, actually." Mrs. Gibson pushed her tea cup aside and laid the newspaper on the table, her bony hands trembling slightly.

She started to page through the paper. "Just a minute." She removed a pair of glasses from her housecoat and put them on.

Elizabeth looked at Rebecca and shrugged. I'm sorry, her expression said. They had an appointment at the spa in an hour and needed to get ready.

"Ah, here we are," said Mrs. Gibson, pointing to a photograph with a headline above it saying, 'Have you seen this man?' "That's him," she said triumphantly. "That's the man you have been asking about, the one who comes here."

They both leaned closer and read the caption beneath the photo. 'An age-enhanced photo of the missing Mungo Joudry.' They went on to read 'Last seen almost twenty years ago following his notorious performance at Carnegie Hall in New York, speculation in academic and musical circles is that Joudry is the mystery composer behind the newly discovered *Anonymous Sonata* soon to be performed by the Ontario Symphony Orchestra...'

"But that's incredible!" said Elizabeth.

"It makes sense. If he's the one Mrs. Gibson says she's seen here, and he's the composer of the music you found in your basement, it must be him!" Rebecca could hardly keep the excitement from her voice.

"Are you sure, Mrs. Gibson? How do you know it's the same man?" asked Elizabeth.

"I know my eyes are not very good anymore. But I'm pretty sure. I have seen him through the window sitting at your piano. I... I think its him. Oh dear. I hope I haven't upset you."

"No, no, you haven't. It's not your fault. Here drink your tea before it gets cold."

Rebecca had been reading the article further. "Elizabeth, it must be him. It says here he was accused of plagiarism and then went into hiding almost twenty years ago. He was considered to be a musical genius. The article says he claimed his friend's work as his own."

"But how would he have got into my house? And why?"

◆◆◆

Alexia was bored. She didn't have much to do in Toronto besides find Mungo, and that hadn't proved very successful so far, and Sebastian hadn't arrived yet. She looked around the coffee shop and bit into her croissant wondering how to fill her day. She wasn't very good at sleuthing, she realized. She wondered if she should take another walk to the harbor and see if he showed up at the boat.

Her phone started ringing and pleased to have a distraction she hastily dug it out of her bag. It was from the dance company. She tapped the answer button.

"Alexia, hi. It's Carla here."

"Hi there, what's up?"

"Nothing much. Everything is quiet here until rehearsals start for the new show. How are you doing?"

"Oh, I'm fine. Sebastian's joining me for a few days. He has an audition with the OSO. What can I do for you?"

"Some guy called late yesterday looking for you. He was pretty insistent actually. I told him I couldn't give out your number, but I said I'd pass on the message. He said his name was Mungo Joudry, strange name, hey?"

"What? You're kidding me! Did he leave a number? What did he want?" Alexia asked rummaging through her bag for a pen.

"He didn't say, but it did sound sort of urgent. I'm sorry I didn't call last night. I got distracted and only remembered when I got in this morning. Have you got a pen?"

"Yes, go ahead." She pulled a paper serviette towards her and quickly scribbled down the number. "Okay, that's great, thanks Carla. Yes, yes, I'll let you know my return date. I'm not sure. It kind of depends on a few things but I'll be back before rehearsals start."

Alexia could hardly believe that she actually had a number for Mungo. What were the odds? She immediately dialed it, her heart racing. It rang just four times and then she heard his voice. "Alexia is that you?"

"Yes, I just got your message. It's such a coincidence." Now that she was talking to him she realized that she hadn't really planned what to say. "I'm...well, I'm in Toronto. I came here to look for you. There's something I need to tell you."

"There's something I want to talk to you about as well. I was hoping you could help me. I'm in a real bind." She didn't reply. "Can we meet somewhere? Where are you?"

"I'm in a coffee shop. Downtown."

"Do you know where the St. James Cathedral is? There's a park there."

"Yes, I think so…I can find it."

"I'll meet you there, by the fountain in the park, in an hour," said Mungo.

She left the coffee shop with a sense of uneasiness. She was getting closer to the moment of truth.

◆◆◆

After their lunch the previous day, Blake packed up his things at the boat and returned to the house. Part of him was concerned about Nancy being there on her own since the shower episode she had related to him. Also, he didn't want to concede any ground to this Sven who was circling his wife and he hoped it was a step in the direction of reconciliation with her.

Instead of leaving for the office early the next day, he stayed and had breakfast with her.

"I've been thinking about the thing with Christine," he said looking at her back as she buttered a piece of toast. "I don't want to go to the police, but I could go back to the investigator this Mungo guy hired and see if she can help."

"You mean to find Mungo?" She sat down opposite him.

"Yeah, Christine's killer." He stared speculatively out of the window.

"What a mess. Even if the investigator finds the killer, the police will have to be informed and, at some point, you will be drawn into it. They will find out about your affair with Christine and the blackmail. You can forget being appointed as Head of Ethics for the IPF. And Founder might fire you. Serves you bloody right! You are getting your much-deserved comeuppance!"

"Look Nancy, I know I've screwed up and I'm really sorry. What's important now is trying to fix things," he scraped his chair back and stood up. If she was going to start haranguing him, he was out of there.

"Sit down, Blake, you bastard! If you want my help in fixing things, then sit down!"

He sat. That was something he'd always admired about Nancy. When there was a problem, she rose to the challenge.

"I've got a meeting with the OSO Board and Alfonso today. I'm going to tell them that I think Mungo Joudry is in Toronto. They have an interest in finding him and may pay for the investigation. But we will have to tread quickly and carefully. The OSO doesn't need to know that he might be involved in the murder of your colleague. We have to find him and then find out what he knows."

"Good idea. I'll text you contact details for the investigator. Her name is Meredith Salinger."

"In the meanwhile, I am going to call a security company and get a surveillance system installed. Hopefully he will come back here and the security company will grab him, naked out of the shower if necessary."

◆◆◆

Nancy was in her office rushing to get things finished so she could return home and meet with the security company. The phone rang.

"Nancy, it's Elizabeth here."

"Hi Elizabeth. I suppose you are calling for an update. Things are going very well with the rehearsals and we are holding the auditions for the solo parts today and tomorrow. The publicity campaign is well under way and is attracting lots of interest..."

"Actually it's about the article in today's Globe," Elizabeth interjected.

"Yes. I know it might seem a bit premature to identify him, but most people I speak to think *The Anonymous Sonata* is the work of Joudry. We got an experienced artist to do the age enhanced image."

"The thing is Nancy, I think he might have been at my house. That's why I'm calling. I think it's him."

"Wait a minute. How do you know he has been at your house? When?" Nancy could hardly believe what she was hearing. She felt alarm ripple through her like an electric current. He had disappeared some twenty years ago and now it seems Joudry was infiltrating every corner of her life, on their boat, in their shower and now at Elizabeth's house. Perhaps this was the time to call in the police, it was entirely too creepy. But the downside was that once the police had all the information it would be hard to keep it under wraps and might ruin the publicity campaign. She needed to think about how to handle this...she realized Elizabeth was talking.

"I have this neighbor, she is old and nosy but well-intentioned. When I first found the music, I asked around; anyone who may have been in my house, if they knew anything about it. My neighbor. Mrs Gibson, has a key. Well, had a key. I've taken it back now. She said she'd never seen the suitcase, but she did say something about a man who she has seen around my property. She gets very confused and seemed to be mistaking him for her father, so I didn't take her seriously," she paused.

"Go on," said Nancy, trying to keep the urgency from her voice. "I'm listening."

"This morning while I was having breakfast with my sister - she's visiting for a few days - my neighbor came around with a copy of the newspaper. She insists that the man she has seen at my house looks just the same as the photo of Mungo Joudry in today's paper."

"When last did she see him?"

"I don't know. I didn't ask. It might be nothing and she is very old. Her eyesight is going. But my sister, Rebecca, spoke to Mrs. Gibson the other day and now she seems convinced it's him. She persuaded me to call you. But I'm thinking I should let the police know that I've had an intruder or a trespasser."

"Thank you for letting me know. But as for the police, let's think about that for a moment. Nothing is missing from your home, right? Are there any signs of a break in?"

"No, no nothing like that. I mean Mrs. Gibson could be imagining it. It's quite possible she has dementia, you know, that's why I didn't take her seriously when she first mentioned seeing a man at my house."

"So realistically all you have is the word of the old lady next door and a suitcase you don't recognize in your house," said Nancy. She needed to regain control of this story and when and how much information about

Mungo Joudry was revealed. If the police got involved now it could derail her plans for the OSO.

"Well, yes," said Elizabeth, "but if someone has been in my house..."

"You have your sister staying with you for a while so at least you are not alone in the house. Can you hold off for a few days? I can't go into it right now, but I have reason to believe that Joudry is in Toronto. It seems though, that he still doesn't want to be found. If we alert the police now it might scare him off, and really if he is here, this could help our publicity for the concert tremendously."

"So, you think he could have somehow left the music in my house?" asked Elizabeth.

"It's looking that way."

"But that's weird."

"It certainly is," agreed Nancy. "But look, I have arranged for an investigator to help us track him down. Her name is Meredith Salinger. Can I give her your number? And perhaps Mrs. Gibson will speak to her too?"

"Yes, of course." Elizabeth sounded relieved. "Please keep me informed. It is really creepy to think someone may have been in my house. My sister can't stay with me indefinitely."

"As soon as I have anything firm, I will let you know. Oh, and we have confirmed three performances of *The Anonymous Sonata*, next month. I have two complementary tickets for you, very good seats at the Roy Thompson Hall, followed by a reception for selected guests. Bring a friend or your sister. The concert is going to be sold out."

◆◆◆

Mungo arrived at St James' Park a few minutes ahead of schedule and once again found himself waiting for Alexia and wondering if she would show up. He was surprised when she had said that she was in Toronto. The weather was warming up, but he barely noticed the new shoots peeking through the soil and the new buds on the trees. He scanned the few people walking through the park and made his way directly to the fountain. He walked around for a bit, hands deep in his coat pockets, collar pulled up and the baseball cap pulled low over his forehead.

Finally, he saw her walking at a brisk pace toward the fountain and his heart did a little leap, a mixture of relief and pleasure at seeing her. She strode confidently, her long legs clad in dark denim and a long grey trench coat wrapped around her.

She approached him and he felt the urge to hug her but instead stuck out his hand. The gesture was made even more awkward by the fact that she had gloves on and she appeared uncertain as to whether to shake hands or remove her gloves. He withdrew his.

"I'm sorry," she said, with an awkward laugh.

"Oh, it's okay. It's still a bit cold," he said, anxious to reassure her. "Thank you for coming. Should we find somewhere to sit, or do you want to walk."

"I've already had a coffee, but I would like to go inside somewhere. I walked here and I am chilled to the bone now. Toronto feels much colder than New York was when I left." They walked toward one of the streets bordering the park.

"I didn't expect you to be in Toronto. I thought you'd gone back to New York."

"Well, I did. But I've been thinking, since we last spoke, and there's something I need to talk to you about. I tried to call you, but it seems the number you gave me last time has been disconnected. So, actually, I came to Toronto to find you."

His heart lifted a little at the thought that she had come all the way to Toronto just to see him. They reached a sandwich shop advertising Mediterranean wraps and he gestured toward the door. "Shall we go in here?" She nodded, and he directed them to a table as far from the counter as possible. There were only one or two other customers, the lunch time rush not having started yet.

"Can I get you something?" he asked as soon as she was seated.

"We'd better have something, I suppose. Do they do tea? I've had enough coffee. Steeped with milk. Thanks."

He returned to the table with her tea and a coffee for himself and sat down. He was nervous now to tell her about his problem. He didn't know where to start. How do you tell someone that you think you are suspected of murder? What if she didn't believe him, or worse, if she decided to report him?

They sipped their drinks and after a few moments of awkward silence Alexia said, "You sounded quite anxious on the phone earlier. You said you were in a bind. What's going on?" she asked.

"Why don't you tell me what brought you to Toronto to find me?" he countered.

"No, what I have to say has waited eighteen years, it can wait another half an hour. Your problem sounds more pressing."

He looked at her for a moment and then said, "It's a long story but I'll give you the gist of it. There's someone I know, I suppose you could call him a friend, who was being blackmailed by an employee; they'd had an affair."

Her eyes widened questioningly, she wrapped her hands around her mug of tea, warming them. "And?" she encouraged him to go on.

"Anyway, I tried to help him. We got some information about her. Something she wouldn't have wanted the police, or anyone, to know about. The plan was that I would go to the meeting spot in his place and, instead of paying her off, I would tell her what we had on her and warn her off. A sort of counter-blackmail. We won't tell if she doesn't tell. I went to the meeting place and she didn't show. As I was leaving I saw the woman sitting in her car." He lowered his voice, "When I got closer I saw that she had been shot."

"Oh my God, Mungo," her voice came out as a low hiss. She shook her head in disbelief. "This guy you were helping, is he the one at the boat? I went to that boat where we last met looking for you. There was a man there. He said he was looking for you too, and that so were the police."

"When was this? When did you talk to him?"

"Yesterday evening, after I arrived in Toronto. I didn't know where else to find you, so I went back to the boat. He was there. At first, I thought it was you. It was a bit embarrassing actually. He was in the shower."

"I bet he loved that," said Mungo, rolling his eyes. He could just imagine Blake taking full advantage of the situation. "How does he know the police are looking for me?"

"I don't know. I didn't ask. To be honest I just wanted to get off that boat as quickly as possible. He offered me wine and sat there in his towel, still all wet from his shower."

"So typical of Blake," Mungo shook his head.

"How do you know this guy? Why did you get involved in his blackmail thing? You should have gone to the police."

"I know, I know. It's complicated. But it's too late now."

"What do you mean?"

He sighed, "There's a lot you don't know about me. We haven't had time to catch up properly. It sounds crazy, and I don't expect you to understand, but I wanted to help Blake deal with his scandal, because, all those years ago I didn't deal with mine."

"But why would you...?" she shook her head. He could see that she was confused and frustrated.

"I ran away when Oliver accused me. He was the liar, not me. I didn't want our affair to come out, I wanted to protect you. I was in shock. I didn't see it coming and I didn't know what to do. So, I just ran from the problem, from the media, from you and Oliver and everything."

She stared at him, her eyes wide.

"I don't expect you to understand, but I wanted to help Blake so that I could help myself, to make up somehow for running away when I did. What I do want you to understand is that I didn't kill this woman. He thinks I did. For all I know, he killed her, now the police are looking for me." His eyes implored her. "I don't want to run this time. You are the only person who really knows me. Will you help me?"

Chapter Thirty-one

It was after five o'c clock when Nancy met Blake in the downstairs lobby of the Van Buuren and Co. building. They rode up in the elevator together. Blake was tempted to put his arm around Nancy, but she was still very brittle. She had insisted he sleep in the guest room. She had made it very clear that he was still in the dog house. She'd said that she was prepared to help him deal with this crisis and that after the dust had settled they had some major issues to address.

"What's that you've got there?" asked Blake, gesturing to the folder Nancy had tucked under her arm.

"All the information I could track down on Mungo Joudry. Mostly news articles from about eighteen years ago when he disappeared, the accusation and speculation about what happened to him, that sort of thing. And the few recent ones since the launch of the OSO campaign."

The elevator pinged as they reached the twenty-third floor and they stepped out. "It's this way," he said and led them to the closed door of Van Buuren and Co. Just as he was about to ring the bell, they heard a buzz and the door clicked open.

Nancy looked up and down the hallway and then quizzically at Blake.

"They are probably watching this hallway all the time. Plus, this woman seems to know everything," he said under his breath. They stepped into the reception area and within a moment an inner door opened and Meredith appeared.

"Mr. Beringer," she said extending a hand to Blake. "And you must be Mrs. Beringer."

"Call me Nancy, please."

"Come this way," she said turning. "I have water in my office, but if you'd like something else I can arrange it."

"No, water is fine," said Nancy.

They followed her into her office and sat down; Nancy and Blake on the sofa and Meredith in a chair opposite.

"Now I gather from your call that the OSO wishes to engage me to find a missing person?"

"Well, it's really a continuation of some recent work you have been doing," said Nancy, looking across at Blake.

"Yes. The man, Mungo Jameson, who was helping me deal with the blackmail issue – my wife knows all about it, by the way – we think he is actually Mungo Joudry; the composer who went missing years ago."

Nancy pushed the folder across the table. "Here, this might help."

Meredith picked up the folder and flipped through the pages, scanning them quickly.

She nodded. "Well, he certainly looks like the gentleman you had with you when you consulted me recently," she said, her eyes on Blake.

"We need to find him, as soon as possible, for two reasons. Firstly, it seems that he may have murdered the woman who was blackmailing my husband. He could be dangerous. And we are worried that the police will find out about the attempted blackmail and then Blake will be in their sights."

"And secondly?" Meredith queried.

"If he is indeed Mungo Joudry, then there is a great deal of interest in finding him. Particularly now; with the discovery of a new piece of music which he is believed to have composed. The OSO is about to perform the piece. If we could find him, it would be a great win for the orchestra."

"You do realize that with all the media interest, if he is associated with a murder which involved a blackmail plot, it will be very difficult to keep Blake out of the spotlight," Meredith shot a look at Blake.

"That's the reason we have come to you and not the police," said Nancy. "We understand that you have dealt with some very high-level issues with absolute discretion."

"We always do our utmost to respect the privacy of our clients, but the media is a voracious beast, as I'm sure you know."

"We'll have better control of the story and how it gets out once we have all the information. Will you help us?" asked Nancy.

Meredith stood up and fetched a document from her desk. "These are our terms," she said. "In the case of a missing person we do our best but can't guarantee success, of course. We charge a daily rate, plus expenses; with a success fee at the end should we find the person. We will agree between us how long you wish the search to continue."

Nancy scanned the document and handed it to Blake. Once he had read it he removed a pen from his jacket pocket.

"No, let me," said Nancy. "Best to keep your name out of this if we can." She signed the contract and passed it to Meredith. "It shouldn't be that difficult," she said, "besides his visit to your office, there have been sightings of him in Toronto."

"Yes, I am reasonably confident that we can track him down. We have access to much more advanced technology than was available two decades ago when he was first being sought. Now tell me about the sightings."

Nancy told Meredith about Elizabeth's discovery of the music and her neighbor's suspicion about the trespasser.

"I will follow up directly with Ms. Carey, if you can give me her number please." Nancy found the number in her phone and Meredith wrote it down. "Was there anything else?" Meredith looked from Nancy to Blake.

"There is something else," said Nancy looking across at Blake for confirmation. He nodded.

"I'm listening," said Meredith.

"It seems that someone has been in our house, in our shower actually. A friend of mine popped in to our home to pick something up yesterday. He thought he heard Blake in the shower. Except Blake wasn't home! Someone was in our shower! He called me afterwards to apologize for um…intruding on Blake.

"I wasn't even home at the time," Blake chimed in.

"You are absolutely sure about this? You haven't given a friend or relative a key? Perhaps even long ago and you've forgotten about it?"

"No, apart from the friend who went around yesterday, I haven't given anyone a key. Blake…have you, does anyone else have a key to our house?"

"No, not guilty," said Blake shaking his head firmly.

"Someone has been on our boat too," said Nancy. She looked at Blake.

"I've been spending a bit of time on our boat recently. Things have been... uh... quite busy at work and, uh… complicated..." Blake hesitated.

"You might as well tell her," Nancy snapped.

"With the whole blackmail thing, things have been a bit strained between us," Blake said looking cautiously at Nancy and then back to Meredith "and I spent a few nights at the boat. That's when this Mungo Jameson turned up. I was rather drunk one night and he kind of... uh...revived me. He seemed to know all about the situation with Christine and everything. He offered to help me. I thought he was in cahoots with her. But then when he introduced me to you and he seemed genuine about wanting to help get her off my back, I thought maybe he was just some sort of good Samaritan. He leaned forward with his elbows on his knees and ran his hands through his hair. "But now it seems like he's a killer. God! What a mess."

"But, Blake, tell Ms. Salinger about the woman who came to the boat looking for Mungo Joudry?" Nancy asked.

"Oh yes, that's the other funny thing. So, a few nights ago, I'm on the boat, just got out of the shower and this woman appears. She says she is looking for Mungo Joudry. Weird name if you ask me. She says she met him on my boat, like about six weeks ago or something. Bloody cheek!"

"Did she give you her name?" asked Meredith.

"She gave me this card," said Blake leaning back and digging in the pocket of his trousers. He handed Meredith a slightly creased business card.

"Mmm...Alexia Forsythe," said Meredith turning the card over thoughtfully. "Well, if there is nothing else, I will get my people onto this immediately," she said. She stood, "I will make sure you receive a daily update on our progress."

They said good-bye and the Beringers left Meredith's office.

"That seemed to go okay," said Blake.

"She certainly appears to be efficient," agreed Nancy.

Blake pulled his phone from his pocket and listened to his voicemail. "Shit," he said.

"What now?"

"There's a message from Diane at the office. The police have been there looking for me."

♦♦♦

"You can't stay at your place if the police are searching for you," Alexia said as they left the sandwich shop. "We'll go and pack you some things and then we'll get you a room at the Pantages where I am staying." She paused and studied the hesitation on his face. "What? You know you can't stay at your place until we have got this cleared up. Once we know what is going on we can go to the police with the whole story. If they come for you before and you can't properly explain your involvement, you may find yourself arrested and detained."

"I know, I know. It's just that..." He hadn't told her about his living arrangements. He didn't think she could handle the whole story at once. He was very aware that he was already on thin ice.

"Look, if you are worrying about the hotel bill, I will help you cover it. It will just be for a few days. You said you wanted my help."

"No, no it's not that. You are right, of course. Come on."

They walked quickly along King Street and then south on Yonge, turning west on Front Street toward Union Station. He assumed Alexia would think they were going to the subway, but he hurried them past the station and headed into the *Fitness First* gym. "Wait here," he said as soon as they were inside. He nodded to the young woman at the front desk and pushed his way through the turnstile.

He headed quickly for the men's change rooms. There he found locker 220 and spun the dial on the combination lock. He removed a duffel bag, shoved the lock in the bag, and went out to meet Alexia. He was relieved to find her perusing the notices pinned to the cork board.

"I've got everything I need in here. I use the gym sometimes before or after work. They have good shower facilities. I keep a change of clothes and a few things in the locker."

"You haven't told me where you work," she said.

"There's a lot we haven't discussed. There will be time for that later." They walked up Bay Street, heading for the hotel. "You haven't told me why you wanted to see me," he countered.

"Like you said, there is a lot to discuss and now is not the time. We have to sort out your problem first."

They checked him into the hotel and he was allocated a room on the floor below Alexia's. He stepped out of the elevator.

"Get unpacked and then come up to my room, 304, and we will try and figure things out," Alexia said.

Once in his room, he was pleased to have a few minutes to himself and sat down on the large bed. He put his head in his hands and realized he still had the baseball cap on. He removed it and gave his head a scratch.

Now that he had her support he realized how empty his life had been without someone around to share burdens and decisions with, well, life really. This made him even more afraid of disappointing her. What would she think when she discovered that he was, in effect, a trespasser; worse, a squatter? And now the OSO was about to perform one of his compositions. His name and face were back in the news and the police were looking for him. He fought the urge to run again. What kept him there was that he really didn't want to lose Alexia again.

He went into the bathroom. Like the bedroom it was modern, done out in neutral shades of beige and grey. He rinsed and dried his face. Looking at his reflection in the mirror he had a dreaded sense that the time of reckoning was drawing closer and that he was on an unavoidable path toward exposure.

He heard the phone ringing in the bedroom and went to answer. Who could be calling him here? His hand hovered over the receiver; he picked it up.

"Mungo, it's me, Alexia. I know I said to come to my room, but I've just received a call. I've got to go out and meet someone. Can we get together downstairs later at the bar, at say seven?"

"Fine, fine. I'll see you downstairs later." They rang off. Who could she be meeting, he wondered, maybe a fellow dancer? He was disappointed, but also relieved. He had a reprieve and it would give him some time to figure out his next steps.

♦♦♦

Sebastian was waiting for Alexia in the foyer when she got downstairs. They hugged, and he steered her in the direction of the lobby bar.

"We can sit in here," he said quickly looking around the bar. He found a table but only one chair. The neighboring table had only one occupant but two chairs. "Is this chair taken? Do you mind if we use it?"

A tanned blonde man glanced up from the newspaper which had been obscuring his face. "No, not at all," he said.

"Thank you." Sebastian took the chair and turned to Alexia.

"Would you like something to drink?" he asked his mother.

"No, do you mind, I'd prefer it if we went somewhere else?" she said, casting a quick look over her shoulder.

"What's wrong, Mom?"

"It's nothing. I just feel like a change, that's all." She didn't think Sebastian would react very well if he discovered Mungo was staying in the same hotel as she was, and Mungo still had no idea that he had a son. She felt like she was traversing a minefield and had to tread very carefully.

They left the hotel. They quickly found a coffee shop. Sebastian ordered them each a coffee and sat down opposite her.

"So, why the sudden trip to Toronto?" he asked her.

"Oh, I, uh, just had to see some people," she said.

"Do you have another show coming up here?"

"No, it's not that. How was your flight? Congratulations on getting the solo with the OSO. How long will you be here?"

"Mom, are you sure you are okay, you seem kind of distracted."

"I'm sorry, I am a bit distracted. It's been an odd sort of day."

"I'm a bit distracted too actually. I feel a bit daunted by this solo. I can't screw this up. The next few days are packed with rehearsals. These musicians are so good, Mom, they look at a score and play first time like they have been doing it for years. Mind you, they have I suppose," he laughed, "and Ghiradelli, the conductor, is brilliant. I feel like such an amateur next to some of them."

"Don't say that. Do you think they would have given you the solo if they thought you weren't up to it?"

"Well, no, but I'm sure cost factors into these things too. I'm an unknown and they can pay me a lot less than a Joshua Bell. Also, this has been a bit of a last-minute thing and the big names are booked up sometimes a year or two in advance. This is an inaugural performance, so it is all bit of an experiment for the OSO. You know they think that Joudry composed it?" He went quiet.

"Yes, you told me. I know it is a lot for you to deal with, Sebastian, but wouldn't it be wonderful if your first major solo with a world class orchestra is one of your father's compositions."

"Have you told Dad, what you told me, I mean, that he isn't my real Dad?"

"No, not yet. It's not something I want to do over the phone, and you know how hard it is to get hold of him. Have you spoken to him?" she asked.

"No. I haven't spoken to him for a couple of months. He is such an arrogant shit. The last time I saw him we had a big row. He is always trying to tell me how to manage my career but look at his. He has done nothing for years, advertising tunes! Please!"

"We will sort it all out eventually. I don't want you to be on bad terms with him."

"That's rich, Mom! You and he didn't exactly part on good terms."

"I know, I know, but that was all years ago. We have to move on."

He took his phone out and checked the time. "Talking of moving on, I have to get across town for a rehearsal starting in forty-five minutes. Here, I got these for you," he took an envelope out of his jacket pocket and gave it to her. "Two tickets for the first performance. I hope you can bring one of your dance company friends." He stood up, "I've got to run. The tickets include an invitation to the reception after the show. I'll see you there." He kissed her cheek.

"I wouldn't miss it for the world," she said.

225

Chapter Thirty-two

Sven had followed the woman and the young man with her out of the hotel, but when he saw them enter the coffee shop he had returned to the hotel lobby bar. He couldn't follow them into the coffee shop without raising suspicion.

He wasn't sure who the woman was but when he'd heard Blake shout after her that he'd like to speak to Joudry too and that the police were looking to question him regarding a murder, Sven had followed her to the Pantages Hotel. He had been back and forth to the hotel a few times after that and finally checked in so that he had a legitimate reason for hanging around.

He was relieved to have spotted her this evening. He kept his eye on the entrance and a short while later she returned from the coffee shop and headed for the elevators. He watched her step in and saw that the elevator stopped on the third floor. He took his cell phone from his jacket pocket and dialed Meredith.

"It's Sven,"

"What have you got for me?" said Meredith.

"You know how I told you I have been scoping out the Beringer's boat. Well, I was there a couple of nights ago and I saw this woman arrive. At first I thought it was another one of Beringer's liaisons, but she didn't stay long. I don't know what went down on the boat, but as she was leaving Beringer shouted after her that he was looking for Joudry too, and so were the police who want to question him about a murder."

"Yes, I know she was there."

"What? How can you know? Who is she?"

"I know she was there, but I don't know who she is. What have you got on her?" Meredith asked.

"I followed her from the boat to the Pantages Hotel. You know the one on Victoria Street?"

"Yes, I know it."

"I've been hanging around here for the last day or two. I had to check in so that I didn't raise suspicion about all the hours I have spent in the bar. It's costing me a fortune. I had better sell this story after all the time..."

"What have you got, Sven?"

"I was wondering if you guys could get her name. If I start asking questions here I could blow my cover. I saw her again this evening. She met a young guy, looked like he could have been her son. They went to a coffee shop down the road. Then she came back alone. She's on the third floor."

"I'll get our people on to it. You keep an eye on her," said Meredith and she hung up.

Sven checked the time. He was feeling quite restless and anxious to get on with his article. Things were coming to a head and he was determined to break the story. He was pleased with the coverage the OSO was garnering. There would be more interest and a better market for his piece. Tomorrow he would contact the editors of the national dailies, maybe the producers of *The Fifth Estate*, and start negotiations.

Since Meredith was on the case now he could leave the lobby for a while. He folded up his newspaper and took the elevator up to his room. He went to the washroom and then sat down at his desk. He would work for an hour and then head back downstairs to resume his post and have dinner in the bar.

◆◆◆

Blake was in the office bright and early. He wanted to get a head start on things before it got busy. The last couple of weeks he had let things slide and he needed to get back into the driving seat. He wasn't about to let Simon Parnell wrest control from him. If and when he gave it up, it would be on his terms and only once he had the International Pharmaceutical Federation ethics position nailed down. He was busy reviewing a report for the executive committee when Diane stuck her head around the door.

"Sorry Blake, but that detective is back." She looked at the card in her hand. "A police detective Carl Bradski, and he has someone with him."

"Well, he doesn't have an appointment. Tell him I am busy," Blake said irritably.

"He says it's important. He's very insistent. He tried to see you yesterday," she paused. "I think it's about Christine."

"Oh, all right. Show him in but tell him I only have ten minutes."

A moment later two men entered his office.

He stood up. The taller of the two reached over and handed him a card.

"Detective Inspector Carl Bradski. This is Sergeant Sam Carter. We are from the Toronto Metropolitan Police. If we could just have a few minutes of your time. We have some questions in connection with one of your employees. Former employee actually. A Ms. Christine Hayes. You have probably heard..."

"Yes, yes, all right. Sit down." Blake gestured to the two chairs opposite his desk.

They sat. Bradski continued to loom over the desk in a hawkish fashion, his height not much diminished by being seated. He looked to be in his mid-fifties, grey with a gaunt face and big nose. Carter was younger and as short and solid as Bradski was tall and lean. Good cop, bad cop, thought Blake. *Which is which?*

Diane lingered at the door. "That will be all, thank you Diane," said Blake.

"I was just wondering if the detectives would like something to drink."

"I don't think they have time for that," snapped Blake.

She stepped out and closed the door.

Blake looked at his watch. "So how can I help you?" he asked.

"You are no doubt aware that the body of Ms. Hayes was found at the docks a few days ago. She had been shot. No weapon was found at the scene. She was an employee of Founder Pharmaceuticals. We are speaking to everyone who knew her and, as her boss, we are hoping you can answer some questions for us," said Bradski.

You must be the bad cop, thought Blake. "Well, she didn't report directly to me, so I am probably not the best person to answer your questions. She was in the sales department. I can put you in touch with our Vice President of Sales." He reached for the phone on his desk.

"Ah... would that be..." Bradski flipped through the pages of his notebook, "Eric Smiley?"

"Yes, how the hell...?" Blake took his hand from the phone.

"We have spoken to him already. Thanks anyway." Bradski offered a wide toothy smile. "Really helpful chap, very helpful." He turned to his sidekick, "Didn't you think so, Carter?"

Sergeant Carter nodded in response. "Yes definitely. He filled us in quite well. Very good with people. His name sure suits him. A good guy to have heading up sales, I'd say."

Blake's face was frozen. He stood. "Well, in that case, there is probably not much more I can help you with gentlemen. And incidentally, I consider this a breach of protocol. As the senior executive I should have been informed of your interest."

"We did try sir. We were waiting for you for much of yesterday afternoon. We tried to reach you at home and left messages for you. In your absence your assistant and the Human Resources manager were very helpful. We managed to speak to most of the people who worked with Ms. Hayes. Now we just need a statement from you." Bad Cop bared his teeth again.

Blake felt perspiration gathering on the top of his lip and in his hairline. He resisted the urge to wipe it off. "Well, get on with it then. I have a full schedule today." He sat down heavily.

"How long have you known Ms. Hayes?"

"I don't know. Two, two and a half years. Since she joined the company, I suppose. Surely this is information you would have received from the HR department."

"Yes, yes, of course. But we need to know how long *you* have known her."

Blake glared at Bradski. "Like I said. Probably as long as she has worked here."

There was a pause while he scribbled in his notebook. Blake looked from Bradski to Carter. Carter smiled back at him. Blake looked away quickly.

"How well did you know Ms. Hayes?"

"How well did I know her? How well? How well do you think? She didn't report to me."

"I couldn't say, sir. That's for you to tell us."

"I knew her about as well as I know most other people in the company who I don't work with on a daily basis."

"Mmmm." More scratching in Bad Cop's notepad.

"So, did you dine and go to lunch with most of your employees then?" he asked without looking up.

"What are you trying to insinuate?" Blake exploded.

"It is not our job to insinuate but to gather the facts. We are just trying to establish how well you knew Ms. Hayes."

Good Cop shot him another smile and nodded in agreement with his senior.

"Can you think of any reason why someone would want Ms. Hayes dead?" asked Bad Cop, his eyes now fixed on Blake.

Blake could feed a bead of sweat running down between his shoulder blades.

"No. How would I know what other people would want?"

"These are routine questions Mr. Beringer, and other people in your organization have been far more forthcoming in answering them," said Bad Cop, the wolfish grin appearing on his face but not quite reaching his eyes.

"Well then, if others have been so helpful, you clearly don't need to speak to me." Once again Blake stood up.

Good Cop and Bad Cop both remained seated and looked at him implacably. Finally, Bad Cop said, "Mr. Beringer, you can either answer our questions here, or we can arrange for you to accompany us to the station and you can have your lawyer present. Either way we will get answers to our questions. Where and how we do it is up to you." This time there was no smile from either of them.

Blake could feel his shirt sticking to his back. He wished he could remove his jacket. Instead he picked up his phone. "Diane," he said, "please cancel my next meeting and bring us in some bottles of water."

"But Blake", she said into his ear, "you don't have another meeting."

"Just do it." He put the phone down hard.

A moment later she entered with water bottles and glasses on a tray and gave him a concerned look as she lowered the tray onto the desk. He ignored her, and she left with a quick glance at each of the detectives. He grabbed one of the water bottles and, not bothering with a glass, he uncapped it and swallowed down a few mouthfuls. He wiped his mouth with the back of his hand and pushed the tray toward them. "Help yourself."

"Great. Thanks," said Good Cop, taking a bottle. "It's warm in here," he offered a companionable smile.

Bad Cop meanwhile flipped through his notebook. Apparently absorbed he said, almost casually, "So according to reports we have, you and Christine were quite close. You often had dinners and lunches with her, and many meetings, considering, as you said, she didn't report to you..." He left the sentence hanging.

"Is that a question or a statement?" spat Blake.

"Would you like to explain the nature of your relationship? Bearing in mind that you are not obliged to answer these questions and we could always do this with your lawyer present," said Bradski.

"Look, I was... uh... something of a mentor to Christine. She was new to the city when she started with us. She was eager to learn and to get ahead. She was bright and hard working." He looked from the one to the other opposite, gauging their response. Bad Cop appeared to be recording everything he said. Good Cop nodded encouragingly.

"Go on," said Bradski without looking up.

"Like I said, I became a mentor to her. We became quite close. Probably too close. She became quite demanding." He paused, took a swig of water from the bottle.

Good Cop shook his head sadly. "My wife's brother had a similar situation. Got into a right pickle with the factory floor manager. She turned out to be a real vixen. He nearly lost his job. She got a pay raise." He let out a bitter laugh.

"Thank you, Carter..."

"Sorry, Sir. Just saying one has to be careful these days how things are interpreted."

"Go on please, Mr. Beringer."

"Your Sergeant is right. Things are difficult these days. This whole #MeToo thing has got out of control. I mean a guy can't move these days without putting a foot wrong, getting falsely accused. Everything is being misinterpreted."

Good Cop and Bad Cop both stared at him now unwavering, saying nothing.

"It seems that Christine, Ms. Hayes, got the wrong idea. She started expecting special treatment, bonuses, pay increases..."

"Did you...uh...give in to these demands?" Bad Cop kept scribbling. Good Cop looked around the room as if seeing it for the first time.

"No. No. Not initially."

"But then?" said Bradski.

"I thought if I gave her a promotion and moved her out to Calgary it would be for the best."

"Did she think it was for the best?" asked Bradski.

"Not really. But she was coming around."

"Is that when you agreed to pay her the blackmail?" Bad Cop's pen never stopped moving. Good Cop gave him a bland smile.

"What the...I uh..."

"Mr. Beringer, you would be well advised to tell us the truth. Eventually we will get to the bottom of this and if you have been less than honest with us your situation will only get worse," said Bradski, finally looking up from his notebook.

"How did you...what do you know about the blackmail?" asked Blake. The color had drained from his face, but at the same time he felt something akin to relief flood through him. It seems that he wouldn't be the one to have to break the ugly truth to them.

"Mr. Beringer, it is our job to know things. We are very skilled at finding the facts. Now I suggest you tell us exactly what was going on with Ms. Hayes, from your point of view, that is," said Bradski. "Things are looking very bad for you. I suggest you start talking."

Overcome with restlessness, Blake stood up and paced behind his desk. He turned and looked out the window for a few moments. Taking a handkerchief from his pocket, he wiped his forehead. Then he turned to face them.

"Look, my wife knows what I am about to tell you, but I would prefer if this was not shared with my colleagues," said Blake.

"Your colleagues, I would venture to suggest, are already quite well aware of what goes on in this office. They won't hear anything directly from us, but we can't promise what will or won't be revealed as the legal process follows its course," said Bradski. "If you would prefer to have a lawyer present, we can do this down at the station?"

"I didn't kill her, but I think I know who did." He took a deep breath. He had to make this convincing, he was in a fight for his life.

Chapter Thirty-three

S ven had returned to the lobby bar many hours later the previous night and there had been no sign of the woman he had been following. He'd eventually packed it in and gone to bed. The next morning in the breakfast room he was feeling satisfied with the progress he had made on his article the night before and, barring a few final descriptive details of the forthcoming performance, it was almost ready. He was aiming for publication on Saturday morning, if he could sell the piece.

He had some meetings set up after breakfast to see which media outlets would be interested in the story and hoped that, given the interest in the composer of *The Anonymous Sonata*, he would get a bidding war going between the dailies. *The Globe and Mail* were especially keen, but he hoped he could persuade the *National Post* to bid as well. Maybe *Macleans* for next week's issue, or even *Vanity Fair*. This was just up their street. His excitement was mounting by the minute.

He ordered coffee and a hearty breakfast and opened his laptop to review last night's work. Aware of the restaurant gradually filling up he scanned the room as he bit into a piece of hot buttered toast. He did a double take; a few tables away from him the woman was seated with Joudry. His instinct had been right to follow her. She *was* connected with Joudry.

Just then the waitress appeared with his meal and offered to refill his coffee cup. She blocked his view of their table. He closed his computer and pushed it aside.

"No, no thank you. No more coffee," he said trying to get her out of his way.

"Do you need marmalade or jam, sir?" she asked.

"No, nothing else thank you. This is fine."

"Enjoy your meal, sir," she said flashing him a smile.

As she stepped away he took his phone from his pocket and pretended to be reading something. Keeping it low on the table he angled it toward Joudry and his female companion. He zoomed in as close as he could and quickly snapped a few photos. This was fantastic! He now had a clear shot of the man to help sell his story. He stabbed a sausage with his fork and took a few bites while with his other hand he opened the message app and sent the photo to Meredith.

"He's here!" he typed. "With the woman."

He put the phone down and slid a piece of egg onto the toast with his knife and fork. The phone vibrated next to him. He hastily shoved the food into his mouth, smearing some egg on his chin in the process. He grabbed the napkin off his lap, looked at the screen, simultaneously chewing and dabbing his chin. He felt his stomach clench.

"I know," he read. "Look at the balding man with the blue tie a few tables over to your left."

He swallowed and scanned the room. He spotted the man, who raised his eyebrows and tilted his head slightly toward Joudry and the woman.

Holy shit thought Sven. Now she's watching me watch them.

◆◆◆

The waiter poured coffee for Mungo and Alexia. Alexia ordered granola and yogurt with fruit and Mungo asked for a full English breakfast. When the waiter left he said, "So you are still eating like a ballet dancer."

"I am still a ballet dancer," she replied defensively.

"I'm sorry. That came out wrong. What I mean is, you look good, Alexia. I just hope I can sort this mess out and then maybe we can spend some more time together. If you want to, that is..."

"We will have to see. There is a lot to figure out. I am thinking of making some changes. I can't perform forever. There are fewer opportunities for older dancers. I have been thinking about opening a ballet school."

"You would be a fantastic teacher..."

"Mungo," she interrupted, "we need to talk about *your* future right now. Your situation is the critical one."

"I don't need reminding," he snapped.

"I know." She reached for his hand. "I have been given two tickets for the OSO concert next month. They are calling it *The Anonymous Sonata*. I was hoping you'd come with me?"

He pulled his hand away. "You know I have to lay low right now. I can't go."

"Mungo, it's your composition isn't it? You must've seen the media coverage. Did you know they had your music?"

"I had no idea. I obviously didn't give it to them."

"How did they get it then?" she persisted.

"God, I don't know," he said, struggling to keep the exasperation out of his voice. "I must have left it somewhere. It's a long story. I don't feel like getting into it now."

"You must be so excited though," she said.

"Look, I didn't know anything about it until I read about it in the paper the other day. And I've had other things on my mind."

"But, Mungo, you have to come forward. People need to know it's yours. Don't you see, this might be the answer. People will know that you are innocent," she pleaded.

"Yes. They'll know I'm innocent of plagiarism, but then they'll think I'm guilty of murder."

She was silent for a moment. The waitress brought the meals and refilled their coffee cups.

"Don't you want to hear your music performed?" she asked.

"What is it that you don't get, Alexia? Of course, I do. It's something I've dreamed about ever since Carnegie Hall." He paused, his eyes on her for a long moment, then he looked down and speared a piece of bacon and put it in his mouth. "You know this is not the right time. The police are looking for me. I must prove that it was Blake not me who killed that woman. Or get out of this city, forever," he said, chewing rapidly.

"I know, but that's the point, don't you see? This is exactly the right time." She lowered her voice, "There may not be another time. What if... if they arrest you, if they think you killed that woman? There may never be another chance to hear your music performed live."

Mungo slammed his knife and fork down. "Do you think they are going to nail me for this? For a murder I didn't commit, that I don't stand a chance. My God, d'you think I did it? It was bad enough you thinking I was a plagiarist, but a murderer!" He pushed his chair back.

Alexia's eyes shot around the room quickly. "Mungo, quiet!" she hissed. "Sit down. You are drawing attention." She smiled vaguely toward the room, her eyes resting momentarily on the balding man a few tables over who seemed to have noticed. She gave him a tiny sheepish shrug and looked away.

Mungo pulled his chair in slowly and leaned back, resisting the urge to look around. He picked up his coffee mug and sipped, his eyes fixed on her. "I need you on my side right now," he said.

She leaned forward. "I am on your side. Do you think I'd even be here if I thought you did it?"

He swallowed some more coffee. "Fair enough." He allowed the silence to linger between them for a moment and then, sensing her restlessness, he added, "Look, I'm sorry. All I really want is for you to believe that I'm innocent, that I didn't steal Oliver's composition. But I didn't want to prove my innocence at your expense. I kept quiet because you were with Oliver and I didn't want to ruin things for you. Then when I find out you're no longer with him, what do I do, I drag you into this other mess." He looked across the room and out of the window.

"We have both wasted so much time. Oliver and I were never right together. I wish I'd told him about us years ago. I'm just as responsible for this situation. I was stupid and young and naïve. If I'd told him the truth, there would've been nothing to hide and you wouldn't have had to take the blame." She reached out and covered his hand with hers. He looked down at their hands and then back out the window.

"I want to help you put things right. I want you to be recognized for your work." And more than anything, I want you to know your son, she thought.

"I know you're not a murderer. The only thing you're guilty of is running away and not facing things. I'll stand by you, Mungo, but you must stand up and take your place. You didn't kill that woman and we'll find a way to prove it."

He looked back at her and she sensed his resolve weakening a little. "I know it's risky, but we'll be careful. We can take our seats when the lights are dimmed. Come with me to the concert. Please come and hear your music performed."

He wanted this so badly. He imagined sitting next to Alexia, the anticipation of the audience, the controlled energy of the musicians as they tuned their instruments, the hush of the audience as the conductor stepped up to the podium, his baton poised, the first few notes soaring above the crowd… "Okay, I'll go."

◆◆◆

Sven watched Mungo and the woman leave the room. A few moments later the balding guy took some money out of his wallet, put it on the table, picked up his newspaper and left. Sven shoved his papers and laptop under his arm and followed him out. He got to the lobby just in time to see Mungo and the woman step into an elevator. There was no sign of the bald guy. He quickly crossed the lobby and stepped outside. He saw the retreating back of the guy and hurried after him.

"Hey! Hey, stop!" he shouted. The guy just walked on. Sven quickened his pace. "Excuse me," he said as he drew up alongside him. He continued to ignore Sven. Sven grabbed his arm. "I'm trying to speak to you."

The guy brushed his arm off. "Not here," he muttered and walked on.

Sven stood for a moment wondering if he should just call Meredith. He saw the guy turn the corner onto a side street. Sven followed quickly. He looked around. The guy had disappeared. Sven walked on a few more paces searching, perplexed. As he drew up alongside a dumpster he was grabbed and thrust against it, the guy's forearm across his throat.

"What kind of idiot are you? Do you want to blow my cover? And yours?"

"I don't like being watched. Did Meredith put you on to me?" said Sven trying to pull the man's arm from his neck.

"And I don't like being followed," the man replied. He dropped his arm, "You nearly blew it back there."

"What the hell!" Sven coughed and rubbed his throat. He stepped away from the man.

"I'm not paid to answer your questions. Speak to Ms. Salinger. And stay out of my way."

"I've been tailing that guy in there for weeks, without your help. I just need to know who the woman is, the one who was with him."

The man stalked off down the road.

Still shocked, Sven stared at his retreating back. He took his phone out of his pocket and dialed Meredith's number. It rang twice and went to voicemail. He tried again without success. He cursed and made his way back to the hotel.

◆◆◆

As soon as the detectives left Blake hurried out of his office down the hallway to the men's room, ignoring Diane's concerned enquiry. He relieved himself, washed his hands and seeing his sweaty face in the mirror, splashed his face with cold water. He paced the marbled floors and found himself imagining, instead of marbled opulence and soft lighting, a spartan, cold grey prison washroom, aggressive prisoners trying to provoke him. His heart raced, the sweat accumulating on his brow again. Get a grip, he told himself.

He took his phone from his pocket, quickly finding Meredith's number. The call connected.

"Asshole!" he heard, followed by loud honking. Then "Salinger here. Sorry these idiot cyclists! One just came out of nowhere and cut across me." He heard honking again.

"It's Blake Beringer. I need to see you, today." Blake was not interested in her traffic troubles.

"I'm afraid that won't be possible. I'm on my way to see a client out of town. If you would like, call the office and schedule an appointment."

"Appointment! No way! I need to see you now. This is urgent. The police have just been here."

"Well, that is to be expected under the circumstances. It still doesn't change the fact that I am on my way to another meeting," Meredith replied.

"Where've you got to with tracking our guy down? If we don't find him I'm afraid they'll charge me," said Blake still pacing.

"I am working on it. In fact, we have a number of people working on it even as we speak."

"Good. That's good. So, where is he?"

"This is not information I'm prepared to disclose on the phone. Things are at a delicate stage. We can't have anyone rushing off and spooking him into running again."

"So, you know where he is?" Blake's voice rose in excitement.

"I didn't say that."

"Look, I'm on the verge of being arrested here. I told the police about this Mungo guy, but I don't think they believed me. They've got *me* in their sights."

"Well, let's face it, they have good reason. You *were* being blackmailed by her. That's got to be one of the strongest motives for murder. Your defense is that a strange man you have never met before arrives on your boat and promises to help you deal with a blackmailer. You don't know anything about him, why would he help you? You've got to admit; your story is not very plausible."

"What, wait a minute? But you've met him. You've seen him. You know I'm telling the truth."

"Yes, I've met a man calling himself Mungo Jameson. As for your veracity, well it doesn't seem you have a very good track record. Now if you would just let me get on with my investigation…"

"Look, I'm not paying you to determine my veracity, I'm paying you to find this guy," Blake shouted.

"Well, actually, it's your wife who's paying me. When I've completed my investigation, I'll see that she gets a full report." Blake heard the line go dead. Just then Simon Parnell walked in.

"Morning Blake. Everything okay?" said Simon.

"Just fine," said Blake. "Asshole," he added under his breath as he left the washroom.

Chapter Thirty-Four

Although it was early spring, the night was chilly and the forecasters were even threatening a light snow fall later. As the taxi approached the concert hall Elizabeth saw the crowds, many of them armed with cameras and microphones. She and Rebecca stepped from the taxi both instinctively wrapping their coats around them, their stockinged legs feeling the chill wind. As soon as they stepped onto the sidewalk they were surrounded by a cluster of reporters, many shouting questions at once. "Ms. Carey, is it true that you found the sonata? Is it true that you have never met the composer? How do you think the suitcase got into your house? How long do you think it has been there? How do you feel about tonight's performance? Do you agree that this might be Joudry's work? Have you ever met him? Have you been hiding him all this time?"

Elizabeth had been warned that this might happen and had thought she was prepared, but she barely had time to compose an answer to one question before another was directed at her.

Rebecca took her by the arm and said "Ms. Carey is not in a position to speculate about the composer at this time. Please excuse us." She made her way forward and, as they jostled, the group parted to allow them through.

"Wow, fancy thinking I'd been hiding him all these years. What will they come up with next?" said Elizabeth, relieved to be out of the milieu.

They handed their coats in at the coat check. "Shall we have a glass of wine while we wait, we have twenty minutes at least before they open the doors?" said Rebecca, who was already moving to the bar counter. She ordered them each a glass of red wine. They took their glasses and stepped off to the side, surveying the growing crowd "Do you know anyone here?" said Rebecca, her eyes shining with excitement. "Oh, isn't that Simon Parnell? Remember him from high school? I'm sure that's him."

"Oh hell! I hope he hasn't seen us. He was such a know-it-all. And a bully. Don't look at him, Rebecca," Elizabeth said between clenched teeth. "I don't want him coming over here."

"I won't. Relax. But you must admit, this is rather fun," Rebecca said, "Nancy Beringer got us the best seats in the house. I feel like a celebrity and you are a guest of honor. Isn't this exciting?"

"I'm so glad to have you here. All those cameras outside, they're a bit overwhelming. You look great."

"This is fun. I hope they got my good side," she said, pretending to smile for the cameras. "Do you think they will put this on the news? I must text Ian to tell him and the boys to record it tonight in case we are on TV."

"There you are!"

Elizabeth turned to see Nancy Beringer approaching, carefully navigating the crowd with a glass of champagne in one hand and a bejeweled evening purse in the other.

"Hello Nancy. This is my sister, Rebecca."

Rebecca extended a hand and her gaze travelled from the diamond on Nancy's finger to the one nestled on her chest. She dragged her eyes upward with difficulty. "So good to finally meet you," she said, affixing a smile to her face.

"I'm so pleased you could join us," said Nancy. She turned back to Elizabeth. "There are so many people I want you to meet, and we have a few interviews lined up for after the reception later. There is so much interest. The ticket sales have beaten all expectations. We will probably add a few more concerts to the season. And all of this is due to you! The Executive Director wants to meet you and we have a spot opening up on the Board in the next few months..." she winked at Elizabeth. "I'll see you at the reception after and we can talk some more," she smiled and moved off as someone else caught her eye.

◆◆◆

Blake leaned against the wall, a drink in one hand, and watched Nancy work the crowd. She was stunning and in her element. He sipped his wine and gave his head an inward shake. What had he ever seen in those other women? The diamond pendant he had given Nancy earlier drew admiring glances to her cleavage from men and women alike. He hoped that she would see it for the peace-offering it was and that they could get on to bigger and better things. Though he had to admit, it didn't get much bigger or better than a two-carat diamond suspended on his wife's chest. He hoped she would see it that way. He had enough shit going on and right now he needed Nancy on his side, not opposing him in a divorce court.

His mind returned to the interview with the two police officers the day before. It had been grueling, and he had barely been able to think of anything else since. He swallowed the last of his wine and pushed away from the wall. He needed something stronger and headed for the bar.

He was sure those cops hadn't believed him when he told them about Mungo. They had found out about the blackmail so there was no point in trying to fudge that. They had so many questions which he couldn't answer. Who was Mungo? Where was he? How did he know him? Why would he put himself out there to help Blake? How did he know about Christine? Blake didn't have the answers, so he had to hand it to the cops, it did sound like he was making this shit up.

And that bloody Salinger woman hadn't called him back today either, despite the numerous messages he'd left her. He had wanted to tackle Nancy about his conversation with Salinger, and her insinuation that she would only share her information with Nancy. It was as if the two were in cahoots with each other against him. But given the fragile nature of things with Nancy he had decided against raising this.

A new thought occurred to him. Maybe Nancy was even trying to frame him! Had she *told* Meredith Salinger not to take his calls? How long had Nancy known about Christine? Was it possible, could she have arranged for Christine's murder? Maybe she knew about all the other women and had finally had enough. He was getting paranoid. "Whisky. Double," he said to the barman and swallowed it down before he was barely two paces away. He considered turning around and asking for another one when Nancy appeared at his side.

"I think that's enough, Blake," she said in his ear. Now she was reading his mind! "It's time to take our seats." Just then a delicate but insistent chiming started, followed by a disembodied voice saying "Ladies and gentlemen, the concert will begin in five minutes, please take your seats. Ladies and gentlemen…" He allowed Nancy to take his arm and steer him through the doors.

◆◆◆

Sven stood just inside the main entrance to the building tugging at the collar around his neck and alternately looking at his watch and scanning the street. Where was she? He checked his phone again. No text from her. He hoped he hadn't wasted his money hiring this bloody uncomfortable tuxedo. He tugged at his shirt collar again, straightened the bow tie and peered through the glass doors straining to see if she was coming. He wished now that he had bought his own ticket. If Meredith didn't show up he would miss the concert. She had texted him the day before to say that she had tickets for both of them and to meet her here tonight. She said she had news. When he had pressed her for information, all she'd said was that she would tell him in person tonight and to meet him at the front entrance. He wondered if they were still selling tickets at the box office and was about to go and find out when he felt an arm slide around his waist.

"Did you think I'd stood you up?" her eyes glittered.

"Where did you come from? I've been standing here for twenty minutes." She looked incredible in a long clingy black dress with a slit high up the leg and heels which gave her an inch or two on him, but he was in no mood to compliment her. She had probably been watching him from inside all this time, enjoying his mounting anxiety. He pulled away from her. "We'd better get in there, they are about to start."

They sat down, both scanning the audience. "Tell me if you see him. I'm sure he will be here. He won't be able to keep away," Sven said.

"I've got people in the audience. They will text me if they spot him."

"The things you can do if you have the resources. But remember, I am the one who found him. I have spent almost two years tracking this guy down, single-handedly. Nobody knew where he was, but I found him here. So, tell me, what's the news?" Sven whispered, his eyes still searching the audience.

"Not here. There are too many ears."

Sven was about to object when the lights dimmed, and a hush came over the crowd.

◆◆◆

Alexia and Mungo entered the auditorium moments after the lights dimmed and thanked the usher who handed them each a program and let them in just before closing the doors. Alexia had switched their tickets near the front for ones in the center balcony at the back. She hoped that Sebastian wouldn't notice that she was not in the prime seats near the front.

Mungo looked around, taking it all in. These were not the best seats in the house but from here they were out of sight and he could see the whole auditorium. Every seat was filled. He felt like some sort of emperor surveying his kingdom. And really this was his true domain. This was where he belonged, but not in the back row, he should be up there on the conductor's podium.

The concertmaster walked on stage and took a bow. Applause filled the auditorium. He turned to the orchestra and the oboe sounded an A. As the musicians tuned their instruments Mungo felt excitement well up in his chest and he was overcome with pride. This was his work and even if Alexia was the only one who knew, right now that felt like enough.

The crowd erupted in applause again as Alfonso Ghiradelli walked onto the stage followed by the soloists. He stood for a moment, smiling and nodding, enjoying the adulation. Then he shook hands with the concertmaster and turned to acknowledge the soloists. He stepped onto the podium and the applause found new energy.

He made a slight bow and turned to face the orchestra, his baton poised. For a moment there was complete silence, all eyes on Ghiradelli and then, with the first slice of his baton the air was filled with the sound of thirty violins. The cellos joined in, followed by the clarinets. Mungo knew every note and felt each one pulsing though his veins. This was a journey he knew so well, but this was the first time it was being shared by so many, fulfilling its ultimate purpose. He took a deep breath. He wouldn't have missed this for the world. He took Alexia's hand and gave it a squeeze.

"Thank you," he mouthed, and he felt her squeeze his in reply.

Time stood still, and Mungo was lost in the music as it ebbed and flowed carrying him with it, his eyes moving from Alfonso's shiny black head and precise white baton to each section of the orchestra. It was as if he were conducting them himself, willing each perfect note from each instrument. It was only with the first deep and earthy G of the violin solo that Mungo remembered the program in his lap and he picked it up to see who they had chosen for this solo.

In the dim light he quietly flipped the pages until he came to the biographies. Sebastian Bantry, he read. *Sebastian Bantry? Bantry!* He studied the photograph. He knew this face. He looked up again and stared at the soloist, but he was too far away to see him properly. His eyes back on the program, he skimmed the biography quickly, the words jumping off the page at him. *"Sebastian Bantry, son of musician and composer Oliver Bantry, best known for The Phantom and the Fraud..."* Suddenly all he could hear was the blood thrumming in his ears almost drowning out the music.

He turned to see Alexia watching him, her eyes intense but unreadable.

He leaned in, "Your son?" he whispered, his eyes millimeters from hers, his breath hot on her cheek.

She nodded and said, "Ours. He is our son."

He cocked his head, his brow furrowed, his eyes sharp and quizzical staring at her.

"He is *your* son," she whispered insistently as the music and Mungo's heart rate reached a shared crescendo.

He couldn't believe what he was hearing. He looked at the stage and back at Alexia. He must have heard wrong, the music, the emotion, the stress of the past few days it was all getting to him. He was suddenly claustrophobic; this suit, the crowds, jammed in this seat between all these people, the music... he had to get out of there, he needed some air.

He pushed himself out of the chair.

She pulled on his arm. "Mungo, sit, quiet, people will see you!" she whispered loudly, "You are making a scene. Sit down."

He looked down at her, her eyes imploring him. He sat trying to steady his breathing. He listened to the strains of the violin as it carried across the heads of over 2,000 people. His music being played by his own son, was it even possible? The music washed over him, achingly beautiful, every note reverberating with emotion, one note merging into the next, until the movement ended.

The crowd broke with tradition and into loud applause and when it subsided a voice announced, "Ladies and Gentlemen, this is an unusual sonata and a long one. For that reason there will be a short intermission before we start the third movement. Please return to your seats in twenty minutes." Mungo and Alexia remained seated as most people rose and slowly moved through the aisles to the doors, to find a washroom or refreshment.

Eventually Mungo turned to Alexia and said. "So?" not trusting himself to say anything else.

"Mungo, I tried to tell you. That's why I came back. I wanted to tell you. But then, when we met again… well, you had bigger problems. It didn't seem right to tell you then."

"And it's only taken you, oh, let me see, eighteen years?" he said, struggling to keep the anger and regret from his voice.

"That's not fair, Mungo, and you know it. You disappeared. What was I supposed to do?"

"When did you know he was mine? You could have told me before I left, before everything happened," he said, staring straight ahead.

"I didn't know. Not for sure. I mean, he could have been Oliver's. I was hardly going to say to Oliver, 'Oh, by the way, I'm pregnant, but it might be Mungo's.'" She paused. When he said nothing she went on, "As he grew up, Sebastian looked more and more like you. And his talent, I mean, you just heard him. He's way more talented than Oliver ever was. He looks like you and he plays like you. I think Oliver suspected when Sebastian became a teenager. We both did. Every time I looked at him, I saw you. And so did Oliver."

"Oh God…" said Mungo, finally, with his elbows on his knees he rested his head in his hands.

"Oliver never said anything to me, but he could barely tolerate Sebastian. Sebastian tried so hard to please him, but nothing was going to win him over. Eventually Sebastian gave up trying."

Mungo sat up, "Alexia, I am so sorry. God, what a fuck up. If I could only do it over again."

"We all made mistakes. I see that now. After we met on the boat I had a lot to think about. At first I never wanted to see you again." She looked at him, "You have to admit, you were a little crazy…"

"What changed your mind?" he asked.

"Seeing you again after so many years stirred up all sorts of things for me. For the most part I had moved on with my life. Moved on from Oliver. I never expected to see you again. No-one knew if you were alive or dead. Sebastian only ever knew Oliver, I mean, as far as he was concerned Oliver was his father. But in recent years their relationship had completely broken down." She looked away from him, her eyes tearing.

Mungo reached out and touched her, gently massaging the back of her neck. "I'm so sorry," he said. "I was so fucking caught up in my own disappointment. The longer I was away, the harder it became to go back. I always imagined you so happy with him. After what we had shared and after what he did to me, I knew I couldn't face him again without ripping your life apart. I didn't want to do that to you."

"When I thought about what you told me on the boat, that the music was yours, I realized how jealous Oliver had always been of you. You were the real musical talent. He stole that from you. And in a way I allowed him to steal me and Sebastian from you. Once I knew where you were and that you were still alive, I had to give us all another chance. That's why I was so desperate for you to come to the concert tonight," she said. "I just wanted you to hear your music performed and to hear your son play it before, before…"

Mungo articulated her unsaid words, "Before I'm arrested for murder, you mean." His voice was rough.

"Mungo, I told Sebastian. I told him that you are his father. I needed to tell him first."

"I want to meet him," Mungo said.

"Of course you must. I will speak to him and we can set something up for…"

"No. Tonight. I want to see him tonight," said Mungo.

"There are too many people here. This is too public, it's risky," she protested.

"Tonight Alexia. I might not have another chance."

Her protest was cut off with the chimes followed by "Ladies and Gentlemen, the performance is about to resume, please take your seats…"

Chapter Thirty-Five

"Are you sure you want to do this?" Alexia leaned towards Mungo as they moved with the crowds out of the auditorium.

"I'm more sure of this than anything," he replied.

By the time they got into the reception it was filling up and people jostled behind them to get in. They moved out of the main thoroughfare toward the back wall. "Wait here, I'll get us a drink. I need one," said Mungo.

"No, it's better if I go. Stay here at the back," said Alexia. "And I'll see if I can find Sebastian."

Mungo watched Alexia weave her way through the well-heeled crowd, his eyes instinctively scanning the room for anyone who appeared to be paying him too much attention. Now he was searching also for the young man who he had just learned was his son. What do you say? Mungo wondered. Should he shake his hand, give him a hug, apologize for having been absent his whole life and congratulate him on his performance? Nothing had prepared him for this moment. He still couldn't believe it was true. But this was not something Alexia would lie about so it must be true. He studied at the program again, as if for confirmation, still open on the page with Sebastian's photo. The strong resemblance in the photo to himself as a young man was unmistakable. And wow, could he play! He was filled with pride remembering the beautiful music which came from Sebastian's violin. He had a son. His son was a talented musician. His world had expanded in an instant and assumed a meaning it had never held before.

He'd arrived feeling overwhelmed and excited that he was going to hear one of his compositions performed for the first time since Carnegie Hall and now he'd discovered he had a son. It felt almost as if he was being re-born, getting a second chance to be a musician and a father.

He felt at once elated and sad. He had missed out on so much. He thought of all the years which had passed; he had a son who had grown up into a young man and a talented musician and all the while Mungo had been hiding from the world. He hated himself for his cowardice, he hated Oliver for what he had stolen from him, his credibility, his career, the woman he loved and a son. He had a son, a son... he had a family. His mind raced. He imagined a home, family meals, birthday celebrations, Alexia and Sebastian by his side. He had lost so much and suddenly gained everything. It was still possible...

Alexia appeared at his side, slightly breathless, and handed him a glass of wine. "The orchestra hasn't come in yet. There will probably be some speeches. They have a podium set up at the front and I see a few media here too with cameras and badges." She took a quick sip of wine, looking at him over her glass. "What did you think, Mungo? Wasn't it fantastic?"

"The best night of my life. Things have changed so much since I saw you at the market. I have a son..." he shook his head, took a sip. "What do you think he will say? I mean, what should I say when I meet him? What should I do? What is he like? Do you think he will like me?"

"Slow down Mungo. It'll be fine. We'll handle it. You have a lot of ground to cover and you can't do it all tonight."

"Wait, does he even know I'm here?" he asked.

"No, I didn't tell him. He just knows I'm bringing a guest."

"I can't screw this up Alexia. You know what they say about first impressions. This is the most important meeting of my life. Maybe this is not the right time..." Then he thought about Blake, Christine and the police. This might be the *only* time. Suddenly that earlier vision of a family and normal home life dissolved. He felt desperate. He looked at Alexia, his eyes pleading.

She put her hand on his arm, "I know, when he comes in I can have a word with him and we can slip away, find somewhere quiet to have a talk, maybe get something to eat."

"Mungo, don't look now, but you see that guy over there, the blonde guy? His hair sort of sticks up in shaggy points."

Mungo nodded. "What about him?"

"I think he tried to pick me up," she laughed. "He was next to me when I fetched our drinks from the bar. He started talking to me while I was waiting, asked me if I was here with someone. He sounded kind of sexy, Scandinavian."

"I hope you told him you were taken," Mungo said, jealousy joining all the other emotions swirling around inside him.

"Am I?" she said.

Mungo slid his arm around her waist and pulled her toward him. He kissed her softly at first, then his tongue found hers, soft and slippery and so sweet. He had waited so long to do this. Now, with his world both expanding and about to collapse he seized the moment greedily. "There," he said, "now he knows who you're with." He looked at her, conviction growing *I cannot lose you again.*

◆◆◆

Blake had his eye on the slim waitress weaving between the guests effortlessly balancing a tray of champagne-filled glasses. Her hair was almost pitch black, sleek and glossy, straight-cut across her back and it swayed as she moved. He imagined running his hands through it. As she passed by him he reached out and lifted a glass from the tray. "I'll have one of those," he said, his eyes fixed on her chest.

As she moved on he heard a voice in his ear, "You like that one too, do you?" He turned to see Simon-Bloody-Parnell, a lizard-like smile across his face. Simon's wife was a few feet away, laughing with a group of well-dressed urbanites.

Blake' eyes were ice-cold, "Simon. What brings you here?"

"Well," Simon drawled, "this is *the* social event of the season, old chap. Nancy's done a great job for the OSO. You must be very proud. Congratulate her for me, will you." He gave Blake a patronizing pat on the back and turned back to his wife's group.

Blake threw back the last of the champagne in his glass and stalked through the horde to the bar at the back of the room. Fuck the champagne. He needed that whisky.

"Scotch, double," he said to the bartender, "and make it the Macallan 18. Put it on Nancy Beringer's tab. I'm her husband." The OSO could pay for his bloody drink. He watched the bartender pour out the double measure. The thought of standing around and listening to the self-aggrandizing speeches which were sure to follow nauseated him. He stood with one elbow on the bar counter sipping his whisky and surveyed the room. There was literally nobody here he felt like speaking to and he certainly didn't want to have to make conversation with the likes of Simon Parnell. He realized he was sick to death of the self-satisfied stuffed shirts who populated board rooms, concert halls and country clubs. They were locked in a never-ending game of parading their good-fortune while simultaneously resenting others for theirs. He was toying with the idea of leaving and spending the rest of the evening on the boat when his eyes settled on a couple standing against the back wall. "What the... Well, I'll be ... it's fucking Mungo!"

"Excuse me, sir. What was that? Can I get you anything else?" said the bartender, wiping the counter with a damp rag.

"No thanks. The evening is about to get a lot more interesting," said Blake, pushing away from the counter and taking his cellphone from his pocket. He searched his contacts, found the number and hit dial. "Yes, is this Detective Inspector Bradski?"

◆◆◆

Just then there was some activity at the front of the room and Nancy stepped up to the podium. The background music, which had barely been audible above the bonhomie of the excited crowd, went quiet and Nancy said, "Ladies and gentlemen, music lovers, friends and sponsors of the OSO, my name is Nancy Beringer. I am proud to be a director of this wonderful musical institution and I am pleased to welcome you all here this evening. Wasn't that a most magnificent concert, made even more so by the unique quality of the music and mystery surrounding its composer. Please raise your glasses in a toast to congratulate our orchestra and our maestro, the great Alfonso Ghirardelli." Nancy waved her glass to the side of the room where a group from the orchestra had assembled. The room buzzed with cheers and clinking glasses. There were nods of acknowledgement and bows. Alfonso Ghirardelli stepped forward beaming and bowed with a flourish.

"Thank you, thank you ladies and gentlemen. And thank you all for being here and supporting your orchestra," Nancy continued. "I think you will all agree from the wonderful turn-out this evening that the arts are alive and well in Toronto. We sold out our tickets for this evening within days. Based on the strong response, we have adjusted our schedule for this season and will be adding three more performances of *The Anonymous Sonata*. Please be sure to tell your friends and family. Ticket sales for the additional dates will open on Monday." Nancy paused for further cheers and applause. "Before I hand you over to our maestro who would like to say a few words about the music itself, I am pleased to introduce to you the person who, aside from the mysterious composer, deserves special thanks for bringing this music to us. An avid amateur musician and Toronto-lawyer, ladies and gentlemen please welcome Elizabeth Carey."

As Elizabeth stepped onto the podium to further murmurs and applause Mungo felt his stomach lurch. He took a deep sip of wine and almost choked. He suppressed a cough. A few heads turned in his direction. "Are you okay?" whispered Alexia, "do you want to leave?"

He shook his head, no. He was red in the face and handed Alexia his glass as he pulled a handkerchief from his pocket and wiped his mouth, partially obscuring his face from the few quizzical and some irritated glances around him.

"… a chance discovery as I was clearing my basement one day this past winter," Elizabeth was saying. "You hear from time to time about people who discover old paintings in their basements or valuable antiques in a dusty attic, but these stories have the quality of a fairy tale, so unlikely are they to happen. Well, every now and then, apparently fairy tales come true."

"Over the next couple of weeks, I played the sonata on my piano at home. I became quite captivated and convinced that it should be played by a professional orchestra and heard by many." She smiled and turned slightly toward Nancy, "So, I brought it to Nancy," she paused for some brief applause. "Now you too have shared in my enjoyment of this unusual and unexpected sonata. We have tried to find out the identity of the composer and how it ended up in my basement. While the OSO has a sense of who composed this piece, we may never find out how it came to be in an old suitcase in my home. An angel, a phantom, an uninvited guest, who knows. All that remains, I guess, is to say thank you to whomever left it there." Once again, the guests clapped and cheered.

Alexia leaned forward and whispered in Mungo's ear. "You haven't told me about this. Did you put the suitcase there? Do you know her?" She was studying him closely. He wished she wouldn't. The room felt very close. He pulled the collar around his neck. Stupid uncomfortable garment. "Mungo?"

"It's a long story. Not now," he whispered back.

Elizabeth moved back, and Nancy stepped toward the microphone. She waited for the applause to subside. "Thank you, Elizabeth. I can see we have a lot of interest in the room, perhaps Elizabeth will agree to stay on for a while and take questions afterwards, but for now, ladies and gentlemen, I will hand the floor to our maestro, Alfonso Ghirardelli."

Alfonso stepped up to loud applause and stood for a moment basking in the adulation. "I have conducted for audiences in Vienna, Berlin, London, New York, Chicago and Sao Paulo and I can honestly say that never before has a concert generated this degree of intrigue. I would like to say that it is because of my special ability to interpret the music, to bring the multiple strands and sounds of an orchestra together, to lead and inspire and to get into the head of the composer, but in this instance I have to concede that this evening the interest resides with the composer rather than the conductor," he affected a self-deprecating bow and continued. "This getting into the head of another musician has been harder because his identity is unknown. However, having spent every waking hour over the last six weeks immersed in this music, I think I can shed some light on the kind of person who could write music like this." He paused for effect and the room was silent, waiting for his next words.

"The composer of this music is passionate about sound, a highly creative and eccentric individual, one who is not capable of following the crowd or a trend, a person of great sensitivity, even fragility, a person given to the unexpected and unpredictable, one who does not follow the rules. Even in the creative and volatile world of the arts, where we expect and respect deviance, it is my belief that the creator of this music is spectacularly unorthodox," again he paused and surveyed the rapt audience. Camera flashes went off and he looked directly into a photographer's lens, giving her a moment to take the perfect picture. "Yet it takes true musical genius to create such harmony out of discordance, such peace from music so powerful and it takes a deep understanding of the rules in order to break them and remake them into something so beautiful and unique," Alfonso paused again allowing his words their full impact. The room remained silent, all eyes on him. "Ladies and gentlemen, fellow music lovers, while I am not one hundred percent certain, and there has been much speculation in recent weeks about this sonata, but I believe I know who composed *The Anonymous Sonata*."

Mungo was leaning against the wall. The room swam in and out of focus, Alfonso's words seeming to come at him from a great distance.

"We can leave? Do you want to get out of here?" Alexia whispered.

"No. It's fine. I'm done running," he said.

Alexia held his hand. "Good."

"In the same way that we can distinguish an artist's work through brush technique and texture, choice of color and subject, rhythm and pattern, the emotional quality of the artwork, so too we can identify a composer by the notes, rhythm and emotional color of the music. It is my belief, ladies and gentlemen, that the person who gave us *The Phantom and the Fraud* is also the composer of this remarkable *Anonymous Sonata*."

The energy in the room was palpable; the audience both desperate to react and to remain silent so they could hear what else Alfonso had to say. "And no, I do not believe that *The Phantom and the Fraud* is the work of Oliver Bantry, who has produced *nothing* since he claimed to have composed that masterpiece," Alfonso's voice rose with indignation "but rather the much maligned and missing Mungo Joudry. It is clear now, ladies and gentlemen, that Mungo Joudry is alive and well, still working and still missing." The room erupted into loud conversation, cheers and clapping. Blake moved quickly though the crowd to Nancy, took her by the arm and whispered insistently.

Alexia said to Mungo, "I think perhaps... let's just step out for a bit, get some air."

As they were about to move Sebastian approached them, "Mom, Mom. Isn't this crazy! I've been looking for you."

"Sebastian. Congratulations darling. You were wonderful! I am so proud of you." She gave him a hug. "There is someone else here who is proud of you," she said, tentative now, turning toward Mungo. "This is, this is Mungo Joudry, your..."

"I know ... my father." Without taking his eyes off Mungo he said to his mother, "You didn't tell me he would be here. This is surreal." Time stood still for all three of them and the rest of the room faded into the background. Finally, he extended his hand. "Very pleased to meet you, an honor."

Mungo looked into his face, a face so familiar, yet new. "The honor is mine," he said and took his hand. "You have a remarkable talent. Here," he said, shrugging awkwardly, and opened his arms. Sebastian hesitated just a moment and then stepped forward into Mungo's embrace.

"Oh my God, my son. I never knew," Mungo said into Sebastian's ear. "Your mother told me during the concert. I never knew. I am so sorry and so happy. There is so much to explain. You must be angry with me." He became conscious that he was shaking and let Sebastian go. He looked at Alexia and saw silent tears making their way down her cheeks.

Sebastian stepped back and turned toward his mother. His eyes, like hers, were wet. "We were thinking," she said, "I mean, how would you like to go somewhere quiet for a meal, where we can talk?"

"Yes, yes great," he seemed relieved. "I'll just get my things..."

He was interrupted by the sound of a man's voice. They all turned. Blake had stepped up to the podium. "Excuse me for interrupting, ladies and gentlemen..."

"Oh God," said Mungo. "Let's get out of here. I've had enough. I want to talk to Sebastian." Mungo took Alexia's hand and they started to move toward the doors.

"If I could have your attention for a moment, please," Blake said. The room quietened. "My name is Blake Beringer, I am the husband of Nancy, and she has kindly allowed me to make this announcement. I have reason to believe that the man of the hour, Mungo Joudry, is in fact among us this evening." There was a collective gasp. "He has been unobtrusive, but he is here! If you would all turn to the back of the room, toward the left corner, he is in the company of our violin soloist," Blake said with great satisfaction.

"Leaving so soon, Mungo!" Blake's voice boomed over the sound system, he took a swig from the whisky glass in his hand. "I don't think so, why don't you come up and say a few words for your audience? There is much you have to answer for. If you manage to get a good look at him, ladies and gentlemen, you might see that he bears an uncanny resemblance to the man who is being sought for questioning in connection with the recent murder of Christine Hayes!"

The room erupted with hundreds of voices speaking at once. Concert-goers were jostling for a better view of the back corner while simultaneously trying to keep an eye on the unfolding drama up front. "You might even have got away with it, except you couldn't keep away, could you. Well let's see how far you get this time, hah!"

Nancy stepped up. "That's enough Blake!" She pulled him away from the microphone, but her voice could still be heard over the general hubbub. "You are disgracing yourself and embarrassing me."

Blake yanked his arm from her grasp and stumbled off the platform. "Oh, fuck off, Nancy."

Simon Parnell appeared next to Nancy. "Here, let me help you, Nancy," and he steered Blake away from the podium.

"You have had too much to drink again, Blake. You don't do yourself any favors," Simon said.

"Leave me alone, you pernicious prick," spat Blake. "I want to see that guy get his comeuppance. You have no idea what he has done to me."

"You are the author of your own misfortunes, Blake."

"Oh God, now you sound like my wife. I want another drink."

"Your wife is a fine woman," said Simon.

259

Meanwhile Mungo, Alexia and Sebastian were trying to get to the exit. Their way was barred by a solid crowd that had formed around them. Cameras were flashing and reporters were shouting questions, several reception guests were taking photos with their phones. "Is it true that you are Mungo Joudry? Did you murder that woman? Why did you do it? Where is Oliver Bantry? Did you compose *The Anonymous Sonata*? Where have you been hiding out?"

"Mom, Mungo…? What's this about a murder? What the hell is going on?" Sebastian was trying to elbow their way through the crowd.

"It's nothing, I can explain. Let's just get out of here," Mungo said.

"What do you mean nothing?" Sebastian said.

"Not now, Sebastian." Alexia admonished. They were through the auditorium doors and into the lobby.

"I find out my father is not my father, that my real father composed the most significant piece of music to come out in the last twenty years, and when I get to meet him I find out he is accused of murder! Talk about 'spectacularly unorthodox'. Ghirardelli had that right!" Sebastian exploded.

"Are you the son of Mungo Joudry?" a blonde reporter with a Scandinavian accent called out. "Sebastian Bantry, Sebastian, could you give us a comment for the record please?" He shoved a card in Sebastian's pocket. "Call me, we can talk later. I can tell you what's going on. I know where your father has been."

"Who are you?" Sebastian shot out.

"Check your pocket. Call me." He held his hand to his ear, simulating a phone call. He was maneuvered out of the way.

"We have nothing to say. No comment," said Alexia.

"Step aside please, step aside. Police. Step aside. Police." They were almost relieved to see the uniformed officers who parted the crowd like Moses parting the Red Sea. They moved forward toward the main exit, but they were stopped by a tall man who held up his hand and showed them a card. "Detective Inspector Bradski, with the Toronto Metropolitan Police. Well now, Mr. Joudry, we've been looking for you. It seems that people have been looking for you for quite some time. I'd like you to come with us please? We need you to help us with an investigation into the murder of Christine Hayes."

"Are you arresting Mungo Joudry for murder?" a reporter shouted as Mungo, Alexia and Sebastian were shuffled out of the door, surrounded by uniformed officers.

Chapter Thirty-Six

As they were hustled into the lobby, the uniformed officers kept the persistent onlookers, mostly reporters, back.

Bradski turned to them, "So, Mr. Joudry, we need you to answer some questions relating to the Christine Hayes investigation. Clearly this is not the right place. We need you to come down to the station where we can do this in private."

"Mom! Wait, what the hell is going on here?" Sebastian said looking from his mother to Bradski and then Mungo.

"This is a police matter, please step back," replied Bradski, "this doesn't concern you. Who are you?" A uniformed officer stepped forward to move Sebastian back.

"He's, he's my son. But he knows nothing about this. Leave him out of it," said Mungo.

"Right, well, get his details in case we need him later," Bradski said to the officer.

"But, where are you taking him?" Alexia said.

"To the SCI Unit. Just for questioning at this stage. Here's my card." Bradski handed Alexia his card, took Mungo by the upper arm and walked him to the door.

"Mungo, call me," Alexia shouted to their retreating backs. "I'll get help."

"Mom what's going on? What's this about a murder? Why do they need to speak to Mungo?"

"Okay folks, show's over," a large policeman boomed trying to disperse the curious crowd. "Move on please, move on."

"We can't talk here. Let's go to my hotel. Get your things and I'll meet you outside once I've got my coat."

"This is fucking weird!" Sebastian said.

Alexia joined the queue which had formed at the coat check fighting the temptation to forgo her coat and just head for the exit. She looked at her watch, almost eleven. She wondered what the SCI unit was and how long they would keep him. She looked at the card; Specialized Criminal Investigations. Oh God, it sounded so serious. She would call her lawyer in New York in the morning and ask if he could recommend someone for Mungo. She just wished the whole nightmare was over. How could she help him prove his innocence? She felt a gentle nudge on her arm.

"Excuse me. I think I can help you,"

"No, it's fine, I can wait…" she turned to see the spiky haired Scandinavian at her side. "Oh, it's you. You were at the bar. You're one of those reporters. I have no comment."

"I'm not looking for a comment. I'm an investigator. Well, an investigative reporter. I've been following your friend, Mr. Joudry, for a while. I really think I could help you and maybe you can help me."

"What do you mean? Who are you?" Alexia felt her indignation and distrust rising like bile in her throat.

"Look, I am doing a story. I've been working on this for months. It will be published regardless. I have been researching Joudry for a long time and I can fill you in. But in return, I would like to speak to you and your son. We can't talk here." He pressed a card into her hand. "Call me. I can help you." He turned away with a final insistent nod and she watched him walk across the lobby to an attractive woman with long chestnut hair. They spoke quickly, she nodded, and Alexia watched as she took her phone from her purse and made a call. They moved off.

Alexia finally pulled on her coat and headed for the exit. She spotted Sebastian some distance along the sidewalk, violin case in hand and hunched into his coat. She looked around and was relieved that the reporter hadn't hung around. She had his card if she wanted to talk. She caught up with Sebastian.

He said, "I've called an Uber. There he is," he pointed. They climbed into the car and it drove off.

◆◆◆

"That is some story," said Detective Bradksi. "I've heard some pretty inventive ones over the years, but this one takes the prize. What do you say Sergeant Carter?"

"Certainly entertaining, sir. Almost worth leaving the comfortable home hearth and Netflix on a cold night for this one," Sam Carter smiled enthusiastically.

They were sitting opposite Mungo at a table in a sparse but functional interview room. Mungo was cold. His coat was probably the only one left at the coat check, he thought bitterly. He rubbed his hands vigorously up and down his thighs to generate some warmth and to try and calm their shaking which was probably as much from cold as from anxiety.

Sergeant Carter slurped loudly from a mug of coffee. "More coffee?" he smiled at Mungo pointing to his mug. Bradski was flipping back and forth through a notebook, a quizzical frown on his face.

"No thank you," said Mungo. Even though it would warm him up, he was awash with coffee, having already consumed three large ones since he'd been there. They'd been over and over his story the whole night. He was exhausted but wired. He assumed they were too.

"So," drawled Bradski, his eyes still on his notebook, "it looks like we've got you for "trespass, breaking and entering, murder, illegal entry into the country…oh, and it seems way back when you were wanted for plagiarism." Bradski looked at him now, his face suffused with satisfaction.

Mungo sat back with a deep sigh and ran his fingers through his hair, even more unruly now than usual. He thought of Alexia and Sebastian and the family life which he had never achieved. If he could get out of this, he might yet have a chance at something resembling normality, get to know his son, maybe Alexia would give them a chance…he had to convince them he was innocent. "Look, you've got what you want. I have cooperated fully and answered all your questions over and over to the best of my ability. Now it's your job to either charge me and make a case against me or release me. I'm telling you that I did not kill that woman. When I found her, she was already dead. As for the trespassing, I'm not sure of the law, but you don't have any proof other than what I have told you and no-one has lodged a complaint. If necessary, I will recant that statement. As for the plagiarism, if you speak to any serious musicologist they will tell you that I composed both the *The Phantom and The Fraud*, as well as *The Anonymous Sonata*. I'd give my right arm to see Oliver Bantry perform a composition like that, let alone compose it. In fact, give me a few weeks and I will compose something else, especially for you, and then we will see how far you get with your plagiarism allegation. As for the illegal entry into Canada, well I'll take my chances with that one. The worst they can do is deport me, which frankly, is just fine with me. Now, either charge me or let me call a lawyer. I'm not saying anything more." He pushed his chair back and stood up as if to underline the end of their conversation and hoped that he appeared more confident than he felt.

Just then, there was a knock at the door. Carter stepped outside for a moment and stuck his head back in. "Sir," he beckoned.

Bradksi stepped into the corridor and closed the door behind him. "Apparently there's someone downstairs who says they have important information relating to the Hayes murder," said Carter.

◆◆◆

Nancy was standing staring vacantly out of the kitchen window, across the deck and into the garden, waiting for the coffee pot. She was in her dressing gown and slippers, her arms wrapped around her, tired and bleary-eyed. The sky was a pale wash of Payne's Grey and she was looking forward to the warmth and color of spring.

She had slept badly, her mind a confused myriad of dreams merging with snatches of waking thoughts about the night before. Blake had lain next to her fast asleep and snoring loudly, his brain no doubt soaked with all the alcohol he had consumed. She had no idea how his body managed to sustain it. One of these days it would catch up with him. Her thoughts came to a jarring halt as Sven appeared on her deck. For a moment she thought she was seeing an exhaustion-induced hallucination, but then he tapped on the window.

She opened the door. "What are you doing here?" she protested.

"I know it's early, I'm sorry. I need to talk to you. I need to tell you something before you see it in the papers."

"What are you talking about?" She clutched the collar of her robe drawing the sides together.

"I need to tell you something. Please, can I come in? It's important."

She opened the door wider and stepped aside to let him pass.

"Blake is upstairs. He's still sleeping. He'll probably sleep for hours. He had too much to drink again last night. Do you want coffee?"

Sven nodded. "Thank you."

"Sit down." She poured two mugs of coffee and set the cream and sugar on the table. She sat down opposite him.

They doctored their coffees. She took a sip and circled her hands around the mug. "So, what is so important that you had to come and see me at seven thirty on a Saturday morning?"

"It's about last night."

"Last night. I'm still trying to process it all… wait, how… were you there?"

"Yes. I saw the whole thing. The music was fantastic by the way. Hopefully it won't be overshadowed by everything else that followed."

"I know. But we have more concerts scheduled and I'm sure we will sell them out after this. We may even have to add some more. But I'm guessing you didn't come here to discuss music at this hour?" said Nancy. "Perhaps you just wanted to see me at my early morning best?" her hand went instinctively to her hair.

"Nancy, you forget that I have painted you. I have seen you like few others have. And I'm not looking too good myself." His hand brushed his stubble. "I haven't slept, to be honest. I was working."

"The muse had you in her grasp? What are you painting?"

"Well, actually, I wasn't painting. You remember I told you I'm a freelance writer."

"But you're also an artist."

Sven put his mug down. "I am an artist, it's just that's not how I earn my living. I sell stories. I invest a lot of time into researching the stories that most full-timers can't do because they have short-deadlines, or they can't interest their editors in them. I cover my own costs and then charge a lot for each big exposé. And the thing is... I've been working on a story about Mungo Joudry."

"What?"

"I've been searching for him for a couple of years and tracked him to Toronto. That's why I came here. I found out where he used to hang out and started following him. At first I thought he lived here." When Nancy didn't respond, he went on, "When I say here, I mean, *here*, in this house." Sven swept his arm around the kitchen.

"What are you talking about? Why would you think he lived here?" Nancy's voice rose.

"Then I realized that he sort of did and didn't."

"I don't understand."

"I watched him come and go from your house regularly. He arrived in the morning, let himself in through this door." He tilted his head toward the kitchen door.

"Are you serious? How?"

"He has his own key. He'd spend a few hours here and then leave again about mid-afternoon. At first I thought he lived here and was just working shifts or something."

"Oh my God...!"

"Then I did a bit more research and found out about you and Blake. That you had no children and there was no-one else registered at this address."

"Wait a minute... you knew me, I mean about me, before we met at the art school?" She stood up quickly, folded her arms, glaring.

"Yes, that's partly why I wanted to come here and speak to you. I kind of followed you too."

"You what?"

"I joined the art school to get to know you. I wanted to understand what your connection was to Joudry. I thought that, well, with your ties to the music community, that maybe you were hiding him."

"What?" Nancy exploded. "Why didn't you just ask me?"

"I'm sorry Nancy, I know how this looks."

"How this looks! How it looks! You mean how it is! You snake. You befriended me, I allowed you into my home and you painted me nude. I trusted you. I liked you. I slept with you, for God's sake! All this just so you could research your, your article! Get out! Get out now."

Suddenly Blake appeared in the doorway, naked but for a pair of boxer shorts. "What's going on? Who is this?"

They turned to see him, rubbing bloodshot eyes, his hair mussed.

"Oh Blake, go back to bed. Or at least put some clothes on."

"I heard you shouting. Are you alright?" He moved toward Sven. "What's going on here? Who is this?"

Sven shot a cautious glance at Nancy. When she said nothing he stood up and held out his hand. "I'm Sven Svenson. I'm an investigative reporter, I wanted to talk to Nancy about…"

"Sven," said Blake sharply. He turned to Nancy "This is *your* Sven?" To Sven he said, "Get the hell out of my house!"

"Blake, calm down," said Nancy, but she was relieved to feel her rage shift now that Blake had taken it on.

"Don't you tell me to calm down!"

Nancy sat down and pulled out a chair for Blake. "He's got some information about Mungo Joudry. He says Joudry's been living in our house."

Sven looked from one to the other and back again and then at the door. Right now he would have liked nothing more than to 'get the hell out' of there.

Blake went to the counter and poured himself a coffee, then he sat down.

"Would you two like to tell me exactly what the fuck is going on in my house?" snarled Blake.

"Actually, not only your house. I've seen him on your boat too," said Sven.

"Fuck me!" said Blake.

"This is starting to make sense, right, Blake? You met him on the boat. When he said he'd help you with Christine," said Nancy.

"Do you mean Christine Hayes?" Sven sat down, reached into his pocket and pulled out a notebook and pen. "Do you mind if I…?"

"Put the fucking notebook away," Blake said between gritted teeth. "If I see one word of this in print, I swear Christine Hayes won't be the only one with a problem."

"Okay, okay." Sven closed the notebook. "The thing is, part of the reason I'm here is because the story will be on the front page of *The National Post* today."

"What story?" Nancy had gone white. "We'll sue you for defamation! Blake did not murder that woman. Joudry did. If you were there last night you'd have seen him go off with the police."

"No, no. I didn't connect Blake with the murder. At least not in today's article. The next one will go into more detail about the murder. I'm working with an investigator; she's one of the best in the city. Today's story deals more with the fact that he has been, shall we say, residing in your home. But, it might come across that you two have been hiding him."

"Hiding him! You make it sound like we're harboring a felon!" Nancy screamed.

"Well, it might turn out that he is one," said Sven, nodding.

"Oh my God, could this get any worse." Nancy rolled her eyes heavenward. "Wait a minute - you said female investigator." She shot a look at Blake. "That wouldn't by any chance be Meredith Salinger?"

"How do you know?" asked Sven, watching them both closely.

"If I find that she leaked this to you, I'll sue you both out of business," said Blake, his finger inches from Sven's face. "You certainly know how to pick your boyfriends, Nancy," he spat. He stood and went to the counter for more coffee. He reached into a corner cabinet for a bottle of whisky and added a liberal splash to his mug.

"Oh, don't even start, Blake. What about your girlfriends? Blackmail, murder. You, in fact, are the one who got us into all this. And don't you think you had enough to drink last night?"

"Now don't *you* start, Nancy."

Nancy turned back to Sven, ignoring Blake, "We had no idea that he was staying in our house," Nancy protested. "How could he? Why would he?"

"That I don't know," said Sven. "I was hoping you could tell me." He reached into his pocket for his notebook again and stopped when he saw Nancy's glare.

"I've got dates, times, photos of him coming and going. Everything," said Sven looking from one to the other, rather pleased with himself. "I assumed you knew he was here."

"But why didn't you just speak to me about it? Why go ahead without asking me?"

"I was going to. I just needed to find the right time to tell you, you know, why I joined the art school."

"Art school?" said Blake.

They both ignored him, and Sven went on, "Then there was the walking in on Blake in the shower and all that." Sven shot a cautious glance at Blake. "I thought I would just give you some time to sort things out. Then when the whole story broke last night I had to go to press with it before I lost my scoop. As it is, it'll be in all the media today, but at least I have some information that others don't have."

"Oh fuck!" moaned Blake, still leaning on the counter. "What a story." He reached for the whisky once more, this time not bothering with the coffee.

"I know, right?" said Sven. "I think I've got enough material for a book. Sometimes you just strike it lucky."

Chapter Thirty-Seven

Alexia was awoken by thumping on her door. She was momentarily disoriented. "Mom, mom, wake up," Sebastian's voice. She sat up. The room was still dark with only a thin sliver of light from outside framing the blinds. "Hold on. I'm coming." she said. She switched on the bedside light and picked up the wrap at the foot of the bed. Shrugging it on, she went to the door and let Sebastian in. He had a cup of coffee in each hand and a newspaper clamped under his arm.

"I went to the gym downstairs and then to the Starbucks," he said as he walked past her and put the coffees on the desk in front of the window. "I saw this." He unfolded the newspaper and handed it to her. He turned to open the blinds and she saw a photo of Mungo and an article about the concert. "Did you know about this? He has been living in other people's houses. He is one crazy guy…I mean, who does this kind of shit?"

"Wait. Let me see..." She sat on the bed, rapidly skimming the article, hardly believing the words she saw in front of her. "Oh my God…" she rubbed her eyes and then went into the bathroom. When she had finished she splashed some water on her face, dried it and came back into the bedroom.

Sebastian handed her the coffee. "So, what do you think?" His tone was argumentative.

She sighed, sat down and took a tentative sip. It was good, only slightly sweet and not too hot, just the way she liked it. "Until about two months ago, I hadn't seen him for years. Not since before you were born. There's a lot we don't know about him, but I'm sure there must be some sort of explanation."

"Yah, sure, like he's a…a sociopath!"

"You don't know that. You don't know him."

"Damn right I don't. And based on this," he pointed at the newspaper, "I don't want to."

"I know this is hard, it's hard for me too, but he is your father. I do know that for sure. I should have told you years ago, but he was gone, maybe even dead, and I thought there was no point in upsetting you and Oliver."

"And now apparently, I have two fathers and I don't like either of them. First one is a plagiarist, then he disappears, then oh no, the other one is the plagiarist and the first one is a murderer and a trespasser. What's next?" He stood up and headed for the door. "Great job, Mom."

"Sebastian, wait. Please!" but he was gone, the door shut firmly behind him.

◆◆◆

"Van Buuren and Co.," said Bradski affecting thoughtfulness as he turned Meredith's card over to read the other side. He recognized her name but wasn't going to give her the satisfaction of letting on. His department had crossed paths with the outfit before and, while he hadn't met her, he'd heard that Meredith was a tenacious investigator who was inclined to rub his colleagues up the wrong way.

He sighed and rubbed the back of his head. He was grappling with what to do with Joudry. He had not been able to give them a fixed address and Bradksi figured that, with his past history, he was a flight risk. He wasn't sure they had enough to charge him, but they certainly had good grounds to continue questioning him. Although Joudry had agreed to speak to them without a lawyer present, he sensed that they had reached the end of that particular road and he would clam up soon. Despite himself, he was inclined to believe the guy's story. It seemed too strange to have been made up.

He sighed again and nodded to Meredith, "Okay, we'll use my office," he said.

He turned and the three of them headed down the hallway, through the open plan area where most of the desks were unoccupied at this early hour, to a small office along the side wall.

Bradski lowered his lean frame into the chair behind his desk and thought longingly of his bed and the comforting warmth of his wife, no doubt still asleep. "Please. Sit," he said weariness making his voice impatient. "Carter…" he said nudging his head in Carter's direction.

"Coffee, Ms. Salinger?" enquired Carter.

When she declined Carter took the empty seat alongside her and pulled it out to the end of the desk.

"So, you say you have information pertaining to the Hayes murder?" Bradksi was too tired for small talk.

Meredith leant down and took an iPad from her bag on the floor. She logged on and clicked on the *National Post* icon. She clicked on a story and put the iPad on the desk in front of them.

The headline said *Mungo and his music found in Toronto.* "Read this. Then I'll fill you in on the rest," she said.

Bradski sighed and pulled the reading glasses from his top pocket. Carter pulled his chair in and leaned on his elbows. They skimmed the first few paragraphs and scrolled down "…sudden reappearance at the OSO's performance last night…*Anonymous Sonata* attributed to Joudry, previously accused of plagiarism…indications that he has been in Toronto for years…seen coming and going from the home of big-pharma CEO Blake Beringer and his wife OSO-board member, Nancy… manuscript found in the home of Elizabeth Carey suggests he has been living there too…questions whether they were aware…fugitive lifestyle…currently a person of interest in the recent murder of Christine Hayes…"

"Seems to corroborate…" Carter started. Bradski shot him a look and he shut up.

Bradski removed his glasses and started polishing them with a soft cloth from his desk. "I don't see how this helps us, Ms. Salinger."

"While his behavior is certainly suspect," she said, "I don't believe he's responsible for the death of Ms. Hayes…"

"With all due respect, Ms. Salinger, what you believe or don't is immaterial to us. If you have new information or facts which are material to the case, then we are interested, but we are not here to discuss your beliefs."

She bent down to pick up her bag and pushed her chair back.

"I'm sorry," he held up his hands in apology. "It's been a long night. Why don't you tell us what your interest is in this case?"

She shot them each a deliberating look and then sat back in her seat. "A few weeks ago, a man calling himself Mungo Jameson came to see me, apparently on behalf of a friend who was being blackmailed. Shortly after that I met with him again, along with his friend, Blake Beringer, the CEO of Founder Pharmaceuticals." She paused, assessing their reaction.

Bradski nodded, "We do know about the blackmail. What we don't know is who killed the blackmailer."

"The first step when we deal with blackmail cases is to find out as much as we can about the blackmailer. What I found is that in a past life Christine Hayes was Christine Meyford. She was previously employed as a pharmaceutical sales rep in Vancouver where she started embezzling funds from her employer. She involved a co-worker, Thomas Young, in her scheme. Just before the embezzlement was discovered, she resigned, moved away and changed her name to Hayes. She had covered her tracks very well at work leaving all the evidence pointing clearly at Thomas Young. He was a sitting duck. Took the blame and was convicted. Six months ago he finished a three-year prison term at Ferndale in British Columbia."

She watched Bradski who was by now scribbling away in his notebook. "I have it all here, in this report." She pulled a folder from her bag and placed it on her lap.

"So, you think it's this Tom Young who killed her?" asked Carter.

"We have gone back over his movements since he left B.C. He was unable to secure any full-time work and quickly made his way to Toronto. He was staying in a hostel. Two days after her murder he left town. Security cameras in Hayes' building show him hanging around off and on for weeks before her murder."

"Do you know where he is now?" asked Bradski lifting his phone.

"He left Toronto on a flight two days after the murder…flight number…" she flipped through some pages in the folder on her lap and gave him the details, along with his full name and last known address in Vancouver.

Bradski relayed these to the person at the other end of the phone line with instructions that they start a search for him. He put the phone down and said to Meredith: "Why didn't you come to us with this information sooner? You do know it is an offence to withhold information relating to a crime."

"We only finished our investigation yesterday. Last night after Joudry was identified, I rushed to finish this report and here I am. We have not withheld anything. On the contrary I am handing over to you a comprehensive dossier which should improve your case clearance rate for the quarter." She handed Bradski the folder.

He flipped through the pages quickly, frowning and muttering. "Weapon?" he said looking up at her.

"We think he secured an unlicensed firearm from connections made while he was in prison. We have an informant who tells us he made contact with a few ex-convicts here in Toronto. Their names are in the report."

"Well, you certainly have done your homework, Ms. Salinger."

Chapter Thirty-Eight

Rebecca helped Mrs. Gibson up the front steps and into the house. "Elizabeth has the coffee on and these are the best chocolate croissants in all of Toronto," she said. "Here, let me help you with your coat. No, no, leave your shoes." She eased the coat off the old woman's shoulders and they moved into the kitchen.

"I've already had my egg, but I suppose I can manage a croissant."

"Oh, go on Mrs. G. Of course you can. Bikini weather is still a ways off," teased Rebecca.

Mrs. Gibson giggled. "Oh, my dear, this body has never seen a bikini."

Elizabeth got up from the kitchen table to greet them and pulled out a chair for the old lady. "Coffee for you Mrs. Gibson, or would you prefer tea?"

"Coffee please. Rebecca has been telling me about all the excitement last night. Ooh. I wish I had been there."

Rebecca placed the croissants on a plate on the table.

"It was very dramatic, especially when Blake Beringer took the microphone and pointed out Mungo Joudry. And, as if on cue, the police arrived." Elizabeth handed her a coffee.

"I think Beringer had already called the police," cut in Rebecca. "It seems you were right Mrs. G. He must have been the man you've seen here. How else could his music have got in Elizabeth's basement?"

Mrs. Gibson's eyes sparkled. "So, I'm not so dotty after all, am I? As my old mother used to say, 'everyone needs a nosy old neighbor to look out for them'."

"Indeed, they do," Elizabeth reached out and gave Mrs. Gibson's shoulder a gentle squeeze.

Just then the doorbell rang, and Elizabeth went to answer it. Moments later she showed Detective Bradski and Sergeant Carter into the kitchen.

"These are the policemen from the concert last night," said Elizabeth. "They say they have some news about Mungo Joudry, the composer."

"We can do this in another room, if you prefer?" said Bradski.

"No please, don't worry. This is my sister, Rebecca, and my neighbor Mrs. Gibson. They both know all about the suitcase with the music. In fact, Mrs. Gibson says she has seen him. Here."

"Have you indeed?" said Bradski, "We might need a statement from you?"

"Oh, my dear," Mrs. Gibson's hand went self-consciously to her neck.

"It's nothing to worry about. All in good time," said Bradski.

Rebecca caught sight of Sergeant Carter's eyes resting on the plate of croissants. "How rude of us. Can we offer you some coffee, a croissant?"

"Don't mind if I do," said Carter.

"Not for me thanks," said Bradski, "been drinking the stuff all night. At this rate I'll be lucky if I next sleep in June. Wouldn't say no to a croissant though."

Rebecca passed the plate around while Elizabeth poured Carter a coffee.

"Please, have a seat." Elizabeth gestured to the vacant chairs. They sat. "You say you have some information for us."

Bradski nodded, swallowing a mouthful of croissant, crumbs falling onto his shirt. He brushed them off. "It seems you may already be aware from your neighbor," he tilted his head in Mrs. Gibson's direction and took another bite of croissant, "...as you know we took Mr. Joudry in for questioning last night in connection with the Hayes murder."

"That poor girl," said Mrs. Gibson, her eyes wide.

"We can't say much, we are still investigating, but it looks like she wasn't that poor..." offered Carter.

Bradski shot him a warning glance and he shut up.

Just then Caprice walked into the kitchen and stretched. He went to his bowl and drank and then looked balefully at Carter who was in his favorite wingback chair by the window. After licking his paws, he jumped onto Carter's lap and settled in.

"Oh, you don't think this composer killed her, do you? The one who's been in Elizabeth house!" Mrs. Gibson's voice quivered.

"Well, we are not sure yet, and like Sergeant Carter said, we are still investigating. He maintains he didn't kill her. But what he did confess to was trespassing. It seems he has been living here, in your house, part time, for years. Not only yours but also in a few other homes in the city."

"What do you mean living? How can that be?" exclaimed Rebecca.

Elizabeth was very still, her eyes fixed on Bradski.

"Apparently, after the first one, which came about, he says, unintentionally, he targeted the homes of people who were out all day, typically where the couple both worked full time, or single like Ms. Carey here. No kids. People with boats and cottages. People who travelled a lot, were away often, people with homes in Florida, that sort of thing. It's more common than you might think. Well, not the trespassing, but the long absences from home. Once he had observed them long enough, studied their routines and gained access to their homes, he says it's easy enough to predict their comings and goings, vacations, weekends away. You read their mail, listen to their voicemail, check their email…people who live alone don't…"

"Oh my God! Are you saying he was doing all this, here, in Elizabeth's house? Oh my God! Elizabeth! This is too creepy. I've been telling you for years you should get married, have some kids, a life, not just a job. None of this would have happened if, if…you didn't live alone…!"

"Rebecca. Please. Not now." Elizabeth held up her hand. "If Detective Bradski is right, I haven't been living alone."

Sergeant Carter nodded. He reached over to the plate. "Do you mind…?"

Rebecca handed it to him absently, her eyes on Bradski. "You are sure about this? I mean, there isn't some mistake?"

"I'm afraid so. His story has been corroborated by a private investigator who has had reason to look into him."

"And there's this." Carter put the croissant down and reached for a rolled-up newspaper in the pocket of his jacket. He flattened out the morning's *National Post* on the table and pointed to an article. "This guy, this Sven

Svenson, is a freelancer reporter. Odd name, if you ask me. He's been following Joudry for months. He's seen him here, at your house. It's all in here."

"I did tell you, my dear," said Mrs. Gibson.

Rebecca reached for the paper and started reading.

"It does explain the suitcase and the music…" said Elizabeth.

"We will need the suitcase. As evidence. And if we could look around, Ms. Carey?" Bradski rubbed his eyes. He really wanted to get home.

"Evidence. Evidence of what?"

"Trespass. We assume you do want to press charges?"

"I'm not sure. I think I'd like to meet him first."

"Elizabeth!" Rebecca looked up from the newspaper.

"Wouldn't you want to meet the man who composed that incredible sonata? To think he could have composed it here, in my house."

"He did say that part of the reason he chose your house was because you have a baby grand?" Carter nodded. "And because you work all the time and because he likes your cat." He stroked Caprice gently. They all watched Caprice settle in more comfortably and start purring.

Chapter Thirty-Nine

Blake opened the front door and lifted his suitcase over the threshold. He stood for a moment on the porch, squinting into the weak spring sunshine. He flipped up the sheepskin collar of his leather jacket. *Summer couldn't come soon enough.* As soon as it warmed up, he was taking the boat and heading for the Caribbean. He would need some crew, unless he could persuade Nancy to change her mind. He lifted his suitcase and headed for the car. He unlocked it and lifted the suitcase into the trunk. As he stood up he saw Nancy standing in the open doorway, her arms folded, against the chill or him, he couldn't be sure. Probably both.

He went back onto the porch. "So, Nance, you sure then? You won't come with me? There is still snow at the cottage and the skiing should be good."

She shook her head. "We've been through this again and again."

"It could be good for us. Time alone, really alone, for a change. We could try and work things out. I won't be bothered by work. Now that Simon-bloody-Parnell has my job. God, he must be crowing. This is exactly what he has wanted for years. He fucking engineered it…"

"Blake this is exactly why I won't come with you. It's over and you can't even see it. Simon Parnell did not engineer this. You are the author of your own misfortunes. The Board of Founder couldn't possibly keep you on after this mess, sleeping with your subordinates, blackmail and murder. You just don't get it. You need some time on your own to do some soul-searching, if you even have a soul…"

"When did you get to be so fucking hard, Nancy?"

"Twenty-five years married to you hardened me. I need some time on my own to find my soft core again. Hopefully it is still there somewhere."

"And what are you going to do here on your own? You are not safe with this Mungo character…I still think we should press charges for trespass."

"I've changed the locks, Blake, so your key won't work when you come back. And neither will his. I will be fine. I've spoken to him and he is pretty decent in an odd sort of way. It seems he has done more over the years to look out for me than you ever did."

She turned and closed the door firmly behind her. Blake heard the lock click into place.

♦♦♦

Errol Joynt had one elbow on his desk, a cigarette in his opposite hand and a steaming cup of coffee next to *The National Post* in front of him. *Well I'll be jiggered.* He took a long draw from his cigarette and looked out the window, his eyes narrowing against the glare and the smoke. *Well I'll be jiggered*, he said again and looked back down at the paper. He read on for a few minutes alternately shaking his head, sucking on his cigarette and slurping his coffee. He was startled by a knock on the door. He quickly stubbed out the cigarette and put the ashtray on the floor next to him. "Yes. Come in."

The door opened and Sven stepped in. He recognized him immediately as the man who had come with Nancy Beringer looking for *The Ice Princess* a few weeks ago and he was pretty sure he had seen him around since then on the docks.

Errol stood up. Sven put out his hand. "Sven Svenson," he said. They shook. "I see you have been reading my piece." He pointed to the newspaper.

"This is yours?" Errol asked.

Sven nodded. "I'm a freelancer. I've been working on that for ages," he said. "Mind if I sit? I actually want to talk to you about this story, if you have some time, that is?"

"Sure. Pretty quiet around here until the season starts up. Should be a couple of weeks yet." They both sat. "Coffee?" asked Errol.

"Great. Black, no sugar."

Errol swiveled his chair around and poured coffee from the pot on the shelf behind him into a mug. He swiveled back and handed the mug to Sven.

"Thanks." Sven took a pack of cigarettes from his shirt pocket and offered one to Errol. "Nice little set up you have here. Cozy with a good view of the water."

Errol took one and reached for the ashtray on the floor. He tipped the debris into the trash can beside him and placed the ashtray on the table. They both lit up.

"Not supposed to smoke here," said Errol, the cigarette wiggling between his clenched lips as he spoke. "But I'm here on my own mostly so no one seems to mind."

Sven nodded.

"Sven Svenson. That's an odd sort of name, if you don't mind me sayin'."

Sven nodded again. "My mother's idea, apparently. I'm from Sweden. You from around here?"

"Nah. I'm from Labrador. Used to be a fisherman. But, you know fishing has all but died out there, so I came to Toronto for work, nearly thirty years ago now. Been around boats all my life. The weather's better here though," he laughed. "What brings you here?"

"This story," said Sven, gesturing to the newspaper. "Long after everyone forgot about him, I started searching for Mungo Joudry and found him hiding in Toronto. In other people's homes. And boats and cottages."

"He's one strange guy," said Errol.

"And this is only the beginning of it," agreed Sven. "There's lots more to this and I'm putting it in a book. That's where you come in. I was hoping you could help me."

Errol raised his eyebrows, "Me?"

"He's been coming and going here for a while. I mean, you don't miss much, I was hoping you could fill me in, give me your impressions, when did you first see him, that sort of thing. And I'd love a look around the boat, maybe get some photos…?"

"We…ell. I'm not sure about that. I'd have to check with the Beringers."

"We can get to that. I just need a quick look around. You know, to get the feel of it, the layout. But that can wait till you're ready. Really, if you think about it, you are in a unique position. You've seen this guy. He's been coming here for a long time. And the Beringers, now there's an interesting couple. You have been dealing with them for years. Blake is quite a character too. I would be happy to acknowledge you in the book, of course."

Errol took another sip of coffee and a long draw from his cigarette. "Well now, let me see..." the smoke escaped his mouth as he spoke. "The Beringers first got *The Ice Princess*..." As Errol leaned back in his chair and put his feet on the corner of the desk, Sven flipped open his notebook.

Chapter Forty

Elizabeth turned the car into her road, drove past the trees which were still bare but were starting to show the first tiny green buds of spring. She pulled into the driveway. She loved this neighborhood and her home, even more now than she had when she'd first moved in. She was always filled with an unlikely combination of peace and anticipation when she arrived home. Today that feeling was amplified.

She parked the car and shut the door. A second door closed, and she walked round to open the trunk.

"I'll get it," he said and lifted the small suitcase from the trunk.

They walked into the house and no sooner were they through the door than Caprice appeared weaving himself between Mungo's legs and purring loudly. He bent to stroke the cat and the purring increased.

"I suppose I'm going to have to get used to playing second fiddle around here," Elizabeth laughed.

Mungo straightened and looked at her apologetically, but Elizabeth was smiling.

"This is really awkward," he said. "It's awfully good of you, after everything. I mean, you really don't have to. I would have made a plan..."

"Oh, I know you would have made a plan. You've always managed in the past," she softened her words with a teasing smile. "To be honest, I'm tired of living on my own. My sister is right about that, I do need someone. Not that I have been living alone, have I? Now we are just making it legitimate." She reached out and gave his arm a squeeze. "Come on, no more lurking about in dusty basements for you." She headed upstairs.

Mungo picked up the suitcase and followed her upstairs.

"I've put you in the room Rebecca normally uses. Don't worry, I've changed the sheets. Rebecca is furious with me. Not because you are in her room, but because of the whole thing."

Mungo paused on the stairs. "Elizabeth, are you sure?"

"I've never been more certain of anything in my life."

Still he hesitated. Caprice stopped next to him on the stairs.

"Look, even Caprice wants you to stay." They continued up to the bedroom.

"Rebecca's not here. I dropped her off at the station this morning. She says I am taking a huge risk. She thinks I am totally crazy. I told her I need some crazy in my life. For too long I have been following all the rules and where did it get me? I'm a workaholic spinster with a cat. God what a stereotype! I told her to stop worrying. I said 'if he was going to do anything bad to me, he has had plenty of opportunities before now'. She couldn't really argue with that. There's lots of space in the closet and a bathroom through that door. What am I saying? Of course, you know this already." She was aware that nerves were making her speak too fast. She wasn't nervous about having him there. She was nervous that he may decide to leave. "I have a bottle of Dom Perignon in the fridge. I've been saving it for a special occasion. I'll go and open it while you freshen up and then we can drink to new beginnings."

◆◆◆

When Elizabeth left the room, Mungo walked across to the window and looked down on the street. He put his hands on his back and arched into a stretch. It had been a long night and he had also spent much of the day at the police station. They had transcribed his statement, which went on for pages, and he had signed it. Alexia's lawyer had contacted him and referred him to a local solicitor. He had no idea how he would pay for it, but that was a problem for another day.

He was so relieved when Bradski had come in and told him that they had a lead on another suspect for Christine's murder. He nearly leapt up and kissed the man. He felt the faintest stirrings of faith in justice and the natural order of things. Meredith Salinger was an impressive woman, despite her abrasiveness. If it hadn't been for her, he would still be suspect number one and stuck in a jail cell. He definitely owed her. With no fixed address and his history, he would have been considered a flight risk. They would never have granted him bail. God knows how long he would have been locked up while they figured out the mess, if ever.

He could see that Bradski was reluctant to let him go but they didn't really have enough to charge him. And the lawyer had been very insistent about that. Between the lawyer and Elizabeth, who said he would be at her address, Bradski was finally persuaded. He felt a debt of gratitude to them and to Nancy. Both Elizabeth and Nancy had refused to press charges of trespass. Blake, on the other hand, would have been happy to see him rot in jail for Christine's murder and then he wanted to press charges on top of that.

Elizabeth's voice interrupted his thoughts. "Mungo, the champagne is getting warm."

"Be right there," he replied. He went into the bathroom and washed his face with cold water. His beard caught in the soft towel as he dried his face. He longed for a shower, but it could wait.

He went into the kitchen, Caprice close on his heels. Elizabeth had set out a plate of cheese and crackers the champagne glasses twinkling in the late afternoon. She had lit some candles and he could hear the soft strains of Vivaldi's Spring from the *Four Seasons* coming from the living room. She handed him a glass and held hers up to his, "Cheers."

"Cheers," he said. Then impulsively he leaned forward and kissed her cheek. She turned so that his lips just touched hers before they both pulled away. They both covered their momentary embarrassment sipping from their glasses.

"Let's sit," she said. She offered him some cheese and he realized that he was starving. He couldn't remember when last he had eaten anything. Caprice leapt onto his lap and curled up. "I was asked to give you this." Elizabeth handed him an envelope which had been lying face down on the table.

He looked at her enquiringly, but she just shrugged. He opened it and read:

Dear Mungo,

By the time you read this I will be on my way back to New York. I am very relieved that you will be somewhere warm and safe tonight and that it looks like you are in the clear.

It has been a very eventful and difficult few weeks and we both have much to sort out. I think it is best if we do this separately. It was a shock seeing you on the boat and everything that has happened since then has been rather overwhelming. You have led a strange life since New York and I am not quite sure what to make of it.

I am happy that your music has been acknowledged and that you met Sebastian and heard him perform. You have certainly not lost any of your talent and you must be gratified to know that it lives on in Sebastian too.

Sebastian will be staying on in Toronto to complete the Anonymous concerts. Please give him some time to come to terms and get used to the fact that you are his father before contacting him. Perhaps once the investigation is complete and your life has normalized he will be open to meet with you.

Alexia

He folded the letter and returned it to the envelope on the table. He looked down and stroked Caprice. He wasn't really surprised by the letter, though he was disappointed. He couldn't really blame her. She was angry, and she had every right to be.

He picked up his glass, took a sip and held it up to Elizabeth, "To new beginnings," he said.

"To new beginnings."

A moment later they heard a phone ring. "It's probably Rebecca checking up on me." She crossed the kitchen and dug around in her purse which was on the counter near the door.

"Hello...Oh yes, hi Nancy... Yes, yes everything is fine. He's fine," she said, her eyes resting on Mungo. "Tired, I think. How are you? ... You must be pleased with how the concert went, despite everything. You certainly got the publicity you were hoping for… That's great…two more…that is a long run for the OSO. Oh, that's a good idea, but well, I don't know…I will ask him…Yes, I'll talk to him…He will probably want to think about it… No, I don't think he has a number. Use mine for the time being… Okay, yes, I will let you know… sometime next week. Have a good evening, Nancy. Bye."

Elizabeth sat down again. "Congratulations," she said, "That was Nancy Beringer. The OSO have added two more concerts to the schedule. That will make it six in total. They are inviting you to be a guest conductor. They want you to conduct the last performance of *The Anonymous Sonata*. Somewhere near the end of March. She said they will set the date to suit you. I told her you would think about it and we'll get back to her.

Mungo's felt his chest fill up. He felt it might burst. He took a deep breath to give his heart some more space. He would conduct for his son. He would invite Patricia. Maybe Alexia would come back for the concert. He took hold of Elizabeth's hand. "Thank you," he said.

◆◆◆

Although the air was crisp, the early morning California sun warmed the sidewalk and felt pleasant on his back. The pavement café was filling up quickly this early on a Sunday and he watched the waitress skillfully navigate the tables with steaming lattes and plates piled with croissants. He stretched a leisurely arm out for his coffee mug and returned his attention to the newspaper, turning the page. He took a sip of coffee and almost spat it out. Choking it down and coughing at the same time, he stared at the page. Mungo's photo stared back at him. The headline read "Joudry confirmed as the composer of *The Anonymous Sonata*." He quickly scanned the article. The final line jumped out at him "We have found the phantom, now where is the fraud?" Oliver Bantry pulled ten dollars from his wallet and left it on the table. He put his cap on, pulling it down low, donned his Ray Bans and quickly left the café with the newspaper under his arm.

ACKNOWLEDGEMENTS

My sincere thanks to Dan and Emily. You have both encouraged, advised and inspired me throughout the process of writing this book. Thank you to my sister, Bev, and to my friends and fellow book lovers, Juliet and Sarah, for your keen eyes as beta readers. Thank you to Courteney, my youngest daughter, for the cover design.

And thank you to my husband, Andrew and my daughters; Ashleigh, Bryony and Courteney for your steadfast belief and unwavering encouragement in my creative endeavours.

Printed in Great Britain
by Amazon

85879348R00171